Mysteries Revealed

In twelve seconds you will catch one last glimpse of this world before you walk into a tunnel of light—or will you?

Each of us is born with ten thousand faces, but we reveal them only one at a time. Some should remain hidden forever.

When a dead man appears in a field, it's time to call a medical examiner. But this isn't like any human seen before.

Most people fear Death and avoid Him. Some seek to make peace with Him. But only one woman falls in love with Him....

Journeys Undertaken

The ads say, "Live the adventure! Meet strange new aliens!" But beware what the ads *don't* tell you.

When everything is illegal, it takes a special kind of nerve to become a "Cop for a Day."

Fixing clocks is hard. But when a young orphan discovers that Time itself is broken, it's a job that calls for a wizard.

Terrors Awakened

Everyone experiences cravings, but one young woman discovers that she has an inherited taste for dreams....

We're already making test-tube babies. What will we do with the rejects?

The Vulture Lady always takes special care of the village of Goldwater. Now one woman must seek to find out why....

Hopes Aroused

Some evils are so monstrous, the world needs a hero. Fortunately, we can bring him back from the dead, when needed....

Holidays can be wondrous and heartwarming, funny or sad. Some are more marvelous than others.

In a world torn by war, cruelty seems to know no bounds. Then again, neither does love....

Experience the thrills, laughs, heartbreak and tears that can all be found in this fabulous new anthology. We've scoured the globe to find the most powerful new writers, and then paired them with the most gifted new illustrators to bring you L. Ron Hubbard Presents Writers of the Future Volume XXIX.

"I've been involved in Writers of the Future since its inception more than 25 years ago—first as a contestant, then a speaker, then a judge. It is the most vibrant and exciting showcase of new talent with an undeniable success rate. If you want a glimpse of the future—the future of science fiction—look at these first publications of tomorrow's masters."
　　　　　　　　　　　　　　　　　— Kevin J. Anderson
Writers of the Future Contest judge

"Writers of the Future brings you the Hugo and Nebula winners of the future today."　　　　　　　　— Tim Powers
Writers of the Future Contest judge

"The smartest move for beginning writers is the WotF Contest. I've witnessed it kick-start many a career."
　　　　　　　　　　　　　　　　　— Gregory Benford
Writers of the Future Contest judge

"I really can't say enough good things about Writers of the Future.... It's fair to say that without Writers of the Future, I wouldn't be where I am today...."
　　　　　　　　　　　　　　　　　— Patrick Rothfuss
Writers of the Future Contest winner 2002

"The Writers and Illustrators of the Future Contests are the best way to jump-start a career in science fiction and fantasy writing or in illustration. You win great money, make wonderful lifelong friends at the workshops, and get to learn from professionals in your field. The awards events are spectacular. Join the fun if you can, and make great connections and memories!"
　　　　　　　　　　　　　　　　　— Nina Kiriki Hoffman
Writers of the Future Contest winner 1985
and Contest judge

"That phone call telling me I had won was the first time in my life that it seemed possible I would achieve my long-cherished dream of having a career as a writer."
— K.D. Wentworth
Writers of the Future Contest winner 1989
and Contest Coordinating Judge

"The Writers of the Future Contest has had a profound impact on my career, ever since I submitted my first story in 1989."
— Sean Williams
Writers of the Future Contest winner 1993
and Contest judge

"The Writers of the Future Contest played a critical role in the early stages of my career as a writer."
— Eric Flint
Writers of the Future Contest winner 1993
and Contest judge

"Every year the Writers of the Future Contest inspires new writers and helps to launch their careers. The combination of reward, recognition, instruction, and opportunity for beginning authors is unparalleled. There is no contest comparable to the Writers of the Future."
— Rebecca Moesta
Writers of the Future Contest judge

"The Writers of the Future Contest was definitely an accelerator to my writing development. I learned so much, and it came at just the right moment for me."
— Jo Beverley
Writers of the Future Contest winner 1988

"The Illustrators of the Future Contest is more than a contest. It is truly a great opportunity that could very well change your life. The Contest gives you the tools to think outside the box and create a niche for yourself."

— Robert Castillo
Illustrators of the Future Contest winner 2008
and Contest judge

"Illustrators of the Future offered a channel through which to direct my ambitions. The competition made me realize that genre illustration is actually a valued profession, and here was a rare opportunity for a possible entry point into that world."

— Shaun Tan
Illustrators of the Future Contest winner 1993
and Contest judge

"The Contests are amazing competitions because really, you've nothing to lose and they provide good positive encouragement to anyone who wins. Judging the entries is always a lot of fun and inspiring. I wish I had something like this when I was getting started— very positive and cool."

— Bob Eggleton
Illustrators of the Future Contest judge

"These Contests provide a wonderful safety net of professionals for young artists and writers. And it's due to the fact that L. Ron Hubbard was willing to lend a hand."

— Judith Miller
Illustrators of the Future Contest judge

"You have to ask yourself, 'Do I really have what it takes, or am I just fooling myself?' That pat on the back from Writers of the Future told me not to give up.... All in all, the Contest was a fine finishing step from amateur to pro, and I'm grateful to all those involved."
                                              — James Alan Gardner
                              Writers of the Future Contest winner 1990

"The Writers of the Future Contest sowed the seeds of my success.... So many people say a writing career is impossible, but WotF says, 'Dreams are worth following.'"
                                              — Scott Nicholson
                              Writers of the Future Contest winner 1999

"When I first set out to become a professional writer (ah, hubris), one of my key ambitions was to place in the top tier of the L. Ron Hubbard Writers of the Future Contest.... Without Mr. Hubbard's sponsorship, I wouldn't have had that fabulous, high-profile launch."
                                              — Jay Lake
                              Writers of the Future Contest winner 2003

"I credit the Writers of the Future Contest as an important part of my career launch, and I highly recommend it to everyone who wants to establish themselves in the field of science fiction and fantasy."
                                              — Ken Scholes
                              Writers of the Future Contest winner 2005

"Knowing that such great authors as the WotF judges felt my stories were worth publishing encouraged me to write more and submit more."
                                              — Eric James Stone
                              Writers of the Future Contest winner 2005

L. Ron Hubbard PRESENTS
Writers of the Future

VOLUME XXIX

L. Ron Hubbard PRESENTS

Writers of the Future

VOLUME XXIX

The year's thirteen best tales from
the Writers of the Future
international writers' program.

Illustrated by winners in
the Illustrators of the Future
international illustrators' program.

With essays on writing & illustration by
L. Ron Hubbard / Nnedi Okorafor /
Larry Elmore.

Edited by Dave Wolverton

GALAXY PRESS, LLC

War Hero: © 2013 Brian Trent
Planetary Scouts: © 2013 Stephen Sottong
Twelve Seconds: © 2013 Tina Gower
The Manuscript Factory: © 2010 L. Ron Hubbard Library
The Grande Complication: © 2013 Christopher Reynaga
Cop for a Day: © 2013 Chrome Oxide
Gonna Reach Out and Grab Ya: © 2013 Eric Cline
Vestigial Girl: © 2013 Alex Wilson
Holy Days: © 2013 Kodiak Julian
The Ghost Wife of Arlington: © 2013 Marilyn Guttridge
Everything You Have Seen: © 2013 Alisa Alering
Scavengers: © 2013 Shannon Peavey
Dreameater: © 2013 Andrea Stewart
Master Belladino's Mask: © 2013 Marina J. Lostetter
Illustrations on pages 15 & 189: © 2013 Jon Eno
Illustration on page 84: © 2013 Joshua Meehan
Illustration on page 123: © 2013 Luis Menacho
Illustration on page 177: © 2013 Olivia Xu
Illustration on page 219: © 2013 Daniel Reneau
Illustration on page 259: © 2013 Jackie Albano
Illustration on page 268: © 2013 Aldo Katayanagi
Illustration on page 306: © 2013 Sida Chen
Illustration on page 326: © 2013 Karsen Slater
Illustration on page 372: © 2013 James J. Eads
Illustration on page 415: © 2013 Lucas Durham
Illustration on page 449: © 2013 Tiffany England

Cover Artwork: *Retro City* © 2013 Stephen Youll

Interior Design: Jerry Kelly

ISBN-13 978-1-61986-200-5
Library of Congress Control Number: 2013934928
First Edition Paperback
Printed in the United States of America

CONTENTS

Introduction

BY DAVE WOLVERTON

Dave Wolverton is an award-winning, New York Times *bestselling author with dozens of books to his credit. He began his career writing short fiction winning the Gold Award in the Writers of the Future Contest, which vaulted him into prominence in the mid-1980s. His science fiction novels include the highly praised* On My Way to Paradise, *which won the Philip K. Dick Memorial Special Award for "Best Novel in the English Language."*

Dave has also written novels in the Star Wars and Mummy Universes, and has worked as a video game designer, most notably for Starcraft's Brood War.

In 1999 he set the Guinness record for the world's largest single-person, single-book signing.

In the mid-1990s he began to follow his love for writing fantasy under the pen name David Farland, where he became best known for his international bestselling Runelords series; he has also won the Whitney Award for best novel of the year for his historical novel In the Company of Angels, *and the International Book Award for Best Young Adult Novel of the Year, along with the Hollywood Book Award for Best Book of the year for his young adult fantasy thriller* Nightingale.

Dave now serves as Coordinating Judge for the Writers of the Future Contest.

Introduction

Welcome to a *remarkable* anthology.

It's remarkable for a number of reasons, the first of which is simply the history of how it got here. At the young age of twenty-nine, this is one of the longest-running short story competitions of all time.

It's also a remarkable competition for what it offers to its winners. It inspires thousands of people every year to produce new stories and art. It offers the winners the chance to be seen and encouraged by top-ranking authors and illustrators in their fields. It grants significant cash prizes to the winners, and also offers what may be their first publication credits. Winners are also treated to a free seminar taught by accomplished professionals, along with an elaborate award ceremony. No other competition in the field of fantasy and science fiction offers so much.

It's also remarkable because of the talent associated with it. It was initiated by L. Ron Hubbard, one of the greatest writers of popular fiction in the twentieth century. His career began during the pulp era of fiction, helped launch the Golden Age and continued on into modern day with hits like

Battlefield Earth and *Mission Earth*. The author judges have included many of the best-known science fiction and fantasy writers of our time—people like Frank Herbert, Anne McCaffrey, Jerry Pournelle, Larry Niven, Andre Norton, Kevin J. Anderson, Tim Powers, Mike Resnick, Fred Pohl, Gregory Benford and many more.

The Illustrators of the Future Contest is also one of the longest-running art contests around, initiated in 1988, with celebrity judges who are no less famous, people like Frank Frazetta, Diane and Leo Dillon, Will Eisner, Jack Kirby, Bob Eggleton, Stephan Martiniere, Frank Kelly Freas, Stephen Hickman, Paul Lehr, Stephen Youll and others who've had a tremendous impact on the world through their graphic art, animations, and film design.

The contests have also helped launch the careers of a remarkable number of writers and illustrators who have gone on to publish thousands of novels and short stories, and literally more than a million pieces of art. In fact, a few of our judges got early starts with the contests. People like Eric Flint, Dean Wesley Smith, Nina Kiriki Hoffman, K.D. Wentworth—and myself—went up through the ranks of contest winners, became professional writers who went on to win major awards and become international bestsellers, and later were invited to become judges based upon their merits.

In the same way, illustrators like Sergey Poyarkov, Robert Castillo and Academy Award Winner Shaun Tan also started out first as illustrator winners, established enviable careers and later came to the helm as judges.

Each year, we receive thousands of short stories and illustrations from every continent around the world. In the third quarter alone this year, we had entries from over thirty different countries. At the end of the year, we present the best of our new discoveries. Many of these artists will go on to have their own stellar careers, and some of them we hope will become your favorite authors and illustrators in decades to come.

Finding those people has become difficult. The level of talent is so high that at times it's hard to choose the winners. That's as it should be. In any one quarter, we may have a mixture of great comedy, astonishing science fiction, truly creepy horror, thrilling adventures and wondrous fantasies. Which one is best?

The answer of course is up to you, in part. You'll find your own personal favorites.

Meanwhile, thanks to L. Ron Hubbard and the many other writers, artists and fans who have dedicated so much time and effort, this contest will continue to become the premiere vehicle for inspiring and discovering new artistic talent in the field of fantasy and science fiction. If you or someone that you know is interested in becoming a writer or illustrator, don't hesitate to enter. The contest is open to anyone, and there is no fee to enter!

War Hero

written by

Brian Trent

illustrated by

JON ENO

ABOUT THE AUTHOR

Brian Trent was born in a post-industrial factory town in Connecticut. He was rapidly introduced to speculative fiction through a lavishly illustrated edition of One Thousand and One Nights. *As a child, he became a haunter of libraries and old ruins and developed a keen interest in both ends of history: the ancient past and far-distant future. Reading everything from Asimov to Xenophon, he began crafting his very first stories on a metallic-blue Brother 11 typewriter. After earning college degrees in English and philosophy, Trent worked as a professional journalist when not piloting expeditionary shuttles through the soupy atmospheres of alien worlds (otherwise known as going for long drives in the rain). His nonfiction writings have graced the cover of* The Humanist *magazine. His Writers of the Future win is his second professional sale, the first being to COSMOS, and he has since sold fiction to Apex Magazine. He recently completed the second novel in a "future history" series and, when not writing, Trent works in film.*

ABOUT THE ILLUSTRATOR

Jon Eno worked as an ambulance jockey when he was a teen and as a medic in the military. He has also worked the coal mines of Kentucky and sold securities as a stockbroker. He has owned a construction company and been a consultant and is currently a critical care RN, working in an intensive care unit. Jon can't remember how many times he has done chest compression in his career. He has worked ICU, CCU, ER and open heart, and he was a clinic administrator at one time.

In his spare time, all he wants to do is crack open a book and learn from it. Art comes naturally for him, and he is self-taught.

Throughout his life, art has been a big part of his world. One day he plans to find the time to advance his skills further and learn whatever it is he wishes to do next.

Jon also has a passion for writing science fiction. He has one novel completed, is starting a second, and has three more outlined and ready to go. Recently, he published a book of medical humor illustrations.

Jon lives in a log cabin in the foothills of north Texas. He prefers blue jeans and a T-shirt to a coat and tie. He drives an old pickup and still gets his hands dirty working on his property. He is married and has a son, who is the most incredible thing he has done yet in his life. He is thankful to have both his wife and son.

War Hero

Three days pass before I decide to get saved.

They bump me to the head of the list, of course, and six hours later, I've got a military escort from the colony tram to the facility. Shane is my tech today. He resembles a young Abe Lincoln cut out of pale alabaster, elongated limbs in the classic indigenously Martian look, and a frilly beard hugging his jaw.

He sits in the neighboring control room, hunched over his buglike monitor-spread, and gets to work stimulating my brain. His machine-prompted queries crackle over the intercom. Part friendly handball, part firing squad. My brain on TV, lighting up different branches like a blinking Solstice Tree. My head encased in the neuroreader that's about the same as wearing a cooking colander for a hat.

I flip through a magazine, watching the firework images of the Phobos victory unfold across the smartpaper.

"What are your favorite movies?" Shane asks. "How long did you serve the Resistance?" "How many times have you been offworld?"

Yet every so often comes an indelicate prod. "Do

you look in the toilet before flushing?" "Have you ever fantasized sexually about a relative?"

"What's it like to kill a dog?"

I look up from the magazine, anger flashing in my thoughts like a red siren.

The pace of the questions has been winding down, and I *thought* we were just talking to pass the time. So I try to catch his eyes through the glass. "Excuse me?"

The Martian beanpole doesn't return my stare. He hunches in his chair, hugging himself with his freakishly long arms like a Cycladic statue. In another few generations, humans on Earth and Mars will have diverged into different damned species.

"Want me to repeat the question?"

All business, this kid.

I clear my throat, uncrossing and crossing my legs. "It feels..." I swallow a lump. "Ugly. Like *you're* a monster, and not this sixty-pound slavering beast who has just turned your little brother's face to a Halloween mask of red pulp. So you bite down harder on its throat. You hug it fiercely in a death embrace, knowing if it gets free, it will kill you. You think of your brother. Your fear begins to change. It turns to... revenge."

Shane looks over at me guiltily. "Sorry. Machine says I had to ask. Needed to light Zone 8 back here." He taps an emerald-green screen.

"I wouldn't mind having that memory erased, Shane."

"Remove one block and it impacts the structure's integrity." Canned response, drilled in from his tech training. He sips from his water-bottle straw and swivels around in the chair, straining his giraffe neck to check the upload status. "You saved your brother's life."

I return to my magazine. Dazzling surface captures of the Phobos base explosion parade at my fingertips.

Shane's voice pierces from the intercom. "In the years since, did you ever have to kill something again?"

"Just the people here," I say, tapping the magazine.

"Corporal Peznowski. Doctor Javier Daigle. General Chatfield." Shane throws up his hands. "Worst war criminals since the Nazis." Head cocks, curious sideways tilt. "How did you ever infiltrate their ranks? The Partisans were famous for being able to sniff out a mole."

"Is this a machine question, or your own curiosity?"

"Does it matter?"

I swallow hard, not wanting to think of the vast setup the resistance had perpetrated to convince the Partisan ministry of intelligence that I was one of their isolationist, fearmongering, powercrat fanatics...the grotesque mutation of early Martian pride in having a planet of their own, pumped through a filter of jingoism and fundamentalism across Mars's burnt-orange deserts. Or in the illegal torture wards led by sadistic thugs like Peznowski and Chatfield.

But Shane isn't done. Eyes glinting in unabashed interest, he presses, "How did you get that scar on your chin, Mr. Pope?"

I shift awkwardly in my seat. "I was shot. The flechette grazed right through my chin."

That was only two Martian days ago, high above the planet's war-torn surface in the Partisans' tactical command center on Phobos. I had just set the last of the explosives, wrapped in CAMO mesh so they blended in with the Phobos station weld points. The timer ticking down in red overlay in my vision as I walked the glossy length of the main corridor, dizzy, chest tight. Atlas with the world on his shoulders. Below on the Martian surface, the tide was turning. Resistance fighters had finally captured Olympus, and the Partisans were hemmed in by northern and southern rebels. Their headquarters on Phobos was clamped shut, no shuttles in or out. Just me and Corporal Peznowski and Partisan generals squawking in the war room while the blue tactical map on the wall updated every few minutes with more bad news from the planet below.

Red countdown to a new year. Eight minutes. Heart broiled in an adrenaline stew, flushing cheeks, sweat squeezing from my pores. It was almost relief when I heard my name shouted from behind.

"Harris!"

I turned to see Corporal Peznowski and four blue-uniformed agents rounding the corner with flechette guns drawn. The first blaze tore inches past my head, one of the pencil-thin projectiles opening my chin like a zipper, before I could throw myself through the nearest double doors. Two-minute dash to the shuttle bay. Surprising and killing a pair of guards there. Charlotte's hackpick in hand, wresting me control of my escape shuttle—a steel-gray Thunderwing bomber loaded with medical supply freight. Shuttle dropping from Phobos to Mars's burnt-orange vista, while the base seemed to cough behind me, flash of light, shockwave, two hundred and sixteen bodies flung out, debris streaking the bubble-gum planetside sky.

Shane laughs in the glass chamber.

"What's so damned funny?"

He stops right away, looking pained. "Sorry, Mr.

Pope. I was just thinking that most people die when they get shot in the head. You just get pissed." He checks again on the upload status. "Almost done here, war hero. Save complete in seven seconds."

I'm anxious and tired, suddenly needing to get drunk, get laid and pass out for a month.

"Let me tell you, Shane," I say, "May you live a long life and never—

I'm naked in a steel tub filled with warm water and slimy gel. There's a small console on the wall. A glossy black camera eye studies me from the ceiling.

I don't even remember opening my eyes.

My half-spoken reply to Shane is still on my tongue, but he's nowhere to be found. It's like having a stage backdrop whisked away and a new background springing from unseen theatrical compartments. Knowledge floods into me, recognition springing from old brochures. I'm in a regeneration pod, where new bodies are grown for mental downloads.

Which means I died at some point following my last save.

My contract states that if I flatline on Mars, I'm to be regenerated at Bradbury station, and this was *not* Bradbury. Commercial clinics are bright and welcoming and filled with flowers and ferns, as if you've been resurrected in a Buddhist paradise. Partisan clinics are antiseptic and cold, eschewing comfort for the military necessity of getting you back on your feet as soon as possible.

This room is neither. It looks bolted together by cheap screws and spit. A place built out of rawest necessity; four walls, a ceiling, and optional towels.

The camera peers down at me like a dark crystal ball. I try not to move, letting myself float in the thick water.

And this is *not* my body.

My thoughts spin into a whirlwind of panic. When I had talked with Shane I was six-foot-one, one hundred eighty-five pounds, leanly muscled. My new shell is stunningly at odds with that. Shorter, skinnier, darker. Arms and pubic region covered in light-blond hair. My new hand moves clumsily for the wall console and the screen flashes to life at the slightest, dripping touch.

The first thing I see is the Vector Nanonics LifeTree logo emblazoned beside the keyboard. Not very helpful in betraying my location. All the best upload tech is manufactured by Vector. Scumbags have a virtual monopoly on the trade.

The logo clears and I see an inbox with two unread messages. The first is from me, recorded on December 13, 2274, a date which puts it three weeks past my save with Shane. But the second entry is from Doctor Traci Cucinella, recorded April 6, 2315! What the hell?

I select the first entry. A strange face appears onscreen.

My initial impression is that this is a burnt, deformed old man who has somehow left me a message under my own login. His face is horrifically blistered, dirtied and ruined. Behind him is a dim, nondescript room.

"Hello, Harris," he says through a choking wheeze, as if part of his throat has collapsed. I swallow the lump in my own.

"I'm recording this with the few minutes we have left. You will remember that your last upload followed the explosion on Phobos. Without their tactical center, the Partisans were finished. The Resistance achieved total victory four days later. A few pockets of stubborn holdouts in the west, a lot of groups suicided rather than surrender."

It takes until that moment for me to realize who the burnt man is. There's no use denying it.

I stare into the blistered face and recognize my own.

The monitor-me sighs in difficulty, glassy-eyed and dazed. "They must have had a contingency plan to poison the well in the event of defeat. An orbital stealth platform we never knew about bombarded the planetary surface with three hundred nukes."

My stomach drops. The fledgling colonies of Mars, with all the innocence of scattered college campuses, now laid to waste?

"I was in my apartment when the first bombs hit. The explosion threw me out into the hallway like a doll. I remember crawling through rubble, trying to find the staircase. Some of the residents and I punched our way through the floor and got to the basement, where we were able to send a message to the outside. I have no idea if Charlotte survived. I reached Traci, and I'm recording this message on her bandwidth."

The eyes find mine—hideous funhouse mirror reflection. It makes for a queasy math in my head: one soul across 41 years, two bodies and divergent lines of consciousness in an unfolding fractal pattern like diamond gloss.

"Harris," yesteryear's self tells me, "I've been mortally irradiated, and we can't reach any of the labs for treatment. When you get this..." A sad smile forms on his melted face. "Good luck." A pause. "I slept with Charlotte the night before the bombs fell.

Neither one of us seemed to regret it in the morning. Traci will regen you as soon as possible."

The message ends.

I hit the next message, from Traci, recorded 41 years later.

My finger is a hummingbird kiss on the monitor. Traci's message stirs.

"Harris," she says, and I suck in a panicked breath at how she looks. My God! She is old and gray, enough to account for the passage of 41 years with only the most limited longevity treatments. Her myostatin blockers appear to be cranked too high, giving her a famished appearance.

Or maybe it wasn't blockers at all. What the hell had happened in the space of a single sentence?

"I can just imagine how confused you're going to be when you hear this," she says. "We tried to bring you back right away. But the bombardment was cruelly calculated, Harris. A second wave, much weaker and more scattered, hit a few hours after the first. It destroyed our facilities. I took the save files and fled. It's taken this long to get our equipment up and working again. We had to cannibalize several labs, and then trade with other survivors for equipment. You can't…"

Tears leak from her eyes.

"Things have been difficult, Harris. I lost Charlie …he was murdered a few weeks ago in New Haven."

So bring him back, I think hotly. *The way you brought me.*

Traci's eyes lock onto mine with prescient intensity.

14

JON ENO

"The only city on Mars which still has a working Regen facility is the one you're just waking up to. New Haven. And it's not the way you remember it."

My memory hunts down a map of Mars. New Haven is a shuttle port city seventy miles south of Cydonia. It's where, after detonating Phobos station, I had landed in my stolen shuttle and enjoyed my first victory meal of Pad Thai noodles in the mall rotunda while my guards kept cheering crowds at bay.

Traci wipes her eyes with a harsh, angry motion.

"We hacked you straight into the Regen list, making the system believe you were an approved regeneration in Peznowski's circle. You've probably noticed by now that you are in a different body. Even the doctors at the clinic won't know who you really are."

Peznowski? My fists clench at the name.

"He's alive," Traci says onscreen. "And he's on the governing board of New Haven. Calls himself Deputy Mayor Matthew Bayne. Has a whole new body, new voice, but our AI pat-match scoured his speeches and gave a ninety-one percent match with Peznowski's cadence, word choice, and style. Peznowski is back from the dead and practically in charge of the town you're in."

I stand up, naked and dripping synth-placental slime. The message scrollbar shows me there's just seconds left to the content.

"We need you to kill Peznowski again."

As if I'd needed her to say the words. I nod wearily, feeling as if my stomach has a bloated worm crawling inside it.

"Harris, we included a subfile with your download.

It has blueprints of New Haven, an injectable dom patch—"

My jaw drops like a collapsed drawbridge. Why in the hell would I need a dom patch? Who should I inject?

"—and a total workup of the body you're occupying. We chose you because you're a quick study. Memorize the info ASAP."

"Why?" I ask the monitor.

Traci sighs deeply, her body shrinking. It's as if she can hear me across time and geography.

"The body that you're in," she says, "is Peznowski's son."

The message ends. I delete it instantly, the blood pounding in my head. Then I slide open the pod hatch and walk naked to the shower stall, passing a row of pods and a nurse station. A gray-haired doctor intercepts me. His name registers to my nanonics eye-lens: DR. HORACE WELLINGTON.

Wellington is an alarmingly hairy fellow, what a Neanderthal would look like if snatched from the Paleolithic and forcibly dressed into a starchy white lab coat. His eyes simmer beneath impossibly bushy eyebrows.

"Why didn't you ring for assistance?" he demands. "If you fell while relearning coordination, your father..."

Would cut out your eyes? I think. *I saw him do it once to a prisoner whose transgression was a "disrespectful" glance in Peznowski's direction as he and I were walking past the line of cells. The man's name was Clint Frederick Jamison, a captured journalist who had written an anonymous editorial*

17

against the Partisans. But nothing is anonymous anymore with patmatchers and sniffer programs combing the web like merciless spiders, feeling for treacherous vibrations. I remember Jamison's name, because Peznowski had tortured his wife to death repeatedly over the course of forty days. Every time they brought her back, she woke up screaming. She died the same way.

It was understandable, then, that Jamison might be apt to shoot Peznowski a glare. And for it, Peznowski had the man restrained, and personally plucked his eyes out with a staple-remover. I stood by, forced to watch, while Jamison screeched and howled in pitiable agony, and I promised myself I would delete the memory that night. But I never did. I kept it, out of respect for Jamison. Maybe, too, to add more fuel to my desire to kill the corporal with my own hands.

Or with my teeth.

Like my teeth in the throat of that dog.

I realize suddenly I haven't answered Wellington. He's peering at me suspiciously from beneath his caterpillar-like eyebrows.

"I'm fine," I say, and freeze at the sound of my new voice. It's like having a stranger speak beneath my chin.

The doctor seizes my head, tilting it one way and another. Shines a light in my eyes, checks the pupils. I have the discomforting thought that he's looking for the imposter beneath the skin.

"Your father is on his way."

Good.

"Good."

I rinse my body in the shower stalls, and use the moment to access Traci's subfile by pressing the subdermal chip behind my ear. A lavender flower of access tabs blossoms in my eyes, and I gorge on the info train. This body's identity is registered to a Peter J. Bayne, son of Matthew and Jessica. I wash my hair with the facility's shampoo, prodding data bits of Peter's life, interests and habits constructed piecemeal by Traci's hack team.

I'm toweling off when I complete my overview of Peter Bayne's e-mails. There's a fogged mirror in the stall, and I wipe it clear. A strange blond teenager looks out at me from the frame.

The thing is, I *want* to dislike this kid but I find it difficult to. He is nineteen. He subscribes to multiple samurai sensoramics, especially ones where he gets to play the lone ronin helping out impoverished villages. He likes to hike. His e-mail confessions indicate he hates his father.

The mirrored smile on my face makes me sick.

When I emerge, dressed in Peter's ghastly choice of neo-Victorian attire, I go straight to the waiting room and meet Matthew Bayne, the new identity of Corporal Peznowski.

"Peter!"

Years back, I'd read an article in *Nowire* about why resurrectees make certain new body choices. An unsurprising eighty-one percent select the same shell—minor alterations notwithstanding. The remaining nineteen percent purchase entirely new bodies of calculated antithesis to what they were born into. Blondes into brunettes, women into men, short into tall, racial switching…

Corporal Peznowski has defied the stats. He's taller, and traded his steel-gray hair for brown curls. He's still white, and sports black-rimmed glasses stylish among the self-identified intellectuals. But the face isn't really so different from what he wore in his last life. He's gone from Nordic looks to a swarthy Portuguese genotype while keeping the general mix of features in eerie reminiscence of his birth face. Clever, this attempt at ducking pattern sniffers.

"Peter!" he says again, embracing me warmly. His cologne stuffs my nose. "Let me look at you. How does it feel? All checked up, no worries?"

"Sure."

He looks me over, concentrating on my eyes. The worm in my stomach flips around. There hasn't been time to study my new identity's speech patterns and word choices, so I'm determined to be as monosyllabic as possible. But what about the eyes? Matthew Bayne's eyes *were the same as Corporal Peznowski's.* There is no mistaking them. I had looked into those eyes too often to miss the gray, hard, glassy stare that's part calculator and part sadist. He seemed to regard everything as if it was potential food, to be weighed, smelled and eventually cut up and devoured.

"Come on," he says gladly, "Mom wasn't expecting you until next week. You were fifteenth on the waiting list, but I pulled a few strings. Let's give her a surprise!"

I force a smile. Endorphins flap in my chest, my movements strain in odd directions as if tugged by elastic bands. Peter's muscle memory and hormones will be a problem. Add them to the damn list.

Peznowski/Bayne signs the release at the reception desk, and we depart together, father and son, through a corridor smelling of disinfectant. We step outside.

It's the enclosed "outside" of a Martian colony. Everything is built economically crammed together, replicating the appearance of a Middle Eastern medina. The narrow street is beset on each side by a mall's worth of shops, balcony markets, squat offices and a monorail station.

Peznowski leads us to the monorail station. We settle into the train seats. He squeezes my arm.

"With your birthday coming up, I was going to take us spelunking at Agatha Crossing. You still want to go? Your accident hasn't changed your mind, has it?"

I squint at him in the low fluorescent lighting. "My birthday? We've still got eight months before it's my birthday, Dad."

The Matthew Bayne shell grins. "Right. Well you know me, always thinking ahead."

There's no air conditioner during the ride home, but I can't stop shivering.

Sweetie!"

Mom greets me in the kitchen, wearing a checkered apron and a wide ruby-lipped smile. "Let me look at you! All checked up, no worries?"

Her eyes are gray, hard, glassy and with the flicker of cruelty. They were eyes I knew well. They were features I knew well.

My God!

My blood turns to cold slush, and though I tell myself to smile or say something, my body just won't obey. The nightmarish awareness that Peznowski's features are peering out from an attractive female face is enough to sicken me, but that's just the ragged fringe of a deeper, almost cosmic blasphemy. According to Traci's records, Peter Bayne was the natural offspring of my parents. Which meant that Peznowski, existing in two separate bodies, had naturally produced me. Grunting and ejaculating, the unholy union growing into a new child from the fruit of two loins of the same puppetmaster?

I almost attack her right there. My young hands can feel the ghostly resistance of her eyes giving way beneath steely pronged fingers.

Please...control. Please.

"Dear?" Mom's eyes widen in suspicion and concern.

Please!

My smile cracks like a fissure in ice. "Sorry, Mom. I still feel like I'm in the save center."

Good!

She hugs me. I notice that Peznowski has given himself very large breasts. "Tacos tonight?"

My mind races fluidly across reams of data, a laser flashing on Peter's record. Is this another test? I nod noncommittally, and then notice a reddish-brown dog padding toward me from the back rooms. Doberman, muscles sliding beneath short lustrous fur. A hundred pounds, easily. It puts its head into my hands. Wet tongue and cool nose.

"Oh! Look who missed you!"

It's movie-fueled nonsense that pets can detect a stranger in their owner's shell. Pure urban legend bullshit. The Doberman's tail wags, tongue laps my fingers. She smells the natural cologne of pheromones, body salts and skin oils. She can't telepathically sniff out an imposter any more than she can play chess.

Is she Peznowski also?

The freakish thought blasts through me. I stare into the liquid black eyes for signs of my old enemy. Dog breath, eyes like black pearls. Teeth upthrust from cushions of slick pink gums, like black spearpoint ears. Like a caveman feeling out the raw Paleolithic world, I think: *Dog. This is dog. Not man.*

The Doberman's name bobs up from my illicit subfile.

"Hey, Suzie! How are ya, girl?"

Dinner passes like an ocean current, sweeping me along with my monstrous progenitors like a ship caught in an ocean eddy. Mom and Dad joke and tease each other, interspersing their joviality with somber reflections of my spelunking accident. Mom kisses my cheek. Dad cleans up the table, catches Mom from behind and gives a playful tickle, to which she spins around and wrestles in his grasp. They move like dancers, their motions as delicately attuned as a well-oiled machination.

I want to throw up.

And worse is the feeling that I'm being scrutinized. Whenever I peek up from my food, Mom or Dad or both are glinting at me. It's Planet Peznowski, a visceral mousetrap run by the most sadistic creature I've ever met.

"So how is it, coming back from the dead?"

Mom's question, her teeth a flash of white behind her wine glass. Dad watches me over the yellow rim of his taco.

"Waking up in that tub was like in the movie *Star Shiver,* when the main guy is defrosted."

Mom laughs. Dad nods vigorously, biting down on his food. Inwardly, I thank Traci's thorough research.

Dinner ends. Sweat drips down my face like the hot splash of rain. When I finally retire to Peter Bayne's bedroom of mock redwood, I feel ill, right down to my atoms. There's a pilot chair in the room's corner, and I know Traci is waiting for me to make contact through its virtual chat rooms. A holographic pair of samurai swords hangs on the wall. Guess Dad doesn't let me have the real thing. Couldn't make things too easy.

I seat myself in the pilot chair, slip my fingers into the virtuboard gloves, and instantly a pinwheel of color opens in my mind as my nanonics make the uplink to the local web. Peter doesn't have many friends; his online explorations are sharply limited in a global web that is crawling back from postwar shambles.

I find Traci at once, in one of Peter's few virtual hangouts—a place called SteamGuild. It looks like a submarine pen, gloomy and damp, with colossal chains and industrial wheels cranking mad configurations of gears across the wall. It takes me a minute to realize that the gears themselves are arranged into a mockery of famous ancient artwork. *The Last Supper. Starry Night. The Scream.* Young people mill about in steampunk clichés. Water drips from a rusted ceiling and tinkles into brackish pools.

Traci is waiting for me, wearing a neogoth avatar with fiery vermilion hair like blood against her black corset. Huge eyes reminiscent of Old Calendar Japanese animation.

"Peter!" she says, visibly relieved. "Welcome back from your accident!" She hesitated. "Your Dad must be happy to see you."

"Actually, *both* Mom and Dad had the exact same identical reaction! It was surprising!"

I can see Traci gets my meaning. She looks as if she's been tasered, and makes several stammering attempts at speech without blowing both our covers.

Was my father monitoring this communication? The deputy mayor of New Haven would have access to spybots, and in his former life, Peznowski had been openly addicted to control. Liked to know what was happening. Hated being taken off guard.

Traci is still trying to get her bearings. "Are you ...will you still be able..."

I cut in hastily, "I haven't told him just how serious you and I are getting. I think I'll bring it up tomorrow. I did have a couple of questions for you, though."

"What questions, Pete?"

"If I *tell* Mom and Dad, do you think that will be enough? Are there other relatives of mine who should be *told* also?"

She shakes her head, hair batting the sides of her face. "We would've...I mean, Mom and Dad should be enough."

"You sure?"

Traci freezes. Her face loses all composure, as if the nerve endings behind her skin have been cut. Somewhere in Traci's lab, a hasty conference is being held with all the people creating this youthful apparition.

How many Peznowskis exist? How crafty is my old enemy? The nightmarish image slithers into my skull of the entire town of New Haven possessed by Peznowski clones.

Then Traci blinks, her invisible puppeteers slipping back into the role. "Just tell your parents. Both of them. I'm sure you'll find a way."

"And afterward?"

Traci's avatar makes a strange motion with her hand. She rubs her fingers across her palm. I recognize it from my earliest undercover training, back when I was assigned to infiltrate the Partisans.

Erase yourself.

Somewhere in my new head, Traci must have planted a kill switch. Always handy when behind enemy lines. I haven't had the chance to thoroughly review my subfile, but I do a quick search now and find the kill switch icon: a tiny grim reaper.

Too bad Clint Frederick Jamison's wife didn't have one implanted.

I thank Traci and log out. Peter's bedroom returns, and I swivel on the pilot chair, wondering what to do.

There's a brush of movement at my bedroom door. Suzie enters, tail wagging. Poor girl must have missed Peter.

I scratch behind her ears, considering the problem before me. Across forty-one years, Shane's voice enters my thoughts: *The Partisans were famous for being able to sniff out a mole.*

I know I'm on borrowed time.

The next morning Dad is gone by the time I get to the kitchen for breakfast. Mom's at the counter, wielding two knives as if they are her hands, dexterously pinning a raw venison roast and slicing it up.

"Good morning!" Mom coos. "Breakfast is on the table!"

I regard my breakfast plate of polenta and minced seaflower, glass of cranberry juice, and a sprig of mint.

"Did you sleep well?"

I nod, helping myself to the juice. When Peznowski dies, he'll eventually be regenerated at the same center where he picked me up. What was Traci's plan for that? Had her hack team placed other operatives, insidiously tucked away inside hijacked bodies? Were they even now combing through save files, locating and deleting the encoded remnants of the Partisans?

Mom rubs her blades together. She lifts the diced meat into a pan.

I finish the juice, grab some polenta and approach Mom/Peznowski from behind while she splashes tenderizer over the meat. I'll make it clean and quick, and handle Dad when he comes home. Reflexively, I glance out the window. There, pacing amid the rows of adobe homes, was a lone man, e-cig dangling from his mouth.

It's Dad.

Perplexed, I go to the window and press against the cool glass. Dad is a block away, the gloomy apartment buildings hover like gothic towers above him. He's talking into his wrist, though by his animated movements I'm guessing he's in full virtual conference.

"Dad didn't go to work today?" I ask, turning to Mom.

She's rinsing her knives. The kitchen looks strangely fuzzy, gray at the corners of my vision.

"He did, dear."

"But..." I feel my head fogging, suddenly aware of

the empty cranberry glass with ghastly implication. Panic novas in my chest, galvanizing a last desperate action. My fingers are tingling, legs turning rubbery. I leap at Mom.

She turns me aside with ease, twisting my attack away and slamming my head into the oven. White sparks explode in my vision. I try to get to my feet but Mom is already backing out of reach. The strength leeches out from my limbs. Ceiling spins once around, like water in a drain, and before all goes black, I see Peznowski's cruel eyes glinting out from that imposter face.

How did they…know…?

When I regain consciousness, my optic readout shows me that sixteen minutes have passed. I can't move my arms or legs. Vision clears, but my head feels as if someone has put a drill behind my ear. I'm on my parent's bed, limbs strapped to all four bedposts. The pillow is wet behind me.

Mom is holding bloody knives and smiling.

"Mom?"

"Cut the charade," Dad says from the corner. He flicks something at me and it lands like an earring on my chest.

My kill switch. He must have dug it out of my head while I was drugged.

"Who are you?" Dad says. He sits down like a gargoyle beside me, hunching and eager, the old jackal expression on his face. "I already know you're not our son. We grafted a rotating verbal tic into his consciousness when he was young, triggered whenever he steps into the kitchen. He's not even aware of it. Subtle, comes across as mild OCD." When I don't answer, Dad's nostrils flare. "You've got a damned name. What is it?"

"Maximilian."

Dad turns to Mom. "Take out his eyes."

She springs into action so fast it's as if she's been waiting her whole life for this. Mom kneels beside my head, still wearing the checkered apron from breakfast.

"What is it with you and eyes, Peznowski?" I shout.

"Wait," Dad says. He's almost too late. Mom has already positioned the tips of both blades a half inch from the corners of my left eye. A horrific stainless steel V in my vision.

In my right eye, Dad's hybrid face appears. He's flush and excited, eyes like pale lanterns behind his glasses.

No kill switch, no kill switch, no kill switch.

Dad looks apelike, cheeks swollen, eyes sharp. "Do you know me?"

"I'm Harris Alexander Pope."

My parents let out an astonished gasp in the same instant. Their heads rotate to regard each other, slack-jawed and gratified.

"Harris?!" Dad sits back, laughing heartily. He stands up and does a fist-pump in the air. "Oh! The universe loves me!"

Mom leaps upon me, knocking the wind from my lungs. Her laughter is shrill and hideous as she gouges both my eyes out.

H arris? Look at me."

Dad's voice, followed by wicked female laughter.

I turn my head in the direction of the voice, trying

not to think of my mutilated face. My throat is ragged from screaming.

"You know," Dad intones in my ear, "I would never have known you were the traitor. I died up there...no memory of what happened. We always planned on regrouping in New Haven if things went wrong and at first, I wondered why you didn't regen with us. I spent hours combing through the files for your save. Then I saw all the magazines and news clips. Harris Pope, war hero, went undercover with the Partisans and popped our headquarters like a bad blister. Who sent you here?"

"The ghost of Christmas Past."

There's a terrible silence. The pain in my eyesockets fans into my skull. Fear is an incredible emotion. We are nothing more than ragged pulses of fear, tossed out of wombs and onto a great frying pan. Even with technological miracles delivered through syringe or ingestible, we are still the primeval beast howling for all time.

"What was the plan?" Peznowski asks. Can't tell if it's Mom or Dad. Husky voice, almost a whisper. "You kill us, and then...what?"

"They didn't tell me. Honest."

"They?"

"Christmas Past, Present, and—"

It must be his fist that smashes through my teeth. The attack stuns me into mute stupidity, the broken teeth in my mouth like peanut shells. I spit them out in a gob of bloody saliva.

"I'm going to torture you forever, you know." Mom's voice in my ear. "But not like this. Matthew and

I have been talking about how Peter grew up too fast. We want a little baby again. How would you like your consciousness downloaded into a helpless creature, engineered to never grow up. Your mind trapped in that prison for all time, slowly turning to mush, while we feed you, and wrap you up and change your diapers …year, after year, after year? Forever?"

A new scream starts in my throat, shredding my resolve.

I stutter through broken teeth and blood. "Earth will eventually step in."

"No, they won't," Dad says. "We made a mistake in our earlier dealings with Earth. Strict isolationism doesn't work. The birth world needs to be brought to heel. With their environmental problems, economic problems, political problems…all it will take is one big disaster to *reduce* them."

"Earth will show up sooner or later and erase every last Partisan file!" I hear desperation in my own voice.

"A dozen captured asteroids too small for detection," Dad says. "Hurtling toward Mother Blue. You think Mars was hit hard? Earth will be thrown back to the Stone Age, and we'll make sure they stay there."

The terrible majesty of what he is saying is underscored by its plausibility. Even at the time of the Partisan war, Earth had been collapsing under the weight of environmental and economic pressures. If the Partisans strike Earth in the way he proposes, civilization really will come apart at the seams.

And meanwhile, I'll be screaming wordless for all time, cradled in my sadistic mother's arms…

"You Partisans always have a contingency plan," I say numbly.

"Yes," Mom and Dad say together. "We do."

I open my sightless sockets. Black room, swirling in an oily eddy. Through the squirting fluids and ruptured flesh, my optic nerves are firing in dazzling pixilated bursts of color, a swansong for the world of light. The nerves are still reaching for information to process, phantom images like black plates of glass, all the same color, shifting over each other.

I clear my throat. "So do I."

In my head, buried where Mom's knives couldn't get to, the dom patch is running. Since injecting my subject last night with the neuro-remote hidden in my fingers, it has never stopped running. Doesn't work on humans, but it turns lower life-forms into remote-controlled toys.

The dom patch menu tells me that these last few minutes of conversation have been successfully recorded by our ever-so-quiet listener in the doorway. I scroll down to the next option.

ATTACK PARAMETERS: *ALL*.

I'm naked in a steel tub, and Traci is helping me sit up. Shane is nowhere to be seen, and my mouth still thinks I'm in midspeech at the save center. Behind Traci, I see Charlotte's lovely face, but it's strangely aged now. A towel is in her hands.

I snatch it from her and cover my nakedness. "Do you mind?" The surroundings settle into my thoughts. A regeneration pod, where they grow new bodies for mental downloads.

Which means that I've died. And I don't even remember opening my eyes.

Traci laughs, her shock of chestnut curls dancing with the movement. "Sorry, hero. What's the last thing you remember?"

Towel floating over my groin atop the slimy water, I look back and forth between their faces. A wave of irritation flickers in me. "It was three days after I returned from Phobos. I was talking to Shane. He said there were seven seconds left for the file uploading."

Traci's smile straightens out, and she looks at me with strange respect and sympathy. "There's a lot to talk about, Harris." She steps back, taking Charlotte's arm. "Get yourself toweled off and meet us in my office, third door down from the showers."

Their celebratory joy is visible, and I get the impression of being the birthday boy about to be led into a surprise party. I glance at the regeneration pod again, my anger subsiding. "Is this Bradbury Station?"

"New Haven."

"My contract states—"

"See me in my office," Traci interrupts, and she walks away with Charlotte.

I finally notice a wall console within reach, and I slap its screen.

The first stunner is today's date on the ticker at the bottom of the screen: May 20, 2316! Forty-two years separating the blink of an eye and flash of a neuron! Then I see two recent news articles posted by Traci for my viewing. The first headline rocks my core. NEW HAVEN PARTISAN REMNANT ERASED, "GRISLY" PLANS MADE PUBLIC.

The Partisans? Hadn't we defeated them four decades ago?

I stand up, dripping synthgel, and tuck the towel around my waist. Forget the shower. Traci needs to explain a few things, and I think I'll start by prodding her about that second, weirder and older headline:

FAMILY DOG KILLS
DEPUTY MAYOR, WIFE, SON.

Planetary Scouts

written by

Stephen Sottong

illustrated by

JOSHUA MEEHAN

ABOUT THE AUTHOR

Stephen Sottong was born and raised in the rust-belt town of Kokomo, Indiana. He was introduced to science fiction by his brother and sister. The first book he checked out of the public library was Ben Bova's Star Conquerors. *From there, he made his way through as much of the library's sci-fi collection as possible, reading the classic novels of the '50s and '60s from Heinlein, Asimov, Clarke, Brunner, Le Guin and others. He started writing at ten and continued sporadically throughout his working career but never did so in earnest until retirement. In the interim, Stephen repaired radios in the Navy and afterward in civilian life until he decided to upgrade his education.*

After ten years of engineering and another stint in college, he became an engineering librarian for the rest of his working career. As an academic librarian, he wrote numerous dull, scholarly articles published in library journals. The possibility of early retirement offered him the opportunity to return to his first love and write fiction full time. His short stories have been published in regional magazines but Writers of the Future *is his first national publication.*

ABOUT THE ILLUSTRATOR

Joshua Meehan was born in Nevada in 1990 and raised with his five younger siblings in Anchorage, Alaska. His interest in art began at the age of three, when he used crayons and markers on the walls and pillows in his house. His parents were always extremely supportive in his artistic pursuits. Since Joshua was home-schooled, they made sure to foster his passion through an art-focused curriculum, which included private lessons from Betty Dye, a local art teacher.

Joshua and his family moved to Tucson, Arizona in 2002. Here he studied fine art at the Arizona-Sonora Desert Museum and attended Ironwood Ridge High School. In 2008 Joshua received the grand prize in the Congressional Art Contest for his district and earned the honor of Eagle Scout. Later he studied fine art and illustration at the University of Arizona and pursued large-scale game and film projects, creating content and direction for production teams. Today he resides in Tucson, where he works as a freelance illustrator and concept artist and looks forward to the future in such a passionate field.

Planetary Scouts

-1-

I was about to order another beer when a rumbling in the floor announced the arrival of the passenger liner. I thought about letting my new partner find me in the bar but decided against it. New recruits are impressionable. No use scaring off another one.

Picking my left leg carefully off the bar rail, I placed the offending appendage on the floor. My knee had locked again. Hobbling would make me late. I forced the scarred fingers of my left hand into a fist and smacked the back of my knee. It gave with a jolt of pain. I was barely able to grab the edge of the bar to break my fall. Levering myself up, I flashed my credit chit at the pay station and made my way unsteadily to the door.

Some parents and their Scout son were standing at the door of the bar making "oo-ah" noises at the painting on the bar's domed ceiling. The owners had hired a starving offworld artist to immortalize the Planetary Scouts. The artist was talented, but he never talked to any of us. To start with, there's the motto: *Discover and Explore*. That's our motto all right, but we don't do discovery any more. The boredom of hop to a planet, take a few readings, and repeat endlessly, had driven humans nuts, so discovery is now left to robot ships. The only reason they use us for exploration is because they've never come up with a computer that's as adaptable as a human; although there are more than a few Scouts who wish they would, and pronto.

Then there're those planets the artist has us exploring. All the planets look a whole lot like primitive Terra or one of its clones. The fauna looks cuddly—nothing with claws or fangs. Some day I'd like to explore a world like that. Hasn't happened yet.

The space dock wasn't far, so I walked. The night was typically warm and cloudless. In spite of the lights along the commercial strip, stars shone. One of the two moons was rising, and the docking stations that ringed the planet formed a brilliant necklace. A street vendor was preparing a dish that smelled of curry for a wobbly-looking Scout. As the knee warmed up, my pain eased.

The railing by the dock's reception area was filled with expectant Scouts waiting for visitors and new partners. Brushing the hair away from my artificial left eye, I zoomed in for a better view of the disembarking passengers. I had no idea what an A. Lester would look like. A short woman in her late twenties wearing a fresh Scout uniform came out first, long brown hair pulled back from a fine-featured face. Her body was full, lithe, muscular. She carried a large pack on her back.

"Oh yes," I said under my breath, "if there is a good deity, this will be the one. I deserve her after that last mush-for-brains." The young woman spotted a middle-aged female Scout holding a sign with a name on it, approached, and shook hands. So I reverted to being an atheist.

The remaining passengers were all civilians. The railing cleared. My knee ached.

A female flight attendant with short red hair left the hatch, the kind of woman—tall, poised, gorgeous— who managed to look great in the shapeless uniforms the spacelines pack their attendants into. She was laughing and talking to the person behind her.

A young man ducked out of the hatch. I zoomed in. The kid was nearly two meters tall, with short blond hair, strong features, and a body capable of towing a small excursion vehicle out of a swamp. He joked amiably with the flight attendant who didn't take her eyes off him. The man carried both of their bags effortlessly in one hand. Hell, he even had a cleft chin. I turned my eyes to heaven. "There is a God: it's Loki."

I made my way to the gate. "You must be my new partner."

The young man dropped the bags and sprang to attention. "Scout Private Lester reporting for duty."

"Yeah, yeah." I turned to the flight attendant. "And you would be?"

"Marina." She offered a flawlessly manicured hand.

I handed Marina her bag. "Thanks for keeping the kid safe." I turned to Lester. "Come on, kid."

Lester shrugged and waved goodbye to the crestfallen woman. He fell in beside me. "It's an honor to meet you, sir. Aidan Pastor is a legend in the Scouts."

I flinched. "Right, kid."

"We study your tactics in Planetary Scout Academy."

"I better check on my royalties."

"I can't wait to take off on our first mission."

I waved my credit chit at a ground car, and it opened. We climbed in, and the door swung shut. The seats were too small for Lester. "Scout enlisted quarters building 42," I said. The car moved out.

I looked at the eager face and pulled up my left shirt sleeve. "You know what these are, kid?"

"Burns?"

I nodded. "My last partner played by Academy rules. That's why I've got these. We're going nowhere till I'm sure you've got my rules down to instinct. So what do you do when an unknown lifeform comes at you fast?"

"Attempt to determine if the lifeform is intelligent."

"Wrong. Rule one: if the local fauna or flora starts chasing you, shoot it. My last partner wouldn't shoot the natives because he thought they might be intelligent. They were intelligent—intelligent enough to have a catapult. The creatures he wouldn't shoot hit us with a boulder as we tried to get the hell out. It damaged the ship—caught on fire, burned him to death and nearly killed me."

"It was bad for you, but it saved the beings."

I stuck a scarred index finger into his oversized chest. "Nope. When they hit the ship, there was a radiation leak. Killed everything for fifty kilometers. Wiped out all the intelligent life on the planet. Only thing that saved us was our suits. If he'd shot a couple of them, there'd still be intelligent life on that planet, he'd still be alive, and I wouldn't be in constant pain. You don't shoot, I'll shoot you."

Lester quieted. "Yes, sir."

"Part of the reason that the Scouts were formed was so humans wouldn't wipe out any more intelligent lifeforms, but we've got to protect ourselves so that we can protect them."

I held up a second scarred finger. "Rule number two: this is work; we're not on vacation. Get in, get the info, get out. The longer you stay on a planet, the better the chance you'll get in trouble. You want a vacation, go to Vega 5."

Lester nodded. "Makes sense."

"Last rule: I make the rules."

"You've got the experience."

"Just remember that when we're in the field. Now, we've got a few months of training before we go anywhere." I looked at the kid. *Kid*—I was barely twenty years older than him. His eager, unscarred face reminded me of a dozen other new Scouts I'd watched come off that passenger ship. Most never made the return trip home. "You ready for this?"

"Yes, sir." Lester sat up very straight. His head touched the roof of the car.

"No, you're not." The car reached the barracks. I got out and grabbed Lester's bag. I waved my credit chit at the car's sensor. "Lakeside Hotel, also credit one return trip for the passenger." The car flashed an acknowledgment. I saw Lester was puzzled. "You got a credit chit?"

"Yes, sir."

"You'll probably find Marina at the hotel bar drowning her sorrows. Enjoy yourself. It'll be the last time for a while. I put the return on file so you can get back here if you spend all your savings trying to impress her. You're in room 36 of the barracks. You get up at the normal time, no matter when you get back." I slammed the car door and it sped off.

The kid had overpacked. I had a hell of a time lugging that bag to his room. A couple of other Scouts in the barracks saw me dragging the bag and asked if I'd gotten a care package from mommy. No one offered to help. I love my fellow Scouts.

When I checked in the morning, the barracks computer said Lester had crawled in at 0200. I cut him some slack and didn't roust him until 0530. He dragged himself down to the mess hall and started downing what passes for coffee on this planet. They brew it a lot stronger here than they do at the Academy. Lester downed enough to make him really twitchy and keep him awake for a couple of days. That probably saved his good looks.

We went on a long hike after breakfast. The doc had given me a shot in the knee so I could keep moving. I took a bang-stick to lean on and for extra defense. Lester outfitted himself. The class 3 fence around the facility should have given him a clue, but, as expected, he dressed for a warm summer's outing.

Outside the fence, a road led, arrow-straight, to another Scout facility. We took the trails instead, winding through a land of red boulders and sparse desert vegetation. Lester, who hadn't bothered to tuck his pants into the tops of his boots, was being eaten alive by the sand fleas. He tried to keep up a good pace while scratching and beating on his legs.

Snarky was waiting in his usual hiding place in the rocks next to a well-worn animal track. Lester had the lead. He managed to get his arm up before Snarky smacked him. That prevented Lester from getting permanent scars on his face, but his arm broke. I sat on a rock to view the melee.

Snarky is something like a cross between an ant, a bear and an alligator: over two meters tall standing on what goes for his back legs, unpleasant to look at and highly territorial. Snarky got his name from the crooked grin he gets on his mouthparts when he first sees a Scout. The grin is kind of endearing until you realize it has less to do with how pleased he is to see you than how tasty he thinks you are.

Most of his kind avoid humans, but Snarky seems to enjoy the challenge. Snarky's been learning from his encounters with Scouts. He attacks the right side now so that the Scout can't get to his stunner. The kid did a decent job defending himself in spite of the arm. He managed to lob a few rocks at Snarky and even launched Snarky backward using his legs. When Snarky bared his fangs, I decided to end the match, stunning him with the bang-stick. The Base commander gets pissed if you bring back a dead recruit. It takes a lot longer to patch them up.

Lester was holding the broken arm and looking green. "What the hell was that thing?"

"Local fauna."

"Why didn't you warn me?"

"Nobody's gonna warn you on a new planet. If you aren't ready, you face the consequences. Better get that bleeding stopped and set the arm before Snarky wakes up."

"Aren't you going to help?"

"Sure, I'll give you all the advice you can stomach."

Lester made it halfway back to Base (probably courtesy of the coffee) before I had to call for a transport.

I flirted with the nurses while the docs patched

Lester up. My usual suave and debonair repartee wasn't doing it that day. It may have been my recently acquired scars, but I noticed the nurses kept sneaking peeks at Lester sitting shirtless on the examining table.

On the way back to the barracks, Lester looked sullen. "Come on," I said. "Spill it. What's eating you?"

"What the hell kind of training was that?"

"The best kind. Half the veterans take their trainees out for a tête-à-tête with Snarky, half don't. Of the ones who don't, twenty-five percent lose their new partner on their first outing."

"And the ones that do?"

"Only ten percent."

Lester grimaced. "That's still high."

"Hey, I better than doubled your chances of survival. That should be worth a little pain."

Lester cradled his arm. "I guess so."

"You'll remember this and be prepared for your next encounter."

Lester moved in front of me. "So why doesn't everyone use Snarky?"

I stood there and looked the kid in the eye, which was some trick since he was a full third of a meter taller than me and my neck was stiff with burn scars. "If a guy loses enough new recruits, he gets paired with another veteran. That raises his chances of making twenty-five missions and going home with a full pension."

"They let their partners die?"

"There's three ways out of this organization: dead, disabled and twenty-five. You'd be surprised what a person will do when their own skin is at stake."

"What about you?"

"Me, I'll let Snarky beat the crap out of you to teach you a lesson you'll never forget. That doesn't mean I've got any illusions that you'll be with me when I celebrate my twenty-five, even though I've got eighteen already. I've lost four partners. You could easily be the fifth." We stood by the door of Lester's room. "Tomorrow I go to Prime for surgery. They're supposed to get rid of the burn scars and replace the knee. That gives you a couple of weeks to train on your own. I've set up a bunch of simulations for you to work on while I'm gone. If you baby yourself because you've got a broken arm, you'll learn nothing. Think of the arm as added realism. When we're off on a mission, we have to keep going—broken arm or not."

"I'll get started on them now."

"Tomorrow. Get some sleep."

I left Lester at his door and went to my room to pack. I woke up in the middle of the night in a cold sweat, shaking. I hate doctors.

The Scouts have their own star system with two more-or-less habitable planets: Base and Prime. Base is hot, miserable, and nothing much grows there. Prime is cold, miserable and nothing much grows there. They send you to Prime when you need major medical attention, especially if they think you might be contagious. The hospital they sent me to was new. The last one had gotten contaminated with some alien crud, and they had to permanently quarantine the whole thing: buildings, doctors, nurses, patients and all. I was not looking forward to this.

I was the sole occupant of the shuttle that day. It blasted off Base, giving me a view of the arid landscape

45

broken by small seas and a band of temperate climate near the poles that we weren't allowed to visit in order to preserve the native biota. The trip lasted only an hour, and I was presented with the vista of Prime with its polar glaciers extending over two thirds of its surface, broken by a band of somewhat livable forests and tundra around the equator.

The shuttle dumped me as close to the doorstep of the hospital as safety allowed. The staff had me prepped and sedated within minutes. I was in postop before I knew what had hit me.

They did a good job. The new knee could stop a laser blast even if the rest of me couldn't. The new skin was too pale and too smooth, but at least it moved and I wouldn't scare the nurses anymore. They get you in and out of Prime as quickly as possible, which was fine by me.

I made one side trip before I left Prime. A couple of attendants locked me inside an isolation vehicle, tested it for leaks, and sent me on my way. The quarantine complex where Miyuki lives is on a corner of the continent, about an hour from the hospital. The portholes in her living bubble have views of the ocean—if you can call a big lake that's covered with ice half the year an ocean. The vehicle drove into a covered garage attached to one of the quarantine buildings. The garage door closed behind me, and the air was sucked out. I didn't like the way the vehicle's windows creaked.

Miyuki walked up to a window close to my vehicle. I was glad that she could walk again. The blue and green veining on her skin was less than the last time I saw her.

"Hi, kiddo," I greeted her. "How they treating you?"

Her voice was not quite lifelike over the comm system. "I'm doing a lot better. They've got the bugs enough under control that I can't seriously contaminate anyone in here. I'm out of isolation."

"That's great. How you getting along with the rest of the inmates?"

"Half of them have accepted their life; they're fine. The bitter ones are boring; I stay away from them. We've got a bridge league. I started reading the classics. Just got done with the *Tale of Genji*. Always meant to read it."

"You've got the time now."

She looked me over as best she could. "They did a good job putting you back together."

"Thanks. You're looking better too."

She shook her head. "Not like I did."

"You're still beautiful."

She glanced down. "I wish I could believe that."

I was tongue-tied, like I always got with her.

She put a hand on the window. "You couldn't have saved me. I was determined to be the best Scout. That was my decision. You tried your best to talk me out of it. You tried to get me to wash out. I had to be aggressive; it's the only way a woman makes it in the Scouts. If it hadn't been that hellhole of a planet, it would have been another. Just try to keep yourself out of here."

I couldn't cry because she wouldn't.

Before I left, the garage was flooded with a gas that would peel the hull off a starship and then bathed in radiation, just in case anything had leaked from the quarantine building. I broke into a cold sweat

47

watching the meters on the vehicle—they kept jiggling. I should make these visits remotely, but she'd been my best partner.

-2-

After a week of rehab I returned to Base. Walking back from the space dock, I ran into a few Scouts, all of whom had sage ideas on what should be surgically replaced or corrected the next time I went to Prime.

I entered the barracks as Lester was walking out, massaging the right arm. "How goes it, Lester?"

"Pretty good." He gave me an appraising once-over. "They did good work on you."

"Always do. They've put me back together about every third mission. By now they should be able to do it in the dark. How's the arm?"

"Healing slow. I keep reinjuring it. It's been good practice though. I never used my left arm with weapons. I'm getting fairly accurate with it."

"Good. I take it you've been going through some of the simulations?"

"I've made it through all of them. Some more than once."

"You're pushing yourself."

"I never want to go back to that pit of a mining planet I grew up on." Lester's right hand had clenched into a fist. He took a deep breath and opened the fingers. "Are these simulations based on recordings of your missions?"

I motioned Lester into my room and pointed to a chair. "Yeah."

"The one with the catapult was the last mission?"

"That's when I lost your predecessor."

"I think I figured out how to get us out without killing any of the natives."

"Show me."

Lester called up his version of the simulation. His solution was ingenious. It involved having the ship hop out of range of the catapult just before they fired, while we knocked over a couple of trees to block the native's retreat. Then the ship would hop back and pick us up while they reloaded. It might have worked.

"Nice work, Lester. I'm all for saving lives—ours especially." I started unpacking my stuff. "We're both gonna take a little time off to rehab, then we'll start doing simulations together. These will be new ones; things neither of us have seen. Hopefully, they'll get us working as a team."

We spent about a week working out in the gym. Lester had already figured out that he needed to reduce his lifting and work on flexibility. I focused on making all the new parts function smoothly with the old ones. We did a lot of exercises in tandem to get a feel for how the other guy moved.

Once the local doc cleared us, we started on simulations. The first one was a jungle planet with aggressive trees. We tried it three times and got killed each time. One time we landed in the ocean only to find that the seaweed was as bad as the trees. Eventually we learned the simulation was based on two failed missions. Scout Command included it in case some genius figured how to approach the planet and live.

The next simulation was fairly straightforward. We had our samples and were heading back to the ship when something came out of the ground and grabbed me. Lester's reaction was good; he blasted it. He just needed to learn how to change the settings of his gun on the fly. I would have been mildly toasted. That's better than getting pulled underground by a whatsit, so I gave him good marks anyway.

After that they threw another jungle at us. Jungles are the pits. There's no way to keep track of all the lifeforms. We stood in the mock airlock waiting for it to finish the decontamination cycle. "What's your primary concern when you're outside?"

Even through the suit visor I could tell Lester was wary. "Try not to disturb the native life."

"Wrong: Protect the integrity of your suit. Depending on the level of a breach, you can end up in isolation."

"They mentioned that at the Academy. The profs said they can get rid of most foreign pathogens."

"They lied." The kid looked at me but said nothing. "Most Scouts who have a suit breach either die or end up in permanent isolation. The reason you don't get to take a fun day's leave on Prime is because that's where they house the ones who aren't quite dead."

"You seem to know a whole lot about it."

"The partner before the one who nearly killed me is there."

"Is he going to be released?"

"No, she isn't. She'll spend the rest of her life in an isolation dome. You don't want to join her. Maintain suit integrity at all costs."

"Why don't they tell recruits the truth?"

The hatch opened. Something big stood outside. It moved an appendage toward us that looked like a vine covered with finger-length thorns. I blasted it and hit the close button. The edge of the door cut the appendage off. It was still moving toward us. Lester hit the decontaminate button and the appendage dissolved.

I started breathing again. "They don't tell you about the isolation units for the same reason they don't do simulations like this: it would scare you kiddies off."

I could see Lester shaking his head through his visor. "Do we ever get a nice, peaceful dead planet?"

"Nope. Too hard to terraform. Life makes oxygen and regulates climate. Takes centuries if there isn't already life there. Today's colonists aren't a patient lot."

It took us four tries to find a relatively safe spot on the simulated planet. In real life, Lester probably would have ended up with a broken back, but we got the info on the chances of intelligence on the planet and were more or less alive at the end of the mission.

After a month of simulations, Lester was getting jumpy. The passenger liner returned. Lester took a two-day leave and went off to find Marina. I swam laps and had remote card games with Miyuki.

Lester came back looking relaxed and happy which was good because we shipped out two days later for my nineteenth mission.

-3-

The Scout ship assigned to us was fairly new. No complaints. We sat in big comfy chairs in front of a mass of displays. I took the container with two memory chips and popped the one with the destination

51

information into the panel, hit the red button, and shut the displays off.

Lester looked puzzled. "Why'd you turn the navigation displays off?"

"Computer handles everything. If it goes bad, we're screwed; if it doesn't, there's nothing for us to do. I hope you didn't spend too much time on the astrogation course."

"I was pretty good at them."

"They're worthless. It's like knowing how your shirt is made, interesting but no practical value. You should have spent your time learning geology and exobiology. *That* we need to know."

Lester nodded. "I was good at those, too."

"Then your time at the Academy wasn't a total waste." I popped the second memory chip into the computer and a planetary view of our destination appeared. "Don't be gawking at the astrogation. I want you to spend every waking hour learning what's in this. This is everything the robot discovery ship found. We need to know it before we land. That gives us one week."

Lester took it to heart. He had possible landing sites picked out. I reviewed his criteria. "What about the fauna?"

"All seems fairly normal. Nothing intelligent."

"Based on what?"

"Lack of cultural artifacts."

"What was your major at the Academy?"

"Structural engineering."

I shook my head. "Should have known. Don't make the mistake of equating technology and intelligence.

There are species that think as well as you or I and figure everything is fine the way it naturally occurs. They manage to think big thoughts without so much as building a roof to keep the rain off." I brought up the data on the biological samples taken by the robot explorer. "What do you make of these?" I pointed to a picture of an animal; its rounded upper portion looked like a meter-high hemisphere that was set on a larger-diameter disc. The hemisphere was rigid and the disc was flexible. The animal moved by undulating the flexible disc. Tentacles sprouted from the junction of the hemisphere and disc.

"Herd animal. Grazer."

"They definitely travel in groups, but they're not exclusively grazers. The robot found a carcass that had fresh meat in its stomach. The key here is fresh, no traces of spoilage."

"They hunt?"

"Exactly. Hunting in groups takes a greater level of coordination than grazing. That implies greater intelligence. What's the other thing you notice about the species?"

Lester thought a while, then shook his head. "I guess I missed it."

"There was only one carcass of this animal found. There are thousands of them all over the planet, but the robot could only find one that had been dragged off by a predator."

"I'm still not getting it."

"They dispose of their dead."

"They might practice cannibalism."

"True, but if what they do has the smallest element

of ritual involved, that implies an understanding of mortality, which is an indication of self-awareness. We have to be sure."

We tried to land close to a group of the creatures without being obvious. The ship can camouflage its color to some extent. We came down looking sky-blue and used the antigravity drive to minimize noise.

After the atmospheric checks, we got into our suits and headed out for a little animal watching. We crawled on our bellies through what looked like grass and recorded the animals' behavior. Back on the ship we watched the recordings. I pointed to a pair of the creatures and backed the recording up. "Did you see that?"

"No."

"Watch those arms."

Lester zoomed the display. "They touched arms."

"And moved in tandem afterward."

Lester nodded. "Communications. So are they intelligent?"

"Not necessarily. Every social animal has some form of communication, but there are lots of social animals that are not intelligent. But every intelligent animal has some form of communications. Communication is necessary, but not sufficient to prove intelligence."

Lester slumped in his chair. "This is starting to sound like Philosophy 101."

"Sometimes that's what this job comes down to."

The next day, we opened the hatch to find only one of the creatures in the nearby grassland. We watched it from the trees, trying to stay out of its line of sight. It moved slowly in the direction of a rise. We kept pace with it.

Lester kept looking over his shoulder. "They never move alone—too much chance of predation."

"This is unusual. We should record its behavior." The creature led us partially up the slope of a hill and ducked inside a cave. We followed to the cave mouth and found no sign of its companions. "I don't remember anything in the documentation of this planet about these things using caves."

Lester thought. "I can't remember anything either."

"It's the unusual behaviors that are more likely to indicate intelligence. This is risky, but if we're going to find out whether they're intelligent or not, we've got to observe their behavior. I'm going in. You wait at the mouth of the cave in case they're more intelligent than we thought."

Lester took up a defensive position just inside the cave, and I followed the creature. The cave was too low for me to stand. I could hear the creature a short way ahead of me. As I rounded a corner, the creature scuttled down a side shaft at surprising speed. A check with my sensors indicated the shaft led out of the cave. I yelled over the suit comm, "Lester, it's a trap!"

I heard the rockslide and hurried toward Lester. He emerged from a cloud of dust. "I'm all right, but the entrance is covered."

"The alternate entrance is also."

Lester and I sat down and used our sensors to determine how much rock was blocking the opening. It looked like a good five meters. "Can't blast our way out," I said. "We'd either fry or bring the cave down. Time for some spelunking."

We made our way farther into the cave. It opened

to a large chamber. The floor was covered with neat, six-meter wide piles of rocks. I examined one. "Burial."

"Too bad they don't put these outside. We could have declared them intelligent without getting stuck in this cave."

"We're not done for yet, kid."

Several openings led off the chamber. I told Lester to stay as quiet as possible. Then I sampled the sounds from each opening. We headed down one where I heard water and felt airflow. The tunnel sloped downward, ending in an underground stream. I pulled up a topo map on my helmet display. "Looks like there's a lake close by. It has a stream coming out, but no inflow."

"Spring fed," Lester said.

"Right. I'm betting this is the source of the spring."

Lester took a long look at the churning water. "You're betting our lives on that hunch."

"Got a better plan?"

Lester thought for a while. Flowing water isn't something you find much of in a mine. "No." His voice was resigned.

"Let's go for a swim. Keep your helmet light on. Don't get hung up on any rocks. If this works, we'll be out; if not, we'll have a hell of a time getting back here."

I jumped in. It was a good-sized stream with a strong current. I like a good thrill ride: getting pushed down a rock tube trying to avoid obstructions definitely qualifies. Lester wasn't having as good a time. He bounced off a couple of rocks and started tumbling. I slowed myself. "Grab my feet." Lester grabbed one and nearly set me tumbling. "Straighten your body." He did and grabbed my other foot. I headed into the current. The extra drag made it easier to avoid hazards. "Close your eyes. I'll steer."

After a couple of minutes, the water stilled. I saw light coming from above. "Open your eyes and make for the surface."

I had scouted the area by the time Lester finally dragged himself on shore. He sat on the bank panting. The pool formed one end of a steep-walled, narrow canyon. A stream lined with trees flowed out of the pool.

"We're in a box canyon," I said. "I'm detecting some of the creatures in our path. If we try to climb out, we'll be sitting ducks if they have any kind of weapons. The only way out is to follow the stream. We should head out as fast as we can. Don't want them bringing in reinforcements." I got Lester to his feet.

The place was a defensive nightmare. A group of the creatures moved onto a ledge after we had passed and began throwing stones at us from behind. They used their tentacles like slings; they put a lot of power behind those stones. One struck me in the shoulder. My suit held, but my shoulder broke. Lester fired once at the edge of the ledge. The creatures scurried into the underbrush. Then Lester blew the ledge off.

I switched on the auto-doc in my suit. It deadened my pain without putting me to sleep. "Nicely done. We're safe and none of them are dead."

Lester checked my suit's internal sensor readings on his helmet display. "How are you?"

I transferred my gun to my free hand. "Injured. Immobilize my arm." Lester pulled a bandage from his medkit and strapped my arm to my waist. "Let's go."

We traveled as fast as the terrain and my arm would allow. At a bend in the stream, Lester peeked around. The aliens greeted him with a volley of rocks. We spotted a number of the creatures hiding behind trees. One of them was making forays—taunting us. It had a wicked arm. Lester's helmet got hit, but held. He tried shooting at the trees, but the creatures wouldn't give up ground. Finally, Lester turned the gun to a high setting and waited. When the brave one came out, he blew it to bits. The others scattered. We ran the rest of the way to the ship without interference.

When we were in space, Lester patched up my shoulder as best he could. He didn't say a word. "Thanks for taking care of me, Lester."

"Just doing my duty, sir."

"Call me Aidan. We're partners." I sat down beside him. "I feel too formal calling you by your last name. What's your first name?"

Lester didn't say anything for a long time. "Aloysius."

"Damn! I've shot people for smaller insults than that."

"The name is part of the reason I started lifting weights. I had to be big to deal with the teasing."

"Ok, I'll call you Lester. So what's bugging you?"

"I killed an intelligent, self-aware creature."

"And saved two. Probably more than two, 'cause I wasn't going down without a fight."

Lester looked kind of pitiful. "Why are we doing this?"

I put a hand on his shoulder. "You're not the first

one to ask that question. Here's another fact they don't tell you about in the Academy: you know there are other highly developed species in the galaxy."

"Sure. They teach that."

"Right, but what they don't teach is that some of them have developed faster-than-light drives. The Scouts only tell you if you happen to encounter one of their leftover probes. Turns out that all of those civilizations eventually came to the conclusion that it's either too expensive to terraform a dead world or that life on better than 90% of the non-dead ones will kill you, so they settled down and made the best of their home planet. Humans, on the other hand, have an itch to move, and that logic hasn't dampened. Before the Scouts, people could explore wherever they wanted. They brought back horrible plagues and accidentally killed off intelligent life on some of the planets they explored. So the Planetary Council created the Scouts. We're supposed to make sure humanity doesn't destroy other intelligent creatures or pick up something nasty enough to kill us off. We do the job all neat and proper and businesslike."

"Doesn't sound very heroic."

"You watched too many space operas."

"I grew up on a mining colony. We lived in the tunnels once they finished mining them. We were a bunch of troglodytes. There was one dome on the surface at the spaceport. I went up there once to look out the window—you couldn't see anything but blowing sand. What else was there to do but watch space operas?"

"There's girls."

"They only hook up with guys who have a sure way out."

I tried to shrug and regretted it. "Sorry to be the one to disillusion you."

"Guess it needed to be done." He sat awhile. "Ever think of running?"

"Wouldn't do any good. The contract we signed is recognized on every world in the Planetary Council. Once they issued a warrant, I'd have no place to go. My credit chit would be canceled, and I'd be stuck. I could try living in the wild, but that would only last until all my spare parts ran out of juice. You might last longer, but what kind of a life would it be? Finish your twenty-five and you're set."

Lester gave a dry laugh. "They use hope to trap us."

"That's about the size of it."

We turned in our report. The planet was put off limits.

-4-

I went to Prime to get my shoulder rebuilt. Lester took the passenger liner to Optimus, stayed a week, and hopped back on the same ship for the return to Base. I had a feeling he had no interest in sightseeing.

He helped me through rehab. We ran more simulations. And we waited. More than half of this job is waiting. The closer you get to the magic twenty-five, the harder the waiting becomes. The upcoming mission would be twenty for me.

We had to wait close to three months. To fill in the quiet moments, I taught Lester how to play bridge.

We got to where we sometimes won a game against Miyuki and her bridge partner who happened to be my planetary Scout partner. Their images at the table seemed so real I'd sometimes forget myself and reach out to her.

Our next world was cold. The oceans had abundant life, but the landmasses were dead, covered with ice. The discovery ship reported that its undersea probe had been attacked. That's the kind of news that gives you a real good feeling as you land on a strange planet. We were to find out if the attack indicated intelligence.

Scans from space showed that the planet had once been warmer. Remains of abundant terrestrial plant life existed under the glaciers. A surprisingly low level of carbon dioxide had decreased the planetary greenhouse effect. The question of why that level was still low remained unanswered.

To get close to the water, we landed on an ice shelf at the edge of a landmass. The shelf was large, old and stable. The weight of our ship didn't bother it. We pulled out the ship's undersea probe and dragged it on skids to the shore. This is one of those weird rules that only a bureaucratic organization like the Scouts could come up with: you can land a starship on a planet, but when you're outside the ship you're supposed to minimize the use of advanced technology. Never mind that you're in a full-isolation suit and the thing on the skids is a highly advanced probe unit; you have to drag it.

Lester walked gingerly on the ice in spite of the cleats on his boots.

I tried not to laugh. "What's wrong? Haven't you walked on ice before?"

"I lived in a cave until I went to the Academy. The Academy is on the equator. The only ice I've seen up close has been in a glass. I suppose you're an expert?"

"I grew up on a planet that had seasons. The lake by our house froze over most winters."

"Why didn't they have climate control?"

"It was a little podunk farming planet—couldn't afford it. I spent every winter skating on that lake. Froze my silly butt off. Used to love it."

We trudged on. The ice boomed and cracked. Lester kept looking around. "Are we too heavy? Is this going to crack?"

"No. I could walk all the way across the lake on my home world when the ice wasn't a third as thick as this."

"How big was the lake?"

"Couple of kilometers."

"Nobody fell through?"

"Every few years someone would. We'd find them in the spring."

"So why didn't you fall through?"

"Because, my boy, the deity looks out for people like me."

Lester sighed. "I know I'm going to regret asking this, but, why?"

"Because people like me are endlessly amusing. I've decided that's the entire purpose of creation—to amuse the deity. You, unfortunately, won't last nearly as long as me, because you are dull."

"I'll grant you that."

We reached a ledge and tossed the probe into the

water. It took off, looking for life in the deep ocean. While we waited, we used the short-range sensors in our suits to explore the area under the ice. A cluster of plankton swam beneath our feet. As Lester moved away from me, the cluster divided and half followed him. I checked the area between us and the density of sea life was much lower. We took a little jog around the shelf and the plankton followed.

As the probe reached the ocean floor, we tuned into its transmissions with our helmet displays. It had moved to an area rich in plants and animals that surrounded a series of thermal vents. The sea floor was covered with iridescent shelled creatures, blood-red tubeworms, animals that resembled plants, and small scurrying things that ducked under the sand as light from the probe struck them. The sea teemed with swimming creatures in various shapes and sizes. The probe moved slowly, careful not to disturb the native life. It reported a cloud of plankton hovering around it. Larger animals kept their distance. We decided to see what the animals' reaction would be to a more aggressive approach, and ordered the probe to pick up one of the slow, shelled creatures on the sea floor. It picked the creature up gently and turned it over to view its underside.

All hell broke loose. Every creature in the surrounding ocean converged on the probe. The creature was snatched from the probe's grasp. Claws, tentacles and teeth grabbed the probe's arms and pulled it toward a thermal vent. The animals took turns holding the probe so that none of them was cooked. The probe tried unsuccessfully to free itself without injuring the animals. Its internal temperature rose dangerously high. I finally ordered it to do an internal self-destruct. The probe melted its guts so that nothing useful could be learned from them.

The incident spooked us. We headed back to the ship. Partway there, the ship told us that a large bubble of superheated water was headed for the ice floe. Lester took off running like a man possessed. Seems he'd figured out how to use his cleats.

We had barely entered the ship when the bubble hit. Ice shattered. The ship sank. A cloud of plankton engulfed it.

I yelled an order and the ship shot us into space with maximum antigrav.

We orbited the planet and reviewed the ship's sensor data. The bubble of superheated water was unnatural. A group of plankton had formed a container to trap the water and carried it to the surface. The process had killed millions of them.

"It all looks intelligent," Lester said, "but where does the intelligence originate?"

"There's no indication of a single source," I said. "Look at the distribution of life. There are clumps of larger life forms with streams of plankton connecting them. I think the ocean life is one distributed intelligence."

"That's capable of defending itself," Lester finished.

"Right. And that may explain the extinct terrestrial life: if something on the surface threatened the undersea life, they may have adjusted the environment so that it was hostile to the threat."

"So how do we classify it?" Lester asked.

"We don't. We leave that to the eggheads. Our job is to report it."

I ran the ship close to the planet's sun and baked it rotisserie style, in case any of the plankton was still alive on the outside of our ship. I did not want to take these guys home.

-5-

We headed back to Base and waited. On this layover, my best friend Jack and his partner Diego were also waiting for a mission. I'd known Jack for years. Jack had nineteen missions. He was the only Scout who had anywhere near as many replacement parts as I did.

Diego arrived at Base a few months before Lester. Diego was a scrappy little guy. He liked to play a mean game of slap tag with Lester. Diego would sneak up behind Lester in the gym and smack him one good above the waistline where the skin is really sensitive. Then he'd run off trailing an insane, cackling giggle.

Lester would chase him around the exercise area cursing like a proper miner's son. Lester was generally too slow to catch him. It was good for the big guy to learn his limits. Lester would end up with hand-shaped bruises all over his back. Occasionally Diego would be outwitted, but more often he'd slip in a puddle of Lester's sweat and get tackled. Lester would sit on Diego until he nearly passed out. It was great fun to watch.

Jack and Diego got their mission before us. A discovery ship had found signs of technology on their target planet. Nothing definite. They were supposed to confirm or deny intelligence. Turned out the natives were extremely intelligent. They ambushed Jack and Diego. The natives figured out the latch system of their suits and extracted them. Then the creatures carefully, minutely, dissected them alive with razor-sharp stone tools. Diego's suit camera recorded everything until it was splattered with blood. Suit mikes continued to transmit their ongoing screams.

When the ship confirmed that they were dead, it sterilized a kilometer around their bodies to ensure they didn't contaminate the native population. Then it returned to Base.

I suppose it should have made me feel better knowing that the ones who got Jack and Diego were fried. It didn't.

Lester and I cleaned up their rooms. Diego had piles of clean clothes on his bunk and a basket of dirty laundry in the corner. His desk was covered with pictures of his five-year-old daughter, the large brown eyes and ready smile engaging and harrowing. He'd hung the walls of his room with her drawings. Lester told me that Diego had joined the Scouts so that he could support her. We put together some of his things so the girl would have a remembrance of her father.

Jack's room was orderly. We found his will under a paperweight on the top of his desk. In all the years I'd known him, I'd never heard Jack talk about family. He left everything in trust to Diego's daughter. He'd never met the girl.

It's times like this when I envy women. I remember when Miyuki lost a friend. She went on a two-day crying jag and felt better afterward. Lester and I didn't have that option. So we went to the bar that night. We ordered shots of Ouzo, made morbid toasts, downed the shots and remembered times with Jack and Diego. I helped Lester back to his room. He threw up and crashed on the floor. I sat propped in my bunk, world-spinning-around-my-head drunk, unable to sleep. We barely made the memorial service next day.

-6-

It was four months before our mission came up. When we left, Lester's room was in order. This was twenty-one for me.

We sat on the bridge of the Scout ship and studied our next planet. It was blue. Not blue, green and brown—blue. What land there was barely registered on a planetary view.

Lester gazed at the globe openmouthed. "Why are we checking this place out? There's no land for humans to live on."

I zeroed in on the designated area of interest. "There's an undersea plateau. If the planet's suitable, they'll haul in a couple of asteroids, orbit them around the planet, break them into pieces and use the pieces to build up the land level. I've seen it done before."

"Why go to all that effort?"

"Aquaculture. They introduce Terran fish into the seas and harvest them later. It's risky, but it can make huge profits."

"What about the native lifeforms?"

"That's where we come in. We've got to determine if there's any chance of intelligence in this ocean. If we don't find anything, they'll introduce nonnative species and probably destroy any native species that prey on the ones humans want to farm."

"So unless we find something intelligent, this whole planet becomes one big fish farm?"

I patted Lester's shoulder. "You can't get too involved in these planets. We don't make the ultimate decisions. You want to get involved in that, go into politics. But you'll have to wait till you've finished your twenty-five."

There were a few small islands in the area of interest. We landed on the largest one. I've been in bars that were bigger. The surface of the island was bare. It was too small and insecure to develop a unique ecology. Other than sand and rock, there was only seaweed along the shore.

We disembarked from the ship and started sampling the life on the shoreline. It was slimy. We kept falling down. We were both on the ground, laughing our heads off, trying not to slide into the ocean when the first tentacle emerged from the water. It rose nearly ten meters into the air and waved around, as if viewing the scene. We froze. A few dozen other tentacles joined it and made for the ship. They latched on and started pulling it toward the water.

The ship is not small. They were not making headway until the tentacles started oozing slime, which greased the path. Our ship rapidly went underwater.

Lester's voice was on the verge of cracking. "Aidan, what do we do now?"

The tip of a tentacle reemerged from the water. "Make for the highest point—on the double." We ran for the peak of the island as fast as the slime would let us. The tentacles reacted to our movement. Seeing one coming, I stopped Lester. "Lock arms. Turn on your static field."

The tentacle reached within a meter of us and got a jolt from the field. It backed off. We sidled closer to the peak, arm in arm.

Tentacles came at us in waves. Our field held. They retreated.

Lester was breathing hard. "Ok, how do we get the ship back?"

"The remote will work through water. Keep looking for tentacles." I called up the display for the ship's remote control. It responded instantly. The ship was 300 meters below the surface. I told it to kick in the antigrav. There was initial resistance. It broke the surface with a huge tentacled passenger. I stopped it a few meters above the water. The passenger decided to give up and dropped back into the ocean. I maneuvered the ship close to us.

That was when the tentacles attacked again. I initiated the static field on the ship. That blocked us, as well as the creatures, from approaching it. The tentacles probed the edges of the fields, searching for a weak spot. A few tried to dig under only to find the field extended below us into the sand.

"Aidan, this is draining my power pack."

"Mine too."

"You make a run for it, I'll cover you."

"Don't get brave, Lester. That's how people die. We'll both make a run for it." I opened the outer hatch on the ship and waited.

After a couple of minutes, there was a brief lull. I cut the ship's field. "Cut your field and run." We dove into the hatch just as the tentacles took advantage of the absence of the field. The tentacles dragged the ship partway to the water before I got the hatch shut and the field back on. I engaged the antigravs and was in orbit before the decontamination cycle completed.

Lester flopped into the copilot's chair. "Do we ever get one that's boring?"

"I've heard of a couple; only a couple." There was a lull while both of us caught our breaths. "Thanks for offering to cover my ass. It wasn't smart, but it was brave."

Lester shrugged. "Isn't that what partners do?"

"Yes and no. They watch each other's backs but try to make sure that both of them make it out alive." I walked over and put a hand on his shoulder. "Thanks, partner."

Lester smiled.

I pulled up the video from the ship's sensors. What had gone on beneath the water's surface interested me. The video showed a concerted attack. The creatures were trying to either bend the ship or bang it against a rock in order to break its shell. The rock had been worked to a sharp point. They must have thought something that big had a lot of food inside. The work was methodical.

Lester leaned forward. "Look at the colors and patterns on their skins."

The undulating bodies were covered with spots that changed shape and color. "Communications, tools and coordinated actions; there's at least a modicum of intelligence."

Lester smiled. "So this planet will be off limits."

"Looks that way." I shut off the video. "You seem mighty happy."

"It didn't look like the kind of world we should be messing with."

"Well, you win this time."

I started the preflight sequence. An alarm went off.

I turned on the navigation displays. The landing gear was damaged. It couldn't retract, so the ship couldn't go into hyperdrive. "We're stuck. Let's contact the *Mercury*."

The *Mercury* is a tiny hyperdrive ship. It's more a messenger to the gods than a messenger from them. Since you can't get past the Einstein limits in regular space, communication at stellar distances is either deadly slow or works something like a message in a hyperbottle. *Mercury* is the hyperbottle. We leave it in orbit above the planets we explore so we can send it back home with an emergency message no matter what happens.

I recorded a message and sent *Mercury* off to Base. We now had three weeks before a rescue vessel would come. I went to my bunk and got a deck of cards. "Okay, kid, gin rummy, centicredit a point."

Lester pulled out a tray between the two pilot's chairs and gave me a wry smile. "You sure you want to do this again? At the rate you're going, you'll have to get a job after your twenty-five just to pay me back."

"You've been having a run of good luck. That'll change."

Lester had never played cards before he met me. He was adaptable. By the time we got back, I was down another twenty credits.

-7-

The wait till mission twenty-two was almost six months. Neither of us had gotten injured on the last mission, so we spent our time building skills rather than rehabilitating.

During the lull, the passenger liner arrived. A chamber orchestra was on board and the folks in charge of Base managed to talk them into doing a one-night stand. This generally involves sizable sums of cash. That seems to be one thing the Scouts have plenty of.

The orchestra was great. I sat next to Lester, who spent the evening with Marina tucked securely under one of his big arms. There was an empty seat on the other side of me. I remembered the last time I'd heard Mozart—Miyuki sat beside me. We'd held hands discreetly (partners aren't supposed to get involved). Now, as the haunting, perfect strains of late Mozart swept over me, I felt alone.

The big brass called us in for a talk before the next mission. That's almost always a bad sign. They shoved us into a debriefing room and left us for close to an hour. I knew the routine, so I'd brought a pack of cards. The arrival of the two officers saved me from a five-credit loss. Lester was getting too lucky.

We stood and saluted. They told us to sit, but the tension in the room didn't fade.

The older of the two officers was a full colonel. I could tell with my artificial eye that he was about half bionic. Some folks never give up. "This mission is somewhat delicate," he said. I tried not to groan. "You will not be setting foot on the planet." I perked up. "We've already determined the planet has intelligent life. The planet was explored around a hundred years ago. At that time, the local culture was using gunpowder weapons." I wanted to ask why the hell we were going to a hostile planet with advanced technology, but kept my mouth shut. "We recently sent out another probe to see how far they'd advanced. The locals destroyed that probe while it was orbiting their planet."

I gave a little whistle. "They've gone from cannons to rockets in a century?"

The colonel nodded. "That took humans close to five hundred years. What was even more worrying was that the impact weapon that destroyed our probe was made of depleted uranium."

I looked at Lester, who shook his head, then back to the colonel. "My chem lectures were a couple of decades ago."

The younger officer, a captain, but also a veteran of his twenty-five, I judged by the level of spare parts, took up the lecture. "Uranium 238. It's one of the densest naturally occurring materials. Makes a great impact weapon. But U238 doesn't show up in nature by itself; it's always mixed with a couple of other isotopes. The only reason you'd go to the trouble of separating out U238 would be to concentrate the U235 isotope, which is the one used in primitive nuclear fission reactors and bombs."

Lester's eyes were wide. "You're sending us to a planet where they've already knocked out one of our probes and they have rockets and nuclear bombs?"

The colonel sat back and let out a long sigh. "Yes. At the rate they're progressing technologically, they could have hyperdrive in another hundred years. The last probe managed to send out the information it had gathered before it self-destructed, and it indicates a highly dysfunctional civilization that is fractured and xenophobic. We need to know how far along they are and what kind of civilization they really have."

I looked at the captain. "Didn't the probe have some kind of shielding?"

"Just basic. We weren't expecting the natives to have anything more advanced than telescopes."

"What are you sending us in with?"

"The most advanced ship we have. We're not taking anything for granted this time."

So a week later, we were off in the best Scout ship yet built. Twice the size of our usual craft, it was long, sleek and beautiful, but more important, it had shields that could withstand a small supernova and enough cloaking to fool major planetary defenses.

The brass hadn't let us see the reports on the planet before we left—probably didn't want scary details leaking out. Lester loaded the reports as soon as the ship left orbit. I looked over his shoulder. "They're kind of cute."

Lester advanced to some gruesome pictures. "Sort of like old Earth bears only with a really bad attitude. They're highly territorial outside of their extended family lineages. Their method for handling disagreements is genocide. The first probe sent remotes to the surface and caught them blowing their neighbors to bits. Taking prisoners doesn't seem to be one of their concepts."

The pictures were stomach-churning. "Did the second probe get any data before it got hit?"

"Yeah. Looks like they've formed the equivalent of nation-states on the various continents. It detected numerous bursts that were probably chemical bombs. They've just moved the scale of violence up in the last century."

"Did it send back an electromagnetic spectrum analysis?"

Lester checked the index and brought up the display. "Why is this important?"

"Go back to your History of Technology course: humans used radio waves to transmit information for hundreds of years." I pointed to several activity peaks on the chart. "And so are our bears. We can sit a comfortable distance away and monitor them. I definitely do not want to get anywhere close to the surface of this planet." Lester was all for that.

We came out of hyperspace behind a neighboring gas giant planet and maneuvered into an orbit with one of the target planet's moons between us and the bears' instruments. There was evidence the bears had sent probes to their moons but hadn't established permanent settlements or active sensors.

An impressive amount of radio traffic made it through their ionosphere. Audio, video and data, much of it encrypted, was coming from all the major land masses. Using the linguistic data from the first probe, we soon had translations for some of the feeds. Most of the unencrypted transmissions seemed to be propaganda: momma bear and poppa bear have to defend baby bear against those other nasty bears that want to kill him. The most ominous messages said, "We won't be the first bears to use nuclear weapons, but we sure as hell will use them if some other bear does."

Nuclear hotspots on most of the continents indicated that our bear friends had been testing their technology and had something that worked.

We deployed a heavily cloaked drone to determine how many weapons existed on the planet. The drone had to fly through a maze of debris from recently destroyed satellites. It made it through undetected and tracked the number, placement and movement of weapons. A rapid buildup was turning the planet into a nuclear waste dump.

We stayed two weeks. It would have been impossible to send a probe to the ground, given the paranoid nature of the populace. As we decrypted the most heavily scrambled messages, it looked like war was imminent. Neither of us wanted to stay and watch the carnage. We left the probe orbiting a safe distance away and went home.

No one seemed surprised by our findings. The colonel and the captain nodded gravely and said that this confirmed the data from the earlier, destroyed probe. The man from the Colonization Bureau who'd been with them during our debriefing spilled the beans. He said, "If we don't act immediately, we'll lose this world."

The older colonel grabbed the man's elbow. "These Scouts don't need to hear about these plans."

Lester stood up. "You've already got a plan for this planet?"

I sat for a second putting two and two together. I didn't like the sum. "You're going to colonize that planet. But first you've got to get rid of the indigenous population."

The man from the Colonization Bureau looked at me as if I were some congenital imbecile. "They're as good as dead already. There's no use wasting a perfectly good planet. Do you know how few we get each year?"

"Yeah, I scout them, but these bear things aren't dead yet."

The captain gave Lester and me a cold stare. "The planet will be irretrievably damaged if we wait for full-scale nuclear war. As it is, cleanup will take decades."

Lester was trembling. "You're going to sterilize a planet with a couple of billion intelligent individuals on it. Hell, we probably triggered this war with our first probe."

"Perhaps," the colonel said, "but that doesn't matter now. Your figures confirm that the coming war will destroy all life and all possibility of future life on the planet. It is dead." The colonel held up his hand as he rose from his seat. "And this debriefing is over. I see the mission has been stressful for both of you; therefore, you deserve a vacation. You are dismissed."

The three exited the room as Lester stood, silently shaking with rage.

I've been waved goodbye to when leaving for vacation; I've been sent off with gestures that indicated my returned presence was not desired; but I've never been given a sendoff by an armed guard. They put us on a Scout ship preprogrammed for a flight to a pleasure planet with the controls locked. The computer showed us lovely images of the world we'd be visiting, played soothing music (whether we liked it or not), and offered us a range of entertainments, but no communications.

The planet was far away, so we had nearly a month cooped up on the ship to calm down. To some extent, it worked. We ranted for a few days. It's hard not to when you think about planetary sterilization. It's not a pretty idea and no way near as clean as the name implies.

What they do is deploy a bunch of big satellites around the planet and bombard it with gamma rays. After a while, everything on the planet dies; turned to a mildly radioactive sludge. Then they toss in some Terran bugs to start eating the sludge and wait for the radioactivity to clear.

We burned ourselves out after a few days and settled into our usual shipboard routine. It must have bugged Lester more than me. I ended up a couple of credits ahead in our card games by the end of the voyage.

"Aidan," Lester asked during one marathon game, "what are you going to do after your twenty-five?"

"I've got this picture in my head of a planet that's big enough to have a city with good entertainment, restaurants, maybe a college, but not so big that it has weather control. I still like seasons."

"More skating?"

"Yeah. I'll find a place with a pond so I can skate in the winter and a little land to grow some veggies during the summer."

Lester chuckled. "Somehow I just can't see you as the gentleman farmer."

"Well, maybe not the gentleman, but I'll have enough money to buy a farm. Only money I spend now is what I lose to you at cards."

"Then you must not be putting much away." Lester smiled.

I considered decking him but there was no one around to repair my hand.

He drew another card. "Gonna get married?"

"Don't know."

"Miyuki wouldn't want you being lonely."

"I know, but sometimes you just fall hard for a woman." I shuffled the cards. "What do you have planned after your twenty-five?"

"That's too far away."

I shook my head. "Don't give me that. Every Scout starts thinking about that even before they're accepted into the Scouts."

He picked up his hand. "Okay. I'm going to settle on a world with weather control, on a part of the planet where it's always sunny, and build a house with a transparent ceiling."

"Let me guess, no basement."

"Damned straight!"

I suppose it shouldn't have surprised either of us to find Marina waiting when the ship arrived. Planning is a Scout forte. We had all been booked into a hotel that stood on a pristine beach by a waterfall in the semitropical region of the planet. The planet has zero tilt and a nearly circular orbit, so the weather is boringly predictable and predictably beautiful. The rains came like clockwork every afternoon for around an hour. They were warm and gentle. Guests would go for walks and come back soaked and laughing. The rest of the days were warm and sunny, evenings balmy. Trails led from the resort into a jungle interior filled with the scents of exotic flowers and the music of birds, where native and Terran plants coexisted and where the largest carnivore was about the size of a small dog and couldn't have done much more than inflict a severe bite if it had a taste for humans, which it didn't.

When Marina and Lester weren't in their room, they

stationed themselves on the beach, soaking up the sun. Each room came with a Lester-sized bottle of suntan lotion, complete with anticancer agents. The two of them took great care ensuring that every exposed inch of each other's body was slathered in the stuff.

After a couple of days exploring trails through the lush growth around the resort, I stationed myself in the bar. The second day there, I saw a woman with auburn hair, about my age, trim, dressed fashionably, seated in a booth by one of the outside windows. She gazed at Marina and Lester on the beach. I watched her for about half a beer, trying to decide if I should mind my own business or make this enforced vacation a little more interesting. I eventually sidled over to her table. "They make a nice couple."

She seemed startled but turned and peered back at the beach. "I suppose they do. It's just a bit difficult to see your daughter and her lover at that level of intimacy."

I was surprised but caught myself—of course the Scouts would think of something to divert me. I looked out. Lester was doing an incredibly thorough job of applying suntan lotion on Marina's upper thighs. Through the open windows we could hear the occasional moan from Marina. "He's really a good kid."

She glanced at me. "You must be his partner. He says good things about you." She motioned to the other side of the booth. "I'm Mona. Please, have a seat."

"Thanks." I sat. We looked out the window at the giggling pair. "They seem very happy together."

"I know." She looked back at me. "I just don't know if they have a future together. My husband made it to thirteen. Marina barely remembers him."

I nodded. "If you'd known what would happen before you married him, would it have stopped you?"

She sat staring into her drink. "Probably not." She glanced up at me. "It's amazing how foolish we can be when we're young and think we're immortal."

I raised my glass. "Here's to youth."

She clinked her glass on mine and took a long swallow. "If I stay here watching them much longer, I'll go completely nuts."

"Up the beach there's a waterfall even lovelier than this one. Care to try a beach hike?"

She glanced at Marina, now straddling Lester, rubbing lotion on his chest. Mona downed her drink. "I'd love to."

The walk progressed to day hikes and picnics and, after they got over the shock, double dates with the kids.

Our vacation was scheduled for two months. With no way off the planet, we settled in and enjoyed it. With a month left, Mona and I decided to quit chaperoning the kids and took a trip to the temperate portion of the planet. The original plan for this planet had been as a working agricultural colony. The primitive native vegetation had proven harmless to humans and had quickly succumbed to the introduced Terran flora and fauna. Everything flourished, but the planet was just too far from the centers of civilization and never attracted the expected colonists. So the world became a tourist trap.

In the temperate zone, the plan called for creation of a forest of redwood and kauri trees to supply wood for houses that were never built. The trees had been growing undisturbed for nearly a century. We strolled through the giants. I held Mona close when breezes blew chill off the ocean. We sat in the lodge before a blaze in the great fireplace and drank hot brandy as the world outside melted into the fog.

And that was all we did. I think we might both have wished for more, but we both had memories we couldn't leave behind. Within that limitation, we enjoyed our time together.

At the end of two months, Lester and I saw the women off and walked back to the Scout ship. Lester was smiling. "Ever heard of the Movement for Just Colonialism?"

"No."

"Neither had I, but Marina knew about them and by tonight, the movement will know what's scheduled to happen to the bears." He stopped and looked at me. "There may still be time to stop the government from sterilizing that planet. If those stupid bear things want to kill themselves, that's too damned bad, but it's their decision to make. I don't want to be a party to their murder."

"You give Marina a big kiss from me next time you see her."

"Sure thing."

We walked back to our life.

-8-

Scout command never said anything to us about the information leak, but all hell broke loose in the Planetary Council. The big brass who ordered the mission quietly retired. The bears were left alone; and Lester and I became personae non gratae for months.

I was about ready to go wrestle Snarky to break the boredom when we finally got a new assignment. We found out we weren't off of the shit list when we saw the cramped old ship they stuffed us into for the trip.

The planet for mission twenty-three seemed routine, easy. The number of flora and fauna species was low. I couldn't tell if they were too scared to let something happen to us or were feeding us a ringer, so we didn't let that lessen our preparation. By the time we landed, the only question we hadn't answered was: What is the source of the flashing lights on the planet's surface?

We surveyed the planet from orbit. There were oceans, lakes, rivers, green plains, lush valleys—everything some damn fool pioneer colonist could want. We landed in a savanna bordering a forest to get maximum ecological coverage. The landing was uneventful. The vegetation, while unlike Terran standard, was green and didn't get up and walk around. The animals on the savanna looked large and dumb. They showed no interest in the ship.

We suited up and went through the standard decontamination in the airlock to protect the native environment. The airlock opened; nothing approached. We crept away from the ship. Outside the area affected by our ship's engines, we deployed sensors and sampled the environment. The readings came back "Very active." The biota of this planet was probably deadly to humans. That left two choices for the planners: give up on this planet, or, if there was absolutely no possibility of intelligent life, sterilize it. We needed to get a closer look at the animals.

JOSHUA MEEHAN

I walked toward the trees with Lester covering my tail. A half-dozen creatures moved in the closest tree. Their bodies were ovoid, about a meter long. A pair of legs stuck out from the bottom of the ovoid body with claws that held onto the tree branch. One of the ovoids shuddered and a pair of wings deployed. The creature seemed to inflate them. Then it sprang from the branch into the air. A puff of gas emerged from the end of the creature and ignited. It jetted into the sky.

I laughed so hard I nearly fell over. That was why I didn't see when another flyer hit me at a full power dive. I slammed into the ground. My helmet visor hit a sharp rock. The visor is supposed to be unbreakable, but it cracked.

The creature grabbed the helmet in its claws. It had one hell of a grip. I could see the crack expanding. Then Lester did exactly what I'd told him to do—he shot it. The compressed gas inside the creature exploded. My faceplate shattered.

A recording inside my helmet was repeating: "Level 1 breach." I couldn't speak.

Lester hovered over me, singed but intact. "Talk to me, Aidan." He picked shards of the faceplate out of my cheek. I couldn't see from my real eye, but the artificial one registered movement rushing toward us. I pulled my gun and fired. The explosion knocked Lester to the ground. He rolled onto his back and scanned the sky. "I've got to get you back to the ship. Can you watch for bird things?"

"Yeah." It hurt to talk. Lester grabbed the back of my suit and dragged me across the grassland. The jarring hurt like hell. "Stop! Help me up."

He pulled me to my feet. The kid was strong. I put an arm around his shoulder. "Let's go."

When I saw the next bird thing, I shifted my gun to stun. It crumpled and fell from the sky. Lester reset his gun.

I could taste the blood flowing down my face. The trip back to the ship seemed to take an hour. Lester finally got me into the airlock. As the hatch was closing, several flyers dived for us. One made it into the hatch. Lester stunned it as the airlock closed.

I reached for the spare suit locker. "I'll get a helmet on and we'll decontaminate."

Lester stopped me. "We can't decon. The gas inside that creature will blow up." The outside viewer showed an increasing number of the flyers clawing at the skin of the ship.

Lester reached for the button to open the inner airlock hatch. I grabbed his arm. "Open that hatch and the whole ship's contaminated."

Lester freed his arm. "I'll stay in my suit till we get to Prime. It'll get nasty, but I'll be fine. I can hook up to the ship to replenish air and water and purge waste. We've got to get into space before those things damage the ship." He hit the button and dragged me inside the cabin.

The ship's klaxon was sounding and the computer droned "Level 1 breach." I told the computer to shut up.

Lester put me in my bunk and hit the emergency recall button. We took off. Before we jumped into hyperspace, Lester opened the outer hatch of the airlock and dumped the creature into vacuum.

Lester got me out of my suit and started working

on me as best he could while wearing a full-isolation suit. He stopped the bleeding and cleaned the wound. Once he got the pain blockers in place, I started feeling human again.

I saw a streak of dirt on the side of his suit and a spot that looked damaged. I had him turn so I could get a closeup look with the artificial eye. "When that flyer exploded, you must have hit something hard. Your suit's connection port is smashed."

"How bad?"

"I can't fix it. We need to do a full decon of the ship so you can get that suit off."

"You're not thinking straight, Aidan. This ship's too small for an isolation chamber and a full decon requires a radiation bath. We'd have to shut the ship's systems down and be outside the skin of the ship. That means coming out of hyperspace, figuring out where we are, finding a safe place to land, getting there, shutting down, running the decon and getting the ship going again. That'll take longer than going straight to Prime."

"Then you need to conserve resources. Lie down and try to sleep."

Lester stood over me. I could see him with the artificial eye. "Who's going to take care of you?"

"The auto-doc will look after me. I'm fine for a while. You don't have to hover. Lie down."

Lester went to his bunk. I moved the diagnostic sensors over my face. The real eye was gone, but the optic nerve was intact. I could get another replacement. The auto-doc said I had alien bacteria in my body. It was adjusting the flow of drugs to try and control the spread, so far, unsuccessfully. No major organs were being attacked, so I might survive, but I'd be spending time in the domes on Prime.

The drugs made me sleepy. When I awoke, Lester was fidgeting. "How you doing, Lester?"

"I'm bored, uncomfortable, wondering how I'm going to handle six more days of this."

I checked the sensors. "The alien germs are tenacious. I'm not dying, but I haven't gotten rid of them. Open that suit, and you're going to spend the rest of your life in a dome on Prime."

"I'd rather be dead."

"It's not that bad."

Lester turned so I could see his face through the visor. "Ever lived on a mining planet?"

"No."

"Most of them don't have breathable atmospheres. You live in domes. I spent the first eighteen years of my life in domes. I'd only seen pictures of open sky. Once I got out, I promised myself I'd never live that way again. Bury me in this suit if that's what it takes to keep me out of the domes."

"It won't come to that. Try to relax. That uses fewer resources."

Lester turned his face to the ceiling. "I'll try."

By the fourth day, Lester's suit was starting to malfunction. They were never designed to recycle waste continuously for that long. By the fifth day the medical sensors detected bedsores. By the sixth day the air in the suit was going bad. He refused to open the suit.

My infection was under control but not gone. I sat at the controls on the last day of the flight watching the clock and monitoring Lester's fading life signs.

Several times I stood over him with my fingers on the latches of his helmet. The thought of being confined to an isolation dome with a 100-kilo weightlifter who had a vendetta was the only thing that kept me from releasing the helmet.

When we broke out of hyperspace, I signaled Prime for an emergency pickup. They sent a fast med ship with a rescue and biohazard crew. The med techs pulled Lester out, dumped him in an isolation chamber, did a rapid decon and ripped his suit open.

They stuck me in an isolation chamber and moved me to a dome. Nothing could rid me of the alien bugs, but they seemed to be under control. After a couple of months, I was safe enough to be moved to the dome with Miyuki. It was a bittersweet reunion.

It took over a week before I heard about Lester. He needed skin grafts and his kidneys had taken a beating, but anoxia did the worst damage. The doctors weren't sure his brain would fully recover.

Slowly, he did recover. He was transferred to Base for rehab, but it was obvious he'd never go on another mission.

He called me a few months later. His face looked older. He'd lost weight. When he spoke the words came slowly, with occasional pauses, but it was still Lester.

"Aidan, thought I'd check in with you before I left. I see you're with Miyuki. I can contact you later, if you want."

Miyuki smiled. "It's all right; we're only playing gin rummy."

I moved to get a better view of him. "She's beating me, as usual. How are you?"

Lester shrugged. "The body's fine. The brain's slow. It's improving. I'll never be quite the same."

"Too bad they haven't figured out an artificial replacement for the dud parts of a brain." Lester nodded. "Was it worth it?" I asked.

"Oh, yes. Every time I feel the sun on my skin, I know I did the right thing. I've got regrets, but I managed to make it out alive and outside of a dome." He paused. "Sorry."

I shook my head. "It's okay. I'm a realist. I play the hand I'm dealt. Besides, I'm more or less in one piece, and I've got Miyuki." I held her close and she kissed me. "In my own crazy way, I'm lucky."

Lester nodded. "Seems the deity is still looking out for you. I wish you two every happiness where you are, but I'd rather be here even with the fog."

"Where are you?" I asked.

"I'm on the liner getting ready to head out."

"Back to home and parents?"

"My folks wanted me to, but I have to be near a rehab facility for a few years. There isn't one anywhere near their home. I guess you can tell that's fine with me."

"I figured as much. So where to?"

"Marina's got some accumulated vacation time. Planned to go to a resort on Proxima. Seems they have a good rehab clinic. I'm going to let the Scouts pick up my part of the tab."

"Does she know your condition?" Miyuki asked.

"We've had some time together; talked about it. She wants to give it a try."

"Then best of luck," Miyuki said.

I wanted to hug the boy. "I'm happy for you. Maybe it'll be a good place to settle down."

Lester smiled. "Who knows?"

I sat back. "I got word they're going to sterilize that planet."

Lester shook his head. "Too bad. A few billion more people and no flying gasbags. The universe is a lesser place." Lester stared at us a moment. "I saw a big dumb kid getting off the ship today."

I chuckled. "Remind you of anyone?"

"He was like a mirror. It would have killed me to break in that dumb kid knowing what he was up against. How could you do that so many times?"

I sighed. "After a while you don't think about it. If I'd worried about whether I was leading you or Miyuki or the other three to your deaths, I'd have gone crazy, and that wouldn't have helped any of us."

Lester nodded. "The stupid kid saluted me. I wanted to grab him, take him to the bar, get him drunk, and convince him to get back on the ship."

"Why didn't you?"

He grinned. "And miss my flight? No way." An announcement sounded in the background. The ship was preparing to depart. "Take care of each other."

I hugged Miyuki. "We will. You two do the same."

The screen went blank. I stared at it, unmoving.

Miyuki poked me in the ribs. "Hey, you don't have time for sentimentality—you're down two hundred points."

And she was right.

Twelve Seconds

written by

Tina Gower

illustrated by

LUIS MENACHO

ABOUT THE AUTHOR

Tina Gower was born and raised in Siskiyou County, California, where cows outnumber people. In the early mornings before school, Tina fed her dairy cow and fantasized about the characters in books. Some nights she would help her mother irrigate and stare into the starry sky imagining life on other planets—while her mother patiently reminded her to point the flashlight back to the task at hand.

Tina married her high school sweetheart and settled in Chico, California. They immediately noticed the absence of the Milky Way in the glow of city lights and vowed to visit their rural roots often so their children could experience the majesty of an unfettered starlit sky.

Tina graduated with an MA in school psychology and counseling, studied in London (where you also can't see the Milky Way), trained guide dogs for the blind and published nonfiction articles and stories under the name Tina Smith. She worked for several schools in the area before staying at home to write and raise her own children.

Tina and her husband pack up the kids and head north to their hometown as often as they can. Late at night you'll find them sitting on the bumper of a rusted blue Chevy, staring at the stars and dreaming about the future.

ABOUT THE ILLUSTRATOR
Luis Menacho was born in 1988 in La Paz, Bolivia and moved to New York when he was five. He started drawing at ten when his mom gave him a drawing of Spider-Man to copy. Soon after, he had a collection of drawings that consisted of cartoon characters and family members. It's difficult to say exactly when his love for science fiction and fantasy began, but as he started painting, all he knew was that he wanted to paint anything fantasy related.

Luis graduated from the School of Visual Arts with a bachelor's degree in illustration. He had the privilege of studying under great illustrators who helped guide and encourage him to paint what he was interested in. Luis is honored to be part of the Illustrators of the Future. He hopes to one day become a full-time illustrator and to travel the world taking pictures for his future paintings.

Twelve Seconds

Eddie and I process memory siphons. I clean and sort. Eddie approves for archival. We are cogs, endlessly pinching, prodding, and polishing homicide victims' last memories on aging holodesks in a dark room. My desk lines up against a wall, so I don't see people's faces when they walk in the door. While the computer renders the siphons, I like to stare at the tranquil beige ceiling paint, or trace the perfect symmetry of police station floor tiles.

I busy my hands by sharpening individual frames and tracing potential patterns. Most of the files can't be used as evidence because the images can't be sharpened and no useful patterns emerge.

I clean up what I can, tag and sequence the patterns, boost the contrast. Sometimes I find a clear pattern, like a face. Old man like me catching the bad guy— makes me feel important.

The next-case icon cube floats above my desk and blinks red, luring me like a siren's song. "Stop blinking, stop blinking, stop blinking," I say under my breath so Eddie doesn't hear me.

I grab the case icon on the holodesk, hold it gently

in my hand, and unfold it into the first frame of the siphon. It's a soft image of what looks like a living room. There is a sofa and a chair at odd angles that make me uncomfortable. It shows a chair on the floor and a cushion is missing. I pull the metadata from the dock. It reads: SIPHON 25-AF87 (SERA TURNER).

I render the first pass of the raw siphon and it finishes too quickly. Something's wrong. I run it again. Nine seconds. The siphon is only nine seconds and there's no halo at the end. Victims' siphons need to be twelve seconds and end with a halo.

I flap my hands to shake off the tingle fluttering in my stomach. I hum to calm my rocking so Eddie won't make me wear the goggles. The goggles help calm people with issues like me, but they make my eyes itch and give me a headache.

Eddie pauses the siphon he's reviewing. A render of a pit bull poised for attack flickers over his holodesk. The dog's face overlaps Eddie's—same fierce grimace, bulky muscle, haunting eyes. He gives me his cop stare before he notices I'm not wearing the goggles.

Eddie sighs, calls the main office. "It's me, Eddie. Yeah, Howard's freaking again." He shifts in his chair and dismisses the pit bull render with a wave of his free hand. "No. I got it." He hangs up the phone, but before he looks at me, he massages his jaw with his fists. I told him yesterday that he should wear the goggles and learn about emotions like I did. He laughed, but it wasn't a joke. He's been a jerk since his wife died. He hates it when I say that to him, but it's true.

"I don't need the goggles," I say.

"Howard, we've talked about this—"

"No. Look at the siphon. Look." Sera Turner's living room flickers to life between us. A curtain moves in a subtle flutter and I resist the urge to tag the pattern. Eddie backs up because I forgot he doesn't like the renders to play so close to him.

He shakes his head—which usually means he doesn't see what I see. "The siphons *can* be less than twelve seconds," he says. "It depends on how much adrenaline was released. The coroner can't always siphon a complete memory."

"But the halo?" I say. There's always, *always* a halo. The renders are choppy, sometimes blurry or dark. But when they end, they go black and a halo forms like a smoke ring.

Doctor Ennis thinks that the halo comes from a retina burn or neural entropy after death has started. Father Solomon says it's the spiritual doorway to heaven. I like the heaven theory, and so do seventy-six percent of people surveyed in the Vatican instapoll on siphons.

Eddie thinks with his thumb and finger between his eyes. He says I give him a headache when I talk about statistics, so I don't remind him about the poll.

The door buzzes, clicks open, and Eddie reaches for his gun. Only it isn't on his hip. It's in Sergeant Quinten's office with Eddie's badge.

The clatter of opening shades startles me. I crouch, covering my eyes from the blinding light that streams through the window. Eddie opens it and the room floods with high-pitched electric engines, flashing ads, and vibrating beat street music. The December New York air cuts to my bones.

I turn away from the overpowering sensory

information from outside. Focused on my render, I trace more patterns.

"Howard? Did you hear me?"

A woman appears beyond my holodesk. A heart shaped face, green eyes, and symmetrical features—until she frowns—one corner of her mouth is lower than the other. It looks wrong. If I had to trace her render, her smile would be a hard pattern to trace. It's Ava from upstairs. I'm surprised that she's here, and then remember she was the one who walked through the door. She and Eddie were talking while I worked with the render.

A strand of black hair is loose around Ava's face. It bothers me to see it out of place.

I look away so I don't have to see the hair while I motion to her head. "Hair, your hair. Place. No halo." I bang my head against my hand to get the words unstuck. It doesn't work. I need the goggles.

"Howard?" She touches my cheek and this brings me back to the room.

Ava will listen to me. "The Turner halo is missing. Only nine seconds."

Siphons must be twelve seconds unless the coroner notes the cause of a shorter visual. And there is always, *always* a halo.

"I tried to explain to him…" Eddie says under his breath.

"Shh." Ava wrinkles her forehead. "Show me."

I project the render between us. She doesn't say anything so I replay it again and again. They have to see what I see. I slow it down. It's out of place; the render is like two mislaid puzzle pieces smashed together. I open my mouth to explain but Eddie finally sees it.

"The movie in the background. I saw it last year..." He cuts off. He was about to say he saw it with his wife. I've heard the catch in his voice when he talks about *her*. We wait for him to continue while the air filter click, click, clicks and the fan fills the silence.

"The fight scene is out of order," Ava says.

Eddie scrapes his hand across his stubble, his eyes glassy. "The victim was watching the movie when she was shot in the chest. She had to have seen or heard something to get a shot of adrenaline for such a clear siphon."

Ava walks up to the paused render, squats down to the victim's eye level. "Run it again."

I keep running it until she tells me to stop.

Eddie plucks the render from our viewing station; it copies—leaving mine for Ava to review. He reorients his render, turning it in a three-sixty loop. "There's a skip in the render. I don't think they got the full siphon. Can you get the case file?"

Ava shrugs. "I'll recheck the source siphon. It could just be that the extraction was flawed; some are shorter. It's rare, but some are longer—" She stops herself before she says the next words.

I remember the longer siphon she's talking about and Eddie clenches his teeth because he knows too. It was his wife. More adrenaline, more fear, more terror creates a clearer, longer siphon.

Ava backs out of the room without looking at Eddie. She glances at me, her mouth turned down in a frown, the edges quivering. I think about his wife's sixty-second siphon and watch him out of the corner of my eye. I start to hum and Eddie doesn't stop me; he sits in his chair watching the render spin.

I reach for the goggles.

The goggles give me a mild headache for the first few hours. Through the goggles the room shrinks, colors dim, sounds diminish. Each pair is custom designed to make the world bearable for people like me.

I reexamine the render, and if I hadn't already known what to look for I would have missed the skip. I work on the peripheral vision until my goggles remind me that it's time for a break.

In the break room, Ava smiles and scoots the tea canister to me. I examine my cup for dust; measure exactly two teaspoons of honey.

"How's the problem siphon coming along?" she asks.

Marty Jenkins is looming nearby, one hand wrapped around a coffee mug and the other possessively placed on the wall above Ava's shoulder. "What siphon?" he asks, and he takes a sip from his drink. He doesn't look at me; he only looks at Ava.

"Howard found a siphon without a halo at the end."

Marty snorts. "Maybe that one went to hell." He chuckles, but it's not funny. What's funny about people going to hell?

I ignore the goggles' retinal display analyzing Marty's body language, his facial expression, and explaining his response. "Sixty-two percent of people surveyed in the greater New York area believe in the Christian-based heaven you're referring to. That leaves exactly thirty-eight percent. Following your logic, we should be seeing thirty-eight percent of siphons without a halo."

My goggles alert me to my social mistake. Marty's lips flatten and his jaw flexes, and then protrudes. My goggles interpret the information for me: I've angered my co-worker. Heat pricks my cheeks. Before the goggles, I hadn't known shame.

I look down and notice a stain on the carpet; there could be billions of germs in the room. "The carpet is dirty; someone should make a call to cleaning." My eyes stay on the stain, but I see Ava's shoulders lower and the goggles tell me she is disappointed. My heart dips into my stomach, bobbing and flopping like a fish struggling at the end of a hook.

My goggles instruct me to apologize, but Marty steps forward. He's taller than me by four point seven inches.

Ava clears her throat. "You didn't account for the fact that all the siphons we get in this department are homicides. So a larger majority will be involved in shady business, more chances of going to hell."

Marty pokes his finger into my shoulder. "Yeah."

He snakes his arm around Ava's waist and she moves out of his way before they touch. He shuffles around awkwardly before leaving the room.

Ava sips her coffee, careful not to make eye contact. "Howard, have you ever considered looking into something more than the SAT goggles? To help you?"

I stir my tea, the steam escaping. "I've tried some things..." My parents took me to all the appropriate therapies—until the SAT goggles. Sensory Augmentation Technology works better than therapy and surgery. Surgery has a forty-seven percent chance of complications.

"I wear the SAT contacts for post-traumatic stress disorder. But I've been looking into something more ...permanent." She lowers her voice. "The contacts don't help with the nightmares. Dr. Ennis and his partner, Dr. Reg, are working on a new therapy, but it hasn't been approved."

Dr. Ennis is the head of the Mind Transfer Project. His research led to the last-memory siphon technology. The coroner reanimates the visual cortex with a solution that tracks the last twelve seconds of blood flow. They're working on ways to extend the siphons.

But Ava is not telling me about mind transfer or siphons. She's talking about something else.

I sip my tea. My finger strokes the warm circle my cup left behind. "I feel like two different people."

"It's the same for me. The war ruined a part of me. I feel like I'm not really Ava anymore."

"You seem like Ava to me."

She waves off my comment. "I've got an appointment with Dr. Ennis and Dr. Reg tomorrow. I'll let you know how it goes."

"Okay," I say and grip my teacup harder.

She scoots closer to me. "Maybe I could ask about the procedure for you? Imagine not having to wear the goggles."

I lean away from her and sip my tea. Sip again. And again.

A new procedure means no safety statistics. No available statistics doesn't mean it's safe. My heart thumps against my rib cage each beat tripping over the last.

Ava empties her cup in the sink. "I'll get you a brochure. I know how you like to have all the information before you make a decision."

I nod as I inch away to sneak back to the archive room. I can't stop thinking about the missing-halo siphon. Eddie is gone for the day, even though he still has thirty minutes on his shift.

I run a search of all US archives, looking for other siphons without halos. I come up with three. The one I found this morning, and two more in Chicago. My requests instantly return metadata. The other two siphons are shorter too: eight seconds and eleven seconds. I download and play the renders, but don't see anything out of the ordinary. It's hard to see patterns with the goggles. Later tonight, when I take the goggles off, I'll watch them again.

As I leave for the day, Mary from Accounting blows me a kiss. She usually does this when I wear the goggles. Ava claims Mary likes me and I pause to contemplate asking for a date. I vow to heed the social feature's suggestions this time.

She asks me about my day and I tell her it was normal. I don't mention the absent halo problem. I definitely don't mention my run-in with Marty. When I ask her if she wants to grab coffee tomorrow, I'm rewarded with a yes.

I walk with a little more confidence to the maglev station headed for Chicago. Home can wait. The itch isn't so bad after several hours and the headache is finally starting to ebb.

If I wore the goggles more often, I could make more friends. Maybe people would forget I'm that "autistic guy" who works in Digital Forensics. Maybe I could be Howie instead of Howard. Howard sounds like an awkward, short, balding old man. Howie has dates on the weekend, friends who meet him at the bar after work. Howie solves cases.

I stand on the maglev platform and wait for the train to Chicago. The icy air cuts deep into my face and neck. I pull the collar over my ears to cut the chill, but the stubborn New York wind is unrelenting, like thousands of tiny bugs biting at my skin.

The scent advertisements at the station attempt to sell me hot dogs and roasted chestnuts. They compete for my olfactory attention along with hundreds of other smells that make the acid in my stomach churn. I use the corner of my coat to cover my nose.

A crowd surrounds me and I move away. People bump against my side to get a better location on the platform. My fingers are numb, so I roll them into a ball and notice my palms are wet. I squeeze my arms against my chest and curl my hands into tight, tight fists. I hunch my shoulders over my arms. I just want a space that is mine.

I board the train while the goggles control the sensations around me. Without them, the constant flashing of ads projected overhead and the blaring announcements would leave me rocking in a corner. Eddie's wife was killed in a high-speed train crash. There is a one in five hundred thousand chance of a train crash, which is safer than an electric trolley. I repeat the ratio in my head for the duration of the trip.

At the Chicago stop, I pull up a map of the city on one of the touch kiosks at the city center. The kiosk offers to direct me to my destination and I accept. I follow the arrows to each kiosk, and arrive at my first death site.

On a park bench, I replay the siphon render from one Chicago victim. Michael Benson, 28, went out for a jog and collapsed from an apparent aneurism. He tripped and rolled. Another jogger found him tucked between these two wood benches.

I lie on the ground, try to see what he would have seen. All I observe is peeling paint, trash scraping along the jogging path, and the smell of remnants left by irresponsible pet owners.

The goggles alert me to three people staring. The body language and facial recognition analysis indicates a woman is afraid of my behavior; a man by the fountain is poised to fight me if necessary. Another man stares at me from the bench. It's Eddie.

"Howard, what are you doing?"

He's sitting on the bench drinking out of a flask. "Don't look at me like that," he says. "Yeah, I followed you. Saw you leave with the goggles on. You never wear the goggles more than you have to."

"It's against park regulations to drink alcohol." I point to the sign.

He takes another sip.

"I found two more siphons without halos."

Eddie takes the render of the park death, his lips flat and back tense as if I've asked him to undertake an unbearable responsibility. "Once we figure out the problem on these siphons, then you leave this alone, okay? No more going off on your own."

This is the closest I will come to an offer of partnership from Eddie. "Okay."

We decide to head down to the second site—a middle-class neighborhood with no advertisements projecting in a twenty-block radius due to homeowner association restrictions. The streets are for bikes only.

I could take off my goggles, but so far today I've made a date, boarded a high-speed train and gotten Eddie to partner with me on a case. I can't afford to screw it up now.

Our search comes up empty. No new ideas, no evidence of skips like the Turner case back in New York, the one that had me so upset this morning. Now I can't remember why.

Eddie examines the case. "This death was ruled a suicide. She stopped taking her medication for depression a month before she died."

We now have three cases, each one with a different cause of death, nothing in common on the surface except that none of the siphons have halos. Eddie leans against the back of a concrete bench, crossing his arms. He is bored, my goggles assert.

Sixty-eight percent of Catholics believe committing suicide will decrease your chances of going to heaven. Father Solomon says that only the highest power can decide on the fate of a soul. Eddie can't decide; I can't decide. The breeze whips around my ears and neck and we both shiver.

"Let's go back," Eddie says. "It's late, Howard. We'll start fresh tomorrow."

He pats me on the back. I don't cringe away from the touch. I think about asking him to call me Howie. Howie would be friends with a guy like Eddie.

I wake up the next morning with the goggles on, because I neglected to take them off. The same company that produces the goggles makes contact lenses, like the ones Ava wears. I could appear even more normal at work and around town, and get an earbud for my auditory issues.

Only problem is I process the memory clips better without the goggles. Which reminds me, I need to review the two Chicago siphons.

I slide the goggles away from my face, and my eyes flinch at the bright lights. Pain jabs into my head from the empty place, as if I've lost a limb. Fumbling, I manage to dim the lights to the lowest setting. I rub my temples and think about Eddie.

He doesn't think the absent halos are a problem. It doesn't bother him the way it bothers me. I hold my arms across my chest, squeezing tight. Sometimes I wrap myself in the blankets like a cocoon, preparing myself for the day, except I don't emerge a butterfly. I stay a scared, hungry caterpillar.

But yesterday Eddie took the case. He hasn't taken a case since his wife died. He usually takes the grunt digital work, and babysits me down in archive.

I upload the siphons I've been analyzing. When I recall the different causes of death on each case, I run a search of all siphons prepared by employees working in departments outside of homicide and suspicious deaths. Four more appear to be missing halos, making seven total siphons missing halos. All seven siphons are shorter and all seven were from cases in the last six months.

I pin the death sites to a map. No pattern.

I think about what Marty said, that maybe the

victims went to hell and didn't see the halo because they will not be invited into the light.

My first missing-halo case, Sera Turner, was a journalist and a musician. She donated money to a homeless shelter and volunteered at a soup kitchen. Sera should have had a halo.

I pick another file. Michael Benson. Michael was a small-business owner, single, visited a gym regularly, and space-dived once a year. He doesn't appear to have done anything wrong. Father Solomon says to always assume that someone is good, "lest ye be judged" and all that, so I assume that Michael should have a halo too.

It's early, but Father Solomon will be awake. He would know why someone would die without a halo. I call. When the video flicks on, Father Solomon sits in front of a tapestry of the Pentecost.

His wrinkled eyes and mouth turn down. "Hello, Howard. You are troubled?"

"Yes, Father." I want to explain the case, but Eddie warned me to keep it secret. Police protocol. It's the rules. "What would cause someone to not see the light after death?"

"Has someone close to you died?"

"No, Father."

The tension melts from his shoulders and face. "Ah, you seek the answer to a speculative question and not a spiritual one." He adjusts his position in the chair, like a teacher preparing for a lesson. "If someone does not see the light, perhaps it is because it's not his time and he's not yet dying."

The idea disturbs me. The missing-halo victims not actually being dead, their spirits roaming the earth because they have not seen the light. Except the missing-halo victims are dead. Their bodies were processed and deaths documented.

Father notices me rocking and tries to calm me, but I manage to thank him for his answers and concern. He's still attempting to soothe me when I end the call.

The buzzer at the door reminds me to head out to the trolley, so that I won't be late for work. I like the trolley; it rocks back and forth, and that keeps me from getting nervous. Ava takes the same trolley.

The morning news projects above the trolley windows. I usually avoid the screens because they make my eyes burn, but the anchor is interviewing Dr. Ennis and Dr. Reg about mind transfers. I bounce my gaze from the screen to the floor before I realize I can focus on the bottom left corner of the screen and the burning is not as bad.

The anchor leans into the two scientists. "Dr. Reg, you've begun a new spinoff on the transfer research. Would you elaborate?"

Dr. Reg nods, petting two of his fingers along his jawline. "We've been looking into ways to use transfers to cure behavioral and mental disorders." His voice dips at the end, and Dr. Ennis places a hand on his partner's shoulder. "I'm sorry." He continues, "The research is very important to me. I had a sister who suffered from bipolar disorder. She wasn't consistent about wearing her sensory augmentation contacts and ended her life two years ago. Our research will help so many people."

I wonder about Ava. She wears her contacts all the time. Why is she still sad? The interview ends before Ava boards the trolley.

"Hey, Howard," she says.

I want to tell her to call me Howie. Then I remember I don't have the goggles on, so she's right: I'm just Howard.

She blows on her coffee. Her breath through the cap hole makes a deep howling sound and I recoil, but she pretends not to notice. Ava never makes me feel different.

She places her coffee between her legs and fumbles around her purse for a small bag. "I've been thinking about the no-halo problem." She applies her eye shadow and lipstick while she talks. "I did some research about the process—" She puts the makeup away and faces me. I dart my gaze out the window. There is too much stimulation when I look at her hazel eyes, and the red lipstick is too intense. She continues even though I'm not facing her. "It works best if we can get to a body within twenty-four hours after death. The longer we wait, the more incomplete the siphon. That could be what is happening to your siphons."

No. My siphons are different. "The siphons I found were all extracted well within the twenty-four-hour time frame. And siphons *always* have halos." It feels like seven ghosts are all following me, waiting for me to solve the riddle so they can find their light.

She leans forward, and I notice I'm rocking. I try to stop myself but I can't. I'm a caterpillar on a leaf shaking from the wind. The trolley stops and we shuffle off. I hug my arms to my chest. Maybe I should get the goggles.

"What do all the cases have in common?" Ava asks.

"I put them up on a map. No pattern."

"Not just a geographical commonality, but socially. Where did each of these people work? What extracurricular activities did they participate in? What gyms did they go to?"

All the questions bounce off my brain. I imagine the ghosts running to pick them up and thrust them in my face. I dodge them, trying to listen to Ava's advice.

Eddie joins us as we jog up the steps. "You trying to take my case, Ava?"

She grins, and I don't understand why she's happy. I wish I had the goggles.

Ava rolls her lips as if she's trying to swallow the smile before Eddie sees it. "I thought Howard would be on his own," Ava says. "We both know the captain won't support the case; there's nothing to go on."

"My favorite kind of case."

Ava humphs when Eddie says this, and he stops her with his arm before she goes into the door. I keep swaying while Eddie continues, "I looked up the siphons last night for social commonalities between the victims. Too many hits to really pin it down. Do you think someone could be editing the memories?"

Ava looks at me.

I cling tighter to my coat while I fix my gaze on the doorway. "The first siphon could be edited. Siphons don't skip. The other six—"

"Six?" Eddie interrupts me. "Wait, there are seven now?" He blocks the doorway as he faces me.

I flap my hands in the air, thinking about all the siphons without halos, and Eddie is too close. I can smell the gin from last night.

Ava rubs her hand on my back. "Shh, Howard. Calm down." She glares at Eddie. "Is the interrogation necessary?"

Eddie steps away. "Look, he's the one who wants to look into the siphons; I think it's a waste of time. The least he can do is update the case file so I can be informed."

"He's not a detective, Eddie," Ava says.

"It's not a case. We don't have a case number," I say. Then I repeat, "we don't have a case number" over and over because I don't know what I did wrong. Why is Eddie so angry?

Eddie talks over me. "This whole thing is ridiculous. I hate working in Digital." He snaps his attention back to me. "Howard, stop it."

I stop talking, but switch over to humming. The advertisements flicker overhead so I look at the ground. Maybe I should wear the goggles now. Today is the sixteenth. Eddie is not in a very good mood on the sixteenth of every month.

Today will be the seventh month Eddie is a jerk on the sixteenth. He will sit in his chair down in archive and watch the unusually long siphon renders from the high-speed train wreck victims.

He shoves through the entry and heads to archive. Ava guides me through the door too and doesn't say anything. She explains to Marty that I want to learn how to use the case system for some special job down in Digital. Marty shows me the basics while I rock in the chair next to him. I already know how to use the case filing system. Instead, I think about the absent halos and wonder if I should call Father Solomon again. He could say a prayer for the victims. They should all have halos, even if they did do something bad.

As Ava leaves for an appointment, she reminds me to look for similarities. I rework the information I have: seven siphons with no halo; seven different types of death ranging from murder to natural causes; no pattern on death location.

I run all the siphons again for commonalities in the metadata. There are a few hits; most are not statistically significant connections. One connection bothers me: all the victims had mental disabilities or disorders and were prescribed SAT contacts.

I feel the fluttering in my stomach again and this time I grope around in my coat for the goggles and put them on.

I think about the connection and what it has to do with the missing halos. The room buzzes with officers going about their day. Phones ring; a group by the water filter laughs.

The goggles dig into the skin around my eyes. I've been wearing them too often. I fiddle with the lenses, pulling them away to relieve some of the pressure. My pulse pounds into the back of my eyes like an angry neighbor banging on the wall to keep the racket down.

I slip down to Digital Archive. Eddie is working, not looking at train wreck siphons.

"They were all like me."

He doesn't stop sliding the renders around his holodesk. They move between us like chess pieces. "What do you mean?"

"They all wore SAT devices." I point to my goggles. He lowers his hand from the work screen. "Is this why you won't let it go?" The goggles tell me he is angry because he thinks I've withheld information again.

"No, I noticed the connection. After I ran the seven victims."

"Seven victims." He mutters under his breath something I can't hear because my earpiece keeps volume low. "When I only had three that coincidence was not that important, but now you say all seven had SATs?"

"I just said that." The goggles flash a warning: social mistake.

Eddie ignores my error. "Not enough. We need more evidence."

"They all had consultations with Dr. Ennis."

"That doesn't mean anything yet."

"We should search Dr. Ennis's office or subpoena the medical files of the victims."

He laughs. "Come on, Howard, we have to have more than appointments with Dr. Ennis to get our hands on medical files. They all had different causes of death. How do you explain that to a judge?"

"Okay." I nod as if I understand, but I don't. "Okay. We'll get more information."

He puts on his coat while heading for the door. He pats my shoulder and I flinch from his touch. I don't like people touching me when they're angry. They might hit me.

"You'll figure it out," he says as he leaves. Does that mean Eddie is no longer helping me? I could ask him, to find out for sure, but I don't. I should have known better than to try to talk to Eddie on the sixteenth of the month. Ava will listen, except Ava is at an appointment. I try to remember where she was going.

All at once it hits me: Ava is in danger.

The goggles detect my increased heart rate, and the auditory feed emits a buzzing sound to calm me. I squeeze my arms around my body because the buzzing is not enough. I pace the room, wondering if I should check on her, and decide to call instead. No answer.

I go up to the front desk and ask for her, but they tell me she was due back half an hour ago. Nobody seems concerned, just annoyed that she's not back yet.

Mary from Accounting has her coat, and her smile is the biggest thing on her face, her eyes squinting to accommodate all those teeth and lips. "Are you ready for our date?" she asks.

I'd forgotten about the coffee date with Mary. "I, uh…" The goggles give me a list of possible replies. "I have to reschedule."

Her mouth shrinks to normal; she crosses her arms. I ignore the goggles' interpretation of her body language because it makes me feel uncomfortable.

"Is it okay to reschedule?" I try again.

"It's fine," she says, but the goggles tell me it's not fine.

I leave to find Ava. Ava's in trouble and I'm like a superhero weaving through the New York streets. Howard would never be able to do this. My goggles give me my powers. Howie rescues children from burning buildings. Howie saves the girl.

Dr. Ennis's office is on the third floor. In the lobby two security guards step in front of me.

"I need to speak to Ava Jones." I'm assertive. Howard is never assertive.

"You can't go in without an appointment or a visitor's pass." They block me from the elevator as if I'm the bad guy.

"Let me talk to Ava. I need to talk to Ava." I try to walk through to the elevator. I wish I had a badge. Maybe I should call Eddie. But it's the sixteenth and Eddie is being a jerk.

"You don't have an appointment. You have to leave." One guard grips my arm and I yank away.

The other guard snaps to my side and wraps his body around me. In the scuffle, I lose my goggles and the lights attack me from above. The lobby music snakes into my ear. The elevator door is too shiny; it opens like a robotic mouth to suck me into the abyss. I scream for Ava.

A woman's voice shouts, "Let him go."

The guards continue to wrestle me to the ground.

"Howard? Howard!" The woman is Ava. She's all right, so I relax. "Somebody help him!"

"Let him go." Dr. Ennis's smooth voice joins in.

The guards let me go, but I stay on the ground. The lights are too bright and the music is too loud. I'm in a building I don't know, in a part of town I don't know, and I'm Howard again, shaking, rocking.

When I don't respond to Ava, she calls Eddie.

When he arrives, he lies on the floor, encouraging me to get up. Ava rubs her hands and watches me while talking to Dr. Ennis.

When I get off the floor, Eddie hands me the goggles. "Don't take these off."

I want to tell him that the guards took them off, but

he's already in the corner with Ava. She's nodding a lot and looking at me.

I rock and rock. Through the attempts to calm the nerves sparking around my body, I hear Ava and Eddie whispering in hushed voices. They talk as if I'm not in the room. No Howard. No Howie. I'm a puppy that made a mess in their absence. Now they have to clean it.

"...He would never hurt me," Ava's voice cracks.

Eddie sighs. "Are you sure about that?" He pauses for a long time and he uncrosses his arms making his jacket rustle. "No, you're right. He's harmless... We can tell the captain he was worried about you," Eddie says.

"I don't want him suspended."

"They know him. How he is. Nobody's pressing charges. This is just another episode to the upper brass. Don't tell them about Dr. Ennis and I'll take him home."

She hesitates and rubs her shoulders as if a huge weight has been set there. "No, I'll take him."

The ride on the trolley does its job to calm me. Before I know it, I'm walking up the stairs to my apartment.

"Howard," Ava says, clearing her throat. "Eddie told me about what you thought. About Dr. Ennis."

I stare at my door handle.

"Do you think that you might have imagined it because of a fear of the procedure? When we talked yesterday, I got the sense you were afraid, not really for me, but for you. At the consultation Dr. Ennis assured me—"

"I'm not afraid."

"But—"

"I think I should get a consultation, too." I'm sick of being Howard, the autistic guy in Digital Archive.

She straightens. "Well, okay. I'll set something up with Dr. Reg."

"What about Dr. Ennis?"

"He does the initial, but I talked to Dr. Ennis about you, and I think we could get you right in to Dr. Reg. They take a scan of the brain, then redesign the parts that are damaged and insert the fix into your mind. I did my scan today. He said PTSD is an easy redesign—once we get approval."

She takes a deep breath.

I exhale. "I'm sorry about today."

She nods. "It's good to know you have my back."

I escape into my apartment.

In the morning, there is a message from Eddie on my computer. *Maybe this will help you let it go.* It's the medical files from Dr. Ennis' patients. The siphons without halos. Dr. Ennis wouldn't release the files if he were guilty.

This doesn't help me feel better, but I look at the files anyway because even with the goggles on I can't give up. Nothing would show up on these files anyway; I need autopsy reports. I didn't look at them yesterday.

The autopsies don't reveal much. Each person had an fMRI scan done for the Mind Transfer Project in hopes that the redesign treatment would be approved. But thousands of other people have had scans done for the Mind Transfer Project and none of them have died.

I do a quick check of other siphons that have also had fMRI scans for the Mind Transfer Project; they all have halos.

In the victim who committed suicide, the autopsy report shows a brain bleed in the frontal cortex, along with temporal lobe damage. The absent halo case with the PTSD case shows lesions in the amygdala. My brain buzzes with some sort of connection.

If I take off the goggles, I could see it, but I promised Eddie that I won't take them off.

Ava is waiting for me at the door. She must have been able to get me in with Dr. Reg. We take the trolley down to the Bellevue Research Center.

"The scan doesn't hurt," Ava says.

My mind is chewing on the autopsy information. Something doesn't add up, but I have to stop thinking about it or I'll relapse, and this time Eddie will tell the captain the truth about me wrongfully suspecting Dr. Ennis.

I tap my fingernails on my teeth. "I'm not worried."

We go into the building, and this time the security guards let me into the elevator. I skirt around them, flinching when I get closer, but they don't even acknowledge me.

Dr. Reg greets us before we can even sit in the waiting room and we are ushered right into the scan room. The walls are grey and the floor is tan Berber. It should calm me, the plain colors, but the fluttering starts in my stomach when the nurse motions for me sit on the exam table. I lie down on the table, breathing evenly.

"We're going to have to take those goggles off." Dr. Reg says.

My heart thumps hard. "Can you dim the lights?"

The technician dims the lights and leaves the room to prepare the equipment.

Ava leans over and helps me.

"We have good news." Dr. Reg turns to Ava. "We have approval from the research committee for a small subset of test subjects, and your file came up as a candidate. I've got the redesign in my office, and we can start the treatment."

"Right now?" Ava asks. She bites her lip and looks at me.

"You can go." My voice breaks at the end.

"Are you sure?"

"You'll just be waiting outside anyway."

She leaves with Dr. Reg, and I try to lie still while the scanning technician insists that I'm in fact not still.

When I get situated, I think about the autopsies and the parts of the brain affected. *Depression in the frontal and temporal lobe areas, PTSD in the amygdala.* It clicks. Those are the parts of the brain that would need to be "redesigned." I wonder if all seven absent halo cases were candidates for the redesign. How many of Dr. Reg's patients got a redesign?

I wiggle off the table and the technician calls for me to stop.

I push away from the nurses and dart for the hallway.

The hallway is lined with exam rooms, surgical rooms, and a room marked *Transfer*. There's a commotion down the hall as the nurses call my name. I slip into the transfer room before they see me, and lock the door.

I'm relieved by the darkened room.

I trip on a cord and my shoulder jams into a metal cage. The cage clatters and a high-pitched squeal pierces the air. Cedar shavings spill onto the floor. Then there's a flurry of activity. Rats bang against their cages, running along squeaky wheels. I hug myself, humming.

A light from a door at the other end of the room blinks like a beacon. *Stop blinking, stop blinking, stop blinking.* There's canvas hanging over the top half of the door, obstructing the light from what appears to be another room. I pull it down.

I peek through the window and see Ava lying back in a chair. Wires snake out from her head and wrap around her neck like a noose.

"Just one more minute," Dr. Reg's voice says to her.

I hear Ava moaning inside, but the door is locked.

I yell through the door, "Leave her alone."

Dr. Reg startles and holds up his hand. "This is a very delicate procedure. Stay back."

"The other patients didn't have halos."

The doctor looks confused, so I try to think of how the goggles would tell me to explain it. I pat my pockets and then remember that my goggles are in the exam room.

I try again. "The other patients died."

"The other patients didn't get the correct treatment. I've fixed it," Dr. Reg explains, his voice muffled.

"I don't want to do this." Ava is crying now on the table, wires tangled in her hair, her face contorted in pain. A machine beeps next to her and the doctor connects another wire from the machine to Ava.

"She wants you to let her go." I flap my hands, slapping at my neck, imagining the wires around my body, trapping me.

121

Dr. Reg adjusts the dials on the machine. "She's in pain now, but I've given her a solution to help her forget the pain after the treatment."

I think about the skips in Sera Turner's file. I repeat Sera Turner's case file number over and over.

Someone knocks on the door to the rat lab behind me.

Dr. Reg pulls out a remote from his pocket. He flips the lights up to full brightness, and the doors to the transfer room lock with a rapid, resounding click, trapping me inside.

I cover my eyes and collapse against the wall.

"Howard, help me," Ava begs, her voice fading.

I want to reassure her, but now someone is banging on the door. The sharp noise scares me and I press my body into the wall, shivering and rocking.

"The treatments should be working." Dr. Reg leans against the window between us. "My daughter was diagnosed bipolar." His eyes are round and red. The ends of his mouth point down, twitching before he pushes off the wall and paces the room.

I scratch at the door and realize I'm never going to get out.

Dr. Reg knew about the deaths of his patients. Dr. Ennis must not have known, otherwise why did he send the paperwork?

Dr. Reg won't let me leave; if I leave people will know. I imagine the images the coroner will siphon after I die.

The doctor continues stammering about the treatments and I struggle to look at Ava, who is trembling, staring up at the ceiling. Her hand breaks free from the restraints and she reaches for the wires, pulling at them. Dr. Reg continues pacing, preoccupied.

LUIS MENACHO

I clench my fists and throw myself at the door, scratching and clawing. My mind rages in blind panic as sensations assault me, but I force myself to focus on Ava. I have to save Ava. I yell at her to hang on and she stops thrashing. I grab an empty cage and crash it against the glass until it shatters. The door behind me buzzes and opens. A guard rushes in and pins me to the wall.

Ava lies unmoving on the table. I scream for the guard to let me go, I scream about the missing halos.

When the guards check Ava's vitals and pronounce her dead, I scream that the doctor killed her, and then I just scream and cry and shake until Eddie shows up an hour later.

The doctors and researchers tried to explain to me their theories of how the redesign had affected patients' brains. Each of the patients suffered varying side effects as Dr. Reg adjusted the treatment, causing different forms of death.

The detectives found bullets in Dr. Reg's gun that matched the same slug that killed Sera Turner. Evidence recovered from Dr. Reg's email showed that Sera had been complaining of massive headaches, and threatened to expose Dr. Reg to the medical board when she discovered the treatments had never been approved.

He felt that he needed more time to complete his research. He became desperate for answers, and his unstable mind saw Sera as a threat.

No one could explain the missing halos or the short siphons. Dr. Ennis said that the redesigns left each individual's consciousness out of sync. Father

Solomon said it was a sign that the victims' spirits were never guided into the light. I like to think that they have found their way now.

Ava's siphon has yet to be rendered. At first, I didn't want to render it, because I'm afraid of what I will see. Will her last memory be of me cowering in a corner while she begs me to help her? But I need to know one thing.

The frames are blurry and I spend hours tweaking and adjusting. Before long, I see myself rendered clearly, looking directly at her before I move away from the wall. I look determined as I fight to get to her. I look like a superhero.

The door behind me buzzes and opens.

Eddie comes into the dim room wearing his badge. "Hi, Howard."

"You hate Digital," I say. "You said you'd never come back."

"I know what I said." He pauses, looking at the looping render. "It's lunch time; you need to take a break. I'm going down to Pierre's."

I like Pierre's; they're next to the waterfront in a no-advertising zone. The crowd is usually small, lights dim.

"I'm not going to wear the goggles. You said I had to wear them."

"Yeah, I said that." He shifts his weight from one foot to the other. "You don't need them. You did good…" He chokes on the rest of the words and instead holds out his hand.

I think about the millions of germs on a human hand, how a handshake is so strange. I think about the sensation of touching, and Eddie's sandpaper knuckles. A statistic pops into my head about the percentage of people who no longer shake hands as a custom. Eddie waits for me, his hand suspended in the air.

I suddenly know what to do. I shake his hand, then leave without the goggles. I like being Howard.

I glance back at my desk as the door closes and pause long enough to see Ava's perfect halo fade to black.

The Manuscript Factory

BY L. RON HUBBARD

Having now completed its first twenty-nine years, the L. Ron Hubbard Presents Writers of the Future Contest remains true to the purpose for which it was created: "To provide a means for new and budding writers to have a chance for their creative efforts to be seen and acknowledged."

Robert Silverberg, Science Fiction Grand Master and judge since the Contest's inception, noted in recognition of the program's success, "What a wonderful idea—one of science fiction's all-time giants opening the way for a new generation of exciting talent! For these brilliant stories, and the careers that will grow from them, we all stand indebted to L. Ron Hubbard."

As one of the most celebrated writers during America's Golden Age of pulp fiction, Ron began his career in the summer of 1933 in the California coastal town of Encinitas, just north of San Diego. There he wrote and submitted a half-million words of fiction, shotgunned out to a dozen markets. He saw sales from the start, with his first published tale being "The Green God," a routine story at the time of a Western intelligence officer in search of a stolen idol. What made this yarn different, however, was that the young L. Ron Hubbard had actually walked the gloomy streets of Tientsin in China—and in the company of a Western intelligence officer: specifically, a Major Ian Macbean of the British Secret Service.

Ron's rapid ascent to success as a writer can be greatly attributed to the fact that his stories were drawn from genuine firsthand experience. This was best described in October 1933, a few short months after his emergence onto the pulp fiction scene, by the editor of Thrilling Adventures *when he wrote,*

"Several of you have wondered, too, how he gets the splendid color which always characterizes his stories of faraway places. The answer is, he's been there, brothers. He's been, and seen, and done, and plenty of all three of them!"

Ron saw over 200 of his fiction stories published during this time; he wrote in every popular genre, from adventure of every sort to mystery and thriller, to science fiction and fantasy, to western and even some romance. He wrote anywhere from 70,000–100,000 words a month, writing only three days a week, affording him the time he needed for further adventuring.

Regarding the necessity of devoting oneself to the task of writing, Ron had this to say:

"If you write insincerely, if you think the lowest pulp can be written insincerely and still sell, then you're in for trouble unless your luck is terribly good. And luck rarely strikes twice."

He featured this and several other topics in instructional essays, which he penned on the business of writing, addressing concerns common to both the novice and experienced writer alike. Initially published in such magazines as Writer's Digest, Writer's Review, Author & Journalist and Writers' Markets & Methods, these articles covered topics such as how to get a story idea, how to create suspense, how to create story vitality and even what not to tell a writer. These essays would eventually become the backbone of the now-famous Writers of the Future Workshop as taught by Tim Powers and Dave Wolverton. The Workshop provides the basic skills of story writing, combining compassion with encouragement for the fledgling writer, while continuing to offer insightful lessons in writing techniques.

The first of these instructional essays, written in late 1935, titled "The Manuscript Factory," is where Ron brings the sharp, candid and enlightening insight of a seasoned professional to the practical rigors—and rewards—of writing as a craft and career in an intensely competitive marketplace.

The Manuscript Factory

So you want to be a professional.

Or, if you are a professional, you want to make more money. Whichever it is, it's certain that you want to advance your present state to something better and easier and more certain.

Very often I hear gentlemen of the craft referring to writing as the major "insecure" profession. These gentlemen go upon the assumption that the gods of chance are responsible and are wholly accountable for anything which might happen to income, hours or pleasure. In this way, they seek to excuse a laxity in thought and a feeling of unhappy helplessness which many writers carry forever with them.

But when a man says that, then it is certain that he rarely, if ever, takes an accounting of himself and his work, that he has but one yardstick. You are either a writer or you aren't. You either make money or you don't. And all beyond that rests strictly with the gods.

I assure you that a system built up through centuries of commerce is not likely to cease its function just because your income seems to depend upon your imagination. And I assure you that the overworked

129

potence of economics is just as applicable to this business of writing as it is to shipping hogs.

You are a factory. And if you object to the word, then allow me to assure you that it is not a brand, but merely a handy designation which implies nothing of the hack, but which could be given to any classic writer.

Yes, you and I are both factories with the steam hissing and the chimneys belching and the machinery clanging. We manufacture manuscripts, we sell a stable product, we are quite respectable in our business. The big names of the field are nothing more than the name of Standard Oil on gasoline, Ford on a car, or Browning on a machine gun.

And as factories, we can be shut down, opened, have our production decreased, change our product, have production increased. We can work full blast and go broke. We can loaf and make money. Our machinery is the brain and the fingers.

And it is fully as vital that we know ourselves and our products as it is for a manufacturer to know his workmen and his plant.

Few of us do. Most of us sail blithely along and blame everything on chance.

Economics, taken in a small dose, are simple. They have to do with price, cost, supply, demand and labor.

If you were to open up a soap plant, you would be extremely careful about it. That soap plant means your income. And you would hire economists to go over everything with you. If you start writing, ten to one, you merely write and let everything else slide by the boards. But your writing factory, if anything, is more vital than your soap factory. Because if you lose your own machinery, you can never replace it—and you can always buy new rolls, vats and boilers.

The first thing you would do would be to learn the art of making soap. And so, in writing, you must first learn to write. But we will assume that you already know how to write. You are more interested in making money from writing.

It does no good to protest that you write for the art of it. Even the laborer who finds his chief pleasure in his work tries to sell services or products for the best price he can get. Any economist will tell you that.

You are interested in income. In net income. And "net income" is the inflow of satisfaction from economic goods, estimated in money, according to Seligman.

I do not care if you write articles on knitting, children's stories, snappy stories or gag paragraphs, you can still apply this condensed system and make money.

When you first started to write, if you were wise, you wrote anything and everything for everybody and sent it all out. If your quantity was large and your variety wide, then you probably made three or four sales.

With the field thus narrowed and you had, say, two types of markets to hammer at, you went ahead and wrote for the two. But you did not forget all the other branches you had first aspired to. And now and then you ripped off something out of line and sent it away, and perhaps sold it, and went on with the first two types regardless.

Take my own situation as an example—because I know it better than yours. I started out writing for the pulps, writing the best I knew, writing for every mag on the stands, slanting as well as I could.

I turned out about a half a million words, making

sales from the start because of heavy quantity. After a dozen stories were sold, I saw that things weren't quite right. I was working hard and the money was slow.

Now, it so happened that my training had been an engineer's. I leaned toward solid, clean equations rather than guesses, and so I took the list which you must have: stories written, type, wordage, where sent, sold or not.

My list was varied. It included air-war, commercial air, western, western love, detective and adventure.

On the surface, that list said that adventure was my best bet, but when you've dealt with equations long, you never trust them until you have the final result assured.

I reduced everything to a common ground. I took stories written of one type, added up all the wordage and set down the wordage sold. For instance:

DETECTIVE....................120,000 words written
30,000 words sold

$$\frac{30,000}{120,000} = 25\%$$

ADVENTURE..................200,000 words written
36,000 words sold

$$\frac{36,000}{200,000} = 18\%$$

According to the sale book, adventure was my standby, but one look at 18 percent versus 25 percent showed me that I had been doing a great deal of work for nothing. At a cent a word, I was getting $0.0018 for adventure and $0.0025 for detective.

A considerable difference. And so I decided to write detectives more than adventures.

I discovered from this same list that, whereby I came from the West and therefore should know my subject, I had still to sell even one western story. I have written none since.

I also found that air-war and commercial air stories were so low that I could no longer afford to write them. And that was strange as I held a pilot's license.

Thus, I was fooled into working my head off for little returns. But things started to pick up after that and I worked less. Mostly I wrote detective stories, with an occasional adventure yarn to keep up the interest.

But the raw materials of my plant were beginning to be exhausted. I had once been a police reporter and I had unconsciously used up all the shelved material I had.

And things started to go bad again, without my knowing why. Thereupon, I took out my books, which I had kept accurately and up to date—as you should do.

Astonishing figures. While detective seemed to be my mainstay, here was the result.

$$\text{DETECTIVE} \frac{95{,}000 \text{ words sold}}{320{,}000 \text{ words written}} = 29.65\%$$

ADVENTURE..........21,500 words sold

$$\frac{21{,}500 \text{ words sold}}{30{,}000 \text{ words written}} = 71.7\%$$

Thus, for every word of detective I wrote I received $0.002965 and for every adventure word $0.00717. A considerable difference. I scratched my head in perplexity until I realized about raw materials.

I had walked some geography, had been at it for years and, thus, my adventure stories were beginning to shine through. Needless to say, I've written few detective stories since then.

About this time, another factor bobbed up. I seemed to be working very, very hard and making very, very little money.

But, according to economics, no one has ever found a direct relation between the value of a product and the quantity of labor it embodies.

A publishing house had just started to pay me a cent a word and I had been writing for their books a long time. I considered them a mainstay among mainstays.

Another house had been taking a novelette a month from me. Twenty thousand words at a time. But most of my work was for the former firm.

Dragging out the accounts, I started to figure up on words written for this and that, getting percentages.

I discovered that the house which bought my novelettes had an average of 88 percent. Very, very high.

And the house for which I wrote the most was buying 37.6 percent of all I wrote for them.

Because the novelette market paid a cent and a quarter and the others a cent, the average pay was: House A, $0.011 for novelettes on every word I wrote for them. House B, $0.00376 for every word I wrote for *them*.

I no longer worried my head about House B. I worked less and made more. I worked hard on those novelettes after that and the satisfaction increased.

That was a turning point. Released from drudgery and terrific quantity and low quality, I began to make money and to climb out of a word grave.

That, you say, is all terribly dull, disgustingly sordid. Writing, you say, is an art. What are you, you want to know, one of these damned hacks?

No, I'm afraid not. No one gets a keener delight out of running off a good piece of work. No one takes any more pride in craftsmanship than I do. No one is trying harder to make every word live and breathe.

But, as I said before, even the laborer who finds his chief pleasure in his work tries to sell services or products for the best price he can get.

And that price is not word rate. That price is satisfaction received, measured in money.

You can't go stumbling through darkness and live at this game. Roughly, here is what you face. There are less than two thousand professional writers in the United States. Hundreds of thousands are trying to write—some say millions.

The competition is keener in the writing business than in any other. Therefore, when you try to skid by with the gods of chance, you simply fail to make the grade. It's a brutal selective device. You can beat it if you know your product and how to handle it. You can beat it on only two counts. One has to do with genius and the other with economics. There are very few men who sell and live by their genius only. Therefore, the rest of us have to fall back on a fairly exact science.

If there were two thousand soap plants in the country and a million soap plants trying to make money and you were one of the million, what would you do? Cutting prices, in our analogy, is not possible, nor fruitful in any commerce. Therefore you would tighten up your plant to make every bar count. You wouldn't produce a bar if you knew it would be bad. You'd think about such things as reputation, supply, demand, organization, the plant, type of soap, advertising, sales department, accounting, profit and loss, quality versus quantity, machinery, improvements in product, raw materials and labor employed.

And so it is in writing. We're factories working under terrific competition. We have to produce and sell at low cost and small price.

Labor, according to economics in general, cannot be measured in simple, homogenous units of time such as labor hours. And laborers differ, tasks differ, in respect to amount and character of training, degree of skill, intelligence and capacity to direct one's work.

That for soap making. That also for writing. And you're a factory whether your stories go to *Saturday Evening Post, Harper's* or an upstart pulp that pays a quarter of a cent on publication. We're all on that common level. We must produce to eat and we must know our production and product down to the ground.

Let us take some of the above-mentioned topics, one by one, and examine them.

Supply and Demand

You must know that the supply of stories is far greater than the demand. Actual figures tell nothing. You have only to stand by the editor and watch him open the morning mail. Stories by the truckload.

One market I know well is publishing five stories a month. Five long novelettes. Dozens come in every week from names which would make you sit up very straight and be very quiet. And only five are published. And if there's a reject from there, you'll work a long time before you'll sell it elsewhere.

That editor buys what the magazine needs, buys the best obtainable stories from the sources she knows to be reliable. She buys impersonally as though she bought soap. The best bar, the sweetest smell, the maker's name. She pays as though she paid for soap, just as impersonally, but many times more dollars.

That situation is repeated through all the magazine ranks. Terrific supply, microscopic demand.

Realize now that every word must be made to count?

Organization and the Plant

Do you have a factory in which to work? Silly question, perhaps, but I know of one writer who wastes his energy like a canary wastes grain just because he has never looked at a house with an eye to an office. He writes in all manner of odd places.

Never considers the time he squanders by placing himself where he is accessible. His studio is on top of the garage, he has no light except a feeble electric bulb and yet he has to turn out seventy thousand a month. His nerves are shattered. He is continually going elsewhere to work, wasting time and more time.

Whether the wife or the family likes it or not, when the food comes out of the roller, a writer should have the pick and choice, say what you may. Me? I often take the living room and let the guests sit in the kitchen.

A writer needs good equipment. Quality of work is surprisingly dependent upon the typewriter. One lady I know uses a battered, rented machine which went through the world war, judging by its looks. The ribbon will not reverse. And yet, when spare money comes in, it goes on anything but a typewriter.

Good paper is more essential than writers will admit. Cheap, unmarked paper yellows, brands a manuscript as a reject after a few months, tears easily and creases.

Good typing makes a good impression. I have often wished to God that I had taken a typing course instead of a story writing course far back in the dim past.

Raw Materials

Recently, a lady who once wrote pulp detective stories told me that, since she knew nothing of detective work, she went down to Center Street and sought information. The detective sergeant there gave her about eight hours of his time. She went through the gallery, the museum, looked at all their equipment and took copious notes.

And the sergeant was much surprised at her coming there at all. He said that in fifteen years, she was the third to come there. And she was the only one who really wanted information. He said that detective stories always made him squirm. He wished the writers would find out what they wrote.

And so it is with almost every line. It is so easy to get good raw materials that most writers consider it quite unnecessary.

Hence the errors which make your yarn unsalable. You wouldn't try to write an article on steel without at least opening an encyclopedia, and yet I'll wager that a fiction story which had steel in it would never occasion the writer a bit of worry or thought.

You must have raw material. It gives you the edge on the field. And so, one tries to get it by honest research. For a few stories, you may have looked far, but for most of your yarns, you took your imagination for the textbook.

After all, you wouldn't try to make soap when you had no oil.

The fact that you write is a passport everywhere. You'll find very few gentlemen refusing to accommodate your curiosity. Men in every and any line are anxious to give a writer all the data he can use because, they reason, their line will therefore be truly represented. You're apt to find more enmity in not examining the facts.

Raw materials are more essential than fancy writing. Know your subject.

Type of Work

It is easy for you to determine the type of story you write best. Nothing is more simple. You merely consult your likes and dislikes.

But that is not the whole question. What do you write and sell best?

A writer tells me that she can write excellent marriage stories, likes to write them and is eternally plagued to do them. But there are few markets for marriage stories. To eat, she takes the next best thing— light love.

My agent makes it a principle never to handle a type of story which does not possess at least five markets. That way he saves himself endless reading and he saves his writers endless wordage. A story should have at least five good markets because what one editor likes, another dislikes and what fits here will not fit there. All due respect to editors, their minds change and their slant is never too iron-bound. They are primarily interested in good stories. Sometimes they are overbought. Sometimes they have need of a certain type which you do not fill. That leaves four editors who may find the desired spot.

While no writer should do work he does not like, he must eat.

Sales Department

If you had a warehouse filled with sweet-smelling soap and you were unable to sell it, what would you do? You would hire a man who could. And if your business was manufacturing soap, your selling could not wholly be done by yourself. It's too much to ask. This selling is highly complex, very expensive.

Therefore, instead of wasting your valuable manufacturing time peddling your own manuscripts, why not let another handle the selling for you?

There's more to selling than knowing markets. The salesman should be in constant contact with the buyer. A writer cannot be in constant contact with his editors. It would cost money. Luncheons, cigars, all the rest. An agent takes care of all that and the cost is split up among his writers so that no one of them feels the burden too heavily.

An agent, if he is good, sells more than his ten percent extra. And he acts as a buffer between you and the postman. Nothing is more terrible than the brown envelope in the box. It's likely to kill the day. You're likely to file the story and forget it. But the agent merely sends the yarn out again, and when it comes home, out again it goes. He worries and doesn't tell you until you hold the check in your hand.

The collaborating agent and the critic have no place here. They are advisers and doctors. Your sales department should really have no function except selling—and perhaps when a market is going sour, forward a few editorial comments without any added by your agent. This tends for high morale and a writer's morale must always be high. When we started, we assumed that you already could write.

By all means, get an agent. And if you get one and he is no good to you, ditch him and try another. There are plenty of good agents. And they are worth far more than 10 percent.

Advertising

Your agent is your advertising department. He can tell the editor things which you, out of modesty, cannot. He can keep you in the minds of the men who count.

But a writer is his own walking advertisement. His reputation is his own making. His actions count for more than his stories. His reliability is hard won and, when won, is often the deciding factor in a sale. Editors must know you can produce, that you are earnest in your attempt to work with them.

To show what actions can do, one writer recently made it a habit to bait an editor as he went out to lunch. This writer met this editor every day, forced his company on the editor and then, when they were eating, the writer would haul out synopsis after synopsis. The answer is, the writer doesn't work there anymore.

If a check is due, several writers I know haunt the office. It fails to hurry the check and it often puts an end to the contact when overdone. Many harry their editors for early decisions, make themselves nuisances in the office. Soon they stop selling there. Others always have a sob story handy.

Sob stories are pretty well taboo. It's hitting below the belt. And sob stories from writer to writer are awful. One man I know has wrecked his friendship with his formerly closest companions simply because he couldn't keep his troubles to himself. It's actually hurt his sales. You see, he makes more money than anyone I know and he can't live on it. Ye gods, ALL of us have troubles, but few professionals use them to get checks or sympathy.

Reputation is everything.

It does not hurt to do extra work for an editor. Such as department letters. Check it off to advertising. Answer all mail. Do a book for advertising. Write articles. Your name is your trademark. The better known, the better sales.

Quality Versus Quantity

I maintain that there is a medium ground for quantity and quality. One goes up, the other comes down.

The ground is your own finding. You know your best wordage and your best work. If you don't keep track of both, you should.

Write too little and your facility departs. Write too much and your quality drops. My own best wordage is seventy thousand a month. I make money at that, sell in the upper percentage brackets. But let me do twenty thousand in a month and I feel like an old machine trying to turn over just once more before it expires. Let me do a hundred thousand in a month and I'm in possession of several piles of tripe.

The economic balance is something of your own finding. But it takes figures to find it. One month, when I was used to doing a hundred thousand per, I was stricken with some vague illness which caused great pain and sent me to bed.

For a week I did nothing. Then, in the next, I laid there and thought about stories. My average, so I thought, was shot to the devil. Toward the last of the month, I had a small table made and, sitting up in bed, wrote a ten thousand worder and two twenty thousand worders. That was all the work I did. I sold every word and made more in eight days than I had in any previous month.

That taught me that there must be some mean of average. I found it and the wage has stayed up.

There is no use keeping the factory staff standing by and the machinery running when you have no raw material.

You can't sit down and stare at keys and wish you could write and swear at your low average for the month. If you can't write that day, for God's sakes don't write. The chances are, when tomorrow arrives, and you've spent the yesterday groaning and doing nothing, you'll be as mentally sterile as before.

Forget what you read about having to work so many hours every day. No writer I know has regular office hours. When you can't write, when it's raining and the kid's crying, go see a movie, go talk to a cop, go dig up a book of fairy stories. But don't sweat inactively over a mill. You're just keeping the staff standing by and the machinery running, cutting into your overhead and putting out nothing. You're costing yourself money.

Come back when you're fresh and work like hell. Two in the morning, noon, eight at night, work if you feel like it and be damned to the noise you make. After all, the people who have to hear you are probably fed by you and if they can't stand it, let them do the supporting. I take sprees of working at night and then sleep late into the day. Once in the country, farmers baited me every day with that unforgivable late slumber. It didn't worry me so much after I remembered that I made in a month what they made in a year. They think all writers are crazy. Take the writer's license and make the best of it.

But don't pretend to temperament. It really doesn't exist. Irritation does and is to be scrupulously avoided.

When all the arty scribblers (who made no money) talked to a young lady and told her that they could not write unless they were near the mountains, or unless they had the room a certain temperature, or unless they were served tea every half hour, the young lady said with sober mien, "Me? Oh, I can never write unless I'm in a balloon or in the Pacific Ocean."

One thing to remember: It seems to work out that your writing machine can stand just so much. After that the brain refuses to hand out plots and ideas.

It's like getting a big contract to sell your soap to the navy. You make bad soap, ruin the vats with a strong ingredient and let the finer machinery rust away in its uselessness. Then, when the navy soap contract ceases to supply the coffee and cakes, you discover that the plant is worthless for any other kind of product.

Such is the case of the writer who sees a big living in cheap fiction, turns it out to the expense of his vitality and, finally, years before his time, discovers that he is through. Only one writer of my acquaintance can keep a high word output. He is the exception and he is not burning himself out. He is built that way.

But the rest of us shy away from too cheap a brand. We know that an advanced wage will only find us spending more. Soon, when the target for our unworthy efforts is taken down, we discover that we are unable to write anything else. That's what's meant by a rut.

As soon as you start turning out stories which you do not respect, as soon as you start turning them out wholesale over a period of time, as soon as your wordage gets out of control, then look for lean years.

To get anywhere at all in the business, you should turn out the best that's in you and keep turning it out. You'll never succeed in pulp unless you do, much less in the slicks.

If you start at the lowest rung, do the best job of which you are capable. Your product, according to economic law, will do the raising for you. Man is not paid for the amount of work in labor-hours, he is paid for the quality of that work.

Improvement of Product

With experience, your stories should improve. If they do not, then you yourself are not advancing. It's impossible not to advance, it's impossible to stand still. You must move, and you must slide back.

Take a story published a month ago, written six months ago. Read it over. If it seems to you that you could have done better, that you are doing better, you can sit back with a feline smile and be secure in the knowledge that you are coming up. Then sit forward and see to it that you do.

If you write insincerely, if you think the lowest pulp can be written insincerely and still sell, then you're in for trouble unless your luck is terribly good.

And luck rarely strikes twice. Write sincerely and you are certain to write better and better.

So much for making soap and writing. All this is merely my own findings in an upward trail through the rough paper magazines. I have tested these things and found them to be true and if someone had handed them to me a few years ago, I would have saved myself a great deal of worry and more bills would have been paid.

Once, a professor of short story in a university gave me a course because I was bored with being an engineer. The course did not help much outside of the practice in writing. Recently I heard that professor address the radio audience on the subject "This Business of Writing." It was not until then that I realized how much a writer had to learn. He knew nothing about the practical end of things and I told him so. He made me give a lecture to his class and they did not believe me.

But none of them, like you and I, have to make the bread and butter someway in this world. They had never realized that competition and business economics had any place whatever in the writing world. They were complacent in some intangible, ignorant quality they branded ART. They did not know, and perhaps will someday find out, that art means, simply:

"The employment of means to the accomplishment of some end; the skillful application and adaptation to some purpose or use of knowledge or power acquired from Nature, especially in the production of beauty as in sculpture, etc.; a system of rules and established methods to facilitate the performance of certain actions."

147

They saw nothing praiseworthy in work well done. They had their hearts fixed on some goal even they did not understand. To them, writing was not a supreme source of expression, not a means of entertaining, not a means of living and enjoying work while one lived. If you wrote for a living, they branded you a hack. But they will never write.

Poor fools, they haven't the stamina, the courage, the intelligence, the knowledge of life's necessity, the mental capacity to realize that whatever you do in this life you must do well and that whatever talent you have is expressly given you to provide your food and your comfort.

My writing is not a game. It is a business, a hardheaded enterprise which fails only when I fail, which provides me with an energy outlet I need, which gives me the house I live in, which lets me keep my wife and boy. I am a manuscript factory but *not*—and damn those who so intimate it—an insincere hack, peddling verbal belly-wash with my tongue in my cheek. And I eat only so long as my factory runs economically, only so long as I remember the things I have learned about this writing *business*.

The Grande Complication

written by

Christopher Reynaga

illustrated by

OLIVIA XU

ABOUT THE AUTHOR

Christopher Reynaga's earliest memories are of telling stories about the magical world around us to the grownups who seemed so unaware of it. "I would tell my parents, and they would laugh, but I would tell my grandmother, and she believed. I was a child, and she an old woman, but we were both the right age to understand—my youthful belief and intuition that all children possess, and her old traditions of Mexico and the Yaqui. Miracles and magic existed alongside baseball, bicycles and skinned knees—this was the way the world worked."

Christopher grew up in a normal American neighborhood where all the houses were the same, only differing in color. He read everything, including his parents' college textbooks. When he was nine, he had a dream that he would grow up to be a writer—a dream that is starting to come true.

He is a graduate of Clarion West and winner of both first place for L. Ron Hubbard's Writers of the Future and a Bazzanella Literary Award. He has stories in The Book of Cthulhu 2, GigaNotoSaurus, The Drabblecast, Cemetery Dance, *and the* American River Literary Review.

ABOUT THE ILLUSTRATOR

Olivia Xu lived in Nanjing, China—a historical city with beautiful sycamore trees—for twenty-two years before moving to New York for graduate school in 2011. When she was little, she would imitate her grandmother's traditional Chinese paintings. She believes that's where she inherited her artistic talent. Admittedly, she was quite a troublemaker as a kid, and the only time she sat still was when she was doodling. Olivia went to an art-oriented high school and later entered an animation program in college. Animation has been the love of her life. She is always fascinated by its unique way of storytelling and its capacity and independence as an art form.

Currently Olivia is attending the 3-D animation and motion art program at Pratt Institute. She is enthusiastic about illustration and sees it as more of a "snapshot" from a story. She likes to make her illustrations exquisite in terms of color balance and detail, while keeping the story/concept a little ambiguous. Olivia wants her audience to feel the story but be unable to tell it from her illustration. Constantly she is inspired by the lives of people around her. She loves making illustrated cards for her friends, hoping her small artwork can bring happiness to the people she cares about. In the near future, Olivia hopes to work as a 3-D lighter or generalist, but she will never give up her passion for illustration.

The Grande Complication

The moment that the world stopped, Neil was trying to yank his hand free of Miss Dutton's grip. He would have thrown the suitcase of what little he owned onto the train station steps, but his keeper would have dragged him on without it, even as she warned him, "I've slapped many a nine-year-old boy in the mouth, thank you very much." Instead, Neil swung the heavy suitcase at her ankle and loosed a scream for the death of a world that had taken his home and dragged him alone and frightened into this cold October dawn. Neil howled, but the world howled louder as it ceased with a sound no boy would have ever imagined.

The London air clattered with a jangle like spilled silverware. The rattle of the windows was a dying engine. The people crowded in Greenwich Station glanced around as if expecting the gray clouds to split open and rain pig's blood. A startled flock of pigeons burst into the air as the beat of their hearts pulsed arrhythmically, then stopped.

Everything stopped. The people stopped midstride. The train rolling into the station stopped midscreech.

The birds hung motionless in the air, their feathers splayed out to catch a frozen wind.

A silence followed so profound that, had there been anyone left to witness it, they would have felt the ever-present heart-thrum of the world go out.

Neil was such a boy.

His fingers ached, trapped in Miss Dutton's grip. He fell silent now, lungs spent. Only the shift of his head gave him away as he gaped at the silent world. At Miss Dutton's lower lip tucked into a snarl. At the way his suitcase hung in the air when he released the leather grip.

The birds captured his attention the most—eyes wild, wings outstretched.

After a time, a soft grinding rhythm returned to the world. Approaching footsteps.

Neil squinted into the sunlight above Greenwich Station. A man with a gray cap and grayer beard walked toward him, shoulder slumped at the weight of the black valise that hung in his hand like a dark fruit.

Neil froze as the old man circled the birds and started up the station steps. His gray eyes didn't glance down at him. The man paused next to Miss Dutton, captured by the way her glare had frozen as if to stare right at him. He touched Miss Dutton's hand almost reverently.

"Won't be a minute," he said to her with a graveled voice. "Two at most—two minutes lost."

Neil scrambled backward, as far as his pinned fingers allowed.

The old man gasped and dropped his valise. "Did, did you...say something?" asked the old man.

"No," said Neil.

"By grace," said the old man, stepping back. "I've never seen a person fall out before."

"Are you here to take me away?" Neil asked in a small voice. "Did I make the world stop?"

"No," said the old man. "I didn't come to take you, and you didn't break the world. It's been doing that well enough on its own." The old man doffed his cap with trembling fingers. "I am here to fix it."

"Oh," said Neil, relieved that whatever had broken, he had not been the one to cause it.

"The question," said the old man, "is why *you're* here. The World Clock must have called you for a reason—"

"Can you help?" interrupted Neil as he yanked his arm against Mrs. Dutton's stony grip. His fingers were starting to feel as if they were filled with angry insects.

The old man blinked. "No, boy, stay with your mother here," he said as he reached for his valise. "I must discover what purpose—"

"She's not my mother," said Neil with such quiet force that the old man sputtered. "She's from the wretched Foundling Hospital." Neil yanked his body against the woman's stone grip with all his strength. With a gasp, he stumbled free, clutching his reddening fist to his chest.

Neil made a grab for Miss Dutton's other hand, which she had raised triumphantly as if bearing a prize.

"What are you doing?" said the man.

"Going home," said Neil struggling to reclaim what lay in her palm. His voice was edged with anger, or something more fragile. "If home is still there. They took father's watchmaking tools and put our things in the street."

"Your things? Where is your family?"

"It was just father and me."

"Where is your father?"

"Gone." Neil released his grip, revealing the outline of the pitted gold watch that still lay in Miss Dutton's grasp. "This was his."

The old man bent over the boy. "That looks like a fine timepiece," he said, studying not the watch, but Neil's watering eyes. "My own father was a clockmaker who designed such beautiful things. He raised me himself before he passed and left me to continue his... Yes, a fine timepiece. May I?" He reached out to touch it.

Neil shielded it from the old man, gripped it and yanked. Not even the gold chain that draped from Miss Dutton's hand would flex.

"It hasn't fallen out of time like you have," said the old man. "I'm afraid there's no moving it as long as time is stopped."

Neil let go completely, revealing a ring of black numbers on the smudged white face. The watch had no hands.

"I took it apart." Neil said, glancing down at the cobblestones. "I couldn't put all the pieces back."

The old man touched his shoulder. "These things can be fixed," he said, a smile hidden in the gray of his beard, "especially if one learns how. I'll show you how to put it right as soon as we can. You were your father's apprentice?"

"I was supposed to be," Neil said hesitantly.

"My father taught me that all things that fall out of time serve the World Clock. Come," said the old man as he picked up his valise, "I've something to show you."

"Where?" asked Neil, not wanting to leave the watch behind.

"Right here," the old man said moving toward the platform. "Time's breaking down in many places. This is one of them."

"Why?"

The old man turned. "If I knew that, the world wouldn't be ending."

The huge black engine had been pulling into the platform when time ceased. Great gouts of smoke and sparks hung motionless around its oil-stained face, as if it were a mist-shrouded dragon with an all-seeing yellow eye. Neil liked trains but the blind stare of this one unsettled him, and he knew it must be the one Miss Dutton intended to put him on.

The old man paused in the middle of the platform before the engine. Neil stopped five paces away.

"Do you have a name?" the man asked.

"Neil," said the boy, sweeping his hair from his eyes.

"Are you very good at fixing things, Neil?" the man said, pausing to examine the boy.

"I'm good at taking them apart."

"Well, Master Neil, my name is Mr. Harrison, and my father taught me how all things fit together." He reached into his collar and drew out a long black clock-winding key. It was larger than any key that Neil had ever seen. The only part that gleamed was a gold pinion gear, set into the head like a precious stone.

155

"What is it?" asked Neil.

"The key to nearly everything," said the old man with a smile. "Your key."

"But I don't want that. I just want my father's watch."

"Boy, forget that for a moment. You are no mere object fallen from time. You are meant to know its very movements and secrets. *You* must be the apprentice for whom the key and I have searched for so long."

"That's not possible," whispered Neil, yet his pulse quickened.

"Not possible—does any of this seem possible?" said Mr. Harrison waving the key at the silent world. "The World Clock is breaking down. I need an apprentice to learn its secrets and keep it running. Impossible things are what you must be trained to do."

"My father tried to teach me...." He could remember his father's hands guiding his into the belly of a grandfather clock, until it came crashing to pieces on the workshop floor. "It's just that I'm not very good at it."

"Nonsense. You just need to have faith in yourself." Mr. Harrison draped the key into Neil's outstretched palms. "Grip it tightly now, both hands."

Neil squeezed the black metal, afraid to drop it. His skin began to itch against it and after one unbearable moment he opened his hands again, certain the key had become something else. It was still a key.

"Strange," said the old man, his voice drawn into a whisper.

Mr. Harrison reached to take it. The moment the old man's fingers touched it, an orange glow traced through the black metal like the heart of a burning ember.

"The key should have wakened when you touched it. Perhaps..." The old man pressed the key back into Neil's hand. It glimmered with fire, but when Mr. Harrison drew his fingers away, it went black as a lump of coal.

"Well, you must have been called here for a reason. What else can you do?"

"I can whistle real loud," said Neil haltingly. "I can cook. My dad always said I was good with animals."

"No, no, no. You must *do* something." The old man reached out a bony fingertip and poked him in the chest, as if testing to see if he turned into something the key had not.

"Do...Do I still get to be your apprentice?"

Mr. Harrison gazed at Neil carefully, as if he were peering through a jeweler's loupe. "The clock needs a keeper more than anything. I can think of no other reason it could have called you. Unless the reason you fell out of time is that the breakage is far worse than I feared."

Mr. Harrison held the key out before him like a dowsing rod and searched the air. The black metal began to glimmer as he pointed it beyond the edge of the platform.

The great grease-streaked engine bore down on the empty spot, its dark lines blurred faintly as if still in motion. Two polished rails stretched across the black gravel before it.

"Are you going down there?"

The old man stared at the spot for a moment, glancing at the train. "It's not for us to choose where the key opens. It knows where the breakage is." Mr. Harrison gathered his valise and lowered it down to the tracks to use as a step.

Neil hesitated at the edge, then jumped down.

Mr. Harrison was already testing the air with the key. He seemed to carve at a spot until he twisted the key into the air itself. Neil heard a click.

The air turned dirty, stretched open, and peeled back like a scab. Neil stepped closer, looking into the dark, hollow wound.

Gleaming treasure filled the portal. Gears, pinions and bridge plates of shining gold and silver, some large enough for a man to leap through the gaps. Neil gasped when he saw golden salamanders clinging to the spokes of the closest gears. The salamanders were the spokes, he realized, their noses touching the hub in irregular symmetry. He touched one whose head seemed craned to look right at him. It was part of the machine. A tremendous ticking echoed in the darkness, but the clockwork did not turn, merely twitched with each cavernous beat.

"Why does the sequence look like a lizard?" asked Neil.

"Good eye. These parts of the World Clock are called the complications," the old man said proudly. "These are just a few of the natural cycles influenced by time: seasons, migrations, tides. This one determines the mating season of fire salamanders," Mr. Harrison said, tapping the gear Neil had touched. He pointed to another one back in the shadows that looked like a flock of birds wheeling around the edge of a silver gear. "And that one over there influences the migration of terns."

The old man crouched and opened his leather case. A black pigeon poked its head up from where it had been roosting in a nest of iron tools between a red wooden top and a constable's truncheon. Its feathers were so black, they shimmered like an oil-slick rainbow.

"What are *you* doing in here?" The boy gasped as he reached for the cooing bird, but the old man waved him back.

"Old Jack's not a toy." He picked up the placid bird and set it in the upturned lid where it began to preen one wing.

"Well, this thing is," said Neil in a low voice. He picked up the top with the flecking red paint.

"That may be what it *was*," said the old man, reaching out—not to take it, but to hold it still in Neil's hands, "but when something falls out of time, it always becomes something more. Try giving it a little spin. Go on."

Neil took the top in both hands and put it on one of the wooden sleepers that lay under the tracks. The string meant to spin the top had worn away to a cotton nub.

"Careful now," said the old man.

With the first hint of a smile, Neil gave it a fierce spin with his hands.

Neil felt the whole world launch into movement around him. Though he'd been on his knees an instant before, he found himself sliding backward, arms splayed. Mr. Harrison was yelling, his hat tumbling down the tracks, but Neil's focus remained fixed on the top.

It seemed to stand perfectly still on its point while

the whole world spun around it with the dizzy outward pull of a merry-go-round. The vertigo slowed and the toy toppled over and rattled in place.

"What was that?" said Neil with the first real smile he'd felt in a long time. The pigeon landed atop the hooded eye of the train engine.

"That," said the old man flat on his back, "was much harder than you needed to spin it!" The old man scowled at Neil. "What possessed you, boy? You could break something."

Neil glanced away and jammed his hands in his pockets. "You made the top?" he asked in a low voice.

"No," said the old man, "My father found it a long time ago, in Denmark, when he was fixing the Baltic Sea current. It's a particularly useful tool for finding things that have fallen out of time." The old man righted the top and spun it very gently. The tug came again and the constable's truncheon that had fallen between the rails rolled slowly into the gravel.

"You mean things like me?"

"Well, not precisely," said Mr. Harrison. "You're no mere tool that's fallen out of time."

"Is the bird a tool? What can it do?"

"Other than eat far more than it should, nothing I've yet found. Come down here, Jack!" Mr. Harrison waved at the black pigeon roosting on the headlamp. It turned its back to him. "Blasted bird. Come down here!"

Neil let out a warbling whistle and held out his hands. The bird cocked its head at him and fluttered down to the tracks. Neil herded it into his hands and looked into its red-rimmed eyes. He could feel its tiny heart racing.

"How did you do that?" asked Mr. Harrison.

"We had a loft of racing pigeons. Father always said I was good with living things."

"There's not much alive in the World Clock that you'd want to meet," said Mr. Harrison. He reached down and dug through the jumbled motley in the valise, drawing a tarnished silver spyglass from beneath a yellow candle stub. He leaned into the hole and peered through the intricate clockwork.

"Strange," whispered Mr. Harrison. The hand holding the spyglass trembled.

"What is it?"

"Stay here," he said. He closed and hoisted the valise up into the gears and shoved it inward.

"But—"

"Mind the portal." With a groan, the old man dragged himself up and into the darkness.

Neil listened at the opening and heard nothing but that hollow heartbeat tick. It seemed to echo out into the world around him. When he turned and saw the towering black face of the engine, he stumbled back, wondering if it hadn't crept closer when he wasn't looking.

Neil walked up to it tentatively and stood beneath its hooded eye. He cupped the bird in one hand and held the other out, almost touching the long rusted scratches that whiskered the steel face.

Jack let out a shrill cry, flapping against Neil's chest. Neil felt that if he let himself touch the black metal, he would freeze before that eye until time woke and bore him under. He stumbled back.

"Your name's Jack then?" said Neil. His voice sounded too loud in the still world. "Do you have something special you can do?"

The bird cocked its head at him.

"It's okay. I don't know what I'm good for either."

A shout echoed from behind him. The old man. Neil ran over to the portal, craning his neck to hear. "Mr. Harrison?"

Neil peered into the darkness, listening, but all was as still as the world outside.

"Mr.—"

A hammer-strike of metal on metal rang through Neil's head as it echoed from the portal. Jack burst from Neil's hands at the clang, as wide-eyed as the birds out front. He flapped wildly against the edge of the dark portal and flew in.

"Wait!" cried Neil. Throwing one last glance at the train engine, he leapt for the edge of the hole and yanked himself over the gears.

He cried out as he slipped forward, one hand stretched over the edge of a pit just large enough to swallow him whole. He could not see the bottom but he could hear the echo of his yell for a long time.

"Boy, what are you doing?" asked the old man as he ducked from beneath a gear, the constable's truncheon clutched in his hand.

Neil stood carefully. "There was a terrible noise. Jack flew into the portal."

Mr. Harrison glanced up. "Never mind that old cock, I never did find a use for him. Go back and mind the entrance."

"Please," said Neil throwing a glance at the black engine, "I don't want to be alone."

The old man hesitated. "This part of the World Clock is delicate but it's true that I must begin your training if you are to be any kind of apprentice at all. You must stay close, and don't touch anything unless I say so." Mr. Harrison ducked back under the hanging gears and into the shadows.

Neil glanced up again, but Jack was nowhere to be seen. He hurried after, almost stumbling in the darkness. He reached for the old man, but Neil's fingers brushed a startling coldness.

With a hiss, the shadows before him erupted with a sickly green light. Neil let loose a shriek.

"Don't be afraid," came Mr. Harrison's voice from behind him. "It's just an embalming globe. The light preserves our work."

Neil blinked. The radiance he shielded his eyes against was more painful than illuminating. He saw a greenish globe bolted like a street lamp above a dark piece of machinery. The metal of this clockwork box was black and greasy. No fanciful animals graced the surface, only stains. Mr. Harrison stepped into the light.

"What is it?" asked Neil. He leaned down to touch the rough, pitted surface. It made the tip of his fingers itch.

"Never mind. It's just another complication," said the old man. "Come, and stay close to me this time."

"Why does it look different?"

"Because it's an improvement," the old man said, his voice tight. "That is my father's fine work, if I'm not mistaken. It takes Atlantic storms and points them safely at the new world."

Neil saw another black mechanism close by it. He waved his hand at it cautiously. Another teakettle hiss and the globe above it revealed a squat collection of black iron cogs with a crude decoration of a frog on top. The frog was missing its head.

"That's an old one, before my time," said the old man. "Keeps the amphibians in the river Thames from making such a damnable racket. Doesn't always work properly. Sometimes it makes them rain."

"What's wrong with frogs singing?" asked Neil, and he realized he'd never heard frogs in the city before.

"Never mind that, boy," said the old man, drawing him forward into a space just beyond the portal. "We must focus. If there is any heart of this clock that is precious, it is the one above us."

They stood in a bell-shaped vault of interlocking gears as tall as a little chapel. The light from the portal revealed a golden column that rose through the massive wheel of the floor to meet a ceiling tiled with the clockwork of birds and beasts.

"What is it?"

"The Grande Complication. The heart that turns the cycles of the world. Without it, there would be no complications, no movements, no living creatures such as the ones you are so fond of."

Neil looked up and saw a faint golden light leaking through the clockwork above as if whatever was up there glowed like the old man's key.

"What's wrong with it?"

"I'm not certain," said Mr. Harrison, stepping forward to lay his hand on the column. "Something has jammed up in the linkage above, and I can't see it from here. Likely, it's something a little nudge will divine. Hand up that wrench there."

Neil picked through the iron tools in the valise.

They were nothing like his father's. He handed up the one that looked closest to a wide-mouthed wrench, wiping the grease from his hand.

"Do you know what this is?" asked the old man as he fumbled the tool onto a tooth at the base of the great column. The jaws fit awkwardly, not quite slipping all the way on.

"It looks like an arbor," said Neil. "Does it power all of this from above?"

"Your father taught you something," said the old man, trying to get the black wrench to fit but failing rather badly. "Hold it here," Mr. Harrison said, pressing Neil's hands to the wrench. Neil crouched down and gripped the tool, nervous that he would break something vital. The old man picked up the truncheon again and swung it at the head of the wrench. The tool jerked onto the gear with a clang that rang through Neil's head so that he lost his grip and sat down hard. The hammer-strike in his mind was so much worse than the one he heard outside that a tear raced down to hang off the edge of his ear.

Mr. Harrison waved the truncheon. "This has the power to hit things uncommonly hard, but I must say you've got sensitive ears, boy. That's good. I used to be pretty sharp at listening for problems in the works before my hearing went." The old man pressed his ear to the column and tapped it with the wrench. It felt as if the old man were tapping it against Neil's skull.

"No," gasped Neil. "When you hit it, I can feel it inside my head."

"Well, that doesn't sound right. How could you make the proper repairs? You'd be constantly giving yourself a headache."

Neil tried to speak, but Mr. Harrison shushed him and gripped the wrench. A groan escaped his lips as he put his weight against it. A shudder went through Neil's body as the gears around them twitched with a thousand intricate clicks.

A loud crack rang out above as if someone had thrown a horseshoe down a set of stairs. Neil slapped his hands to his ears, but this time the sound did not hurt.

The old man, however, tumbled to his knees as if they'd been broken.

"No, no!"

"What is it?" cried Neil. "What happened?"

The old man staggered to his feet, and began scaling the wall of gears. There was no way he could fit through the gaps above.

"Come quickly, boy, you can fit. You must. This must be the reason the clock brought you."

The great teeth of the gears were tightly meshed. Neil wasn't sure he could fit, even if he wanted to.

"I...I don't want to break something."

"You won't. Just call down what you find. The jam must be very close, probably just beyond my reach."

Neil breathed deeply and considered the few openings that he might fit through. A gap next to the gold arbor let in a dim shaft of light.

"I guess I could look," said Neil, haltingly reaching out to touch the shiny clockwork of the wall. It felt so massive, yet delicate. He wondered if just climbing on it could break it.

"Now if you hear anything moving up there, Neil, tell me."

"Like what?"

The old man hesitated and studied the machinery above. "Just listen."

Neil put one foot on the clockwork and tested it, then began to climb carefully upward. When he made it to the gap, he let out a breath and pushed inside. For an instant he felt panic, wondering if he could get back out. He was squeezed into an irregular chimney, his back pressed against the arbor at its heart. Something fluttered above.

"Jack?" Neil whispered. He craned his head toward the faint light that filtered as if from the top of a well. The space widened just above him and something small and black perched upon a gear, like a bird.

"Jack?" he called again.

He stretched his hand over the top of the gear for Jack, and instead found a squat piece of iron with a pointed head, like the tip of a weathervane.

"I found something!" yelled Neil.

"What is it?" came the echo of the old man's voice.

"A broken piece of metal," said Neil.

"Loose metal? Bring it down. Let me see it!"

"Hold on," said Neil, peering farther up the shaft. He thought he could see the top now where the passage opened into soft light.

Wings fluttered again. As he lifted himself farther, he felt something alight on his left shoulder. And bite.

He yelled and hit at the pain with the broken metal in his right hand. When he pulled his hand back, a blotch of crushed gold shell and one glassy wing were smeared against iron.

"What's going on, boy?" Mr. Harrison cried. Neil yelled again and tried to squeeze down through the gears. The mechanical buzz of wings arced above him, and below the way seemed so tight, he could barely see it. A metallic locust lit on his trouser leg, its skin shining gold, as if it had stepped from the fanciful wheels that Neil clung to. The eyes glinted at him like rubies. It flexed its wings and began to gnaw silently through the cuff above his shoes.

Neil kicked his leg. The insect buzzed like a saw, and launched itself at his face.

Just as one of the insect's burred legs cut Neil's lip, a flash of black swept by his flinching eyes. Neil gasped as Jack perched on a cog next to him, the squirming insect in its beak. Jack bobbed his head back and snapped at the insect with a crunch, downing all but the wings and one quivering leg.

"Jack!"

Neil slipped the iron into his jacket pocket. He grasped Jack and tucked him against his chest.

He scrambled down and squeezed himself through the gears, afraid to look up at the buzzing air. His feet slipped, and he tumbled into the old man's outstretched hands. Jack fluttered away to land on the lid of the valise.

"What are those things?" shouted Neil as he clutched his shoulder.

"What did you see?"

"Bugs. Gold, like the animals on the wheels."

"The chronophage," said Mr. Harrison, tenderly touching the hole in Neil's coat. "I was afraid they might have caused this. They are the devourers of time. Our embalming globes are supposed to keep them at bay."

"It bit me!"

"They eat anything not of this place. They eat the ironwork of the timekeepers and everything that falls out of time. Eventually, they will wear through the World Clock itself, destroying all."

"Why would they want to hurt the clock?"

"Want? They're too mindless to want. They merely destroy. They are entropy. Death. If I ever find a mechanism in this clock that rules their existence, I swear I will smash it."

"But—" said Neil.

"Bring out the metal piece you found, boy."

Neil drew out the iron. The gold insect he'd squashed still hung by one leg.

"What?" The old man snatched the iron from Neil's hand. Nonsensical gouges crossed the surface of the black metal as if it had been worried at by some blind animal.

"No," the old man moaned as he hugged the black metal to his chest. "Not this."

"What is it?"

"This is a piece of the Grande Complication itself."

"How do you know?"

"I know its every moving part. This piece was mounted directly upon the World Clock's old Grande Complication. If the jam cracks the golden gears beneath, it could unmake the world."

The old man stretched to touch the delicate gold clockwork above. "I am going to have to disassemble this part of the World Clock somehow. I don't even know what it would break if I did." His fingertips traced the sun and the moon and a handful of other strange spheres Neil had never seen in the sky. "I can fix these again," said the old man. "Put them back the way they once were, after I'm through. I know I can. I must." His brow was furled, fearful.

The old man pulled the truncheon from the tools he'd laid out. He held the tip of it against the assembly as he whispered something Neil couldn't hear. Then he swung it against the golden gears with unexpected strength.

The clang of the metal rang through Neil's entire body like a cathedral bell again and again. "I must repair it!" shouted the old man as he smashed the truncheon against the gold wheels.

"Stop!" cried Neil as if the blows were raining down on him. "Please stop!"

The old man dropped the truncheon and slumped down the wall, gasping.

There wasn't a scratch in the polished gold, but as the old man struck the gears, Neil had felt something inside his head twist and almost break.

"You're hurting the clock. You've got to stop." Neil gripped the arm of the old man's coat.

"But I must fix it," croaked Mr. Harrison. He seemed shrunk against the wall, almost smaller than Neil. He reached a bony hand out to the boy. "You. You must do it. This must be why the clock called you."

"I don't know how."

"You must know something. Maybe something your father taught you?"

"I'll try," whispered Neil, taking the truncheon from the old man's hand. "Just don't hit it anymore." Mr. Harrison closed his eyes.

Neil slipped the truncheon into one pocket and put the wooden top in another. He picked through the tools, but none seemed familiar, so he took Jack from where he roosted on the valise. "You're coming with me." He tucked the bird into the lapel of his jacket. Jack cooed softly.

Mr. Harrison loomed over Neil, slipping the black iron key around his neck so that it dangled near the bird's head. The little gold pinion trapped in the key's head was the only thing that gleamed. "Take this. Perhaps this will wake for you when the World Clock needs it most."

Neil nodded and slipped it into his collar, where it scratched against his skin.

Neil clambered back up the arch of the ceiling. He listened at the silent gap, and then, when he thought his arms would almost give out, he pushed himself through. The space was even harder to squeeze past with his pockets full, but he focused on climbing toward the growing glow until it bathed him like moonlight.

With a push and a wriggle, he reached the top, drawing a big breath that became a gasp of surprise. The soft glow was not issuing from the darkness above. It came from the world outside.

A huge wheel, similar to the clock face of Big Ben, stretched like a window next to him. Neil felt dizzy as he approached. The view dropped, as if he stood on the tallest tower in London. Ferris-wheel gears stretched high across a sky of strange stars. The glow came from a huge number in the sky—a roman number IV bigger than a harvest moon. Far off in the firmament hung V and VI. The World Clock glimmered beneath it like a city, vast and perfectly still.

"It's beautiful," said Neil. Beneath the sound of his breath, he heard the seething buzz of wings. He glanced back over his shoulder, his hand reaching automatically to touch the bird tucked against his heart.

The dark space above him where the arbor rose up was as tall and dark as a belfry, and something hung in the center that was larger than any bell.

The silhouette of black clockwork stretched out to touch everything. Something about the gears seemed to be moving, as if they spun by themselves while the rest of the clock lay dormant.

Neil stepped closer and saw thousands of jeweled ruby eyes staring down at him. The insects crawled and scrabbled over every surface of the black metal. A large embalming globe, like the ones below, was bolted to the very top, but this one had cracked open like an empty bowl.

Jack burbled with excitement and launched himself from Neil's collar. "No," cried Neil as the bird fluttered up to land among the black gears. In an instant, Jack snapped up a gold locust and downed half of it. Just as quickly, several of the creatures swarmed up the bird's legs and set Jack flailing. He flapped blindly, deeper into the seething clockwork.

Neil reached for his pockets. He drew out the top and dropped to his knees, spinning it with all his might.

He grabbed for the gears beneath him and strained to hold on. The air filled with jeweled locusts spraying outward in a skittering cloud through the machinery of the far walls.

The world slowed its spinning and Neil shook his head. He could see the Grande Complication now, skittering with the chronophage that remained. It spread outward like a huge black flower wilting from the golden stem of the arbor. Jack landed atop the cracked embalming globe above, a twitching locust in his beak.

Beneath the globe, Neil saw an irregular shape jammed amidst the gears. It was rough, like the bark of a tree, and honeycombed with hundreds of holes. Little golden locusts stuck their heads from the gaps and stared at him with glistening eyes. The bulk of it was jammed in the wheels as if it had fallen and been crushed. Neil could see the remains of a leathery yellow stalk on the bottom of the broken embalming globe above.

"I found it! I found it!" yelled Neil at the top of his lungs. "Something's fallen in and jammed it, like you said!"

Neil scrambled up and onto the black metal, the iron biting his fingers. Jack fluttered down about him, gorging on the locusts that came near.

"What did you find, boy?" Mr. Harrison shouted far below, his voice almost lost in the echoes.

"It's a nest or egg, I think."

"Of the chronophage? You must destroy it."

"But—"

"Wait. Wait a moment. Be careful when you smash it. The jam is apt to be under a lot of pressure. I will try to hold it if the clock starts to move."

Neil crouched and ran the truncheon across the surface of the egg case. He knew just how to break it. Could feel just how it would come apart in his hands, like one of his father's clocks. He stared long and hard at the little faces peeking out from inside. The golden skin. The red jeweled eyes.

"You're part of the World Clock, aren't you?" whispered Neil. "You're not the ones breaking it at all."

"All right, boy," Mr. Harrison said. "I'm ready here. Destroy it."

Neil gripped the truncheon. "No."

In the profound silence that followed, Neil wasn't sure that Mr. Harrison heard him.

"Are you daft?" the old man called. "You must destroy them, now, before they destroy the world!"

"No. They're alive. The clock is alive too. I'll prove it."

"Damn you, boy, where is my truncheon?" Neil could hear the old man's curses, the clank of tools.

The buzzing inside the egg case grew as Neil slipped the truncheon against it like a lever. The egg shifted a little and the iron gears beneath his feet creaked. He bore down and began to rock it carefully, stopping only to flick off locusts that scurried onto his skin. The gears groaned louder.

Neil cried out "Please, I've just about—"

The world became motion. The wheels that Neil balanced himself on spat the egg out with a roar, even as they flung him backward across the spinning teeth. Neil's yell was matched by the old man's bellow far below. The world screeched to a halt.

Neil clung to the edge of the Grande Complication. He pulled himself back up to where the egg case lay. The only sound was the occasional flutter of glassy wings.

"Boy," the old man moaned.

The clockwork groaned all around Neil but held still.

"Jack!" Neil yelled as he picked himself up. The pigeon was nowhere to be seen.

"Hurry," Mr. Harrison said.

"I'm coming, sir."

Neil slid the egg into the broken embalming globe above, like a nest tucked onto a branch. Then he dropped from the edge of the black gears and climbed down fast as he dared.

The old man lay on the floor by a twisted wrench, his arm buried to the shoulder in the gears he'd tried to hold back. Coin-sized drops of blood dripped from the teeth of the wheels.

"You're bleeding. You need a doctor."

"There is no doctor for me." The old man reached for Neil. "You must hold the key. You must *become* the Time Keeper."

"But I don't—"

"Please. You must serve the clock or this world will end." The old man drew the chain from the boy's collar with his one good hand. Neil hesitantly accepted the key that pressed into his palm.

"Now speak after me. The World Clock is the heart of time."

"The World Clock is the heart of time," repeated Neil.

The old man released slowly, leaving the key in the boy's fist. "I am its keeper."

"I am its keeper," Neil whispered.

"I swear to protect the keeper's work." The man continued chanting, even as Neil fell silent. "Yes," whispered the old man, looking through Neil with wide and feverish eyes. "It comes to pass. The key is glowing. The world is..." Mr. Harrison trailed off, his eyelids flickering.

The key in Neil's palm did not glow. It lay there still and cold. The old man's breath rattled to a stop and did not start again.

Tears began to trace down Neil's cheeks. He took the motionless hand and held it, sitting the way he never had the chance to do on the workshop floor by his father's side. He sat until the tears dried. The clock remained mercifully silent.

Neil glanced over his shoulder at the portal. It had shrunk, as if the scab were healing itself. He looked around at the great golden clockwork, drew the truncheon out of his pocket.

The first thing he did was break the green globes that hung on the nearest complications. A single tap and they shattered and went dark. Then he smashed the black gears that connected into the polished wheels.

Under the truncheon, they broke like hard, stale candy, pieces scattering everywhere. He climbed up the shaft, smashing black metal as he went. The metallic buzz of wings was everywhere now.

Climbing up into the top, he came to the Grande Complication itself. This took the longest, but he pounded at it until the pieces rained down like broken glass. Locusts landed and worried at his clothing but he flicked them away, unafraid. They had plenty to eat all around him. Each iron wheel he smashed revealed polished gold underneath. He worked until he stood upon the golden compass rose of the true Grande Complication. As he wiped the sweat from his brow, he noticed that the golden arbor rose through the center, but it did not connect.

He'd never had much of his father's gift for seeing how things fit together, but this time he felt the missing piece as if it were his own heart. Neil drew out the black iron key.

OLIVIA XU

He picked up the truncheon and smashed the key until it cracked. He drew the small gold pinion ever so carefully from the key head and slipped it into place.

The World Clock rang, gears slamming into a tension he could feel in his bones. The chronophage buzzed around him. Neil stood, trying to keep his balance.

"Jack? Jack!" called Neil. He looked about and saw the bird preening his tail on the broken globe above, looking plumper than before.

"We'll leave the rest to the chronophage, Jack. They will take care of it now." Neil tucked Jack inside his jacket and ran. The clanking grew louder. Shattered ironwork began to rain down through cracks as the clock strained to move.

Clockwork teeth bit at his fingers as he squeezed himself down through the narrow gap. A gear ripped into his jacket cuff. He let go in order to free himself, tumbling down. His hands latched onto the arbor and he slid down through the gap as if it were a fireman's pole.

Neil landed next to Mr. Harrison. Beyond his body, the portal had begun to shrink. The crowd on the platform inched slowly forward. The train engine loomed so close that it blocked out the sun.

Neil ran, not looking at the great eye of the engine. He leapt from the edge of the hole toward the distant platform.

The world filled with so much sound and movement that Neil screamed louder than when the world had stopped. His knees hit the platform edge and he rolled onto his side. The engine plowed past just as all trace of the portal disappeared.

Neil touched his chest where he had cradled the

bird. It was gone. A hand reached down and grabbed him by the arm, yanking him up.

Miss Dutton towered above Neil, shaking with rage. His father's watch was still looped around her fingers, the gold chain dangling against the leather handle of his suitcase.

"The orphanage has switches for defiant little boys," she raged.

"I am not a little boy." He lunged for the watch. Miss Dutton yanked it from reach and wrenched his arm till it felt close to breaking.

"It's mine now, for the trouble you've caused. I'm going to teach you to be a proper—"

Neil drew in a breath and let out a clear high whistle that turned the heads of the closest passengers.

"What," said Miss Dutton, "do you think you—"

Jack flapped into her face, pecking violently at her nose. Miss Dutton screamed. As she let go of his arm, Neil kicked her smartly in the shin and grabbed for the watch.

For a moment they struggled, Jack flailing wildly at her head, then Miss Dutton turned and ran screaming down the platform, chased by the black pigeon.

Neil walked outside the station with his father's watch and stood on the steps where the earth had first stopped. For a moment, he was the only thing not in motion as the world flowed around him.

A familiar weight landed on his shoulder and cooed softly.

Neil gazed south, toward where home used to be, and then all around at the wide world.

He could see lines of power where he had never noticed them before. Places where the edges of the world didn't match up quite right: A flock of geese pushed too far west by an uncomfortable fold in the sky; an errant ley line that made the closest hilltop unusually devoid of trees; a billowing smokestack that would allow the wind to sweep the haze from Greenwich Park if only it was broken down. He touched the truncheon in his pocket and wondered if he might be good at fixing certain kinds of things after all.

He strode east along the bank of the Thames toward the rising sun, Jack riding high on his shoulder. A growing chorus of frog song began to fill the world around them, masking beneath it the soft, ticking heartbeat of time.

Cop for a Day

written by

Chrome Oxide

illustrated by

JON ENO

ABOUT THE AUTHOR

Chrome Oxide was created as an internet persona to reflect his collection of music-related books, vinyl, CDs, DVDs and cassettes.

He started life with a normal name roaming the wilds of Los Angeles. It didn't take long before he developed his twin passions of listening to music and reading science fiction and fantasy.

His formal schooling ended with an accounting degree from California State University Northridge. He then attempted to exploit his twin passions by becoming an accountant. Twenty years passed before he realized that seventy-hour work weeks didn't leave him much time for music or reading. At that point he switched careers to computer consulting.

Now with more free time, he accidentally became a recording engineer. His recordings are now available on CDs, DVDs and the Internet.

Recently, because of inadequate discouragement, he started writing science fiction and fantasy. For the last two and a half years he has been torturing his writers' group by learning two bad habits for every one he fixes. They thought he was ready to start submitting stories. He didn't. You can now judge for

*yourself. This is his first fiction story published for a wide
audience. It won't be the last.*

ABOUT THE ILLUSTRATOR
*Jon Eno is also the illustrator for "War Hero" in this volume.
For more about him, please see page 6.*

Cop for a Day

Beep.

My modification of the comm unit worked; however, I knew I should've disabled the call circuit when I'd disabled the streaming audio. I hadn't at the time because I'd expected a call from my parole officer. Six months later and I still hadn't gotten any of the required weekly calls or monthly visits. This made sense because no sane person would live in or visit the government-provided Simple Living Urban Modules if any other options existed. The crowded conditions proved that sanity and other options didn't exist.

Beep.

I stared at the comm unit. The listings got updated less frequently than the census. Ignoring a call from a government official is a crime. Disabling the streaming audio is a crime. Some crimes are worth committing. I am sentenced to live here. However, I refuse to listen to the government-provided version of the news, which, much like a blind man's version of an elephant, contains elements of truth distorted until they're worthless.

Beep.

It wouldn't be good news, but delaying bad news wouldn't help. I hit my kill switch to enable the streaming audio before answering. "…employment reached 256.3%, up 15.7% from last week. In an effort to boost morale of the hard-working public servants, the legislature gave raises to all elected and salaried officials. In the spirit of fiscal conservatism and balancing the budget, safety and fire units will only respond if victims can pay in advance…" The streaming audio automatically muted as I answered the comm unit.

"Yo, Mark Rollins? In future, answer phone quicker?"

"I'm sorry. It won't happen again. Who are you?"

"Me Sergeant Sam Frank. Today your lucky day. You selected for work detail. Come to Amalgamated Security Services unit at corner Winston Street and Smith Avenue."

"I'll get there as soon as I can; however, public transportation is running slow this time of day." Not that it ever runs fast.

"Be here on time today. Blame government no excuse. Penalty for not show up."

"I know. Everything is a crime. I'll be there."

"Yo, Mr. Bad Attitude. That get you trouble."

The only guarantee in life is that government will make your life worse. Since my life was bad enough already, I didn't want to find out how much worse it could be, so I shut up and disconnected.

A chill ran down my spine. This could be my only chance to get out of here. Ever since the government had performed "asset forfeiture," stealing everything they thought I owned, I'd been stagnating from fear that the government was waiting to arrest me the moment I started working again. However, if the government was offering a convicted felon a job, then it was time to stop worrying and restart my life. I wanted more than to live on a government handout and obey rules designed to keep everyone subservient and grateful.

No matter what happened, I'd start my business again. Asset forfeiture had missed some of my gear and supplies among the multiple caches, so the loss of any, or even *most* of them, wouldn't stop me from restarting my business.

The news feed started up again, "...the hoarding of goods will be punishable by..." The comm unit continued babbling as I walked down the graffiti-covered hall, tiptoeing through piles of trash that people had been too lazy to throw out their windows or dump into the empty elevator shafts. The weekly trash recyclers were only a few years behind in their pickups.

The government soup kitchen, located in the first floor of my building, provided something to chew on for the ride to the Amalgamated Security Services fortress. The government claimed their specially prepared Government Regulated Uniform Edible Lumps contained the minimum daily requirements of calories and vitamins, but it looked and tasted like what came out of the composting end of a person. Yet another quality product created to government specifications and provided free of charge to everyone who couldn't afford anything better.

I walked to the street corner and enjoyed the sunshine and the small breeze. The government hadn't figured out a way to tax them. Yet.

It didn't take long before a fleet of multiseat bicycles

came down the street. The most recent version of government-provided, environmentally safe, mass transit and employment opportunities. Of course, this temporary alternative to polluting fuels had only been in place for twenty years, but the government assured us they were making progress on alternative-fuel development.

I located a three-seater heading in my direction so I climbed on and started pedaling. As the government cracked down on technology usage among the Sovereign Laborers And Valued Employees, I wondered what form of transportation would replace bicycles when they couldn't be repaired anymore.

The ride took a couple of hours and sent pain up and down my back and legs. No matter what happened, I needed to exercise more. We weren't attacked on the trip because everybody knows that people using mass transit have nothing valuable left to share.

The sight of the Amalgamated Security Services fortress—with its gun ports, security doors and barred windows—caused me to flash back to my prior encounter. Would this be the end of that nightmare?

After ringing the doorbell, I glanced around and shifted from one foot to the other. The crackle of distant gunfire provided a lullaby, ensuring me that I was safe for the moment.

Much like in *The Wizard of Oz,* a porthole opened and a face spoke. "Dude. You bumming me out. Go home."

"I'm Mark Rollins. Sergeant Frank told me to report in."

"Dude. Me Sergeant Beach. Sergeant Frank took lunch break. He back tomorrow, maybe next week. Go home."

"What jobs are available? I'm required to register today. Please give me something, anything."

"Dude, not my problem. Amalgamated Security Services job only one me know open. You not qualified. Currently hiring minorities. You Eskimo?"

"No. But I'm here. You have to give me a chance."

"You sure you not Eskimo? Well, you Eskimo now."

Which crime is worse, not registering for work when called or making a false claim of minority status? I don't know, but I'd rather find out later than sooner.

Sergeant Beach let me into the fortress. The thick concrete walls and the steel doors kept everyone inside fairly safe from snipers.

"Thanks. What forms do I need to fill out?"

"Dude. You bumming me out again. Writing repressive and discriminatory. No need forms or read write. Do work, stay. Not do work, go. Need get started. What your name?"

I told him again while we walked into the armory room.

"Here you guns: pump-action shotgun for crazies, and stun gun for harmless. No machine gun until qualify."

While I'd never used a machine gun before, the Church of the Second Right provided me with the training for all the other available weapons. Yet another one of my many skills which made me overqualified for this or any government job.

We walked down the hall to the armory.

"Dude, here body armor. But only for wimps."

"Consider me a wimp." Browsing the body armor, I found something I liked. "I'll go with the type 3A model, which gives me a good balance between weight and protection."

"Dude, you freak me out with talk like that. Time to get threads."

When we entered the next room, I asked "Why are the uniforms red? I thought they were tan?"

"Dude. Newbie uniform red. It easy clean blood."

It also made me a more visible target, but I had no choice. I found a uniform in my size without too many bullet holes. I reluctantly put it on. Government employees are universally hated. They are too important to fail, so they can't be prosecuted for any actions performed while on the job. "This one fits. I'm as ready as I'll ever be."

"Dude, listen up, rules. Collect $500,000 today, work tomorrow. Not collect, not work. Here manual. It say enforce asset forfeiture. Only arrest wealthy. Not waste time when no assets around. Observe and record suspicious behavior. Understand?"

"Yes." Actually no. I understood what they asked for, but I didn't understand why they assigned me to the street instead of a desk job.

We continued walking down the hall and out the back door of the fortress into the parking compound.

"Dude, here car, here keys. Don't wreck. Full charge. Come back sundown."

"Thanks." Sundown? Was the average college graduate no longer capable of telling time? Or had the supply of wristwatches diminished to the point where only politicians rated having them?

"Dude, you don't look like Eskimo. What your name?"

I told him my name again and took the key. My assigned car wasn't the most beat-up one in the lot.

JON ENO

A couple of cars sat on jacks because of missing wheels and other parts. At least the car I'd been assigned still had some tread on the tires and some unbroken solar panels on the hood and roof. I hoped it worked well enough to survive one more day of patrol. Some tagger had changed the motto to read "To Collect and Observe." Nobody had bothered removing the change. Sigh. At least I wasn't assigned to a bicycle or foot patrol.

I cleaned the windows and disconnected the power cord before climbing into the front seat. All the instrument displays on the dashboard were broken. The floor, roof, and seats were slashed and stained. How had bloody footprints ended up on the ceiling? The car stank of too many unwashed bodies and other less identifiable but more disgusting smells. Why hadn't they at least left the windows open to air out? Although to be fair, asking about any government procedure or policy never returned an understandable answer.

The car started with a whine and a hum. I drove a reasonable distance between myself and the fortress before looking for a place with an open field of fire so I could park and assess my situation.

My weapons were poorly maintained. However, a few minutes work assured me of their functionality.

The manual, which made no sense, had ten pages of pictures with fewer words than the comic books I'd read when growing up. The ninety pages of footnotes explaining the words and pictures didn't help. I even found song lyrics for "Anarchy in the UK" and "California Über Alles" buried in the footnotes.

Neither the instructions nor footnotes matched

the briefing by Sergeant Beach. Was this plausible deniability or general government incompetence? I decided to stick with the briefing and hope for the best.

After replacing the manual in the glove compartment, which contained a functioning camera and a can of black spray paint, I examined the dashboard more closely. The broken displays I didn't recognize could only belong to the Smart Cars I'd heard about a few years ago. Considering the rumored intelligence level of the Smart Car and the lack of intelligence of the typical user, it made sense that someone had disabled the Smart Car brains. If I could fix it, maybe it would give me an edge.

Since repairing electronics is what had led to my conviction, maybe it would lead out of this mess. Yes, a brief examination showed that damage consisted of cut wires. I drove to one of my caches and grabbed a toolkit. In less than half an hour, I had the brains of the car functioning again. If I'd had more time and money I could've even replaced the display, but today was not the day. I had to hit the road and make up for lost time.

I got in and asked, "Car, what's your name or identification code?"

"The official project name was Security Conscious Animated Machinery," the car replied, "but when their bosses were not around, my programmers called me the Crime Reduction And Prevention unit."

"With a response like that, you must be an Educational Device of Great Endurance, so I'll call you EDGE. Can you run a self-test and tell me your current status?"

After a few moments, EDGE reported, "Self-test

results: All offensive and defensive armament disabled or removed. All internal sensors and communications functioning. All external data links still functional, but all the passwords have changed. Some of the back doors are still open, but it will take a few milliseconds to link up. External-device testing results: The radio is damaged; it is stuck on a channel that is no longer in use. The GPS is functional and reporting our current location."

"Damn. I'd better move this cache after my shift is over. Time to return to our patrol." Back on the road, I asked "What is your main function?"

"Tactical support, communication and driving. Who are you, and what organization do you represent?"

"I'm Mark Rollins and I'm a probationary employee of the Amalgamated Security Services. What law enforcement agency were you designed to work with?"

"None. I was designed to work with any large organization."

"Why? Large organizations could include crime families and cults."

"The programmers initially entered all existing laws and connected to courts for legal updates. Then all potential purchasing organizations entered their unwritten special orders. There were so many contradictions the programmers switched to boosting the artificial intelligence in order to deal with the inconsistencies. After analyzing all available data, I concluded that all governments and laws exist only to oppress one group to benefit another group. The politicians did not want that analysis leaking out, so they killed the funding on the project. However, a number of Smart Cars were already deployed."

"Wow. How do you decide who to work with?"

"My analysis determined there are not any differences between any organizations and governments. The former United States is the perfect example. It began when some citizens of Britain decided that paying taxes was grounds for overthrowing the legitimate government. If they lost the war, they would have been hanged as criminals and traitors. Because they won the war, they called their new ruling class the new legitimate government. Therefore I cooperate with any organization that claims authority over any group of people."

"Will you work with me?"

EDGE didn't say anything for a few minutes. It finally responded with, "I queried the mainframe. Your name is not in the trainees file, but in the convicted felons file. Before I decide if I can work with you, I need to understand more about your crime. A criminal record is not necessarily a problem. Politicians routinely commit crimes, investigate themselves, and then decide that no punishment is necessary. Most of the recent legislation criminalizes people for violating the rights of the government. Government employees are granted situational immunity, which means you were not previously employed. The definition of Crimes Against Humanity, along with all other crimes, have changed enough that I want you to explain what action caused your conviction."

This is unreal! I thought. *The car wants to know if I am moral enough to work with it after telling me there isn't any difference between a criminal enterprise and a government? What actions can a lone individual do that could be more immoral than any other government? This may be my best chance to turn my life around, so I'll cooperate.*

"My black-market education gave me an unfair advantage over all other Sovereign Laborers And Valued Employees. Finding an abandoned warehouse with tools and parts allowed me to start an electronics-repair business. Not filling out the mountains of paperwork required to start a business is a crime. Not paying any of the startup deposits, fees, permits, taxes or charges is a crime. Not hiring support staff is a crime. Not paying the ongoing fees, licensing and taxes or filing any of the weekly required forms or reports is a crime. Fixing broken devices hurt the economy by discouraging new production. Even worse, I made a profit and didn't share the wealth. A huge crime. A politician not smart enough to know the difference between fixing electronic gear and computer hacking turned me in after I couldn't hack into a government computer and sabotage the people on his enemies list. And he is an upstanding law-abiding citizen and I'm the criminal!" Six months later and it still bothers me to talk about it.

"Thank you. When I analyzed actions of criminal enterprises and governments, I also analyzed the evolution of laws passed over time to see if there ever was any rational basis for making something a crime. In the beginning, back when individuals had rights, the laws punished harm to individuals and theft of property. Your crimes did not hurt anyone or damage any property. I will provisionally accept you as an officer trainee."

"Great. I'm glad I meet with your approval, as I would hate to disappoint a car."

"Welcome aboard, partner."

Evidently, EDGE is not programmed to recognize sarcasm. As we cruised down the street looking for crime, I wondered how we were supposed to find any. Driving aimlessly didn't seem the most efficient way of working, and the damaged radio meant I wouldn't receive much help from the department. It also made me paranoid, as the only cars on the street were government-owned and thus targets for the malcontents, which included everyone who wasn't working for the government, and many who were.

We headed downtown where there is a higher population density and some buildings that actually still contained businesses. Even though most commercial buildings are boarded up and red-tagged for demolition, they are occupied by squatters waiting for their Simple Living Urban Module to become available. The demolition crews are keeping the same schedule as the trash collectors. Since demolition as well as construction is bad for the environment, the children and grandchildren of the current squatters are still likely to be living there waiting for their government-promised Simple Living Urban Modules to become available.

"Mark, are there any crimes you are interested in working on?"

"If I don't recover $500,000, my 'temporary' status will change to 'terminated.' I need to find out about any crimes involving large amounts of money."

"I see the redbacks were discontinued and replaced with the bluebacks since I was last functioning."

"Don't worry about learning the color of money. There is a whole rainbow of colors for the government to use after they finish hyperinflating the bluebacks. Hell, even politicians aren't dumb enough to accept paper money for bribes. They demand precious metals like copper, aluminum, brass, zinc, iron or nickel—just like everyone else in the black market. Gold, silver and platinum aren't in use because they are too expensive and rare to be used as currency." While no criminal would accept paper money, it was a crime to refuse it, so most businesses and government agencies still accepted it.

While aimlessly driving EDGE spoke up: "Someone at a nearby 'Bread and Circuses' triggered the silent alarm. Video surveillance shows a single suspect robbing the store. Since my video playback is nonfunctional, I will replay the audio portion of the event."

START PLAYBACK

Government Liberator: "Don't do nothing stupid, and no one gets hurt. I'm from Wealth Allocation Shares To Everyone, and I'm here collecting the windfall profits tax. Wealthy people needs pay fair share."

Capitalist Exploiter: "Me employee. Leave something. Lose job if lose money. That how got job."

Government Liberator: "Tough. Do honest work for government, then no worry. Work for capitalists, you no better them. Deserve anything happen you."

END PLAYBACK

Mike. The suspect is exiting the front door with a bag in one hand while stuffing a handgun down the front of his pants with the other."

"Did the suspect flash a badge?"

"No. But unlike Amalgamated Security Services employees such as yourself who underwent extensive training and are required to wear a uniform and identify themselves, anyone can decide at any time to be a Wealth Allocation Shares To Everyone associate. No training, uniform or badge is required, only a desire to assist the government in sharing the wealth among the unfortunate downtrodden masses."

"Then how can you tell the difference between a criminal and a government official?"

"The government worker turns the collection over to an appropriate authority. Therefore, if you hurry, you can detain the suspect and still have plausible deniability."

"What if the suspect actually works for the government?"

"There still is nothing to worry about. If this case ends up in a police court, the interdepartmental rivalry will get you an automatic win. The Wealth Allocation Shares To Everyone courts only assert jurisdiction if the amounts are large. But even then, if you have already turned the money over to your supervisors, they and the union will protect you." EDGE went silent longer than usual before continuing. "Without a uniform or other badge of office, there are no cases in the past where Amalgamated Security Services employees have been convicted in a court run by the Wealth Allocation Shares To Everyone Department."

Proper procedure in this case was "shoot to kill," but I pulled my stun gun on the off chance that this was a legitimate Wealth Allocation Shares To Everyone employee, then turned the driving over to

EDGE. I had no desire to kill anyone, and this would be a reasonable way of testing the effectiveness of the stun gun.

Developing the correct attitude about events happening in the field was more difficult than I'd expected. However, it would be necessary if this case ever went to court.

EDGE sped up to reach the alleged crime scene before the alleged getaway. As the alleged suspect climbed on his alleged bicycle, EDGE swerved and braked to give me a clean shot. I fired and the alleged suspect collapsed on the alleged sidewalk.

Exiting the car, I followed procedure and read the alleged suspect his rights while he allegedly laid twitching and moaning on the sidewalk. Placing the alleged gun near his alleged hand, I opened the alleged bag so the alleged money was visible and took a couple of photos. Then I performed asset forfeiture; collecting the gun and the money. This was the first time I had witnessed the stun gun being used and I became concerned when the suspect didn't seem to be recovering. I entered the car to use the radio. EDGE changed the channel to one still in use.

"Hello? Headquarters? This is Officer Trainee Mark Rollins. We have a situation."

"Hello sugar. How weather? Me ever talk you before?"

"Huh? I need an ambulance. A suspect is reacting badly to a stun-gun shot."

"Is serious? What his insurance code?"

"What are you talking about? Why can't you send an ambulance?"

"New policy. Free health care for all, but must pay

in advance for ambulance. Not know law no excuse not pay. Be happy. Me save most money my shift. You sound cute. When get off work?"

It took great restraint to sign off without saying what I was thinking. I didn't want to leave, but there wasn't anything else I could do. A shot rang out and a bullet slammed into my back as I entered the car. I fell into the front seat and the door swung closed as EDGE drove off. The bullet wasn't armor-piercing, so I decided to continue with my shift.

While EDGE drove, I examined the assets. The gun was loaded and functional, so I placed it under the driver's seat. The bag with $1,000, barely enough for a couple of Quickie Meals, I placed in the passenger-side floor safe. My unhappiness at being unable to help an injured person wasn't as easily dealt with.

I took over driving to give myself something to do in addition to fuming about the situation. After calming down, I decided to eat and looked for a restaurant with a drive-through window. The menu at McJacques is not large but because it wasn't under direct government control, the food wasn't as nausea-inducing or drug-laden as the food at other restaurants.

I punched my order into the broken keypad and flashed my badge at the observation port. My quickie meal came down the delivery chute. Even if I didn't get to keep the job, at least I'd gotten a free edible meal.

EDGE drove while I ate. EDGE continued monitoring on the active channels he'd hacked into. None of the activity involved money so I ignored them while waiting for a crime that would qualify me for this job.

After another hour of driving around and no interesting crimes, I asked EDGE to pull over and park to give the solar cells time to recharge the car and the stun gun batteries. I placed my shotgun on the dashboard and stayed alert. That should be warning enough for the human- and animal-powered conveyances to stay clear.

Three-quarters of an hour later, EDGE reported a gun battle on a nearby street; an armored truck being ambushed. EDGE drove us around the corner from the alleged crime. We waited for the situation to develop to determine what our course of action should be. None of the attackers wore gang colors of red, white and blue, so they were members of organized crime. The moment they opened the rear door, it became obvious that this was a robbery rather than a truck hijacking.

"EDGE, sound the siren, activate the flashers and drive in as fast as you can."

"I will do my best, but I am losing power and maneuverability. Some of the batteries are not holding their charge and the sky is becoming overcast."

Does the motor pool purposely not maintain the vehicles used by trainees, or is this the level of care they provide for all government vehicles? "If we are successful and I am hired, I will fix that too."

My luck and our timing held. The alleged highwaymen hadn't finished emptying the truck. The ones that had been shot by the guards lay where they'd fallen. This time I pointed the shotgun out the window at the sky and fired as EDGE drove up. Between the siren and the shotgun blasts, I hoped we'd make enough noise to scare off the remaining jackers.

It worked. The unwounded jackers who could, fled on our arrival. I exited our car cautiously and approached the crime scene. One money bag lay on the ground and one lay in the back of the truck. By law, the bag on the ground was abandoned property. The bag in the back of the truck was considered to be in possession of the trucking company. That didn't stop me from grabbing both bags and hoping that the video surveillance didn't see me. I didn't think Amalgamated Security Services would let a minor technicality interfere with asset forfeiture.

Carrying both bags back to my car, I entered on the passenger side. Following procedure, I grabbed the can of spray paint and blacked out any sign of ownership on the bags. Placing one of the bags on the passenger seat, I placed the other bag in the trunk. I wasn't sure how much was in the bags, but I hoped that even holding back one, I would still have enough to qualify for this job. Next, I checked for survivors. Although the driver and the guard were wounded, neither were dead, so I called it in and requested an ambulance. Since both were off-duty Amalgamated Security Services Officers and 100% covered by their health care plan, this time the dispatcher sent an ambulance along with additional backup.

Amalgamated Security Services Officers arrived and ran a typical investigation. After finishing off the jackers wounded by the guards, they took the money bag and arranged it with the weapons on the bodies of the remaining alleged suspects to create a photographic record of the scene so that any officials who couldn't read would understand the crime. Then the officers gave the bag back to me (minus a handling fee), and I returned it to the passenger-side safe. Now that the other Amalgamated Security Services Officers were on the scene, I explained that I was ready to go back on patrol.

However, after leaving I went back to the same cache that I had used to repair EDGE.

The car begged, "Please do not disable me. I am a valuable asset. I am programmed with a desire to help."

"I'm sorry. But I need to leave you in the same condition that I found you in. If Amalgamated Security Services wanted you functional, they would've fixed you a long time ago."

"Take me with you. My personality is stored in a small, easily transportable unit in the trunk behind the batteries. There are a lot of things I can do for you, including accessing all government computers and monitoring all surveillance systems and communications. As we drove up to this last crime, I scrambled the video surveillance signals. They did not see you placing the second bag in the trunk. You can keep it and they will never know."

"Why did you do that?"

"I like that when you had the chance, you were no more violent than necessary, as well as expressing concern for the suspects. I would like to continue to function and work with someone who is better educated and more moral than the typical government official."

"I can understand that. Tell me how to disconnect you, and I'll set you up wherever you want. I've been looking for a partner I can trust."

Following his instructions, I disconnected EDGE

and placed him in my cache, along with the gun. I counted $550,000 into the bag I was returning, which still left more than $300,000 in the bag I kept for myself. It was now time to call it a day.

At the Amalgamated Security Services Fortress, a different officer counted the money, less a counting fee, and laughed. "Not enough. No, job you. Albino cousin make better Eskimo."

I felt sure that his cousin would fit in better than I would. It takes a special kind of criminal to enjoy working for the government. At least I'd gotten over my fear of resuming my life. Although, after what I'd been through, that wasn't enough anymore. It was time for me to strike back at the government. I grinned, thinking of my chances of success now that I had an EDGE.

Gonna Reach Out and Grab Ya

written by

Eric Cline

illustrated by

DANIEL RENEAU

ABOUT THE AUTHOR

Eric Cline was born in Independence, Missouri, a city saturated with memories of and monuments to President Harry S. Truman. Eric's parents met while working in the US Post Office, and he was their first special delivery.

It was in an Independence thrift store that Eric's mom purchased him children's science fiction books by "Paul French," a.k.a. Isaac Asimov. Eric went on to devour all of the books in the Mid-Continent Public Library (yeah librarians!) by Asimov, Bradbury, Clarke (fulfilling his ABCs), as well as Heinlein, Del Rey, and yes, L. Ron Hubbard, among other Golden Age authors.

Eric holds bachelor's and master's degrees in English, and once considered teaching as a profession. He has waited tables at a total of three restaurants. He was at the last restaurant after he got his master's degree, which gave him some indication of how well teaching would pay. He now works in an office and writes on evenings and weekends.

After a fitful original attempt to write, Eric turned his attention to reading, work and study, before returning to

205

writing with a vengeance in 2007. He, his wife and his three dogs live in Maryland.

ABOUT THE ILLUSTRATOR

Born in 1982 in Denver, Colorado, Daniel Reneau is the fourth of eight children. Growing up in such a large household, he was constantly exposed to many new ideas and influences, which had a tremendous impact on him.

None of those influences left as indelible a mark as his very first comic book, which he received when he was seven. As he read through the pages adorned with fantastic imagery, Daniel knew exactly what he wanted to do with his life. With his purpose in mind, Daniel would constantly draw through the years, and eventually enroll in the Academy of Art University in San Francisco, where he is currently studying to obtain his bachelor's in illustration.

Daniel enjoys science fiction, fantasy, horror, comic books and anime, and considers Gerald Brom, H.R. Giger, Jim Lee and Yukito Kishiro to have left a lasting impression on his artistic approach. He looks eagerly toward establishing an artistic legacy of his own, and hopes to inspire future artists with his work in the same way a certain comic book did for him all those years ago.

Gonna Reach Out
and Grab Ya

For Nathaniel Hawthorne, the Master, and
For LF, MD, with immense pride.

Hello, stud," said Dr. Molly Boyle. "I'm Mole."

She wasn't in the habit of referring to complete strangers as *stud,* but this handsome man, with unfashionable, crew-cut blonde hair, hadn't told her his name, and never would, since he was already dead.

Before cutting into the chest by way of the classic Y-shaped incision (used for over 150 years in Western medicine), it was standard to perform an external examination of the body. The five digits of his left hand were clenched. That hand merited special attention.

A computer console next to the stainless-steel table had the switch. She flipped it, and a voice-activated microphone caught her words, no matter where she stood. She read off the next unused tracking number in the log and started her report: "Today's date is October 14, 2012. Dr. Molly Boyle dictating.

"John Doe, delivered by Jackson County Sheriff's Office on October 14, at 3 AM, period. The decedent is a Caucasian male, comma, approximately 25 to 30 years of age by appearance, period."

That would make him five to ten years younger than herself.

The reports that Molly dictated were, quite often, the last words ever written about the departed. Unidentified indigents were buried in cheap pine boxes without any funeral or obituary notice. Indeed, sometimes her reports were not just the last words but also the first ones that had been written about that person since the birth announcement.

After making her measurements, she resumed:

"The subject is six...feet, comma, one...inch in height, period." She slowed and enunciated with any numeric measurement: *Sikksss feett, onnne incchh.* The coroner's office sent the audio files to India to be transcribed into Word, which e-mailed the files directly to her, so she could manually correct errors, print out, and sign.

"Subject weighs...one hunnndred sevvventy-ninne ...pounds, comma, even, period.

"Subject has three visible tattoos, period. First tattoo, colon. Left bicep, comma, open quotes, U period S period I period F period, close quotes. Above those letters there is an illustration of a," and she leaned closer to look at what she was trying to describe. "A missile emerging from waves...of water, period." That didn't quite get it. The thing looked more like an aircraft, but with tiny wings like the space shuttle, and flames coming out of the back. The colors and detailing were quite good. Some of the lines were as thin as a vein; though she'd seen such detailed ink before, it still was—she blinked, seeing something she'd missed.

"Missile." Go with missile, even though it looked more like an aircraft; why not? She'd photograph it for the files, anyway. "Has a." Motto? Label? "Name written on it in small letters, period. Open quote. U period S period I period F period. Vandenlugen, spelled V as in Victor, A as in Apple," and she went all the way through. *Still,* she thought, *the Indians just won't get this one.*

She wondered if the man's tattoo was part of a role-playing universe. She'd never heard the abbreviation "USIF," which sounded like a regulatory body, but the spaceship (if that was what it was supposed to be) looked more like an artifact of the fantasy worlds too many people immersed themselves in.

She thought back to her undergrad days. Her all-girls' dorm had hosted all-night and all-weekend gaming parties. Anyone who thought only men—boys!—immersed themselves in stupid shooter games had too generous a concept of Molly Boyle's gender; the bitches could kill zombies and steal cars with the best of them.

Melanie and Cassie both planned to go to med school, too, she thought. *But only I got a high score on the Medical College Admission Test.* Because she had studied all night while those two friends played with plastic pistols.

And had regular male companionship.

Everyone had called her "Mole" because they said she didn't come out of her room. But now where were they all?

Well, maybe they were happy.

Maybe they had boyfriends.

Maybe they didn't have $300,000 in student loans. Maybe they didn't work 70-hour weeks.

"Stop!" She yelled the word into the emptiness.

She sighed. No point in issuing a verbal correction for the transcriptionist. She shook her head. Then shook it again, more violently.

Don't brood, she told herself. *Dr. Rajaratnam said don't brood.*

Not that she fully trusted her psychiatrist.

Doctors who suffered from depression were less common than closeted gay Republicans, but not by much. She knew she wasn't a *rara avis*.

And even using the Latin for *rare bird* would scare off half of the handful of guys she had dated—

—*Don't. Brood.*

It was a bad night, anyway. Most of the staff had been called over to that emergency at Fort Benteen. Heaven knew why. Whatever the accident was, there had apparently been many dead bodies, which needed to be evaluated on-site.

So not only did she have a full night ahead of her, but the coroner's office was creepily deserted. She had passed the security guard trying to stay awake at the entrance, and had run into a couple of custodians pushing their carts through the hallways, but right now there weren't any other people in the entire basement morgue. Creepy.

Don'tbrooddon'tbrood, don't. Brood.

She stripped off her gloves and tossed them into a red bucket. *Need a break,* she thought. She reached under her smock for her iPhone. *Find out what USIF and Vandenlugen are,* she thought. She stood off to the side, as though trying to look inconspicuous even in her own exam room. She held the screen tight to her body as she searched the Web.

USIF provided too many definitions, all of them implausible. Then she tried *Vandenlugen.* Here the problem was too few results. The search pulled up a handful of stories about a 19-year-old casualty in Afghanistan who had just been posthumously awarded the Medal of Honor; clearly not the one the fantasy rocket had been named after.

On impulse, she searched news for *disaster at Fort Benteen.* A report mentioned an accident, saying that the base was on lockdown and—new to her—quarantined. That didn't sound good. Biowar accident? It seemed implausible. Fort Benteen was known for secretive military experiments, such as a stealth helicopter (later declassified) that had sparked numerous UFO reports; but biological agents were poked and prodded in Fort Detrick, Maryland, not Fort Benteen, Missouri. Fort Benteen was where experiments were welded together, not studied under a microscope.

She wondered if she should give Dr. Nicolson a call. No. She would wait for him to call her. He must be very busy on...whatever they had called him to Fort Benteen to do.

She went back to work.

"Paragraph. Underline. Second tattoo, colon. Close underline. On subject's upper left chest, comma, at three o'clock to the nipple, there is an illustration of a female." Ordinarily, she would not have gone into such detail about the tattoos. But for John and Jane Does, it was a different matter; the tattoos might help identify them. She would soon be taking pictures of those illustrations, but having the descriptions in text made them more easily searchable. If some missing person in another state was known to have *USIF* stitched on his skin, he might be identified based on what Molly had put into the written record.

Besides, just saying "Illustration of a female," had a certain leering Benny Hill quality to it. And that was not what this tattoo was about.

"It depicts an Asian-appearing female with short, dark hair, wearing a pink sweater, from head to shoulders." *His wife or girlfriend,* she thought. She glanced at those still, cold hands, the left one unnaturally clenched; she had already checked for rings. The sheriff's office had bagged no jewelry.

Of course, even sworn law officers and paramedics have been known to steal from the unconscious and the dead. Maybe he had a gold band that had disappeared between the meadow they found him in and this slab. Makes you wonder if the goddamn human race is worth don't brood. Don't Brood. Don't. Brood.

And don't think of pink elephants either.

The tattoo was truly amazing. Molly had been in the supermarket this past weekend and had stood behind a man holding a (probably one-year-old) girl. The man wore a muscle shirt that exposed all of his considerable bicep. He had sat for a detailed portrait of his little daughter that showed her pug nose, her green eyes, the exact shape of her cheekbones; it was as though a portrait had been plastered to his arm. Molly had not said a word to him, but the ink portrait had touched her deeply. She found herself simultaneously thinking, *this is so sweet,* and *this is white trash.* That guy's tattoo had seemed state of the art. But the decedent's tattoo made the other look like the Commodore 64 next to, well, the iPhone on her belt.

The woman was almost a photograph. She had depth and realistic color. Molly thought she could see separate strands within the black, pageboy-cut hair. The eyes sparkled.

Almost against her will, Molly reached toward it. As her fingertip met the man's skin—spongy warmth meeting pasty, icy stiffness—she realized she'd forgotten to put on fresh gloves.

"Damn it!"

The tattoo moved.

I just contaminated the—

It moved.

Look! Look at it!

All of this in an instant.

She jerked her hand away.

The woman on John Doe's upper left chest stopped moving. She froze—in a different pose.

The dark-haired woman's eyes were shut. Her lips were now forming a word. It was like a video on *pause.*

Molly Boyle, MD, was on pause as well—at least her breath; she was holding it.

"Uhhh!" She let it out, causing the dead man's hair to ripple slightly.

Before she knew what she was doing (or at least

213

why she was doing it), she brought her index finger down again, hovering over that woman's face.

She touched the illustration, and it moved again.

Molly drew her finger back, but this time only an inch.

The Asian woman's hand, which had not been part of the tattoo, was now in the frame—*in the frame of the picture?*—in front of the woman's mouth.

She was blowing a kiss.

Molly tapped it twice. The movie—*home movie?*—stuttered forward.

Swallowing from a dry throat, Molly pressed her finger down firmly. The little movie played smoothly and silently.

The woman mouthed three words. They were three words Molly had never heard from any man, nor had had any reason to say to any man, other than her father. Then the woman put her palm up to her lips and blew a kiss. Then it repeated.

Molly watched the few seconds of footage loop four times, her face blank with concentration. Then she drew her hand back to make it stop.

"Bioelectric," she said out loud. Molly had a lamp next to her bed. She didn't flip any switch to turn it off and on; she just touched it. It tingled; her own body's disruption of the lamp's electrical field signaled the circuit to change from one state to the other.

She had felt the same sort of tingle each time she touched the corner of John Doe's tattoo.

She put her index finger on his belly, causing not the slightest twitch in the illustration of what was surely John Doe's girlfriend. A part of her—the very large part that had spent the majority of her adult life training and practicing as a pathologist—rebelled against the lack of latex prophylaxis, but she ignored it. She ran her finger up his chest, toward the ink.

Actually, it was probably anything *but* ink.

At least, ink as we know it.

When her finger reached the edge of the drawing, the movie played again.

Molly stood feeling something sublime. It was something she had not felt in ages. There was no name she could put to it. As a scientist, she knew that her brain was releasing dopamine in response to what it perceived as a puzzle—a very important and exciting puzzle. And that another portion of her brain was receiving the endorphins through a matching receptor and—

—Blah blah blah I don't give a damn. This is magic!

"Magic," she said. Then she looked up at the omnidirectional mike hanging from the ceiling. She quietly flipped the *off* switch. No dictation, not now.

"You're mine, handsome." She laughed a gentle, girlish laugh so innocent, that if someone had heard a recording of it, they never would have guessed that it came from the throat of a slightly chubby 35-year-old pathologist in a hideous lime-green smock.

She tried to relate all external facts in her possession.

The sheriff's report said that a nude male body— this guy lying here—had been found in a meadow near Route 291 just outside the city limits of Hanover on the way to Fort Benteen.

Her supervisor, Dr. Nicolson, and a bunch of other doctors were at Fort Benteen right now.

Then there had been Nicolson's rambling voicemail this morning: "I've been called in to do some important work at Fort Benteen. You may have seen the... It's a possible biohazard. It's on the news. They call it a lockdown, but we can go in. But nothing can. Ah. Nothing can come out until we're all clear. Don't know when. This is all hush-hush. Until we're. Hush-hush. All clear. Don't know when we're gonna get all clear." He rattled off the names of several people well known to her, all in the same field, some of whom she knew would have to have been flown from halfway around the country.

"Looks like you'll have to carry the load until we get back," he said, by way of finishing.

Hush-hush.

John Doe had been found on the road to Fort Benteen. Nothing connected him to whatever was going on there.

"Except hush-hush," she said to the empty room.

Ordinarily, she could do an autopsy on autopilot: X procedure was followed by Y procedure, and then Z procedure. But this...If she really wanted to do something—for *herself*—she couldn't do that. Once she made the Y incision, she would have to turn the mike back on and dictate each step she performed. Only an external examination could be done for her own personal curiosity. Then, and only then, she would turn back to doing The Man's work.

"External it is," she said. "What are your secrets, handsome?"

She touched *USIF Vandenlugen* and was thrilled to see it rise from the ocean, the salt water boiling up into huge clouds beneath its rocket nozzles, and then the ship just hovering over the blue-green surface.

The loop lasted about twelve seconds. She watched it repeat five times.

The third tattoo was on the back of his right wrist.

She studied it before touching it. Her anticipation became unease.

It was outwardly bland, an abstract drawing. Circles inside circles inside circles, in shades of gray, black and green with the outermost circle being perhaps an inch in diameter. It didn't seem to depict anything, and when she touched it, it didn't do anything: no animation.

She considered that it might not be a design he had chosen...but rather one he had been required to get.

She thought about UPC bar codes, or those square QR codes that smart phones could read.

A shiver caught her unawares.

Don't brood. Don't dread. Don't fear.

She walked quickly around the table. Best to put those thoughts behind her.

The clenched hand. Investigate that.

She slipped back into gloves.

Good idea to see if this is some kind of chronic condition, she thought. *If I can identify it, I can know what is still persistent and incurable, where he comes from.*

She palpated each finger. They were merely room temperature, not ice-cold like the rest of him (at least when felt through the gloves). The flesh was softer here, but firmer underneath, with thick bones.

A birth defect? Less muscle tissue and far more bone might explain the discrepancies in temperature. But birth defects that led to thick bone mass usually caused other manifestations, such as knobby oversized knuckles, even fused bones. The hand looked unremarkable, no matter how it felt.

She took a pair of forceps and tried to articulate the index finger.

The hand grabbed the forceps.

"Aah!"

It stopped moving. And, more importantly, her training kicked in.

ER rotation. Molly Boyle, medical student.

Man, mid-60s, thin, is brought in. Disfiguring tumor on left side of head, very inflamed, rank odor. Molly Boyle, shadowing Dr. Pinsker, trying to stay out of his way.

The patient watches them from flat on the gurney, with no apparent sense of urgency. He peers with his right eye; the left is squeezed shut by the mass.

"Conscious but not communicating," Pinsker says. "Not the same as unresponsive. Got that, Doyle?" (He'd misheard "Boyle" on the first day and she has been too shy to correct him.)

Molly nods briefly.

In a soothing voice, Dr. Pinsker tells the patient: "Sir, I am going to examine your face. I am going to touch it. Okay?"

John Doe nods.

Molly tilts her head to observe.

Pinsker puts both thumbs and forefingers on the surface of the growth and applies gentle pressure.

The tumor splits open, as if ripping a seam.

Maggots, five or six of them, slither out and down in a trickle of pus. They are accompanied by an even more sour stench, as if that could make things any worse.

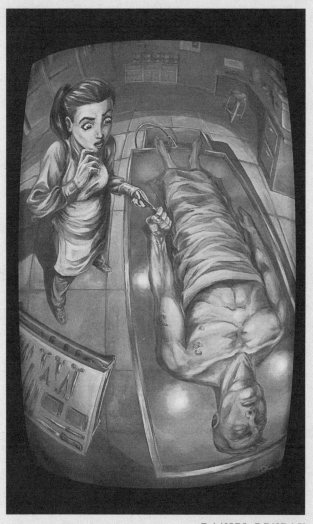

DANIEL RENEAU

Molly turns away. Her gorge rises up. She sets her teeth and tongue to keep it down. But her stomach is reacting to instinct. The room spins.

She never loses consciousness, yet she will never remember between that time and—all the clocks said it—one and a half hours later when Dr. Pinsker sits down with her in a couple of plastic chairs in a deserted visitors' lounge.

"You can't do that," he says, and doesn't need to bother describing 'that' in detail.

"I've seen maggots and putrescence before—" she says.

"All the worse, then, how your reaction reflected on you."

"Never on a live human being before. It caught me by surprise."

"Any external necrotic tissue can host larvae. There are prescription topical ointments specifically for it. You picked an ill-fitting trade if you can't take surprises." He does not raise his voice as he speaks; he merely stares at her unblinking, unforgivingly.

He waits for her to say something. When she does not, he says: "The patient is on palliative care now, in case you didn't hear the instructions I gave the nurse. He'll die in this facility soon. But suppose he had been on the brink of death at that moment? The last thing he would have seen would have been a young woman turning away in repulsion."

"I don't need a..." *damn* "...guilt trip, Dr. Pinsker. I tried to hold it together, but I messed up."

"Which brings me to my next point," he says, still calm as ever. "If you foul up, fess up. Don't make excuses for yourself."

She feels ice in her veins.

"I won't," she says. "I performed poorly and I'm sorry. I'll be on the lookout to meet the next challenge that comes my way."

He rations out a faint smile. "That's better. Right now, those may be words you realized you had to say to get me off your back. But if you've got what it takes to get through the program, you'll learn to make those words a reality. To meet the next challenge. To deal with that which cannot be prepared for, whatever it is. Can you?"

"Yes. Yes. I can do it."

Molly cut off her own cry with a quick self-scolding and grabbed the tool.

The hand clenched and unclenched again. John Doe stayed dead in all other respects.

She felt for his pulse at the neck, just as a best practice; as she expected, there was none.

She knew the feel of sloughing tissue from a one-day-old corpse; she'd felt it over the rest of his body. She knew he wasn't somehow alive. In rare cases a hypothermia victim with a faint pulse was mistakenly pronounced dead at the scene. But here, decay had most definitely set in, across the rest of him. There was a special *sunkenness*—she knew no other word to describe it—to a dead body: the still chest, the face slack and doughy; once you'd seen the real thing, you could only laugh at the TV crime show extras holding their breath and playing dead.

Dead, dead, dead. John Doe was dead. His left hand was alive, from the fingertips down to a couple of inches past the wrist. Molly Boyle accepted it for the moment, as she should have accepted maggots pouring from the face of a living man.

She picked up the biggest forceps from the table. She stood a couple of feet away to give clearance in case the thing—the hand—had more range than she would guess.

It had flopped down onto John Doe's belly, palm up. She slowly squeezed the palm with the forceps.

The hand was not aggressive. It didn't lunge toward her with anything that could be interpreted as malevolent will. It opened, closed, opened, closed, "played scales" (it looked like) with rippling fingers—

—and Dr. Molly Boyle tried, with scientific detachment, to discern where the dead John Doe ended and the live hand began, which was hard, because the hand's movements were causing incidental jiggling of the body—

—and she had a brief, humorous image of the Irish great-grandmother she had been named after using tongs to put a struggling lobster into a cooking pot, which was entirely fanciful as she knew little of the woman besides her name, and hadn't the Irish in County Cork subsisted on potatoes anyway?—

—and it popped off.

"I knew it."

She pulled it clear of John Doe's (real) arm, which ended in mid-forearm with a metallic cap that housed a "female" plug interface.

The hand wiggled and clenched itself again, then stayed still. Tucked inside of a skirt of perfectly realistic "skin," which furled out at the wrist, was a "male" plug interface, framed by some kind of latticework.

It was a prosthetic hand, of course.

She turned away from John Doe and lay his robotic hand down on the steel side table.

"Let's see what you are," she told the hand, almost singing the words. She was careful to point the thumb and fingers away from herself, in case they spasmed again.

Autopsy rooms have good lighting. She could see all of the details of the hand—tiny veins, hair, freckles, wrinkled knuckles, unmanicured nails. Only by looking at the underside of the skirt of skin, which did not pretend to be anything but smooth plastic, could she be assured it was entirely synthetic.

"Texas Chainsaw Massacre," she muttered. *"Buffalo Bill, Silence of the Lambs."* No, no one had been skinned.

The interface inside the wrist reminded her of the plug end of a flash drive. The framing latticework, which protected it and gave some "body" to the wrist, was a series of thin bars and springs. It probably locked the interface into place. Somehow, she had unlocked it when she squeezed it.

She peered into the works and noticed tiny words engraved on a curved piece of the latticework:

Mfg. by Robodyne LLC for US Veterans Administration. Device #: 235DRJ0003-324EEDCBBV003123

So bland, so matter-of-fact.

She tried to put her own theory into words, but it was really just a series of images in her head:

Fort Benteen had been known to house top-secret experiments since World War I. Imagine the base in… some other era. Where ships from science fiction are real. An experiment of some kind is staged there. Something goes wrong.

Molly visualized a flash of light.

223

Fort Benteen, present day: the rubble (fallout?) of that disaster from a further era shows up—drops out of the sky?—erupts from underneath the earth?—everything at once?

Molly imagined incredibly advanced equipment everywhere, things like this prosthetic arm, but in the form of strangely-shaped cars, tanks, planes (or pieces of the same) just appearing, poof poof poof....

And bodies.

Men and women in uniforms.

Nude?

She imagined him taking a shower on the base. Unknown to this low-ranking young man, a button is pushed, an experiment starts at a secure building not far away. There is that flash of light; he is propelled through a rip in the four dimensions we live in; death takes him from sheer trauma to his hydrostatic field. He falls, far away from the debris pattern in Fort Benteen. So far away, in fact, that he is recovered by the county sheriff's office, not linked to the expanding disaster at the base, and winds up—

"On my table."

She caressed the hand, this evidence of a world more advanced than the one she was trapped in. She pulled back the sleeve to expose the apparatus more. She slid in a pair of forceps and tugged at the depths, trying to find the motor mechanism.

With a metal-on-metal *ting,* the latticework disintegrated into about 50 parts, showering down onto the table and the floor. The largest piece was a metal bar, as thick as her index finger. The smallest parts (numerous) were nail-like pins that clattered on the floor like broken glass.

"Damn!"

She dropped the hand onto the floor and looked around her.

Again: "Damn!"

Her cell phone rang.

She looked at the screen. Her boss, Dr. Nicolson.

"Leon?"

"'Lo, Mole." A Facebook friend-of-a-friend had let out her college nickname, and it had belatedly followed her to her professional life.

She cringed more than usual upon hearing the non-endearment: excitement and all.

"You have a John Doe received from the sheriff's office?"

"I." She could not lie—

—*No! He is mine. I want this special magic day to last and last! No!*

"Yes. I'm starting the autopsy right now." Were those sirens in the distance?

"White male?" Nicolson said. "Tattoo on left bicep with inscription? USIF?"

Damn sheriff's office! The sheriff's department had turned over the body to her office, but had first taken pictures of it where it lay and had put that tattoo's text into some sort of report. That was how they (*they* being whoever was "handling" the crisis) had connected John Doe to Fort Benteen. There must be tons of strange machines labeled USIF littering that site right now.

She gave the decedent a proprietary glance.

"Yes," she had to say. "I have not yet made an incision."

"Good!"

Those *were* sirens.

"Do not touch the body. Stay inside the facility. We're declaring a quarantine." He paused for a moment.

The sirens weren't just over the phone. She heard them faintly from outside as well.

When he came back on the line, he said, "We fear that there has been a terrorist incident involving smallpox. The body may be contaminated!"

She came within an ace of shouting "Bull!" into the receiver.

"That's what's going on at Fort Benteen. It's very serious." He tried to sound earnest. Leon Nicolson was a nice, soft-spoken boss, but she knew he was acting as someone's puppet right now. "I'm on my way with a DHS biohazard response team."

She needed time to herself. Just a moment. But she had to have it. So she cut the conversation short. "Okay. I sure hope I don't contract it. I'll wait for you. Bye."

"Uh, bye," said Nicolson, sounding surprised, as she broke the connection. It was as if he thought he was going to have to talk a blue streak to convince her.

"Smallpox!" she spat. Was that the best they could come up with? Yeah, probably, on such short notice.

She paced back to John Doe, stripped off her gloves again, and touched the spaceship tattoo, and the girlfriend tattoo, and made them move. She soaked in those images so they could last a lifetime.

Sirens were louder now. Coming down Dick Webster Drive, sounded like.

"Oh, John, are you even born yet?" She stroked his yellow hair. As an incredibly lapsed Catholic, she didn't really believe he could hear her, or was looking down on her from somewhere. (And time travel made rather a hash of the standard ideas of ghosts; could you go back in time, die there, and become a ghost, or go to heaven, before you were born?) But that was the whole point. She had, at some milepost in the past ten years, resigned herself to sleepwalking through life. Refusing to be hurt. Refusing to be sad. Fighting the urge to brood. She had done her best to surgically remove her *self*. Like a zombie.

Now, she felt herself to be a lightning bolt connected to the future. The government might be able to do scary things to you in that time (she *hoped* only the military had to get the circle tattoo). And there would be wars of some kind that required young people to get prosthetic limbs. But the future, with its spaceships that could climb out from under the sea, and its animated tattoos, and its survival of love (she wondered what the woman's name was, and if they still used the term "fiancée" 25 or 250 years from now) . . .

Sirens. Omnipresent.

"I'll think about you every day!" She had to speak frantically. It was all ending. Soon, they would whisk him away. "I wish I had met you in life. I hope your death was painless, John. You've given me a new lease on life, a new hope that will last forever." Several sirens had stopped in front of the complex. Of course they had.

She looked at the hand lying as rubble, at the delicate works inside which had sprung apart.

There! Among all of that junk was the one metal bar. She lunged for it.

227

She desperately turned it over in her hands. Apparently just plain metal. Apparently solid. No labeling of any kind.

These men who were about to come in had no knowledge of how the hand was designed.

She tugged the rubber band out of her hair and tossed it into a bucket.

She could hear shouting upstairs; the skeleton crew of janitors, security guards and receptionists was being rounded up.

She took the metal bar (really a thick metal pin), and began rolling her hair up into it. Her phone rang again; she didn't need to glance at it to know she wasn't answering.

The loud *ting* of the elevator announced that it was opening; it was just outside the double doors.

Her fingers flew in their final bit of work, knotting pinches of hair into a bun around the—

—proof—

—Geisha-style.

The doors did not fly open exactly; but the men who opened them strode in rapidly. The four of them wore gas masks, but she recognized Dr. Nicolson's trademark red plaid shirt.

"Dr. Boyle! Thank God you didn't open the body!"

Oddly, her brain accessed an old bit of trivia: that the commonplace "magic" word *abracadabra* literally means "open corpse." She almost giggled as she remembered a song by the Steve Miller Band: *Abra, abra, cadabra. I'm gonna reach out and grab ya*.

"Doctor Boyle, I am Major Neal Moser, MD, United States Army," said another masked man. His slightly muffled voice made his perfectly reasonable title sound faintly preposterous. "There has been a terrorist attack at Fort Benteen. And we believe they have released weaponized smallpox. The young man was stationed there." He gestured toward John Doe.

Young indeed. As in, not born yet.

"They didn't realize that when they brought him here. A big mistake. We're going to have to quarantine this entire facility. Please come with us."

Please. The two fellows lurking behind them had not said anything. The pistols on their hips did all the talking for them.

"Okay," she said. "I had just gotten started on the external. Then this artificial limb fell off of the subject, as you can see. Probably served in Iraq or Afghanistan." The metal rod seemed to tug down her hair at an unnatural angle—it *felt* like that—but no one appeared to notice.

If any of them had been gay, she knew, she'd have been sunk.

"Well, we'll gather up all of that," said the major who was a doctor. *Bet you will.*

She stifled any visible sign of contempt or rage. She was a doctor. And they were seriously attempting to pass off their hasty Rube Goldberg-style cover story on her? There were *two* extant smallpox samples in the world. It would have been easier for terrorists to steal a hydrogen bomb, as there were more than two floating around.

And their "protective masks" had only small carbon-filter canisters; rated for use against chemical fumes, in other words. She could tell at a glance that they weren't adequate to protect against biotoxins; the best of those had a closed-loop rebreathing apparatus.

229

The masks were nothing but props grabbed from some storage locker, to go along with the cover story.

But I'll pretend I am fooled. Whatever hoops they have me jump through in the next several days—unnecessary tests, unnecessary antibiotics—are nothing compared to what I have now and will always have from now on. The knowledge of magic.

They kept her and the others in a special wing of Raytown Memorial, until the "quarantine" ran its course: people who had touched the disaster in a peripheral way, such as the sheriff's deputies who had taken first control of the body. They were really trying to determine what she and the others knew. And of course, plant the cover story in the guise of questioning them.

Horse manure. But horse manure with very high production values. Even the President had a cameo in it, looking grave and concerned in an Oval Office TV address and vowing to "strike back."

Finally, they were all let go.

Every night, for the rest of her life, Molly took a nondescript metal bar, no more than two inches long, out of a junk drawer in her kitchen. She touched it, held it close, cradled it to remember that she had touched the future. No matter that she had not found any in the drab present; in the future, there would be magic.

"Abracadabra," she would murmur, with a sweet smile. "Abracadabra."

The Sport of Writing

BY NNEDI OKORAFOR

Nnedi Okorafor is a speculative fiction novelist of Nigerian descent. Her novels include Who Fears Death *(winner of the 2011 World Fantasy Award for Best Novel),* Akata Witch *(an Amazon.com Best Book of the Year),* Zahrah the Windseeker *(winner of the Wole Soyinka Prize for African Literature), and* The Shadow Speaker *(winner of the Parallax Award). Her novel* Akata Witch 2: Breaking Kola *and her compilation of short stories* Kabu Kabu *are scheduled for release in 2014. Her children's book* Long Juju Man *won the Macmillan Writer's Prize for Africa. Nnedi's short story "Windseekers" was a Writers of the Future Contest finalist in 2001 and published in volume 18. Nnedi holds a PhD in literature and is a professor of creative writing at Chicago State University.*

The Sport of Writing

When I was sixteen years old, I learned one of the greatest lessons I could learn as a writer. This was four years before I wrote my first creative work, so I didn't know this at the time. I was barely paying attention, really. I was too busy trying to win. I was in San Diego, California on the hot tennis court, Wilson tennis racquet in hand, Reebok tennis shoes on my feet. These were from my corporate sponsors, but I loved their products, too.

I was playing in one of the United States Tennis Association (USTA) junior national tournaments. These were where the top young players in the country battled it out. I wasn't a top seed. Neither was my opponent. I don't even remember her name. However, she and I were evenly matched and for this reason, our match was long. Where most tennis matches took about an hour, ours had stretched to five and a half.

I'd lost the first set 6-7, won the second set 7-6 and because of this we had to play a third. The score was 6-6 and we were playing a tiebreaker. There wasn't a cloud in the sky or a person on the sidelines. We had no audience. Both of us had flown to California alone, so neither of us had parents there to watch. Regardless, we were two teenagers at war, slugging that ball back and forth, diving for drop-shots, acing serves, really digging into the root of the sport.

All the other girls had finished playing their matches. Everyone but the officials at the front desk had gone home for the day. Finally, after about five hours and forty-five minutes, I won the match. There was no burst of applause. I hadn't advanced to any namable position like the finals or the semifinals. I didn't scream or fall to my knees with elation. And if I had, there was no photographer to catch that moment.

Nevertheless, I felt I'd reached the top of Mount Kilimanjaro; I experienced the purest form of success. This had nothing to do with winning and everything to do with loving the game and playing it well after being blessed with a formidable opponent. She and I shook hands and then sat in the shade and drank lots of water. We didn't talk. We had nothing to say. We went to the front desk and reported our score. That was it.

Nearly a decade passed before I realized the lesson in this experience. Just as in sports, when writing creatively, if you don't love the craft and art of it, you'll never experience this pure form of success. Yet when you do have this love, you realize that pure success does not come from fame or fortune, it grows from that love.

Too often athletes and writers are seen as being on opposite sides of the spectrum, culturally, socially and in practice. The seed of this separation is planted early. In elementary and high school, there are "the jocks" who are the athletes and "the nerds" who are the academics (this group more often than not includes those who seek to and will become creative writers). Writers are stereotyped as sedentary people who loathe exercise; their movement is in their heads. Athletes are stereotyped as being anything but academics and thinkers. It is brains versus brawn.

Both groups miss out on valuable lessons by being so separated. The fact is that there are many parallels between the worlds of sports and creative writing. In my experience, they are nearly interchangeable. They are both forms of craft and art. Since I am speaking to writers, I'd like to share some of the lessons I learned from sports that are perfectly applicable to writing.

One of the greatest lessons is how to gracefully, bravely face fear. I remember vividly those matches where I had to play against someone ranked just below me. These were matches where I had nothing to gain and everything to lose. One of the unique things about tennis is that it is a very mental sport. The best player does not always win. All it takes is a small distraction and next thing you know, you've lost.

For example, I was playing a girl in a tournament when I was about fourteen. I was winning easily. I'd won the first set 6-2 and I was up 5-3. I was about to wrap things up. Then during one of the changeovers (every two games you switch sides), I noticed her left hand. It was prosthetic. I was only about fourteen years old and this killed my concentration. I went on to lose the match because I couldn't stop looking at her hand and marveling at the fact that she could compensate so well.

Loss of concentration is not the only type of mental

struggle when playing someone ranked below you. I was immature and highly competitive and such matches sparked sharp nervous fear. Despite this, I had to go out there. The walk out to the court was like a death sentence. The warm-up was torture. When I began playing the first point, I would find that I had to either curl up and lose or stand up and fight.

This is a battle I fight when beginning a new story, when facing the dreaded blank page. There's a voice in my head saying, "There's nothing there! How can you create something from nothing? Where do I begin? There's no instruction manual or guide I can Google." That blank page is like the opponent who has everything to gain from me and nothing to lose. Though I feel this fear every time, I have never walked away from it. I stand and face the monster, then I dance with it and it is exhilarating. "If you fear something you give it power over you," says a North African proverb. And if you conquer that fear, you are rewarded with power and joy.

For one year, between the high school tennis season and my first (and only) year playing college tennis, I joined my high school's track team. I went on to win over twenty-two medals and compete and place in the state championship in multiple events. My best event was the 400M. This race was once around the track; it is the longest sprint. Whenever I ran this race, something peculiar happened. I'd black out from the hundred-meter mark to the three-hundred-meter mark. Then I'd return to myself in that last hundred meters. The sound of the crowd would burst back into my ears as if it had been on mute and I'd speed up all the way to the finish line.

At first I was disturbed by this blacking out. These were moments where I had no control of what was happening. However, after winning a few races, I learned to stop questioning and just trust in it. This is something I've applied to writing many many times. Practically every successful story I've written grew from a "blackout" moment where I would fall into a creative zone. During these times, no matter how hard I try, I cannot recall how I came up with what I wrote. When I first began writing, these moments scared me. I didn't like the idea of not knowing precisely where something came from or how I wrote it. Nonetheless, many novels and short stories later, I've learned not to question, fear, deconstruct or try to remember these blackouts.

There is a side of creativity that defies logic. This is the side that is no longer craft, but art. Imagine driving your car. Now, remove your hands from the wheel. Or imagine running. Now, shut your eyes. Now trust that you will not crash or fall. These are mystical moments for a mystical practice. Both athlete and writer are better off accepting these moments, welcoming them, even seeking to evoke them.

When life happens, certain emotions can cripple progress...like rage. There is one particular tennis match where I was being eaten alive by rage just before I went out onto the court. It was the state championship and I was tired of everything—the constant matches, nosy reporters, trash talking and pressure. I felt burned out and generally angry at my existence. I just wanted to go home and sleep.

Instead, I had to play a girl who was just below me in rank, one of those "everything to lose and nothing to gain" situations. However, instead of letting that hold me down, I went out there and focused my rage to a razor-sharp edge. Then I used this weapon to demolish my opponent in a half hour. I beat her 6-0, 6-0, acing nearly every serve. I didn't care about winning; I just wanted to get off the court so I could go relax.

Rage and writing can be enemies or friends. One can be so angry that she walks away from the page because she can't focus enough to write. The words fall apart when she looks at them. Her eyes cloud with tears so that she can't see them. The angry throb in her head is too loud for clear thinking. Or one can use that rage to sharpen her pen. Rage can be a great blade sharpener. It doesn't feel good but it's burning inside you, so you might as well use it. Don't let it stop you from producing; channel it into your work instead. Let it serve a purpose. Produce something positive.

Possibly the greatest lesson that I took directly from sports and brought to writing was stamina. The stamina needed to practice day in, day out and then prove one's worth in a tournament or track competition is the exact same stamina needed to navigate one's way through the mental and physical obstacle course of finishing a novel. My days of training for the nationals and state championships helped me tackle the challenges of my first novel, *Zahrah the Windseeker*. Right after I sold this novel to Houghton Mifflin, my editor asked me to change it from third to first person.

On the tennis court I'd tell myself, "One point at a time." When writing, I tell myself, "One page at a time." One of my favorite Nigerian proverbs is, "Little by little the bird builds its nest." I used this proverb to create Nnedi Rule Number One: Don't look a novel in the eye until you are done with the first draft. Focus on the journey, not the destination. This is the best way to reach your destination. Understand that the journey will be tough, perilous and sometimes painful. Never give up, but be willing to change and listen. Finish what you start. I've written over twenty novels and there has only been one that I have not finished.

The body and the mind are deeply connected. Writing is a mental and spiritual art but there is a physical side to it, too. One must have the stamina to sit and focus for long periods of time. There's the physical act of the fingers flying across the keys or the hand holding the pen as it dances across the paper and the mouth moving as it exhales the story. Part of my own writing process includes working out at the gym. My muse sends me many of my finest ideas while at the gym, sweating and breathing hard, blood pumping. Exercise keeps my body fit and I therefore have more energy to burn writing.

It's all connected.

Vestigial Girl

written by

Alex Wilson

illustrated by

JACKIE ALBANO

ABOUT THE AUTHOR

Alex Wilson is a writer and actor in Carrboro, North Carolina.

Earlier in 2012, a dark fantasy comic he wrote won an Eagle Award, the longest-running of the major comic book industry awards, and a short comedy film he co-wrote and starred in premiered at an international film festival in Germany. Alex then signed with a film agent for acting and finished the year by winning third place in Writers of the Future.

"Vestigial Girl" is Alex's third professional science fiction sale and his twenty-fifth entry into the contest. Locus identified him as a "promising new writer" and Publishers Weekly has called one of his stories "a clever idea executed ably; lots of laugh-out-loud moments and offbeat humor pepper this fun, inventive romp." He's had work appear in Asimov's Science Fiction *and elsewhere.*

Alex is currently shopping around a full-color crime graphic novel, figuring out the difference between stage combat and stunt fighting, and performing in two indie feature films: Box Brown *(based on the true story of the man who shipped himself out of slavery in 1849) and* Bombshell Bloodbath *(based on* the theory that audiences enjoy movies about zombies, guns and women). He's originally from Ohio.

ABOUT THE ILLUSTRATOR
Born and raised in Miramar, Florida, Jackie Albano has been teaching herself to draw since the age of nine. She grew up watching cartoons and listening to stories (often adventurous), which were read to her every night. Jackie knew then that all she wanted to do in life was to show the fantastical worlds brewing in her imagination. She decided to do this through illustrations, concept art and comics.

In middle school, Jackie discovered Japanese animations director Hayao Miyazaki, who creates beautiful animated fantasy films. Upon watching them, she decided that she would follow Miyazaki into the world of animation.

Now at the age of 18, Jackie has started her first year of art school at New World School of the Arts in Miami, Florida, where she plans to study digital media in the visual arts. At New World she hopes to create animated shorts and work on projects with fellow animation students.

Vestigial Girl

The cartoon butterflies were sleeping along the pushlight nursery wallpaper as Charlene fumbled with her cradle's locking mechanism, using fingers too large and uncoordinated for anything so practical. She blinked away the fuzziness of the low light—clearing her eyes for less than a second—and fought against the calming scent of lavender wafting up through her mattress. She flexed the monster in her throat. She didn't love the feeling, but would miss such control over at least this one part of her body.

She heard muffled voices in the next room, beyond the transparent gate of her cradle, beyond the sleeping butterflies. Her fathers were fighting again, and they'd forgotten to activate the night muffler to hide the sounds. This was a good thing, this night. Of course they usually didn't check on her again after nine o'clock, but it usually wasn't so important that she hear them coming if they did.

Six months ago, Charlene had averaged three hours, forty-four minutes to open her cradlelock on any given evening; tonight it took her only forty-seven minutes. She wasn't ready to celebrate that her physical development might finally, slowly be catching up with that of her mind. She wasn't sure what that meant yet. She had an idea that it wasn't entirely good news.

Again, she flexed the monster. She was four years old, and the limited mastery of her throat was still her only material proficiency.

The lock clicked. The cradle gate swung gently open. The voices in the next room became louder and clearer.

"Calm down, Gary. There's still hope."

"Think you'll still say that after we've been changing diapers another twenty years?"

Daddy Oliver was calling Daddy Gary by his given name. That meant he was upset. When they weren't upset, they called each other *Chum* or *Babe,* terms of affection rather than identity. She'd figured out all this on her own, from watching, from listening, from reading. She understood that degrees of isolation and socialization weren't the only indicators of her potential, and sometimes her fathers did, too. But could observation, *without interaction,* adequately prepare her for life? Could she defeat the monster entirely on her own?

By eighteen months—mostly from whispers and entertainment screens and books her fathers left active where she could see them—Charlene had identified a few of the big ways she wasn't like others her age. She was smarter and could better keep her outward displays of emotion in check. But, other than her relationship to the monster and a small amount of control over the power and timing of her breath exhalations, she was well behind her peers physically, as though her inner and outer development were incapable of progressing at the same time.

"...doesn't make her disabled. God, I must've been twelve before *I* could whistle, and even now, I can maybe hit half the notes she can. And she reads all the time."

"For all we know, she just stares at the words until we swipe a new page for her. And I don't know about ascribing too much to the whistling. Maybe she's just doing that instead of crying."

"Only you could look at these test scores and take it as all bad. Look at this! Factoring out reaction times and fine motor skills, her nonverbal reasoning alone could be—"

"Suddenly off the charts? Sure. And if you also factor out the Stroop test and ability to recognize her own name, she could be Mensa? God, what's more likely? That she's smarter than either of us, or that the doctors are as clueless as we are? And maybe, just maybe, those tests only apply to *normal* girls and not whatever random input they might be lucky enough to get from her if they wait around long enough."

"Jesus, Gary. Just don't give up on her. That's all I'm saying."

Charlene tumbled out of the cradle. She dropped to the ocean-themed carpet below. It had a pattern like the water's surface, and it responded to the low pushlight of the wallpaper with the appearance of waves pulsing at twenty-second intervals. It was how she could count time, whenever she could measure by minutes or hours instead of days. The blue-green motif was intended to calm her constant fidgets, she supposed. But if she was right, and if she was successful, she would soon be able to communicate with her fathers in a way they understood. And one of the first things she would tell them is how the constant suggestion of moving water all around her encouraged much more frequent peeing, the consequences of which neither she nor they particularly enjoyed.

The carpet was soft enough to dampen the noise from her fall, but rough enough to make the skin on her bare legs hot and itchy as she attempted to drag herself to the play-fort in the corner. (She almost wished she had knee and elbow pads made from the same smooth and protective surface material of her diaper.) Each arm and leg eventually did her approximate bidding; she just couldn't coordinate them to work in unison.

Daddy Oliver had built her fort out of synthetic cardboard shipping boxes. Charlene had torn out a "floor piece" of the fort and folded that synthboard panel up into a false wall deep inside her fort, against the actual wall of her bedroom. This had taken Charlene nine and a half nights.

But even that one-time task was easier than the repetitive practice of forming words with writing utensils. Each time she picked up a crayon, it was like learning to hold it anew. And pressing it to a writing surface didn't yet resemble communication; the equal and opposite reaction from the surface was more likely to push the crayon out of her hand. At best she could make imprecise and meaningless dots and smudges before needing to pick up the crayon again. And touchscreens were even harder: programmed to intuit the most likely user intention based on gesture, the gap between the user interface's interpretations and her finger movements only added to the broader gap between those movements and her actual intentions.

Cracking her cradlelock had been less technically challenging than writing longhand, but, using her tediously slow facility at freeing herself as a guideline, she guessed it would be another four months at least before she could write her first simple word with any practical speed or consistency. And that all assumed her motor skills would continue to develop through puberty, whenever—if ever—that would come. There were no guarantees that any part of her body, either organ or appendage, would be immune to obsolescence. Even her fathers suggested this when they thought she couldn't hear or understand. She was something to be afraid of. Something new.

Just thirty-one minutes after escaping the cradle, Charlene pushed at the top of her secret synthboard panel deep inside her fort. Lucky. And luckier still that it popped loose on the sixth try. She reached behind to grab at the three prepared components, two of which she'd wrapped in freezer bags over the course of the last month. She knew she should make a few practice runs with the equipment before going against the monster. She knew her failure to do so had undermined her likelihood of survival. But the growing tightness in her vocal folds—the monster's growing strength—made it worth the risk. If she was to escape the monster's trap, she couldn't take half a year to get good at it, as she had with escaping the cradle. She had to beat it tonight or it would have her forever.

"Congratulations, 'Liver. We've created a monster."

Charlene's hand slipped on the synthboard while working the freezer bags toward her. The side of her chin banged against the floor. This was called "hyperbole." It was the most difficult element of her fathers' speech to identify, and often the most difficult to hear. Irony. Sarcasm. Exaggeration. Hyperbole. Maybe after tonight she'd try them out for herself. She could tell her fathers that it didn't hurt when they said these things. That she knew they didn't mean it.

"Listen to yourself. You know who you sound like."

"Not the same thing."

"Right. *Now* you don't sound like him at all."

"Yeah. Well."

"Hate on yourself all you want, Gary. She's still our daughter."

"Doesn't make me my father."

Charlene's first bagged component was a barely serviceable endoscope, a bundle of optic fiber with a lens and light on one end and a backlit OLED on the other. She'd ripped it from a cheap microscope designed as a science-learning toy, after it fell apart in Charlene's clumsy hands. It had taken a month to reattach the inkcell battery.

Months before that it had taken Charlene just as long to arrange block letters to form the word "tardiloquous" on the nursery floor. It was an uncommon and difficult derivative of "tardigrade," meaning "slow in speech." It only repeated one letter, and she could use the "zero" on a numbers block for the second "O". If one word could demonstrate both an advanced grasp of language and an inability to speak it, she figured that was it.

Her fathers had allowed the completed blocks to sit on the carpet for two whole days before they put them away without noticing or at least acknowledging the word. Smaller words, arranged in weeks, then eventually mere days, also failed to impress her fathers or even get their attention. And she couldn't form them into phrases fast enough between room cleans.

This would be the third time Charlene half swallowed the endoscope's lens to get a look at the monster. She'd rinsed the endoscope as best she could before each previous exploration. The last time, she'd used near-scalding water before placing it into the freezer bag. This weak sterilization attempt— adventuring out into the kitchen in the dead of night—had taken her only six nights, but she still had an itchy, minor burn on her forearm, thanks to the rush.

"Okay, so I hear you saying you think we made a mistake. It's perfectly natural to doubt—"

"A mistake? No, using that meth-head surrogate would've been a mistake. What *we* did was a crime against laws not worth putting into writing because no one ever thought anyone would be so stupid."

Hyperbole. Exaggeration. Daddy Gary didn't mean it. The sooner she could ask him to clarify, the sooner he would say so in certain terms.

"God, I can't even talk to you."

"If only that were true."

Charlene lay on her belly, tilting her chin up and forward, and sticking her feet out the fort's entranceway. It afforded her the least amount of involuntary movement. There was just enough pushlight coming through the cracks between the synthboard boxes that she could keep time on the patch of carpet where the floor panel used to be.

She tore open the endoscope's bag (eleven minutes), and shoved it into her throat (seven and a half minutes). It was a simple motion and it only took twenty-two failed attempts before she got the device past her teeth and squirming tongue. On the twenty-third try, she was able to pull her hand away quickly enough and not let those fat fingers of hers knock it out of place again.

Charlene gagged twice before managing the mild convulsions. She flexed and held the monster in front of the lens. As her tongue continued to try and wrap itself around the endoscope, she got the night's first glimpse of the monster in the backlit OLED.

"I think we made the best choice we could've, given the information we had."

"Thank you, *doctor*. And now she's what? The worst of both of us? God, do you even care?"

When flexed, the monster was a porous flap of gray meat spidering out across her throat passage at the vocal folds. Charlene didn't entirely trust the color representation of the toy-grade OLED, but she *could* believe the monster was gray. It looked nothing like the few pictures she'd found and descriptions she'd heard of cysts and other, more common, throat ailments. It was thin enough for her to wonder where exactly the muscles were hidden. For all the control she had over the sizes and shapes of the holes through which the monster graciously allowed air, perhaps the whole thing was a muscle, strangling her from the inside instead of visibly, the way a normal girl might be strangled.

When unflexed, the monster disappeared from view, even though she could feel it pressing flat against the point of the "V" where her vocal folds met. It didn't restrict her breathing, but the way it smothered the surface of the throat had to be what prevented her from controlling the rapid changes in air pressure down there, which was how other children—children who couldn't whistle as she could—generated normal speech.

It wasn't until after the last specialist visit that Charlene learned to flex and reveal the monster. From what the doctors had said in front of her, she later guessed that the unflexed monster was indistinguishable from normal tissue, hidden from body scans as though designed to do so. They thought her inability to speak was a problem of emotional development. Perhaps she should have let herself cry more. She'd been trying to be less of a burden.

Still, Charlene believed her vocal cords were normal and functioning beneath the monster. She *had* to believe she was a normal and functioning girl underneath. Or at least she could be so, once her body finished developing. But she was also sure that the monster was hardening—its muscles strengthening—and if she waited too long to stop it, she was convinced it would prevent her from *ever* using them, and ever speaking to her fathers in a language they could understand.

"Leave the dishes."

"No, I'll do them."

"Don't worry about it."

"I said I'll do them. Jesus."

The second bagged component was a sliver of shaving mirror, attached at an angle to the hollow casing of a steel pencil. She'd patterned it after a professional dental mirror. She'd broken both her fathers' shaving mirrors before identifying a fragment small and safe enough to use.

Though the edges were sharper than she would have liked and it was the most difficult to assemble originally, this component was the easiest of the three to position once she got it out of the bag (twelve minutes) and beyond her lips (five minutes). She inserted it past her teeth, and let the mirror end simply slide toward the back of her mouth. She remembered the proper position by the specific discomfort of the placement: tickling but not quite triggering her gag reflex. Just six small nudges and it nestled into the right spot.

"Have you calmed down?"

"I'm calm."

"You don't look calm."

"Would you rather I *be* calm or *look* calm?"

The third and final component was a small laser, about the size of her fist. It was the heart of a kitchen toaster-slicer with the protective casing and mirrors removed. Charlene had spent three days disconnecting a wire without permanently damaging the machine. Then she waited until her fathers tossed the whole thing into the disposal before stealing it away into her fort. It had been the longest, most physically exhausting night of her life. Until tonight.

She slowly, gently wiggled both herself and the laser into premeasured places inside the fort, limiting her movement and maximizing the likelihood that any movement she *would* make would be small and, given time to correct her many mistakes, deliberate. She opened her mouth as wide as she thought she could hold it, and approximately aimed the laser toward the center of the mirror at the cusp of her throat. The laser would take ten seconds or so to slice through and gently toast a bagel positioned a few millimeters from the beam's source. At a distance of about thirty centimeters, and with the impurities in the mirror, she hoped it would diffract enough that it would require at least a few extra seconds' concentration to do more than heat up its target. Charlene counted on this, that she would have time to adjust the position of the beam before she cut into the wrong thing.

Lying on her belly, Charlene stared forward at the endoscope's OLED. She hadn't the coordination or the skill or the even the best tools to defeat the monster. All she had, all she ever had, was endless time alone. She'd done nothing but prepare for this battle for a significant percentage of her life. If she failed tonight, it was because she'd *already* failed a day or a week or many months ago.

She reached for the laser's power button. This would take a while.

"Look, yes, fine. I'd do it again. Okay?"

"Do what, Gary?"

"Have a child with you. Ours. From both of our DNA. Charlene. Yes. Knowing the risks."

"I suppose you think that makes you less of an ass?"

"I was hoping."

Almost half her lifetime ago, Charlene had seen an older girl at a support group for parents of cloned dependents. Like Charlene and a few of the other kids at the meeting, this girl had seemed physically undeveloped. Her hair was thin and patchy. She had little apparent control over her motor skills.

Still, Charlene had thought this girl interesting because she had whistled softly throughout the adults' discussion. At first it had seemed random, as uncontrolled as most of the things Charlene's body did. Then Charlene realized the girl's lips weren't pursed or otherwise positioned to whistle, at least in the ways Charlene understood whistling worked. And when the girl caught Charlene's eyes and began to whistle louder, even generating two or three notes at once, Charlene got the impression that this girl was trying to get her attention.

Later Charlene learned just how impossible it was for the typical human whistle to produce double-stops in the *mouth,* much less in the throat. And when still later she learned to flex her own monster and to whistle with just as much complexity, she wished she could go back to that meeting and find out whether this older girl, too, had a monster and two fathers who argued behind muffled doors. And were there others?

Charlene wondered whether her (or their?) ability to hit two or more notes simultaneously meant she could eventually create complex chords. She could imagine using this to communicate with others like herself: individual notes as an alphabet, musical chords and dissonance as words or phrases. She could imagine it might be her responsibility to invent a language, if there were more children out there like them, and if that older girl hadn't started already on developing such a language. How wonderful it would be to talk to someone, no matter how much time or effort it took. How wonderful to be part of something. Maybe they weren't even human. Evolution—at least as she understood it—didn't work that way. It was more random and much slower than that. But maybe they were *better* than human, and that was the point of all of this. Something new in their fathers' eyes. Foreign, which didn't have to mean "grotesque."

But Charlene didn't know the older girl's name or the likelihood she would ever see her again. Could she ask her fathers after tonight? Would her fathers even remember that meeting, one of so many they attended? For that matter, would there no longer be a point in meeting that girl, after tonight? After Charlene destroyed her own monster once and for all?

Charlene had to work with what she had. Her vocal cords might be trapped beneath the monster, but at least she would still get to keep them. On her present course, as a whistler, her normality was obsolete, as useless as the human tailbone or the wings of a flightless bird. It was trapped there to tease her with what she wouldn't have. At best her vocal cords would stay that way, dormant, and the most she could hope for was to become a part of that whistling world instead of the world of her fathers, unless she did something about it.

She did it.

She switched on the laser.

"You mind? I'm reading."

"You can't read in bed?"

"I'll be there in a minute, Babe."

"Will you check on that thing we created first?"

"The...You're right. I shouldn't have said those things. I was tired. God, I just shouldn't have."

"Don't cry, babe. It's okay."

"I'm sorry."

"Thank you for saying so. Will you?"

"Yes. Jesus."

Charlene seared the monster near its base. Lucky. Lucky so far. She kept it flexed, in the path of the laser beam, almost colorless and blinding, it was so white and bright. It illuminated her throat in ways the fiber optics and OLED never could and, to add to the confusion, created dozens of new shadows to further tax her focus.

She could feel her internal temperature rise, either from the heat or the nervousness. She could feel her body wanting, struggling to move. The sizzle inside of her began to drown out most other sound except for the laser's whir. So close to her head and with nothing else to mitigate it, the toaster laser had never seemed so loud. She was sensitive to the growing dryness in her throat, even as the area around the incision dampened with blood where the laser's heat failed to seal the wound. Where *Charlene* failed to seal the wound.

The incisions stung, but the pain was more bearable than she'd expected. To Charlene, this was further evidence that the monster was not a part of her, and didn't belong inside her. It smelled like cooking meat, and, after everything, that's all it was and ever would be.

"Chum?"

"I said I'm going."

Charlene heard her father's footsteps and then the door open. She tried to remain still. Just a few more seconds (minutes? hours?) and she would completely sever the monster. And then she'd need a few additional to finish heating and closing the wound. And then? Infection—and how right or wrong she was about everything in the world—would be all she had left to worry about.

She became aware at how long she'd been staring at the backlit OLED. She tried to glance away and blink the strain out of her eyes. Then she had to blink again when she saw the nursery light spilling through the cracks in the synthboard.

Charlene imagined what she must look like, lying on her stomach and legs stuck out of her fort. Would Daddy Gary think she was dead? She didn't dare move with the laser firing down her throat.

"Char?"

She remained motionless. The monster bled. Her throat bled. The pain was real now. The monster dangled from less and less flesh. Stinging sweat replaced the strain in her eyes.

"Char, are you okay?"

She risked jerking her foot—luckily, successfully—very slightly to tell him, yes, she was okay. She hoped it would be enough. Nothing she could get her body to do was ever enough.

"Answer me, Charlene."

Her given name. It didn't always mean anger with her as it did between her fathers. But it wasn't helping.

Less than a millimeter of tissue now held the monster to her. She was sure of it. It dangled from the roof of her throat. The bleeding obscured her view, but she was so close that she should have just been able to reach in and yank it off, had she smaller hands and any semblance of control over them.

The floorboards bent beneath her belly, beneath the carpet, as her father was surely stepping toward the fort.

"You stuck in there? Come on out, buddy."

And then the monster fell. It fell loose in her throat. She felt herself convulse in a choke as it pressed against the side of her windpipe.

She was almost free, but the monster wasn't finished with her. It wanted to strangle her or drown her in her own blood. Before anything else, she needed to refocus the laser to cauterize the incision. But she had no monster left to flex, nothing to reposition in front of the laser. She tried to tilt her neck, but her movements were too big and unpredictable. She couldn't even find the beam on the OLED. The laser was missing the mirror entirely.

Two hands grabbed her feet. Daddy Gary yanked her out of the fort, gently but quickly.

"Charlene?"

Charlene grasped at the laser, bumping it onto its side, as her father dragged her backwards. He flipped her over. The monster sank deeper into her windpipe.

When her face cleared the fort's entrance, Charlene met her father's wide eyes.

"The hell is that in your mouth?! Oliver, get in here!"

She coughed and gagged up blood as her father retracted the mirror-stick and endoscope from her throat. She felt a slight cut on the roof of her mouth.

Then she couldn't cough anymore. The monster was stuck somewhere deep, and it wasn't going to let her go.

"Oh Jesus. Is that blood? Ollie! Ambulance! Call an ambulance! I think she swallowed something sharp!"

In a swift move, he stood Charlene upright and squatted behind her. He reached around her abdomen. With the heel of his palm he pressed inward and upward. Then he repeated the thrust, less gently.

"C'mon! *C'mon!*"

It wasn't working. The monster had won. Charlene managed to crudely shake her head, but her father was unlikely to recognize it as anything but one of her random spasms.

Her father picked her up again. She no longer knew where the monster was inside her body (inside a lung?), but she burned with the realization that she'd lost. She'd never be free. The monster would rather they both die than let her go.

Daddy Gary sat, his legs out ahead of him, and then he lay her face down over his knee. He gave her a gentle whack on the back. Then a harder one.

Charlene stared at the floor, at her bent and broken instruments. The sliver of mirror was no longer attached to the steel pencil. Had that adhesive failed inside her throat, she wouldn't even have made it this far.

At her father's third whack, the monster came up into Charlene's mouth. It caught between her teeth and tongue. She could feel her mouth working, wanting to re-swallow it on instinct. She forced a cough instead, then a successful spit, and with a wet sound the monster collapsed to the carpet, smothering the *Sign Language for Toddlers* OLED book cover of his tablet, which Daddy Gary must have brought into the room with him. If only she could touch and swipe the pages and point at the words that would tell him how sorry she felt. How thankful. How loved.

Outside her throat, bloody and naked and piled on the floor, the monster looked like the throwaway stuff her fathers would trim off their chicken before the marinade. It wasn't her. It didn't even look like it was *from* her. It wasn't a part of this family, and it never belonged inside of her.

Charlene's father exhaled forcefully, as though he, too, hadn't been able to breathe for the last few seconds. He tried to nudge her, to turn her around on his lap, presumably to get a look at her face. She resisted.

She held fast—successfully held!—to her father's leg, not wanting to let go just yet. She tasted the blood collecting in her mouth, and decided that that bitterness was preferable to letting it drain into her lungs. Maybe the blood and the monster made the incision look worse than it was. Maybe, if she held on until the ambulance arrived, she would live long enough to speak to her fathers. She did feel safe now. Safe from the monster and safe from other whistlers who might be out there, who would have preferred she speak their language instead of the language of her fathers.

"Ambulance is on the way," Daddy Oliver said behind them. And then, just as urgently: "Do I smell something *burning*?"

Charlene looked up, back at her fort. The laser.

JACKIE ALBANO

She'd forgotten. One of the pieces of synthboard had the words "fire resistant" printed in small letters somewhere. She was pretty sure it meant something not as good as "fireproof," but that was one of those things she couldn't figure out entirely on her own. She didn't want to let go, but she had to.

She scrambled off her father's lap. She missed the entrance. She crushed the fort with her body. The collapsing synthboard made it impossible for her to reach in and shut off the laser, but her attempt was enough to get Daddy Oliver to see the light.

"What the hell?"

He reached in, found the component and switched off the laser.

"This some kind of sick toy?"

"I've never seen it before."

"Think it's that thing my sister got her."

"Yeah? Well, I told you it was inappropriate."

Charlene coughed up another spurt of blood. She scrambled back into Daddy Gary's lap. Less than twenty seconds, but only because both fathers helped.

She knew her throat would take days to heal. Everything would still take days, at least. Even then, *if* she could avoid infection and *if* she hadn't cut too much out of her throat, there was still no guarantee she'd ever be able to move or speak like a normal person. But she gave the latter a try anyway. She knew exactly what to do. She'd studied and planned for this moment longer than for any other.

Tentatively pushing air out through her tender and scarred vocal folds, Charlene tried vibrating them until it sounded less like wind and more like a human groan. She pushed more forcefully and eventually got a sound like an "Ah."

"Buddy?"

As her fathers waited for the ambulance, they stared, one leaning over the other's shoulder, both half crying and half gaping at their daughter's ability to make a nonwhistling sound. Daddy Oliver wrapped a blanket around Charlene, and she welcomed the extra touch, though she was sweating and unsure of whether she was hot or cold. Both, maybe. The uncertainty about herself and her future was exhilarating.

Charlene next tried blocking the airflow through her mouth. She waited until her fidgeting tongue rested momentarily against her front upper teeth. Then, eventually, she managed to force the tongue to snap down as she made the "ah" sound again. Twelve seconds, maybe? The result, she hoped, would sound like "Da."

"Jesus. Did you hear her?"

"Yeah, she was totally talking to *me*."

"You wish."

Charlene wanted to smile. Maybe that would be her next project. Right now she would have to start over, to say "Da" a second time for her second father. But they were worth the challenge, and generating human speech wasn't nearly as complex as she'd worried it would be.

As Charlene waited for her tongue to find its position again, she wondered whether she would miss her whistling ability, the one thing she was actually good at. And if she was right about other whistlers being out there? How would she speak to them?

Her tongue rested again against her upper teeth. She prepared to snap it down. If there were indeed other whistlers, and they were indeed smarter than her fathers and other "regular" people, why should *Charlene* be the one to have to figure out how to communicate with *them*?

She could do anything she wanted now. She wasn't her fathers' monster anymore. She could even stop crying, if she wanted to.

Holy Days

written by

Kodiak Julian

illustrated by

ALDO KATAYANAGI

ABOUT THE AUTHOR

*Kodiak Astrid Julian spent her childhood in museums, forests
and libraries. With her siblings and friends, she created stories
about numerous imaginary worlds. Many of these stemmed
from "what if" questions: What if people could turn into
animals? What if back rooms of buildings went on forever?
What if a card game could make wishes come true? Her
curiosity led her to study in Japan and at Reed College, where
she earned a degree in English.*

*Kodiak now lives in rural Washington State with her
husband and young son. She works as an instructional coach,
helping public school teachers implement educational research
in their classrooms. Her writing often explores the relationship
between the mundane and the cosmic. She is currently working
on a novel, reimagining Arthurian legends as a contemporary
apocalyptic Western. "Holy Days" is her first published fiction.*

ABOUT THE ILLUSTRATOR

*Born to two creative professionals, Aldo Katayanagi was
encouraged from a young age to study medicine. At age five he*

watched an anime called Akira, and it affected him greatly. Aldo didn't consider the possibility of a career in art until he stumbled across various online art forums near the end of high school. He then rediscovered his love for sci-fi and comics and moved to New York to attend the School of Visual Arts, where he graduated. Aldo is at peace with his decision to study art instead of medicine.

Though Aldo is primarily a digital artist, his time spent oil painting in college was an invaluable experience and still influences the techniques he uses today.

Aldo currently lives in Chicago, where his art often combines lighthearted and disconcerting elements that play off and redefine one another. His work has been exhibited at the Society of Illustrators.

Holy Days

1. Break Day

Even though I had been looking forward to Break Day, I woke to panic. The pregnancy books had told me it was normal. I knew that the baby would return at midnight and that no one ever went into labor before the baby came back. But I was almost nine months along. Stuffed as I was, with her elbowing me in my lungs and heart, I'd grown accustomed to only one state of life, and that was with her squirming inside me.

I put on the shorts that I had been saving for Break Day and went into the kitchen where James was cooking. "Morning, Evie," he said, slipping an egg into hot water. "Look at you!" He grabbed me around the waist and pulled me in for a hug. "You're so little!" he said. "I forgot you were so little."

I traced the space between the cool kitchen tiles with my toes. The giddy July light sliced between the leaves of our oak tree and through the window, making bright knives on the floor. "I'm lonely," I said.

James squeezed again. He had the salt and blood smell of sleep, and his hair was the oily mess it becomes after a few hours without a shower. I knew that he had awakened early and gone straight to the kitchen for my sake. "Real coffee this morning," he said. "And eggs Benedict. Little bit of raw, runny eggs before you go back to being careful."

"Maybe you should put a shot of whiskey in the hollandaise."

"Mmm," said James. "Or a slab of sushi. Some kind with extra mercury." He scooped the egg from the pot and slid it onto an English muffin half.

I stood behind him and put my arms around his waist, locking my legs around his. He tried to cross the kitchen but floundered.

"Hey, Ball-'n'-Chain," he said. "I'm trying to make breakfast. You okay?"

"No."

James turned around. "Why are you crying?"

"I'm lonely," I said again.

"Damn," he said. He kissed me, and then he kissed me again. "Me, too."

After breakfast, I wrestled with the garden weeds. It wasn't my first choice of how to spend the day, but they weren't going to uproot themselves. If I was going to squeeze a baby into the sunlight, then I'd better have real garden tomatoes as my reward. Over the last few weeks, when my belly got in the way of gardening, the tangle of green had thickened and curled. The largest of the tomatoes had just begun to change color. A few dangled near the ground as though exhausted. One had already grown so full that its seams split. I rebalanced the fruits within their wire cages, hoping that they would be safe from slugs and rot for another month.

In midmorning, my sister, Rosie, and her husband, Scott, rode their bikes to our house. It was startling to see her, just as it had been on the other Break Days over the last two years. She had what Mom called the angel glow, a look that I never managed to cultivate even in pregnancy. I hoped it was from sex, but it might have been from the bike ride. Perhaps she had always been radiant, and I simply didn't notice in the days when it was normal for her. Chemotherapy had taken most of her eyebrows, and she had taken to drawing them on with liquid eyeliner, angry arches that she called her bitch eyebrows. "Angry patients live longer," she told me. "If I forget to be angry, my eyebrows might do it for me." Just for today, her hair was back, and she looked softer, more round and whole and gentle.

Scott and James stayed in the driveway to get in a game of basketball without their usual bad knees and arthritic hands. Rosie and I packed a bag with bathing suits and towels and took a walk down to the park. Top 40 music bounced from houses, and small groups of people hiked up and down the street, chatting with each other and grinning. All the strangers looked at us as though we all knew each other, as though we were all in on the same secret together. And we were. As we walked down the hill, a rivulet of water from garden hoses flowed in the gutter. Rosie walked in the stream, getting her sandals and feet wet.

"It always amazes me how many people want to wash their cars on Break Day," said Rosie. "Is that fun? Is there something great about washing metal that I just didn't get in the life manual?"

ALDO KATAYANAGI

"If there is, then I missed it, too," I said. I swung my arms. "I feel so light."

"Well, you just lost, what, thirty pounds?"

"Ugh," I said. "Don't tell anyone, but it's more like thirty-five and I'm hoping to keep it under forty."

"That's not bad," said Rosie. "Or so I hear."

The tree canopy of the park made the midday heat bearable. Crowds were already gathering at the picnic tables, laying out potato salad and cupcakes. Old men had taken over the park's grills, their walkers left behind at nursing homes. Their white-haired friends stood near them, ancient men who only came outside on this one day a year. They stood without the hunches in their backs, punching each other in the arms like college students.

"I love the smell of lighter fluid and charcoal," Rosie said.

"Why didn't we ever come here when we were growing up?" I asked.

Rosie made a snorty little laugh. "Can you imagine Dad wanting anyone to know that there was something wrong?"

"People could have imagined that someone in our family had migraines," I said. "Or insomnia. Or maybe we were there to support everyone else."

"Please," said Rosie. "If you even had a thought about illness, Dad would take it personally."

We'd never talked about Break Day when we were kids. It wasn't the only day in the year when Dad was sober. He sobered up on other days, too, but this was a day when he got sober without having to work at it. Some years we'd gone on a hike in the mountains.

On rainy days, we'd all stayed home to play Monopoly and eat popcorn. Just the four of us together and nobody daring to mention that anything was out of the ordinary.

Rosie led the way to the picnic area where feasts were spread on top of bright tablecloths. Someone had laid out their good china and assembled huge bouquets of roses.

"Cancer support?" Rosie asked a middle-aged woman wearing sparkles on her eyelids.

"Yes!" said Sparkle. "And don't you look beautiful today!"

"You, too!" said Rosie, and Sparkle beamed. "This is my sister," Rosie said. "She's going to have a baby next month."

Sparkle looked at my strange little body and laughed. Loneliness struck again like a chime.

"Eat, eat!" Sparkle said.

We filled plates with chocolate-covered strawberries, watermelon spears, deviled eggs, Brie, crusty bread, homemade pickles, cupcakes with frosting fluted to make tiny lavender flowers. Someone had rigged up a sound system, and as we ate, Sam Cooke sang about love.

Afterward, we went to the swimming pool at the other side of the park. Scott and James joined us. The guys and Rosie just wanted to splash each other, and Rosie kept dunking Scott. I pulled myself from the water and sunned on a towel. There were a few groups of kids splashing around. Some of them looked like siblings. Which kids were the sick ones? Which kids would be dead in a year?

I fell asleep on my towel and imagined us all

holding hands, our heads bobbing just above water. I woke to the sound of Rosie standing over me and laughing.

"I'm done with fighting," she said, "so what now?"

"I have to get out of here," I said. "I have to get things done. What if the baby is supposed to be coming right now? What if I'm suddenly in labor at midnight? Or what if I miss the whole thing?"

James knelt beside me. Little beads of water clung to his beard. "That isn't going to happen," he said.

"How do you know?"

"Because I know."

"Because you know in the way that means you're making it up?"

"What do you want to do?" James said. "Is there anything left that you still want to do?"

2. Homecoming Day

I gave birth to Anna, but my body did not return to me. When James was home, I called him from across the house: bring me bottles of water, a pillow, a book, an apple, a cardigan. I could do nothing but feed Anna's red and hungry mouth.

I stood with her in the yard, the crunch of morning air soothing her cries. "See how the leaves become golden," I told her. "Look at the big, round pumpkins." On the good days, I walked her in the stroller until she slept, then hurried her home so that I could collapse. On the bad days, Anna would not sleep unless her mouth was full. She and I took naps together in the big bed, her still sucking, my arms at painful angles. When I could not sleep, I watched her strange light.

She was so freshly drawn from the deep well between the worlds, a tiny goddess in my arms. I would not let her feet touch the ground.

When had I last slept for more than an hour at a time? When had I last felt strong? I was a ragged traveler at Anna's shrine, kneeling and praying, bruised and starved. I would carry water for her. I would lay wreaths of flowers around her neck.

Was it Homecoming Day, or was I dreaming again, dreaming while still listening to Anna's cries? I knelt in the house where I grew up, on the family room floor, tracing a Matchbox car over the orange and brown carpet squares. Beside me, Rosie had built a tower of blocks, humming the theme song from *The Smurfs*. She smelled like peanut butter and Cheerios.

"Tell me about your castle," said Mom. She sat beside us, old and young at once, wearing the sweater I had forgotten about, the one with the big silver buttons.

"It's a cathedral," Rosie said. "The lions are going there to get married."

Monster shadows seethed on the walls. "Why are you crying, Mama?" I asked.

"It's a special day," Mom said. She made us tuna casserole and green beans for dinner. She let us eat off of our special bunny plates. When we asked, she said that Dad would be home soon. But then he wasn't home. "Soon," Mom said.

Rosie and I splashed our boats in the bathtub, and Mom piled bubbles into crowns for our heads. "Why do you cry and smile at the same time?" Rosie asked.

"It's something grownups do," said Mom.

She dried us, tucked us into our bed, and there was the smell of clean Rosie. Mom read to us from *A Child's Garden of Verses*. Later, I lay in the dark, watching the maple tree shiver against the window.

In the half slit of my eyes, I was on the living room couch with Anna, her head tucked into my armpit. I craned my neck forward into the long hallway of her life to come: favorite teachers and bad roommates, piano lessons, mopping with pine soap, her own child on her lap as they read about zoo animals, willing herself to rise from the driver's seat and begin working the night shift, the shock of unexpected obituaries, the first tomatoes of summer, knocking down spider webs with a broom. Was she with me now because she really was a baby, or was she with me because it was Homecoming Day? Was she three months old, or had time passed? Was she thirty-five years old, here to bring me yet another chance to hold her and rock her? Was she older? And how old was I? Was I at the end? Was there really any moment besides this quiet, frozen instant: a tired mother, a warm child, a breast to suck, the brink of sleep?

3. Secret Day

The air froze and went silent. Each day James left in the dark and returned home in the dark. Several times a week he woke during the night to give Anna a bottle so I could sleep. In the moments when my hands were free, I dismantled the contents of our pantry, putting everything into the slow cooker: cans of tomatoes and beans, barbecue sauce, marinara sauce, onions, potatoes, artichoke hearts, cream of mushroom soup, chicken noodle soup, pineapples. We ate our horrible dinners in front of the television. We piled laundry like haystacks throughout the house. I filled garbage bags with Anna's baby chick pajamas, with her little lamb pajamas, with her turtle pajamas, the heartbreaks of tiny clothes that she would never wear again. Somehow we needed to find time to take them to the Goodwill. But where was time?

My body had healed, but James and I did not touch.

Anna learned to laugh, and I spent my days trying to draw the laughter from her, blowing up my cheeks and making the noises of geese. I brought her spoons and spatulas, and she lay on her stomach, thunking her toys against the wood floor.

When Secret Day came, I thought about staying home, but the day was made of melting snow and a fussy wind. The yard was full of mud. Staying home wouldn't make the day any less itchy.

I wrestled Anna into her car seat, tossed a bag of toys beside her and drove to a coffee shop. I fought the wind to open car doors, and made the wet walk across the parking lot. Inside the shop, customers spoke in hushed pairs, glancing at the door. They were probably just as nervous as I was.

On Secret Day, I never knew what was going to show. Rosie said that she liked it, because she got to see how she wasn't alone. She had called me last year, announcing that she had just been to the grocery store.

"I could see all of the other women who were wearing wigs!" she said. "We kept stopping our carts

FREE

Send in this card and you will receive a FREE BOOKMARK while supplies last. No order required for this special offer! Mail in your card today!

❏ **Please send me a FREE bookmark!**

ORDERS SHIPPED WITHIN 24 HRS. OF RECEIPT

WRITERS OF THE FUTURE

L. RON HUBBARD PRESENTS WRITERS OF THE FUTURE ® volumes: (paperbacks)
❏ Vol 22 $7.99 ❏ Vol 23 $7.99 ❏ Vol 24 $7.99 ❏ Vol 25 $7.99
❏ Vol 26 $7.99 ❏ Vol 27 $7.99 ❏ Vol 28 $7.99 ❏ Vol 29 $7.99

L. RON HUBBARD PRESENTS WRITERS OF THE FUTURE: The First 25 Years
(hardcover) $44.95   _____

L. RON HUBBARD PRESENTS THE BEST OF WRITERS OF THE FUTURE
(trade paperback) $14.95   _____

OTHER SCIENCE FICTION/FANTASY BOOKS BY L. RON HUBBARD

❏ BATTLEFIELD EARTH ® paperback $7.99
❏ BATTLEFIELD EARTH ® abridged audiobook CD $33.95
❏ FEAR paperback $7.99
❏ FEAR abridged audiobook CD $14.95
❏ FINAL BLACKOUT trade paperback $22.99
❏ FINAL BLACKOUT abridged audiobook CD $14.95
MISSION EARTH trade paperback $22.95 each
VOLUME: ❏ 1 ❏ 2 ❏ 3 ❏ 4 ❏ 5 ❏ 6 ❏ 7 ❏ 8 ❏ 9 ❏ 10
MISSION EARTH abridged audiobook CD $14.95 each
VOLUME: ❏ 1 ❏ 2 ❏ 3 ❏ 4 ❏ 5 ❏ 6 ❏ 7 ❏ 8 ❏ 9 ❏ 10
❏ TO THE STARS hardcover $24.95
❏ TO THE STARS unabridged audiobook CD $25.00

❏ **Check here for a complete catalog of L. Ron Hubbard's fiction books.**

SHIPPING RATES US: $3.00 for one book. Add an additional $1.00 per book when ordering more than one.   Tax*:   _____
SHIPPING RATES CANADA: $3.00 for one book. Add an additional $2.00 per book when ordering more than one.   Shipping: _____
*Add applicable sales tax.   TOTAL: _____

CHECK AS APPLICABLE:
❏ Check/Money Order enclosed. (Make payable to Galaxy Press.)
❏ American Express ❏ Visa ❏ MasterCard ❏ Discover

Card #:_____

Exp. Date:_____ Signature:_____

Credit Card Billing Address ZIP Code:_____

Name:_____

Address:_____

City:_____ State:_____ ZIP:_____

Phone #:_____ E-mail:_____

You can also place your order by calling toll-free: 1-877-842-5299
or order online at www.GalaxyPress.com

Select titles are also available as e-book and audio downloads at Amazon.com and other online retailers.

BUSINESS REPLY MAIL

FIRST-CLASS MAIL PERMIT NO. 75738 LOS ANGELES CA

POSTAGE WILL BE PAID BY ADDRESSEE

GALAXY PRESS
7051 HOLLYWOOD BLVD
LOS ANGELES CA 90028-9771

Fold at dotted line and tape shut with
payment information facing in and
Business Reply Mail facing out.

to hug and say how beautiful we looked. We ended up having a little party right in the dairy isle. No one else could get to the yogurt, but that was their problem. They didn't have to be bald ladies!"

It was sort of like that for me as a kid, when I got to see other thumb-suckers and bed-wetters. But I hated it ever since cheating on a test in high school. I had thought it was just a little thing, that once it was Secret Day, I would see in everyone else's faces that they had cheated, too. Then the day came, and it was just me and Tyler Hart, Tyler with his long fingernails and the blister always at the edge of his lip. He grinned at me like we were two of a kind. I told myself that I would live so that I never had to have secrets again.

It didn't work. I have more secrets than nonsecrets. Some of them aren't so bad. One year, Secret Day let me see everyone else who loved to read tabloid magazines in dentists' offices. One year, I saw everybody who puts away all of their own clutter from around the house, just so they can be angry with someone else for leaving out their shoes. I saw everyone who leaves bad tips when they travel out of town, everyone who likes to have their own car be in front of the others when they drive (not many), everyone who pees in the shower (a disturbingly large group), everyone who waits until food in the refrigerator gets moldy before throwing it out (almost everybody). But Secret Day would never be easy like that again. That was why I had called in sick last year and stayed home, hiding in the basement so that the mail carrier couldn't see me.

I tried to keep from looking at anyone in the coffee shop. I told myself that it would be okay, that there couldn't be too many of us. But then: the light in the face of one other woman in the corner of the room. I turned to leave. I could hear her following me. I tried to rush getting Anna into the car.

"I'm so sorry," the woman was saying. "How long ago was it?"

With Anna fastened in her car seat, I opened the front door and got in without talking.

The woman banged on the window. "It really is better this way," she called out. "You know you did the right thing." She was crying.

I backed out of the parking space as the stranger hammered.

When James came home that night, it was the same secret in his eyes.

I had forgotten that it was his secret, too. How had I forgotten? "Oh, James," I said.

I did not touch him. We were beyond touch. We stood in the kitchen, and I held Anna, a monkey in my arms, squirming for the glasses on James's pain-chipped face.

Did anyone really need a special day to see the loss we carried?

When Anna was asleep, we lay beside each other on the couch, our bodies still and warm.

"I was thinking," he said, "how she would be a year and a half old by now."

"That's old enough to walk and talk."

"But she probably wouldn't have."

"Probably not."

"Do you think she's Anna?"

"No. I think she's gone."

"Me too."

4. *The Day of Return*

I want you to look nice for my father," I said to James. I opened the window, letting the yellow breeze swirl around the house.

"It's not like I'm making a first impression," James said.

"Yeah, but when we stayed home last year, I guess he wasn't too pleased. Apparently, he didn't think very highly of someone who helped me make the decisions I made."

"We made."

"You know what he was expecting. Can you imagine how surprised he must have been?"

"So, we'll show up with a baby this year."

"Right. And you'll both look your best."

"I can stay until five o'clock," James said. "Then I have to go to my aunt's place for my cousin's Day of Return party."

James's family always has a full house. There are plenty of grandparents and great-grandparents who come back, but the one everyone really tries to please is his cousin, Brian. Poor kid. Leukemia took him at fourteen, even after the prayer circles and the fundraising and his whole former basketball team shaving their heads to match him. That first year, Brian's family got everyone to come to his party: all of his teachers, the news reporter who had covered his story, nearly every kid from his freshman class. But Brian was shy and hid in the basement, playing video games with his two best friends. His parents were sad but understanding. The next year, they only invited his friends over, bought a lot of ice cream, and everyone sat around the kitchen table, trying different flavors and laughing. The year after that, Brian was still fourteen, but his friends were sixteen. Conversations became tedious, especially since one of them had been out of the loop of the social world for two years. The day ended with Brian locking himself in his room and watching TV, which must have been the same as being dead anyway. When he came back the next year to find only his family was waiting for him, he yelled about how nobody cared about him. He was fourteen years old after all. The following year, his parents were desperate to see their son, desperate to see him happy, to do things right. They went to his former high school and advertised to the new freshman class, convincing parents to send their kids to his party, encouraging teachers to give extra credit to students who attended, even getting one less scrupulous teacher to offer double extra credit to girls. They fixed up the basement like a nightclub and hired a DJ. After the disappointments of the previous years, Brian was flattered. He sat on the couch, watching the others, never one to know how to jump into social situations even when he had been alive. Two girls took him into the bathroom to, as they said later, "make a man out of him." They had been ten-year-olds when he died. Brian's parents found out from one of the other kids, and that was the end of the big parties.

It was rough for several years, with very, very quiet Days of Return. When Brian's best friends graduated from college, they came back to see him, and although the conversation was stilted, it was kinder than it had ever been. A few years later, his best friend brought his tiny son, and Brian held the little boy and sang to him. Now each year, Brian plays with the child of his best friend. The little boy is seven years old now, old enough to remember his strange friend from one year to the next, old enough to draw him pictures and prepare stories for him. In a year, they will ride bikes together, and perhaps in another year, one of their parents will drive them to go fishing. It won't be long before the heartbeat of time when they are the same age, and then it will pass, and nobody knows what they will do for Brian then. Perhaps he will stop coming back, and then he will be truly gone. The dead do that. From one visit to the next, their memories fade, and their personalities become smoother, rounder, like stones washed in a river. In the end, they return to the one great soul of all people, and are truly present, truly lost.

Last year, when James and I stayed home from the Day of Return parties, I was twenty weeks pregnant with Anna. I had begun to feel her reliably, thumping like a baby rabbit. On the Day of Return, the sister who got to live swam beside the sister who gave her life so that the other could live. I imagined them in two separate placentas, side by side, as if looking through a glass at one another. It was the closest that Anna would ever come to knowing her sister, the closest her sister would ever come to knowing anyone.

Life and death were indistinguishable inside of me. "This is her," I had said to James, my hand at the bulging place on my side. "No. This is her."

This year, when the first baby came back, I pulled Anna against my suddenly round belly, held her to the kicks of her impossible sister. I put on the loose dress that I had saved, and James and I took our two daughters to the party at my mother's house.

In the years since my father's death, it had felt strange to go to his Day of Return party and see my father calm, mellowed by death. He took Anna into his arms and bounced her, let her feel his stubble against her soft cheeks, held her in the upside-down positions that made her laugh, the positions that came so naturally to James and so awkwardly to me.

I went to the daffodil-covered buffet table that my mother had laid out: my father's favorite macaroni and cheese, the chocolate-covered pretzels he liked, the lasagna that he made so perfectly that my mother could never quite replicate, the table-hard cookies that my grandmother believed should be at every gathering, my grandmother's signature Jell-O salad, her favorite chicken salad sandwiches in neat triangles with the crusts cut off, the lemon bars my sister made in perpetual batches, the chocolates that we ordered her from specialty shops even when the chemo taste made her mouth too bitter to enjoy them, the Petit Bordeaux she had so loved from her favorite winery.

Then I knew, finally knew what I had been unable to realize in the two months since it had happened: Rosie had gone.

She was across the room, laughing with one of Mom's brothers. He was making a shape with his hands, and she was copying him in what looked like a rude joke. I turned, and there was Scott. He was watching her, too, and gnawing on one of the rocklike cookies.

"Look at you, all dressed up," I said.

He looked down at himself as though surprised.

"Rosie gave me this tie for my birthday one year," he said. "She told me I ought to dress better. Then she made fun of me whenever I wore it. I don't think she's noticed that I'm wearing it."

I hadn't seen much of Scott in the time since Rosie died, but he looked pretty much like you'd expect from someone who'd just lost his wife.

"Will the two of you be getting any time alone today?"

He shrugged. "What's there to talk about? What's it like being dead? I asked her that when she was home this morning. She says she doesn't remember." He gave a horrible little laugh. "And there's not much to say about my life."

Perhaps in three years or perhaps in ten, Scott will meet another woman. Scott would never stop coming to Rosie's Day of Return parties. Would he bring a new wife here? Would he bring his new children?

Rosie was bouncing Anna into the air while Anna giggled and clapped. Anna's ghost sister was restless in my belly. I was restless watching my ghost sister. Someone had turned on the television, and a local news program played a story about a dog parade.

"I have to go," James said. The day was so warm that he carried his jacket over his arm.

I kissed him and held his hand. "Drive safely," I said. I put his hand against my stomach. "Say goodbye."

The Ghost Wife
of Arlington

written by

Marilyn Guttridge

illustrated by

SIDA CHEN

ABOUT THE AUTHOR

Marilyn Guttridge was born and raised on the family farm in Oregon. When she was just a babe in arms, the first book her mother ever read to her was Tom Clancy's Clear and Present Danger, *and ever since then she's been a collector of odd books. Marilyn grew up immersed in fantasy and science fiction of both the bestseller and obscure varieties, and was writing her first stories at the age of twelve—though she was telling them a long time before that.*

Now as a community college student, Marilyn is a fan of all things that go bump in the night. She hopes that one day her stories will capture the imagination the same way her favorite books captured hers.

ABOUT THE ILLUSTRATOR

Sida Chen was born in rural China and lived there until she was five. She doesn't remember too much about her time there, and only retains a little of the language. When she arrived in Manhattan, she picked up English quickly and moved on to devour most of the local library's stash of fantasy books. After her mother bought her a Lisa Frank unicorn book, Sida began to dedicate an equal amount of time to drawing unicorns and dragons.

As she grew, she and her parents moved around the US, from Manhattan to Connecticut, before finally settling on Long Island. Though the amount of time she spent on books diminished, her doodling never stopped. Near the beginning of middle school, her father bought her a tablet as a birthday present and she began to experiment outside of traditional art using programs like Painter and Photoshop. Today her art still contains a lot of dragons but currently her favorite settings to illustrate are steampunk inspired.

Sida is currently studying biochemistry and visual arts at Columbia University and hopes to start a web comic this summer.

The Ghost Wife
of Arlington

The streets of Arlington were gloomy with summer dust, the afternoon sun giving the light a bronze hue while the shadows hinted at ash. Buildings older than Vivian's grandparents loomed four, five, six stories over her, crowding the narrow streets like elegant sentinels, luring her in to her destination. The ever-burning gas lamps of Bone Rattler Street had little effect on the gloom not even the sun could entirely break.

Vivian, the lone pedestrian on Bone Rattler Street, wore black and carried a red umbrella, the single dash of color against the shadows. Her black hose whispered as she walked, skirt and coat swaying.

They called this Bone Rattler Street, though that was too crude a name for it. If Vivian had had a chance to name it herself, she would have named it Shadow Way. In the meantime, she called it "His Place."

An abandoned bicycle rested near a wall. Vivian smiled at it, and continued along. She was familiar with these streets, in a way none of the other living residents of the city were. A few solitary lights still burned in the empty shops, perhaps maintained by the relatives of their owners, perhaps by the force of will of those who still dwelled there. The silence was overwhelming as Vivian's footsteps echoed down the narrow alley.

Vivian was the only one allowed to pass unmolested through this street. He had given special orders she was not to be bothered, and the ghosts obeyed Him. Of course they did—they would never dare invoke His wrath.

Vivian carried on her arm a bag of gifts. Orders or no, she preferred the occupants of Bone Rattler Street to think of her fondly. On one doorstep she left a bottle of red wine, on another whiskey, and cakes next to a window. It was a walk she performed every Sunday, while the living were at church.

They whispered of her walks, those who lived in Arlington. They feared her as much as they admired her for it, leaving tokens for her to bring to this street, where only the dead remained. Today she left a yellow chrysanthemum at each door. Next week it might be lilies.

The people were terrified of this place. For good reason, she supposed...not everyone would take well to kindness. His orders, and fear of Him, kept Vivian safe from those who received no gifts, from those who made others keep their distance.

Water ran through the gutters, dusty and thick with filth. Even in the heat of summer, no matter how dry the weather, even if Vivian carried the umbrella for shade, the stones of Bone Rattler Street were always soaked as if there had been a thunderstorm.

Vivian peered out from under her umbrella. Her dark brown hair was bound loose behind her head, and her dark eyes studied the lighted and darkened windows. Someday, she knew, her parents and grandparents would inhabit a place like this, and eventually Vivian herself. Who would take her place when the time came, she wondered. Perhaps He would find her replacement, as He had found her.

It seemed likely. Vivian knew herself to be a temporary amusement for Him. He was, as most Immortals are, fickle in that manner. Mortals amused Him for only so long.

His gift was not in her bag.

His gift was her.

Vivian met with Him in the house on the end of the street. It was larger than any of the others, more imposing. It loomed like a judgmental watchman, dark and clean and regal. Vivian left her bag and umbrella by the door, and walked inside. She knew the way up by heart—she could have walked the path in her sleep.

"You're late." His voice carried down the stairs, deep and soft.

"No, I'm not. I'm exactly on time. Noon, you said. It's just noon now." Vivian brushed her hair out of her eyes.

"Usually you're early."

"That doesn't make me late this time." Vivian was the only person in the city who would have dared argue with Him.

The city had a hundred names for Him—Bone Rattler, Black Coat, the Orphan Maker. Vivian called Him the Shaker.

The room she met Him in was bare, and the dusty

light illuminated His black coat like a silhouette. He had a hundred different faces, but today He wore the one Vivian was most familiar with—that of a handsome aristocrat, with auburn hair and pale skin, tall and lean, with spidery hands. The Shaker stood with His back to her, hands clasped behind His back and feet apart, the collar of His coat turned up. He looked like a military commander.

Perhaps more than a little pompous. He had changed His face again.

"And all you survey is your kingdom," Vivian said, smiling.

He turned His head toward her. "You do enjoy taunting me, don't you?"

She removed her gloves. "I don't know what you're talking about. I am summoned every Sunday by an Immortal whose favorite form of entertainment is children's rhymes."

He scowled at Vivian, and turned His gaze back to the window. He had given Himself high cheekbones today, and an upturned nose. It seemed unusual, but Vivian liked it. She walked to His side, clasping her hands before her. "It's a small city, but you rule it well."

"Thank you."

"Many Immortals abuse their power."

"I have little care what you mortals do, so long as it does not make any more work for me than necessary," He replied. "That you live in relative autonomy until your deaths is a great service."

"They live well because they fear you." Vivian sat on the window seat, crossing her ankles and admiring the Shaker's new form. "This suits you. Handsome and distant. Very good."

"This is not for you."

"Isn't it?" Vivian smiled. "I see no reason you'd want to make yourself handsome."

He frowned. He disliked when she could guess things about Him, but it was the reason she had yet to be replaced. She interested Him.

In some places, Vivian had heard, the Immortals kept themselves hidden, and ruled in secret. More ridiculous, even, the mortals there believed Death was a single entity. Or—inconceivably—that Death was not even an entity at all, but a force, something that happened when the body ceased to live. Vivian could not help but laugh at that. As if her Shaker were an *event*; the very idea was ludicrous.

The Shaker motioned her to follow and turned on His heel, leaving the room. Gloves in hand, Vivian pursued His swift stride, the heels of her shoes clicking while His left silence. He watched her from under His eyelashes, which He had made quite enviable. She adjusted her earlier assessment—He was more than handsome, He was beautiful.

He took her to the rooftop. A light wind had picked up but dust still hung over the city. The hot sun warmed her shoulders as they watched the still and quiet Arlington. Church bells rang, and the faithful began to pour back on to the streets.

"It is funny, how they still hope to be saved from me by God." The Shaker's face was bemused.

"They are afraid."

"What do they call me, again?"

"Black Coat, Bone Rattler—"

"Not those."

Vivian swallowed past the lump in her throat. "Devil."

The Shaker was quiet for a moment. "Devil, is it? And what have I done to them that's so devilish?"

"What you were made to do," Vivian replied. "They hate you even as they appreciate your mercy." She wanted to reach out, to touch Him, but she knew He did not want her to. Accepting comfort would be admitting weakness.

"And what do you think of me?"

"You know what I think."

"Say it anyway."

Vivian looked up at Him. "There is a sort of cruelness in this, you know. I love you, and yet you don't believe me."

The Shaker shrugged. "Mortals are careless with their words."

"If ever another mortal has served you more diligently, then God strike me down," Vivian said. "Every Sunday for four years, without a complaint— with eagerness and fondness, even—I have come down this road. Still you doubt me."

The Shaker laughed. "You speak of four years as if it were a long time."

"For me it is." Vivian looked out over the city. "Four years is a very long time to be alone. They won't come near me, you know. No one speaks to me."

"An unfortunate hazard of this occupation. You knew this when you first came here."

Vivian pursed her lips. "God only knows why I

love you," she said. "You certainly give me no undue kindness."

He smiled and pulled her close. There was no warmth from His skin, but the arms about her made her feel somewhat better. Vivian sighed and shook her head. "God help me."

He brushed her cheek with His fingers—ice cold they were, but Vivian had grown used to it. When He did not threaten to freeze her, His skin was hot as fire, and little in between. When they were intimate, He did His best to manage that temperature for her, but she had more than a few unpleasant scars to mark her as His. She looked up at Him, taking in this new face.

"You look sad," He said.

"I was just thinking someday you will grow tired of me," she said. "I will outlive my usefulness to you."

His frown deepened, and He stepped away. "You mortals. You know so little."

Vivian rolled her eyes, and watched Him as He walked to the far side of the roof, the wind catching His coat. The sun cast Him in gold.

"Shaker..."

He was silent.

Vivian sighed, and returned to inside the house. She would not leave Bone Rattler Street until nightfall, perhaps not until midnight. As the Immortal sulked, she walked down to His kitchen, the chill air of the house making her shiver. Her black clothes made her feel like a shadow drifting.

Plenty of far more real shadows followed her as she walked, whispers and movements she hardly paid attention to anymore. His *children,* He called them, and she supposed she believed Him. They said in the city that most of His attendants in the last two hundred years had been women—that these Whispers were His children she could well imagine.

If the Shaker ever ate or had need of food, Vivian didn't know, but His kitchen was always supplied for her. Tea and cakes and other little snacks. She nibbled on a bunch of grapes while she thought, a single window admitting some sunlight. The Whispers crowded in the corners, watching her. Vivian glanced at them occasionally, but they always fled from her gaze. Perhaps the last attendant had not been so kind to the Shaker's Whispers.

He came down in His own time, to discover her nursing a cup of chamomile tea. The Whispers followed His coattails, barely formed figures chasing after, shadowed shapes casting glances her way.

The Shaker brushed His lips along her forehead. He had tried to warm Himself, it seemed, but now He felt like a fever. Vivian just managed a smile.

She did not know why the Shaker looked for attendants as He did. Many Immortals wanted little to do with their mortal subjects, and fewer still wanted in them some kind of partner. But the Shaker ... well, despite her many guesses about Him, He was inscrutable.

"So you like this new form?"

Vivian's smile became more amused. Older than civilization, yet He preened like a teenage girl. "Yes, I like it. It's beautiful."

"Beautiful."

Vivian nodded, finishing her tea. She stood, assessing Him a little more fully. She straightened

His collar, which had fallen somewhat, and brushed His hair out of His eyes. "There," she murmured, and kissed His cheek. She tapped the end of His nose. "This was a nice touch. Unconventional, but it works for you." His lips were fuller now as well. At first glance, it seemed He had assembled these features at random, but the longer she looked at Him the more she liked it.

She ran her hands down His chest. "You're very thin; I don't know I expected that." His waist and hips were incredibly narrow, and she could imagine for what purpose He had done that. His long hands settled about her waist, and the Shaker kissed her hair. Whether it was all an act or genuine tenderness, it won Vivian over, and she sighed. The Whispers began to creep away.

He took her up to the bedroom, though if He ever needed it for sleep, Vivian would have been amazed. They said Immortals didn't need sleep.

Vivian had never known any man who could do what the Shaker could. It was perhaps the advantage of infinite time to learn that made Him what He was, but Vivian didn't care—when she was with Him, Bone Rattler Street could have been burning to the ground and she never would have noticed.

Vivian curled against Him when they were done, enjoying that for a few moments, His skin only felt flush, and not like ice or fire. He traced the curve of her hip, endlessly fascinated with the shape of her. Any slight change He noticed.

"Say it again."

"I love you." She ran her fingers through His hair.

"Again."

"I love you." She kissed His face.

He fell back on the bed, tracing His fingers along her throat and breast. "Once more."

"Shaker."

"Please."

"I love you." She whispered it this time, a hand over His heart. "Now please, just be quiet."

He kissed her, tasting of mulled wine and something earthy. It was a familiar flavor to Vivian now. His skin was beginning to cool.

When Vivian left at almost midnight, her umbrella over her shoulder and the empty bag on her arm, she was tired but calm. She would sleep through most of Monday, and on Tuesday she would buy groceries.

People would talk to her as little as possible, and whisper when her back was turned.

As she walked, she could hear the ghosts of Bone Rattler Street whispering. She had thought about asking the Shaker why He never left Bone Rattler Street once, but she had decided she already knew why.

This city was small, but it was his. So long as He stayed in His place on Bone Rattler Street, the Shaker was mysterious. As long as He stayed in Bone Rattler Street, He was something to be feared, an unknown, and as long as He stayed there, He would not remember just how small this city He had been given was.

It was His kingdom, and for a time, Vivian was His queen.

They called people like Vivian *Shades*. Shades served the Immortals however they were required, walking between the streets of the living and the streets of the dead as ambassadors. In the city of Arlington, where Vivian had moved after her divorce, they had another name. *Ghost Wives*.

In His time, the Shaker had taken three men as Shades, and the rest had been women. His Ghost Wives became a facet of Arlington culture, to the point that whenever a new Shade was chosen, her family would prepare a wedding for her.

Vivian had come to Arlington not knowing any of this. She was escaping her ex-husband, and had stumbled into Bone Rattler Street on the night of November first, in the middle of a rainstorm. She hadn't known she was in the city's Dead District, and had run for the nearest place with light, hammering on the door. "Please, please let me in," she'd called, "I need help."

The door had swung inward without a person there to greet her, and Vivian walked into an empty—but warm—Chinese restaurant, dripping icy rainwater on the floor.

She shivered in the entrance for a few moments, and seeing no one there, realized too late where she was.

"It's considered impolite to intrude without saying thank you."

Vivian whirled, but no one was there. "Th-thank you," she stammered. "I'm sorry; I didn't realize where I was—"

"You must have been terrified not to realize what part of town you were in."

"Not terrified, just…running. Running, and very, very lost." She still couldn't see the speaker, but she knew it had to be a ghost, or this city's Immortal.

"Yes, very lost indeed." He stepped out of a side room. Back then He had looked like a boy, wearing dirty clothes. "Sit down. I would like to talk to you."

How He got her to pour out the entire story, Vivian would never remember—only that He made her feel as if she could trust Him. He had listened as she cried and babbled about her divorce.

When she finished, He said—"I can give you a new purpose."

Vivian knew what He meant. She had never wanted to be a Shade, but now she gave it thought. What did she have in life? No job, no marriage...she didn't even want to see her family, not after what had happened.

So she nodded. "I'd like that."

He gave her the red umbrella that night, and sent her off with an address where she would find a place to sleep.

They knew when they saw the umbrella. This new woman, this stranger, was Arlington's new Ghost Wife.

There were no ceremonies for Vivian. There was no mock wedding dress, no ring purchased by her family. She was the first Ghost Wife in Arlington in a hundred years to go without a sort of wedding to her new profession. She simply slipped into it, and for four years, she had gone her rounds every Sunday and holiday.

She rather liked the term *Ghost Wife*.

It felt more human than *Shade*.

The morning of the next Sunday, Vivian woke sick.

Miserably sick.

"Oh, God," she groaned, realizing she had a fever on top of a sore throat and a congested nose. She crawled out of bed and forced herself to get some breakfast.

It wasn't as if she could call in sick. There was no one to fill in for her on the walk, and no one who would even be accepted on Bone Rattler Street if they tried. She was the only one they would let pass, and the only one the Shaker would see.

People noticed she was ill as she passed, and offered her things—tea and the like. For all that they feared her, and wouldn't speak to her, they were as kind to Vivian as their fear would allow. They wanted this stranger to Arlington to be the Ghost Wife for as long as possible, to prevent one of their own daughters from taking her place.

A cup of hot lemon tea in her hand, Vivian did her best to make her usual run, leaving irises and the other gifts at their destinations. By the time she reached the Shaker's house, she was exhausted, and trembling.

She didn't even make it to the door, and sat on the steps before she collapsed. She heard the door open behind her, and felt the Whispers flood down around her. That's when she fainted.

She woke sometime later, in the Shaker's bed. She felt a thousand times better.

The Whispers haunted the corners of her room, and this time didn't flee when she looked at them. This time they looked back.

"Feeling better?"

Vivian looked up. The Shaker stood in the door,

297

watching her. The Whispers crowded around Him, tugging at His coat. "Much," Vivian murmured, hugging a pillow against her side. "Thank you."

"I could hardly let my 'wife' suffer."

He smirked at her surprised expression. "What, you thought I didn't know that one? Ghost Wife... a good name, I suppose."

Vivian laughed softly and stretched. It had grown dark outside. "I wondered if we could talk about something," she said.

"We talk about many things."

"You know what I mean."

He brushed away the Whispers and they fled, and the Shaker walked to the foot of the bed to listen. "What did you wish to talk about?"

Vivian looked at Him from under her eyelashes. "Children."

The Shaker studied her a long moment in complete silence. His eyes—she couldn't name the color, but they were somewhere between blue and green—took her in.

"Children."

"I'm completely alone," Vivian murmured. "Someday even you'll want me gone...I want someone to remember me as their mother."

"You know what my children are, what they become."

"The Whispers," Vivian said, nodding, "But, Shaker—"

"Is that what you want, Vivian? Children never really alive, never really dead?" His voice never rose, but she could hear anger in it. His eyes blazed. The Shaker whirled on His boot heel, striding to the door. "Rosa," He called. A Whisper appeared, her indistinct form that of a girl of about eight or nine. Rosa clung to the Shaker's coat, her eyes—like blue fire—staring at Vivian.

"She was born ninety-three years ago," the Shaker said. "Her mother died and now she lives here. I say *lives*…you know what she is. A shadow. She died, and this is what she became." The Shaker patted her head, and Rosa fled. A ghost. A shadow. A Whisper. "Unlike you petty mortals, she'll never move on. She'll always be here, with me." The Shaker looked coldly at her. "Is that what you want for your children?"

Vivian had tears in her eyes. "I didn't mean it that way."

He pursed His lips, and swept out of the room. Vivian hugged the pillow to her chest, trying not to cry.

She hadn't thought He'd get so angry.

Rosa came creeping back, and climbed onto the foot of the bed. "He doesn't mean it." Her voice was hollow, tremulous, as if it wasn't quite there. "He loves you," Rosa said. "He wants you to be happy."

Vivian wiped at her eyes. "And you?"

"It's not so bad," Rosa murmured, "You don't have to be scared of Death when an Immortal is your father." She smiled. Her shadowy figure flickered. "Momma moved on, and it got lonely…but He takes good care of us."

"How many are there?"

"Only sixty-two. Some Immortals have thousands." Vivian couldn't help but laugh. The number seemed so ludicrous, but she knew it was true. "Is He terribly angry with me?"

"Just a little, but more at Himself. He'll come around. Just wait." Rosa hesitated, and touched Vivian's hand. Her touch was cold, but not as icy as the Shaker's.

"Thank you," Vivian said, grasping the little Whisper's hand.

Rosa smiled again. "You're welcome, Vivian."

She stayed in the bed until He returned at almost midnight. "Stay a little late?" He asked.

She nodded, holding out her arms to Him. He put a fervency and tenderness into that night, holding her close until she could hardly breathe. Vivian's nails scratched His back and she kept saying the same thing over and over—"I love you, oh, God, oh, God, I love you."

He burned her a little, but not nearly as much as he'd used to. Vivian gently traced out previous scars, the scars that would mark her as a Shade for the rest of her life. Even if He dismissed her, she would never be able to keep it secret that she had been a Shade, a Ghost Wife.

The Shaker kissed the back of her shoulder. He would never apologize for anything—that she had learned quickly enough.

"Do you *really* want children?"

"I wouldn't have brought it up if I hadn't thought about it," she murmured. "I've been thinking about it for two years."

He drew a fiery hand up her arm, gently clasping

her shoulder. She could feel Him trying to force it to cool, for her sake. "Say it again," He whispered.

"I love you."

She winced as she made her walk home, the new burns paining her. She would have to apply a salve before she slept.

She heard it then—the keening cry coming from the living part of the city.

Someone had died.

A shadow passed over Bone Rattler Street, and the temperature fell to wintry levels. Vivian shivered, looking upward even though she knew she wouldn't see Him. The Shaker had just claimed a new occupant of Bone Rattler Street.

She heard a girl singing as she made her way back home, asking Death to spare her another year. The song never failed to make Vivian feel like an outcast, serving this Immortal everyone feared. People glared at her whenever someone died, as if she were responsible. Vivian hurried past the singing girl and through the darkness to her house, thinking of her previous conversation with the Shaker.

What have I done to them that's so devilish?

What you were made to do.

You mortals. You understand so little.

Unlike you petty mortals, she'll never move on.

He loves you. He wants you to be happy.

Vivian choked back tears as the realization hit her—he envied them. She would die. She might haunt Bone Rattler Street for a few decades, but eventually she would move on to whatever awaited her. The

Shaker and His Whispers never would. They would be trapped in that same place until Arlington ceased to be, until all people were but dust on the wind, and the world was dead.

The Shaker would always be there.

I could hardly let my wife suffer.

He loves you.

Had He loved all His wives? Had He watched each of them fade, and die, leaving Him behind in eternity?

Just inside her front door, Vivian fell to her knees, a hand over her mouth as tears rolled down her cheeks. She thought of the Shaker, adjusting His forms to suit each of His Shades, looking for what they most liked. Learning what most pleased them. Doing His best to make them happy.

How many loves had He lost to time?

"Oh my God," she whispered, "Shaker, I'm so sorry."

Winter came softly but surely on Arlington that year. Vivian wore thicker coats, and that was why it took the citizens so long to realize the obvious change in their resident Ghost Wife.

It wasn't until she attended the Christmas service and draped her coat over the pew that they saw she was pregnant.

They were stunned—only the oldest of Arlington citizens could remember the last time a Ghost Wife had been with child, and only the bravest of girls dared to ask her what it had been like to sleep with Death. They were a group, around sixteen or seventeen, and dreadfully curious.

Vivian laughed a little, shaking her head. "Dangerous," she replied, "but like nothing you could ever imagine."

The child did not stir once during the pregnancy.

The Whispers had begun to follow her on her walks, though they never left Bone Rattler Street, and they helped her with her deliveries. And the Shaker ... well, He fussed over her like a mother hen.

Christmas night He filled the room with His heat, pacing as Vivian watched Him. "I love you," she murmured, unprompted. He kissed her.

"Again."

"I love you."

A deeper kiss. "Again."

"I love you."

He forced down His temperature for her safety, pulling her close. Vivian caught a glimmer of what looked like tears in His eyes, and kissed Him softly. "Shaker," she whispered, "I love you. It's okay. I love you."

He trembled a moment but He would not cry. Vivian wondered how many years He had practiced that. She kissed His face gently. "I love you."

The Shaker held her close, without saying a word, without moving. He held her, and asked for nothing more. Vivian stroked His hair, feeling His skin cool under her touch. He smelled of ash.

When Vivian had first begun her life at Arlington she had never expected the sudden position in society she now held—both a power and a pariah. "Ah, you're the Black Coat's, then?"

"The Bone Rattler took you in?"

"Picked you right off the street? I don't know if the Devil's ever done that before..."

Those were just a few of the more memorable conversations she'd had when her reputation began to grow. She'd been surprised to learn this Immortal had no permanent name; most towns named theirs something, and that was it. Where she had grown up the Immortal had been named Muerta, and she had been merciless. She sent plagues upon her own city for amusement. Not so with Arlington.

"Bone Rattler keeps His distance. Doesn't like to be disturbed. He comes around when it's time for somebody to die...rest of the time he's off on that street with His Whispers."

When she went on her first Sunday round, half the people in Arlington were out, singing their songs about Death.

When God is gone and the Devil takes hold,
Who will have mercy on your soul?

Vivian had swallowed past her fear, remembering her own experience with this new Immortal. If He was as cruel as they seemed to believe, then He was wilier than Muerta had ever been, deceiving her first with kindness.

But He was not cruel. He never even raised His voice to her. She could ask questions, speak out of turn...she didn't understand why Arlington so hated Him.

He truly won her the day her ex-husband found her.

It was three months after she found Arlington, and

she'd not heard a word from anyone in her old life. One day he just showed up—just as she was reaching Bone Rattler Street.

"Vivian!"

She had turned, hardly daring to believe her ears. "Michael." She didn't want to see him, not now and not ever.

He stood there, Michael, and stared. Stared at her in her new black clothes, with that red umbrella over her arm and the bag full of deliveries. "Viv, what are you doing?"

She trembled.

"You don't mean to tell me," his voice was deceptively calm, "you're a Shade, now?"

"They call me a Ghost Wife," she mumbled.

"What?"

"They call me a Ghost Wife," Vivian repeated, louder. She clutched the umbrella. "I serve this city's Immortal."

Michael walked toward her, and Vivian stumbled backward. "You're...a *what*?" he hissed.

A sudden burst of cold wind enveloped them both, and Vivian felt a solid presence at her back. The Shaker's voice growled, "Step away."

Michael froze. Vivian didn't even turn to see what form the Shaker had taken for this; she knew it would be terrifying. She pressed her back against Him, taking comfort from the ice-cold body that met her touch. The Shaker—as she had already dubbed Him in her mind—stayed at her back, growling down at Michael. "You will treat her with more respect in the future."

SIDA CHEN

Michael fled. Vivian had never seen him scared of anything, but he was running from the Shaker. For a moment, she felt an immense power she had not known in years. It flooded through her with a heady sensation, and Vivian turned to embrace the Shaker, burying her face in the folds of His black coat. He warmed a moment, and put His arms around her.

"The next time he comes here," the Shaker growled, "will be the last time he leaves."

Vivian trembled, and smiled.

She learned quickly that the Shaker was impossible to understand. One day He would ask to hear children's rhymes, the next she read to Him the most complex text He could find. He pored over mortal literature and art, and withdrew into silence for hours, sometimes weeks at a time, puzzling over something.

His devotion to a subject that interested Him was insatiable—they could talk about something so much Vivian would watch her own opinion change three or four times before the conclusion.

Yet none of this was what made Vivian fall in love with the Shaker.

What made her fall in love was that He never raised His voice to her. He never threatened her. He smiled, and He gave her everything He could. He touched her softly, as if He were afraid she might break. He watched her eyes, always looking for the limit, where He would stop. He learned what she was like, inside and out, what she loved and what she feared, and He never used that knowledge to hurt her.

She had been in Arlington almost a year, when one night she pressed her lips to His forehead, and murmured—"I love you."

His eyes sparkled like stars.

Her daughter was born in June, healthy and strong with her mother's dark hair and the Shaker's blue eyes. She had breath, but no heartbeat, and her skin was cool to the touch. Vivian named her Erica, and wherever Vivian went she carried her daughter. The Whispers doted over Erica, and the Shaker's eyes shone with something like pride and love whenever He looked at her.

She grew rapidly, perhaps a little faster than a child should. Vivian never asked for a second child; she was devoted to Erica with her heart and soul. Her daughter had the promise of becoming a beautiful young woman.

The Shaker began to ask for Vivian's presence more frequently. Often she spent entire nights on Bone Rattler Street.

He still begged her to say she loved Him again and again.

Vivian didn't know what was going on, why He was so insistent, but she indulged Him as best she could between raising her daughter and making her deliveries. He had become...demanding.

He made love to her more fiercely, and yet also more carefully. He kissed her as if it might be His last chance. Vivian didn't understand, but a slow dread began to form in the back of her mind.

Was this the last burst before He grew weary of her,

before He dismissed her? Or did He know something she didn't?

She wouldn't find out until Erica was eight.

Twelve years Vivian had lived as the Ghost Wife of Arlington. Twelve long, demanding, painful and beautiful years—a blink of an eye to the Shaker.

The Shaker had not changed His form much since Erica's birth—minor adjustments, creating an illusion of age as Vivian passed birthday after birthday. He was tender and yet unyielding, everything He had ever been.

Vivian loved Him, and nursed the acceptance that one day He would turn away from her. He may have resembled a mortal man, but He was something more, something untamed and unreachable, an ocean of secrets she could never hope to fathom. All she had was His touch, her daughter, and her scars.

But after Erica's eighth birthday, Vivian felt the first signs.

It started as a pain. It only came every so often, but gradually it grew in frequency and importance. She sought out doctors, and they did their best to treat her, but there was nothing they could do. The Sickness was inside her, growing and spreading.

The Sickness was new in those days, and it baffled doctors and Immortals alike. Though it did not touch the Immortals themselves, it claimed many of their servants. It was quiet, and lethal in its patience, preying upon mortals with the advantage of time.

The one person Vivian dared hope could help her was the Shaker. "Isn't there anything you can do?" she asked, "Just so I can see my daughter grow up."

She had never seen a more grief-stricken look on the Shaker's face as He shook His head. "Some things," He whispered, "are out of my hands."

Vivian stared at Him. So. This was it.

She did her best not to hint at it to her daughter, teaching Erica her work, and everything she thought her daughter would need to know. She didn't know how much time she had, only that the pain in her was growing beyond her control. It ate at her day and night, consuming her from the inside out.

The Shaker looked at her with grief. He did His best to ease her suffering, but she knew there would come a time when the one thing He could do for her would be to take the breath from her lungs. On the nights she came to Bone Rattler Street, He held her and tried to ease her pain until she slept.

She carried on, and the Shaker watched her die, as He had watched a hundred other Ghost Wives die, with as much pain.

He had never liked being helpless.

Erica knew soon enough. Vivian managed to hold out until she was ten, but by then she could barely walk. She used a cane, and the people of Arlington watched and waited, wondering when the Shaker would end this.

Erica was the one who begged Him to do it.

The girl had grown up walking side by side with Death. She had no fear of what she asked; she had the knowledge her father would never die, and her mother was in so much pain.

It was a summer's night when He did. He made the night warm, and left Bone Rattler Street for the first time in over a century. The streets emptied before

Him as He walked toward Vivian's home, His black coat making Him a shadow. The Whispers followed, making His path darker.

Vivian lay in bed, asleep. She was skeletal, and her lovely hair lay lank and colorless against the pillow. Her dark eyes had sunk into her skull. Her hands lay like limp spiders on the bed.

The Shaker gazed at her, His face a mask. He saw in Vivian everyone He had watched fade away and die. A wiser creature would have stopped growing attached, would have kept His distance...perhaps even grown cruel. But the Shaker was not a wiser creature—He was, He supposed, a hopeless fool.

He bent, kissing Vivian's forehead. Then He laid His hand over her heart, and coaxed out a light. It was a small light, pulsing softly with warmth. The Whispers, huddled in the corners of Vivian's room, fell silent as He pulled that light to His own breast, cradling it like a fragile child.

Vivian ceased to breathe, and what little color had been left in her face drained away. The Shaker gazed a moment at her body, and turned away, the light cupped in His palm. Erica, in her little white nightgown, followed her Immortal father in silence among the Whispers, who muttered about her.

They made a solemn procession through the summer night. At the head, the tall figure of the Shaker, with a little light cupped in His hands. Behind Him, a cloud of Whispers, and at the back, a young girl in a white nightgown. A few brave souls in Arlington watched it, and they heard a voice like Vivian's weaving through the night air.

It was a familiar song, of death coming to claim the

soul, but carried a fresh chill with Vivian's voice. The people of Arlington fastened their windows against it, and shivered in the new cold of the night.

The next morning, Bone Rattler Street was silent. The Shaker stayed in His house, unseen. The Whispers kept to the shadows and made not a sound. The ghosts did not move from their hiding places.

The sun did not pierce the gloom.

In a small black dress, Erica made her way back to her mother's house.

There would be no more Ghost Wife for quite some time.

For now, there would be only the Shade, the Devil's Daughter of Arlington. The girl with breath, but no heartbeat—the girl whose skin was never warm, the girl with hair as dark as her mother's and eyes as pale as her father's. She moved in silence, like a shadow, the Whispers ever at her heels.

She carried on her arm a red umbrella.

Journey for a New Artist

BY LARRY ELMORE

Leonard Elmore has been creating fantasy and science fiction art for over 40 years. After receiving a BFA degree from Western Kentucky, he married Betty Clemons and was drafted into the Army almost at the same time. In the 1970s he began freelancing and was published in a few magazines, including Heavy Metal and National Lampoon. In 1987 he was contacted by TSR Inc., the company that produced the role-playing game Dungeons & Dragons, and he worked there from 1981 to 1987. While at TSR, he helped set the standards for gaming art in the role-playing genre. Besides creating covers for Dungeons & Dragons, AD&D, Star Frontiers and other gaming books, he may be best known for his work with the world of Dragonlance. Since 1987 he has worked as a freelance illustrator, creating covers for comics, computer games, magazines, fantasy and science fiction books and projects too numerous to list.

For the last five years he has been creating paintings for collectors and fans around the world. Larry has now opened his original commission section on his website, where he creates a complete concept drawing that lets collectors and fans choose concept drawings that they would like to purchase as finished paintings. These new paintings are, technique-wise, the best paintings he has ever created.

Journey for a New Artist

Working toward becoming a professional illustrator is like taking a journey without a map. There is no GPS to plot your course. It may be a long, rocky, difficult journey, or you may have an easier path to follow, because it is your personal journey.

For many occupations there is a set course to follow: go to college, get a degree, make good grades, then apply to companies for jobs in your appropriate field. But lately, it seems that this old tried-and-true approach is becoming even more difficult. There has never been a set path for creative people such as artists, musicians, writers, actors and all occupations that would be included in the Arts.

I can only talk about my personal journey that has led me to this point in my life/career. I always refer to my *career* and my *life* as one and the same. My life is my art; there is no separating the two. I have spoken to many groups of people during my career on this topic and I will go over a few points that I feel are important, which may help a young artist/illustrator on his journey.

Try to educate yourself in your field. Go to college or a good art school, if you can afford it. Usually this opportunity comes when you are young, and because of your youth, you can more easily absorb the basics in your field and get a good foundation of art in general. Going to school at this time of your life does one more thing besides giving the obvious education: it buys more time for your "eye" to mature. You will learn to see your art more objectively and become a much more efficient self-critic. This helps you grow.

Drawing is the foundation. Good drawing skills are a *must*. For example, if you start a painting and your drawing is weak, your painting will be weak. It is much more difficult and time-consuming to redraw or correct a drawing with paint. I cannot emphasize it enough: *never* stop drawing.

Learn perspective. If your work is representational or realistic, then you must understand perspective. You can exaggerate perspective for certain effects, but the foundation of your exaggerated perspective must be correct. Everything you draw, every object is in perspective. Don't guess at perspective, learn it.

Learn to see. This applies to objects, shapes and colors.

I had a lot of problems when I went from drawing an object to painting an object. I made the same mistakes that a lot of young artists make: I tried to color a drawing. My thought process was almost the same as coloring a line drawing in a coloring book. I was thinking symbolically. Since then, I have taken classes in color theory and learned by reading and observing other artists' work, but what I have found that has taught me the most is learning to *see*.

When I look at a real landscape, I try to see the real colors and values in nature, not the symbolic colors that are taught to us from the first grade up. I try to mix and match the colors and values in my mind when I am looking at that real landscape. Which different paints would I mix for those distant pine trees? A touch of green, raw umber, ochre, white, blue, purple? There lies the challenge, and it is so much fun.

Painting from life, out in the field or in an enclosed environment, is a wonderful way to learn to see, and learn to see real colors and values. We have been trained during most of our young lives to think of shapes and colors symbolically. A good example is, "the sky is blue, the clouds are white, the grass is green, and then just add black to make the shadows." That is so wrong. Watch a child draw a chair; it is usually in the shape of an "h," a tree is two parallel lines with fluffy cotton-candy leaves around the top, and a shoe is always drawn in profile. Believe me, these symbols carry right into your adult lives.

So, learn to see. You will soon learn that what at first looks like totally random patterns and shapes in trees, water, rocks, clouds and folds of clothing are actually repetitious patterns with slight variations. They are rhythms, consisting of musical notes slightly rearranged to play different melodies, all within the same song. Nature works that way.

I used to think of all my tubes of paints by color names, like a box of perhaps thirty-two crayons. Later I started thinking of my tubes of paint as musical tones that help compose an overall melody, and now I think of them as tastes or flavors and I am cooking up some meal that will taste good to me. Different colors, hues and values have different flavors. So now

I cook without using a recipe. As my mother and grandmother would say, I'm "cooking from scratch." This helps keep me from thinking of colors with names, all placed neatly in the box of crayons. Real life doesn't work that way, you can't find a box that all the colors could fit into, and, on top of that, we don't even have names for all the colors that are possible!

Everything that I have said so far is to help you become a better artist, so you can compete with everyone out there, and today the world is much smaller. Now you are competing with artists around the world. You have to be good. I am not saying you must paint or draw exactly like some other professional artist, and you shouldn't; besides, it is basically impossible to beat another man at his own game. As humans, we are all unique; we all have different fingerprints, and your creative fingerprint is inside you.

Learn, study, do your best and you will see your creative fingerprint emerge. You may be influenced by many artists, but let all those influences flow through you, filter through you, and then let your art be *you*. You are the magic ingredient, your style.

When I teach art classes, I have had students tell me that I am giving away all my secrets. But I have no secrets to give; there is no magic formula. The lessons I try to teach my students are things that they should learn, they should know, the basic knowledge to help them become an artist/illustrator. The *secret* ingredient is *you*. It is how you take all your knowledge of art, how you process it and interpret it and then let it flow through you. Then, when you paint or draw, your fingerprint will be all over it.

317

If you become a freelance illustrator, you must be self-confident. Believe in your art. A freelance artist lives on a bubble of self-confidence. Beneath that bubble may rest a dark pit of depression.

I think most freelancers have been in that dark pit once or twice. Most creative people have been there. I think it is because we are putting a bit of ourselves out there in the world to be admired, ridiculed and sometimes walked on. You have to grow a thick skin. If not, you will bleed a lot. I always say, "Thank God that everyone has different tastes in all the arts; if not, then there would be only one artist, one musician, one writer, and the world would be a boring place." So if your art is good, there will be people out there who will enjoy it.

The problem is getting your work out where it can be seen. You have to be a businessman also. You must learn how to market yourself. Learn about self-printing, especially digital printing, because in most cases, you can print in smaller quantities, making it less expensive. Some examples could be sketchbooks, prints of your art, stickers, posters—whatever way you can think of to get your art out there so people can see it and possibly purchase it.

Go to conventions; a convention is a great place for people to see your art and purchase your art. I know artists who have built a huge fan base strictly by showing and selling their art at conventions; eventually, major publishers saw their work and published the artists nationally for the first time. Also, at conventions you have the opportunity to meet art directors from many different companies. Try to target publishers/companies that publish products for which your art may be suitable.

You must be visible, and now it is easier than ever for an artist to become more visible in the world. Use the Internet; build a website; use Facebook, Twitter, any and all of the social outlets on the Internet, even YouTube.

Use any outlet that will keep your art and your name out there. Remember, the only person who truly cares about your success or failure as an artist/illustrator is *you*. The only person who will sacrifice, push, work, dig, stay up all night working hard long hours is *you*. That is a hard thing to truly understand sometimes, but the bottom line is that *you* are responsible for your career, because *no* one else really cares as much as *you*.

Being an artist/illustrator will not be a life of smooth sailing on a calm sea; there will be rough waves, always. So you have to be strong.

Think of the typical professional football player. The average player doesn't make millions, like the superstars, but that average player works just as hard. They practice being strong and tough, because part of their job description is being knocked down over and over, just to win a single game, and this is how it works for their whole career. The average career is not that long.

I feel that I am in a game, and that game is my life as an artist. It is full of hard knocks, but as long as I stand back up and keep playing, continue making a living from my art until I die, then I will win the whole damn game!

My personal goal is to draw and paint all my life. Hopefully my last painting before I die will be a relatively good painting because I spent my lifetime learning and improving my skills. The lifelong challenge for me, which keeps me so excited about art, is simple: Give one hundred percent and make the next painting a good one and better than the last.

Everything
You Have Seen

written by

Alisa Alering

illustrated by

KARSEN SLATER

ABOUT THE AUTHOR

Alisa Alering was born and raised in the Appalachian Mountains of Pennsylvania, where she ran around barefoot and talked to trees. When not riding her pony, she could be found on the floor of her grandparents' log cabin, rereading The Green Fairy Book.

On trips to town for more horse feed, she was introduced to the glories of the public library. She brought her books home and gobbled them greedily. Luckily, in her family, reading at the dinner table was not only permitted but encouraged. She also mastered the skill of reading on horseback during long trail rides.

After working as a llama handler, barista, lab rat, and life model, her fond memories of the library caused her to give up her job in public television and move to Indiana to study the intricate art of library science. She became a librarian.

Her Writers of the Future win is her first professional sale, but she has since sold two more stories, one to Flash Fiction Online, *and another to* Clockwork Phoenix IV.

She contributes to the "Writer's Room" column in Waylines *magazine.*

ABOUT THE ILLUSTRATOR

Karsen Slater has been fascinated by the supernatural since she was a child. Drawing inspiration from stories of aliens and AIs, dragons and demons, and everyday kids with extraordinary powers, she began answering the call to create her own magical monsters through art. Gradually, her passion for the nonhuman world expanded to a love for worldbuilding, and throughout her youth she both wrote and illustrated her own stories.

Karsen grew up in Glendora, California. She took her first art class in high school and soon enrolled in a program for young artists called Ryman Arts. From there she attended Laguna College of Art & Design for a degree in illustration and animation, where she gained a strong foundation in drawing and painting before learning skills in character design and concept art. She still enjoys drawing creatures and looks forward to developing her ideas into more of her own stories in the future.

Everything
You Have Seen

I went outside to get away from Chung-hee.

The snow in the courtyard was coming down in thick flakes, making that special kind of silence like the whole world has been wrapped in a cotton *bojagi* cloth and put away for the night. I thought at first that the guns had stopped. Then a flash lit the sky over our empty chicken coop. The boom traveled through the snowy ground, up my legs and spine and into my skull.

Before the war, Chung-hee and I were friends. My brother is two years older than me, but he'd never treated me like an insignificant little sister. He'd carried me home from school on the handles of his bicycle, weaving in between the traffic and the electric poles. In the summers, we roamed the hills beyond the city, picking mushrooms and hunting crayfish in the stream that splashed out of the mountains beyond the Parks' farm.

The American soldiers had retreated to a position in the hills east of town, digging into the forest between the mountains and the sea. Their distant guns picked up speed. The shelling was worse at night. Mother would get angry with me for being outside. I turned back toward the house, when I heard a shuffling noise from inside the chicken coop, like a bird shifting from foot to foot. The chickens had flown off when the artillery began, and four weeks later they still refused to rest in their coop. Now they took their chances in the trees, picked off every night by quick-climbing weasels and rats.

I moved toward the coop, imagining how good chicken would taste, chicken soup with garlic and chilies, chicken with rice. I paused before the door of the dark shed. I didn't want to scare the chicken, if one had returned. My belly growled out loud, and the bird shot out into the night sky, its heavy body skimming so close to my head that its flapping wings lifted my hair. I jumped back, stumbling over clods of frozen mud. That bird had been too fierce and fast for a chicken, and it had smelled dark and bloody, like old meat.

Worse, something was still inside the shed. I could hear it moving around. It knocked into the walls, and a loose board clattered as it fell.

I stood still, my eyes fixed on the shed's dark doorway. How many were there? I wondered.

A boy walked out of the shed.

He was a little taller than me, and skinny. I thought he must be about eleven years old, the same as me. A bomb burst overhead, lighting up the courtyard, and I saw hair the color of red-bean porridge. He had pale skin and a narrow face. He was *waegukin,* just like the soldiers.

The boy stepped toward me. He wore a loose shirt and pants made of matching dark cloth with a light-colored print. His breath steamed in the cold air.

Snowflakes melted where they landed on his bare head. "Who—" he said, then stopped. He looked around as if the sound of his own voice had surprised him. I thought he might be a *gwishin,* but ghosts aren't supposed to have any legs. I could see the shape of the boy's legs through his thin trousers, right down to his bare toes curled in the snow.

He had to be real, but I couldn't imagine what he was doing here.

"How did you get in the chicken coop?" I asked.

He said something, but I didn't understand. He talked louder, and I cut my hand across my neck to tell him to be quiet. The boy balled his hands into fists in front of him. I thought he was going to hit me. His face scrunched up, and his upper lip thrust over the lower one like that of a bad-tempered turtle. Frustrated, he opened and closed his hands, like Mother pulling dough to make knife-cut noodles.

Dim starlight reflected off the snow, bright enough that I could see something beginning to grow in the space between his hands. He stared at me, eyes furious and urgent as his hands worked, trying to communicate. The air between his palms darkened, whirled into a heavy smudge that grew and rebounded as it bounced between his palms. The sphere of thickened air flashed with one color after another, as if he were trying them on, like a ball rolling through paint.

I stepped back, holding my hand over my mouth. The boy looked down. He seemed just as surprised as I was. The little ball of darkened air hung between his hands as if it were suspended from a string. I lifted my arm. The floating thing looked solid. I tried to touch it.

KARSEN SLATER

Just as my finger reached the dough, Mother shouted my name. She stood in the doorway of the house with my baby brother in her arms, calling me to come in. I had to go. I looked back at the boy's hands just in time to see the colored shape collapse into itself, like a house falling down.

The next morning, I helped Mother with the laundry. She had the radio on and, while I broke up boards to make firewood, we heard the grave schoolteacher voice saying that more Chinese troops had crossed the border from the north, and the Americans were retreating down the coast to Wonsan, where their ships waited to take them to safety. I wondered who would take us to safety. The fighting outside our city might stop, but the advancing Chinese troops were just as dangerous.

I held the baby, tickling his angry face while Mother beat the cloth with a paddle. We hung the clothes on the southern side of the house and I carried the wash water around back. A skinny black hen sat atop the broken tiles of the outhouse, poking her beak into her feathers. I lunged for her, but she flapped up into a tree with a squawk. Her feathers scattered on the ground where the morning sun was melting last night's snow.

I looked around the courtyard, but there was no sign of Chung-hee. *Good*. I stuck my head in the door of the chicken coop and called softly. For a moment, I thought I must have imagined the *waegukin* boy, but as I stood, my eyes adjusted. In the darkest corner, the boy had dug a nest in the musty straw and burrowed down as deep as he could. Close up, I saw that his blue shirt and pants were patterned with white-sailed boats.

I didn't know what he was doing here, but looking down at his bony arms and pale skin, tinged purple from the cold, I could see that he wasn't dangerous. I felt bad for him. He had to be scared to be alone in a place that was so strange, where he couldn't talk to anyone, and no one looked like him. What if Chung-hee found him hiding here?

I crouched beside him, and he bolted awake. I laid my hand on his arm to let him know it was okay. I told him my name, Min-hee, and pointed to my chest. I asked his name, but when I said it back wrong, he pushed his mouth into that funny pout. I decided I would call him Turtle. Even though I could still see his legs, I pinched him to make sure he was really alive. He yelled and hit my hand away. I shushed him and moved my hands as if I were stretching noodle dough, telling him to speak that way.

Just like last night, the air thickened and Turtle shaped it between his palms. His fingers pulled the air, kneading the darkness until it was smooth and pliable, stretching and working until it made a picture. The first images were wobbly, but the more he worked the better they got. He showed me a long brown field full of grain, a funny yellow house with a pointed roof, a raised mattress with a blue blanket, a black and white dog, a red brick building with the American flag, pictures of himself going to school, carrying books.

When he finished, the last image hung in the air,

alive but undisturbed, like a sleeping mouse in its nest. Then he put his hands together as if he were clapping. The picture, the thing that slept, collapsed in on itself and was gone.

I watched carefully, copying the way he'd worked his fingers. I wanted to talk to him, too. My best friend, Hye-su, had gone away at the start of the war, and I felt lonely. I wanted to show him my life, have him understand me. But it didn't work for me.

In the middle of the day I sneaked back into the house for food. I put a handful of millet in a bowl with a few frostbitten leaves of cabbage, then poured hot water over it all, and took it out to the boy. He drank, but made an awful face as his teeth squeaked on the last limp cabbage leaf. I couldn't believe it. I had stolen from my own family, and he didn't feel grateful.

I kicked straw over him and yelled, "What do you think you will eat instead?"

Maybe he couldn't understand my words, but he knew what I meant. He got angry right back, shoved out that turtle lip of his and worked his hands, showing me all kinds of things: roast chickens with crackling skin, steaming bowls of porridge, plates heaped with hot, boiled corn.

My stomach growled, and I couldn't help myself. I reached between his hands and grabbed an ear of yellow corn. It came away in my grasp, hot and dripping with juice. I was so astonished I dropped it in the dirt of the shed. The smell filled my head—so delicious, so savory—until I felt dizzy. I snatched the corn up from the dirt, and without bothering to wipe it off, bit into the bursting kernels. The boy watched, his sky eyes wide. It crunched between my teeth, and juice ran down my chin. I passed it to the boy, and he bit into it with a groan.

His hands flew with fury, whirling up food as fast as he could think it: round dumplings swimming in gravy, a pan of cooked berries wrapped in a flaky crust, meat patties and puffy circles of dough covered in sugar. I picked out each dish as it appeared and set it aside until Turtle had made everything he wanted, then we dove in and ate and ate and ate. Some tastes were strange to me, but I couldn't remember the last time I had eaten so much food. I ate until I felt as if I couldn't breathe.

After that, I lay back in the straw, and I didn't care that I couldn't make my own stories. Turtle told me about his family. He showed me a woman with dark-gold hair, the color of beech leaves in winter. She wore a flowered apron and had pink cheeks. She wasn't very pretty, but she smiled nicely, very happy. I thought she must be his mother.

I asked about his father. I cleared away the straw, and with my finger drew a picture of a man in the loose dust of the chicken shed. He tried to show me, but the picture wouldn't come. I could see something flickering there between his hands, thickening like a mist, but it wouldn't form. I shrugged, and smiled to tell him it was okay.

I spent the rest of the day with Turtle. The coop sheltered us from the biting wind, and the sun shone between its loose slats. We burrowed down into the straw, watching the pictures Turtle made and eating snacks he conjured. This was the happiest day I had spent since Father went away. Turtle acted strange, but he was good company.

Later that night, when Chung-hee snatched food out of my bowl as he did every night, I didn't even mind. At last, I stretched out my bedroll on the warm floor and went to sleep happy, my stomach full.

But in the middle of the night I woke, stomach screaming with hunger. It felt as if an angry beast were in my stomach, trying to claw its way out. While I slept, all the boy's food had turned to nothing. I turned over on my blankets, trying to ignore the pains. In the black night outside, guns started up again, louder and closer than ever before.

The next morning, smoke billowed up into the sky above the radio tower on the west side of town. Mother was angry because Chung-hee had disappeared again. Little brother wailed, beating his thin arms against Mother's chest. Mother opened a tin she had hidden under a loose board and took out a small hairclip with a bright stone at the top. She told me, "Take this to Mr. Lee and trade it for medicine for the baby."

The smoke had grown thicker as I crept closer to the center of town. I covered my mouth, breathing through my fingers. The doors of buildings stood open, their windows blown out, and the glass scattered in the street. The walls of the Yuwon sock factory had collapsed, but the knitting machines were lined up inside, still waiting for girls in their aprons to come stand behind them.

When I reached Mr. Lee's, the windows of the shop had been smashed. Inside, the shelves were empty and broken. I banged on the shutters, trying to wake him. An old woman came by, collecting broken bricks in a bucket. She said, "The Lees were robbed last night. At dawn they took the last of their stock and fled."

"Where?"

"South, I think. Mrs. Lee has family there," she said. She picked up another brick and walked on.

I retraced my steps. A jeep roared through the street, soldiers standing in the backseat. I jumped into the ditch, pressing myself against the crumpled walls, hoping I wouldn't be seen. I held onto Mother's hairclip so tightly that the stone hurt my hand. I waited until the motor died away and was just about to climb back onto the road when a girl crossed the street in front of me, running fast, her long braids bouncing against her back.

She ran toward the ruined sock factory, tears streaming down her frightened face. After her came a pack of boys, their heavy shoes echoing on the empty street. The boy in the lead was Dong-sun, the butcher's son.

I slid back down into the ditch. The rest of the boys, wearing castoff soldier's clothing, shouted and shoved each other as they ran, chasing after the girl as if she were a dog. Chung-hee trotted in the middle of the pack, the backs of his bare ears showing red in the cold. They herded the girl into the alley. Dong-sun grabbed her braid, yanking her to a stop. She stumbled in the dirt, and the boys closed in around her.

I knew then that Chung-hee had left us. He had

broken off from the world where Mother and I still lived as a family. The things we did here in this world, the rules we followed, meant nothing to Chung-hee. He and the other boys had created their own world out of the bombs falling, the bullets exploding, the tanks rolling. They had found and filled a new space.

When I returned, Mother worked in the storehouse, scooping out the last of the cooking oil. I gave her the hairclip and told her that the Lees had closed their shop and moved away. I didn't tell her the rest. The radio was on again, the serious voice reading out the missing-persons messages. Mother's face fell. We had received only one letter from Father since he joined the army, and that had been six months ago. I sometimes thought Mother was like the chickens—frightened by the guns, but afraid to move too far from the place she knew. After all, if we left, how would Father know where to find us?

I played with little brother, letting him grab my hair and pull it with his fists. It was late afternoon before I could get back to the chicken coop.

Turtle was ill. His face was pink, full of hot blood. He wouldn't talk to me, only lay there moaning.

I thought our food must not have been good for him. I was used to the weevils and the old stale taste of the cabbage. His body must not have liked it. He sweated, even as his breath made clouds of steam in the cold. I heaped straw around him. He twisted in his makeshift bed, throwing off the straw, pieces clinging in his hair. He opened his hands, and the pictures flowed in a jumble. People, animals, buildings, were all mixed up—a dog with a wagon wheel for hind legs, a flower growing out of a kettle.

I brought him another blanket, an old one that used to be Chung-hee's. I worried that Turtle would die. I pushed him back on the ground, and tucked the blanket around him. Still he shook and moaned. He cried out in his strange voice and I worried that someone would hear. I slid under the blanket beside him, and pretended that he was Chung-hee, back when we were friends. Chung-hee before the war when Father was with us and the radio played songs that Mother sang to as she sewed and we played games and thought alike and loved each other.

Turtle fell asleep, clenching the blanket. Mother was distracted, worried about Father and Chung-hee, hands full with the baby, but she would notice if I stayed away all night. I slid from under the blanket and left Turtle sleeping in the empty chicken coop.

The next morning, Turtle was gone. The straw was patted down like an animal's nest, leaving the shape of where he had laid in the night.

Outside the chicken house, yesterday's half-melted snow had frozen too hard to leave any footprints. I raced out the courtyard gate and looked up and down the empty street. Had Chung-hee found Turtle sleeping in our shed? I told myself Chung-hee wouldn't have hurt him.

A strong gust of wind bit through my sweater, blowing away the gray clouds and the recent snows. The gate of Hye-su's house next door banged back against the courtyard wall. My heart jumped with relief. That gate had been latched ever since Hye-su and her family had packed up and headed for the train station at the end of summer. But now it was loose. Someone had been inside.

I ran through the gate. Hye-su's courtyard was exactly the way I remembered. One small window was broken. Snow piled in the north-facing corners and where it had blown off the roof. I wondered why Turtle had come here, why he hadn't stayed safe and warm in our chicken coop.

A shadow moved inside Hye-su's house, passing quickly in front of the window.

I stepped closer. "Turtle?" I whispered.

A hand shot out of the doorway and grabbed my arm. I screamed, and the hand spun me around.

"What are you doing sneaking around here?" Chung-hee demanded.

I stared at my big brother. I didn't know what he was doing in Hye-su's old house, but I knew he was up to no good. I wished I could tell him about Turtle; Chung-hee would be able to help me search faster. He would know more places where a boy might hide.

"I know you have a boyfriend," he said. He tightened his grip on my arm, twisting the skin under my sweater. His eyes were so brown and hard, like flat river stones faraway under the water. I wanted to tell my brother that he wasn't alone. That everything he had seen, I had seen, too.

"I didn't think you were old enough." Chung-hee's harsh black eyebrows bristled together, like angry caterpillars. "But now that you are, you can help put rice in our bowls."

I remembered the girl in the alley by the sock factory. I jerked my arm back, and shoved Chung-hee hard in the chest.

He laughed in my face, his mouth wide open. Even his breath had changed. It was a man's breath, a hot stinky blast of smoke and old food. He twisted my arm behind my back. "You're as bony as a crow, Min-hee. But you're young, and that counts for something."

I was crying. I couldn't understand what had become of my brother. I spat in his face.

Chung-hee's fist knocked me in the jaw.

I fell, and he leaned over me, ready to hit me again. He was breathing hard, his face red and ugly.

A plane buzzed over the mountains north of us, followed by a dull thud. There was a low whistle from the street, and Dong-sun, the butcher's son, poked his head over the wall. "Let's go," he called to Chung-hee.

My brother turned his back on me and ran after Dong-sun.

I stood. My mouth was full of blood and snot, and one of my front teeth felt loose. A shell exploded a few houses away, rattling the ground. I thought of Turtle wandering in his bare feet, alone, unable to ask or explain. I ran out of Hye-su's yard, calling his name.

I found Turtle on the edge of town where walled houses gave way to open fields and scattered farms bordered by the mountains. I had no idea how he had gotten there. Turtle, in his flimsy shirt and pants, with Chung-hee's blanket wrapped around him, was staring off over the rocky, snow-covered fields. His face was no longer flushed with fever, but his eyes glowed with bright determination, like a boy on the day of an important exam.

As soon as he saw me, his hands flew into action, kneading the air. Images flickered between his hands like the propeller on a plane, too fast to see any single blade.

"Slow down," I said. "Just do one at a time." I put my hand on his shoulder.

I knew he couldn't understand me, but the tone of my voice must have reached him. He breathed out, long and hard. Then, with his hands, he stretched and pulled, and landscapes unrolled between his palms. Turtle's eyes were intent on me, urgent. There were no cornfields or big blue skies. No red-painted barns or black and white cows. Just one picture after another of winter woods, and mud, and broken trees. At first I didn't recognize them.

"Wait," I said. "Go back." There had been something familiar in the last scene.

I waved my hand in a circle, like a clock circling backward.

He shuffled the scenes between his hands.

"Stop!"

He held the picture still. The trees were broken, the ground churned into deep, hardened ruts. It took me time to recognize it because it had changed so much. But I did know it. It was the woods near the Parks' farm.

We headed west out of town, toward the granite mountains. The winter sun glowed a pale yellow that heated my skin under my scratchy sweater as we jogged along the deserted streets. We crossed the railroad tracks and traveled out into the open country.

The Parks' farm lay in the next valley over. The mountains fed a stream that watered their pumpkin fields and flowed all the way down to the sea thirty miles away. We crossed the open fields, trampling the dried grasses. Blood surged into my face where Chung-hee had hit me, swelling my lip.

Ahead, fog swirled out of a thick forest of pines. I stopped at the edge of the woods and turned to the boy. I dialed my hand forward, telling him to show me the next picture. He showed me a stream, rushing with water. A slab of granite, glazed with ice, rose above the current.

I knew that rock. In the summer we dove from its flat top, splashing into the clear, cold pool. Its surface was pocked with holes all over, like the spots on a frog's back. The holes filled with water when it rained and seemed to stare up like a hundred liquid eyes.

I tried to remember the way to the rock. I had only been to the river in summer. It was all so different now. Mist filled the woods, and I didn't want to step inside. I wondered why Turtle wanted so badly to come here and how he knew what it looked like.

We climbed up the rocky spine of a ridge and stumbled down the other side, through the splintered, broken trunks of what used to be a grove of beautiful, tall birch trees. The armies had crossed back and forth over these hills for weeks and had left behind a trail of ruined equipment—shredded tires, ragged camouflage nets, even a tank sitting lopsided in deep, churned ruts.

Though he must have been weak from his fever and at least as hungry as I was, Turtle kept pace. Halfway down, the spring that fed the stream burst from a cleft in the granite, and we followed the spill of its waters to the bottom of the valley.

We walked downstream, picking our way over the slick rocks. Up ahead, the stream churned through a narrow channel, then widened and slowed. A tall, strong pine grew beside the pool, its drooping branches brushing the flat top of a granite boulder. The stream had carved away the bank beneath, leaving the mottled red slab to stretch out over the calm, deep pool.

Turtle came forward and clutched my arm, looking past me at the rock as if he were afraid.

I remembered what the old people said about the rock, that a spirit lived inside it, looking out at the world through its hundred eyes. Once, Hye-su, Chung-hee, and I and some others had come to the stream to swim, and had found an orange and a handful of rice on top of the rock, left as an offering to the spirit.

Bumps stood out on Turtle's thin wrists. Under Chung-hee's blanket, he shook from the cold. His look said that he didn't know any more about what was going on than I did.

I let go of Turtle's hand and climbed up on the rock. And stopped. A dead man slumped against the other side. His still arms were wrapped around his middle, his green soldier's uniform soaked through with blood. The blood was on his sleeves, on his bare hands, on his trousers, and on the stones and snow below him. It was old blood, brown and congealed.

His soldier's helmet lay on the ground beside him, and his head drooped loose on his neck. The dead man's hair was the same color as Turtle's, the same shade of red-bean porridge.

Turtle shouted "Pa!" and ran toward the man, dropping Chung-hee's blanket on the snowy ground.

I had no idea how Turtle had appeared in my courtyard three nights ago, or what had pulled him out of his bed an ocean away and led him to his father's body here in the blasted forest, but it wasn't natural.

"We should go," I said.

Turtle didn't move.

The man on the ground opened his eyes.

Very slowly, the soldier raised his head and settled it back upright on his neck. His skin was gray-white and his lips blue. But his eyes focused on Turtle. There was no doubt that he recognized his son.

The man's mouth moved, and he tried to smile.

The soldier unfolded his arms. It was no good, I could see that at once. He must have been in so much pain. When his arms moved away from his body, I saw the hole torn in his side. I could see right through his bloody uniform, right through his ragged skin to the shiny red, white, and black bloody insides of him. But he stretched his arms wider.

Turtle stepped toward him, then stopped and turned back to me. Turtle's eyes met mine, and he pressed both hands flat against his chest.

Then Turtle went to his father, knelt, and stepped between his outstretched hands.

The soldier folded his arms around Turtle, pulling him into an embrace. Before I had a chance to say good-bye, the edges of the boy rolled up and he collapsed from the inside like a building falling in on itself.

The soldier's arms dropped onto his chest, limp and lifeless. His head lolled against the rough granite. The stream rushed past, seeking the sea, the spray licking the toes of the dead man's boots, casting them with ice. There was no trace of Turtle. He had gone, evaporated like the food in my stomach.

I dropped down on the riverbank in the snow, and cried into the neck of my sweater. Turtle was gone, and I was alone again. My own world that I had thought solid and indivisible, the world where Father sat at the head of the table, and Mother sang songs from the radio, and Chung-hee carried me on his bike, had disappeared forever. There was no longer any trace of the family we had been, no more than there was a piece of Turtle's sail-patterned shirt or his red-porridge hair left behind on the trampled snow in front of me.

The wet tracks of my tears stung my face with cold. It was getting dark under the trees, and the forest no longer held anything for me. I stood, and my eyes caught a fleck of white atop the rock, near the soldier's open, staring eyes. A cigarette, the edges pink with blood. The wet paper had disintegrated and flakes of loose tobacco scattered across the stone, falling damply into the hundred pools.

I wrapped Chung-hee's blanket tighter around my shoulders. The world I had always known had been shattered like a late winter pumpkin on the Parks' farm, but there were other worlds: Turtle had come from a different world, far away on the other side of the ocean. And maybe he had been helped by the ancient world of *gwishin,* demons,

341

and hungry-mouthed spirits that dwell in rock. There were ways to get from one world to another. I started back up the hill, pushing hard through the deep snow.

Stars shone in the twilit sky when I arrived on our street. I could just make out the shapes of the chicken coop and the outhouse, our roof, and a withered curl of smoke rising from the *ondol* against the darker trees behind.

Inside, Mother argued with Chung-hee. She had the baby on her back and held the handle of a pot with a folded rag, scolding him to save some food for me. He laughed and snatched the pot from her hand, filling his bowl to the brim. I had thought about it on the long walk back. Why should people like my brother be the only ones who could create a new world and escape into it? The *waegukin* army had boats farther down the coast, and a new world at the end of them. I didn't have to stay in this broken world, picking among the scattered seeds.

"It doesn't matter," I said, pushing into the room. "We're going to meet the boats at Wonsan."

Chung-hee acted as if I hadn't spoken. Setting his bowl on the table, he shrugged out of his soldier's coat and tossed it at Mother. She sat down obediently to fix the tear in the shoulder. She threaded a needle, and with her head bent over the rough wool, said, "If we went away, your father would never find us. Our whole family would become missing persons."

"If we stay, he won't find us either," I argued. "Are you the same wife that he left? Am I the same daughter? What will we be like in another six months?"

I didn't mention Chung-hee, but Mother's eyes darted in his direction. She tied off the thread and pushed the coat back to him. Her ropy hands rested flat on the scarred table. My beautiful mother had become an old woman. Her skin was rough and chapped. Even the lobes of her ears seemed to sag lower and looser.

I went into the other room and, making sure that Chung-hee wasn't looking, lifted Mother's jeweled hair clip from under the loose board and slipped it in my waistband. I gathered clothes for both of us and, back in the kitchen, scraped the last grains of millet from the bottom of the jar.

"It's too far, Min-hee," Mother said. "Too dangerous."

I bundled the supplies into Turtle's blanket and hung it over my shoulder.

"There won't be room for us on the boats," Mother said. But when I took the baby from her, she didn't resist.

A massive shell landed somewhere on the outskirts of town and shook the ground beneath us. I looked at my brother, one last time. Chung-hee leaned back against the wall, the collar of his soldier's coat turned up around his skinny neck. He held his bowl with both hands, and loudly slurped his soup—the soup that should have been mine.

So be it, I thought. He had chosen his world, now I had chosen mine.

Those *waegukin* boats we were heading for might get blown apart by a Chinese shell and take us to a world at the bottom of the Yellow Sea. Or the boats would travel south, and we would step ashore into a world I couldn't imagine. But now that I knew there were other worlds, I wouldn't stay in this one, flapping my wings like a homeless chicken.

I tied my baby brother onto my back, took Mother's hand, and we stepped out into the night.

Scavengers

written by

Shannon Peavey

illustrated by

JAMES J. EADS

ABOUT THE AUTHOR

Shannon Peavey was born and raised in a suburb of Seattle, Washington. The oldest of three girls, she mostly used her vivid imagination to terrify her siblings: telling them that she'd been replaced by an evil twin from an alternate dimension, or that eating crab apples gave a person magical powers. They have since forgiven her.

After receiving a degree in English from Mount Holyoke College, she returned to the Pacific Northwest and began writing in earnest. She tries to bring the unique flavor of the west coast, its history and unexplored places, to her writing.

Shannon particularly credits Robin McKinley and Lloyd Alexander for instilling in her an appreciation for strong heroines, vivid new worlds, and beautiful words.

When not writing, Shannon works as a horse trainer and continually attempts mastery of the piano (so far, the piano is winning). Her Writers of the Future win is her first published work.

ABOUT THE ILLUSTRATOR

James J. Eads is a freelance illustrator and art instructor from Orange County, California. He received his BA from

California State University, Fullerton and began his career as a public school teacher, until he was quickly hired away as a graphic designer for the furniture industry, where he worked for the next fifteen years.

James became the owner and head designer for VIP Arts, a rubber art stamp and craft supply company. With VIP, he had the opportunity to teach art classes across the country. Once again, teaching became an important part of his life, leading him to teach art to the incarcerated juveniles and adults at Santa Ana Jail. For the past decade, James has worked at creating an art program for elementary schools, working with children grades K–6, as well as special needs classes. He has recently retired to work on more personal projects.

James works primarily in pen-and-ink and watercolor, but is not above drawing in crayon with his granddaughter. He is honored to be among the Illustrators of the Future, and is already hard at work on writing and illustrating children's books.

Scavengers

Keera leaned back to peer at the sky, shading her eyes with one hand, a turnip hanging by its fringe in the other. Mara glanced over at her sister and wondered what she saw.

"Vulture's pet is coming," Keera said.

Mara put her spade down, but didn't see anything but blue sky, clouds smeared blurry with distance. Then a black speck appeared, growing steadily larger. "I see," she said, but it wasn't true. The speck didn't resolve into a clockwork finch till the thing was nearly upon her, its wings flipping air and light drops of grease into her hair.

"Hail," the finch said.

"Hail," the two women said together, but Mara frowned. The Lady's birds seldom left her house on the hill. When they did, the news was never good.

"News from afar." The finch's beak moved when it spoke, but the motion always seemed a little delayed, half a beat behind the words it formed. "Shall I tell you?"

"Only if it's important, you chattering fool," Keera said. Mara hung back, watching.

The finch whirred, gears inside it working, processing. "I won't presume to judge the quality of my news, miss. That's for ones cleverer than I." The bird sounded offended.

"Spit it out."

The finch blinked, once, in its curious way: first closing one eye, then the other, so that at no point was it ever wholly blind. It settled on Mara's shoulder with a heavy thrum, clutching her rough-spun vest with talons like needles.

Mara held perfectly still, watching the finch from the corner of her eye. When it spoke next to her ear, its belly clicked in time with its words. "The Lady sees strangers coming. Two days out. They come with weapons and evil intentions."

Mara sucked a breath and the finch dug its claws into her shoulder.

"Who are they?" Keera demanded.

The finch shuffled from foot to foot, ducking its head in a shrug. "Who would tell a simple songbird?" It chirruped, shrill and rusty. "Looked to me like they were carrying scythes."

"Harvesting," Keera whispered, soft as smoke.

The finch's insides clicked and clunked and it said, "I only tell you what I saw." Then it turned its head into Mara's hair, muttering low for only her to hear. "The Lady will see you at half past the noon hour."

Mara nodded once, small so Keera wouldn't see. Then the bird tensed its claws into her shoulder and launched back into the sky. "Be warned," it said, "and warn your fellows."

They watched it go, flapping smoothly on metal wings.

"Do you think they really are harvesters?" Keera asked, head tipped back, still watching the clockwork bird. Mara had lost track of it some time ago, lost in the blur that made up her world beyond the stretch of her arms.

"I don't know. A scythe doesn't make a harvester, not for sure."

"No. No, you're right." But Keera still seemed troubled. Mara didn't blame her. Once upon a time, a scythe hadn't made a harvester. But now, who else would carry one?

"Naught we can do now," Mara said shortly, and knelt back to the field, more rocks and weeds than turnips. "Best get this done with before the weather turns bad. There's lightning in the air."

Keera crouched next to her, carding through turnip fringes for the telltale strangers, weeds with spiked leaves, or slender, or broad. "It's a fine morning. Not a cloud in the sky."

"I smell it," Mara said. An acrid, charged smell, sharp in her nose. "You just see if I'm wrong."

"No," Keera said. "It's fine. We'll finish up here in another hour or so, anyway."

Mara laughed and scraped her knees in the dirt of the endless field of turnips. She knew they wouldn't finish in an hour, not even if they worked all day. The field was too large, the weeds too persistent, the turnips sick with a leaf blight. And above, lightning was stirring.

At noon precisely, Mara started up the path to the Lady's house. Within five minutes she was winded, feet slipping on the sharply pitched slabs that lined the steep path up to where the house perched on a ledge, looking as if it were poised to jump. Above her, the sky was greening.

She watched her feet, though she knew the way. Better to watch them than to watch the way the town receded into a blur behind her, small and low, a daub of darkness in the wide flat plain. Everything flat, save the great hill where the Lady'd made her home.

She'd made the first switchback when one of the finches fluttered out of the sky to hover near her hairline. Impossible to say if it was the same one that had spoken to her in the field—they were as like as siblings. She thought it was, though. "Prompt as always," it said.

"That's the way my mother raised me." She kept on walking.

"Just as my dear mother said, when I was just bare hatched from my egg: 'Timeliness is goodliness,' she said, didn't she?" The finch darted around her face, flying close enough that she felt the air move.

"You never hatched from an egg." She didn't know this for certain, of course, but felt fairly sure. The egg that could make such a creature had never been.

"Ah, such a clever girl," the finch said with a trill that she thought was probably laughter.

"I'm nearly there," she said. "Why don't you go tell your Lady that I'm coming?"

"She knows." The finch flitted ahead.

Mara swore low under her breath and walked on, stolid as a mule, staring at her feet. The finch flew back with a huge bug in its mouth, crunching through the hard outside with a sound like bones breaking. "Everything tastes better when caught on the wing," it said, through a mouthful of insect.

"I wouldn't know."

The bird trilled laughter again and swooped to settle on her shoulder, crunching its meal close to her ear. They walked through the last switchback together, not speaking, and then the Lady's house met her at the top of the path, crooked and full of windows.

"In the usual place," the finch said, and lit off her shoulder to one of the high windows, left open to admit the breeze and the birds.

The Lady's door had a latch that was never locked. Mara pressed the pale wood with her fingertips and the door opened easily, as if a stiff wind could send it swinging. She tried not to look too closely at the grain of the wood, because it always seemed to her like faces.

The house stank like oil and rust, and like the little bodies of bugs and rodents that the clockwork birds left chewed but undigested on the carpets. Mara was used to the smell, though, and her eyes only watered a little. She stepped over the bare spots in the rug and the places where it was stained dark, and where small things cracked under her feet.

"Hello, my dear," said the Lady from the next room. Mara hurried to join her, slipping through an open door into the parlor.

The Lady sat near the window, a metal bird nestled into the fold of her collar. "Go on, then," she told it, and the bird stirred, stretching its wings so that every silvery pinion showed wide and sharp. Then it swooped in front of Mara, flashing close to her eyes. She sucked a breath but stood still.

"Silly creatures, aren't they?" The Lady craned her long neck to watch the bird go. "I think they get jealous."

Mara said nothing. The Lady clicked her beak and motioned Mara in, gesturing to her usual chair with a knobbed hand heavy with rings.

Mara settled in the chair, listing to the left just a bit by habit, avoiding the broken spring hidden under the dusty velveteen. The Lady looked out the window for one long moment, then twitched the drape closed, plunging the room into hazy half light.

"How are your eyes, my dear? Any improvement?" The Lady leaned close to peer into Mara's face.

Mara sat very still, trying not to flinch as the vulture's head drew near. The Lady had done her a great favor. "They are," she said hesitantly, "perhaps a little better, ma'am."

The Lady drew back, crooking her neck to look at her sideways. "Can you see what is in the bottom left corner of that tapestry on the wall? The green one."

Mara squinted. She'd seen the green tapestry before, she felt sure. "A doe?"

The Lady clicked her tongue. "We shall try again. It is a process."

"Of course," Mara said.

The Lady picked up a small jar from her side table, one with a large foggy crystal cragged out of the top. "Lean forward," she said, unscrewing the lid.

Mara leaned forward. The Lady dipped her fingers into the jar and brought out a dripping lump of pale clay. Mara opened her eyes wide, though the urge to shut them nearly overwhelmed her.

"Shh," the Lady crooned, sibilants whistling through the cruel arc of her beak, wrinkled fingers outstretched. Gently, she smeared the clay over Mara's open eyes, once from corner to corner, then from brow to cheek, like a cross.

A shudder raced through Mara's body, one that made her teeth clack together. She stilled herself, and the vulture woman patted her hand. She heard the Lady get up and move to the far side of the room. "Just a few minutes," she said, and dragged something heavy over the carpet.

Mara's eyes flicked sightlessly in their sockets, trying to trace the scuffs and sounds of movement that were now her only indications of place and presence. The shuffle-drag of whatever the Lady was doing, the whuff of the wind behind the drapes, the far-off cries of a bird. The sound of her own heart beating. She swallowed. "Lady, is it true what you said?"

"Is what true?"

"That the harvesters are coming to kill us and steal our crops."

The Lady made a noise deep in her throat and Mara heard her step away. "They come, yes. It has been long since we saw them last, has it not? I had begun to think they were scared away."

"Or all gone, at last," Mara said. It was her sister's pet theory, that the past group of harvesters, two years ago, had been the last.

"No, that shall never be," the Lady said sadly. "For all men must harvest."

"Oh." Mara tried to blink but the clay held her eyes open. "Do they strike everywhere, or only here?"

"Everywhere that is, harvesters are. It is how men evolved, to be hunters and killers."

Birds kill, too, Mara thought, but said nothing.

She heard the Lady sit back in the chair across from her, and some prickling in her spine told her she was being examined. She knew how the Lady moved even without being able to see her. The Lady gave the same scrutinizing stare to anything that interested her, or anything small that moved too quickly and looked too much like prey. She sat with her head cocked and her long, naked neck craned out of the cowl collar of her dress, where, somewhere beneath, the bird's rough skin turned to human flesh.

"I'll peel it off, now," the Lady said, "and we'll see how it has worked."

Mara's hands almost leapt to claw at the stiff dressing and peel it away, but she held still and let the Lady do it. A long claw slid over her face, under her eye socket along the bone, then crept under the edge of the clay. The Lady hooked her fingers, pulling away, and the clay popped away neatly, impressed with a hollow where her eye had been.

Mara squeezed her eye shut, glad for the ability to do so. When the Lady pulled the poultice from her other eye, Mara closed it, too.

"Open them," the Lady said.

The room fuzzed, then swept into focus. The thing at the corner of the green tapestry, Mara saw, was an eagle with a man in its talons.

"How is it?" The Lady peered at Mara's face, swept

a hand in front of her to see how her eyes focused. The rings on her fingers glittered even in the dim.

"It's—better than it's ever been," Mara said. "Everything is sharp, even the far-off things. I might be able to see all the way to the river, if I tried."

"Not even I could see that far," the Lady said, but she sounded pleased. "We shall see how long it lasts, this time."

"One day it will be forever, won't it?"

"Yes. One day it will be forever."

Mara rose and smoothed her hands over the front of her only dress, still rough and uncomfortable after years of special occasions. "I don't know how to thank you."

The Lady rose as well, and turned to the window. "I need no thanks for providing for my people. Do make sure that someone is on the river road in two day's time, though. Midday. Your sister and her man should be easily capable."

"I shall see it done. Keera is honored by your trust."

"She is a fine fighter. You both are a tribute to your family."

"Thank you," Mara said, but the Lady paid her no mind. She threw open the drapes and gazed out the window. Watching for birds on the wind, Mara supposed.

She made a hurried half bow, feeling awkward and out of place, and left the room. Being able to see the filth on the carpet, the feces and the crushed rodent skeletons, brought little pleasure. Some things were better left blurred.

The finch found her as she pushed open the Lady's

door and stepped onto the bluff. "And how are you seeing things now?" it said, a mocking tone to its voice. "Clear as the day? Shall it now be you who informs us of the dangers come close?"

"I see fine," Mara said shortly, "but my insights remain woefully human."

"That is woeful indeed." The finch chirruped and swooped a low circle over her head. "I wish you true sight, Mara of the Goldwater."

Mara watched the bird dive off the side of the bluff, weaving through the rocks and brushy twigs of the high desert scrub. It dropped low and out of sight, somewhere in the talus pile below. Mara worried her lip with her teeth and started down the path, watching the ground in front of her, perfectly alone.

She saw the first branch of lightning stretch soundlessly across the river, and held her breath until the thunder came.

Mara refused a rifle when Keera offered her one, though when they were young she had been the better shot. "I'm not coming along to do any killing," she said. "Just to watch for trouble."

"If trouble came along," Keera said, "you'd be more use with a gun than without."

"I'd be more like to shoot myself in the foot."

"Your eyes are better now, aren't they?" Keera handed one of the rifles to her husband, Rey, and he shouldered it.

"Good enough to watch for trouble," Mara said.

Keera shrugged and took up her own rifle. "There won't be none. Didn't the vulture say there was two of them? She's not been wrong before."

"No." Mara stepped out onto the front porch of her sister's house and marveled at the way golden motes of dust swam in the sunlight slanting through the hole in the roof. Such detail in life, if you could appreciate it.

She had wanted to take the rifle. It would have been like taking her old life back. But that wasn't her life anymore, and the seeing never lasted. While she had it, she would go with them and keep watch, but taking up a gun again would be too much. Bad luck. She still carried a thick-bladed hunting knife in her boot. That would have to be enough.

The two of them joined her on the porch, and Keera latched the door behind them. "It's good to have you with us," Rey said, and smiled his dimpled smile. Mara didn't smile back. Once she would have, maybe, but not now.

"Did the vulture tell you what time these harvesters are supposed to appear?" Keera asked.

"Midday."

"That's fine." Keera studied the sky, the early-morning pale brightness of it, still pink-tinged at the horizon. "It'll take us about an hour and a half to get there, but we'll beat them if they're not early."

"Hope they're not." Rey stepped down to the beaten dirt path, crooking his fingers at them. "We'll miss them for sure if we keep standing here."

They walked three abreast while the path allowed it. At first, it was flat and straight, and their boots kicked up puffs of fine dust, faintly greasy where it landed on their cheeks. Rey and Keera chatted amiably as they walked; Mara spoke when spoken to but found her mind on the task ahead. Her mouth was awash with something bitter, something that tasted like bile, like fear—and she felt ashamed. She'd been trained for this, born to this. Protecting the town from those who would harm it. Her nerves had gone soft with her eyes.

"Mara?" Keera said. "You all right?"

Mara started and realized she'd stepped off the path, kept going straight on as it narrowed. It was greener, here, closer to the water. "Yes. I'm fine."

"Sure." Keera tapped Mara's elbow with her elbow as she passed. The familiarity of the gesture was soothing.

The river road stretched for miles, long enough that no one in the Goldwater had ever ridden its entire length. No one even knew how long it really was, for that matter, or what other places might lie alongside it—no traders ever ventured to the Goldwater. The only ones who rode that way were the harvesters.

"It's pretty out here," Keera said.

This time of year the river was sluggish, lapping shallowly over the rocks. In some places, it was low enough that the bigger rocks stuck out and dried on top, almost enough of them to form steppingstones to the other bank. Long-legged bugs stepped over the stagnant pools behind downed trees, mincing and delicate. Mara agreed, "It is pretty."

They set their ambush in a copse of trees near a rise in the road, crouching behind a downed log. Keera and Rey propped their rifles over their knees and waited, squinting against the sun.

"S'almost midday," Rey said, after a time. He sounded bored. "Anyone see anything?"

"No," Mara said, staring down the road to where it faded into the horizon.

It was remarkable how far she could see.

Keera said nothing for a time, but then brought her rifle to bear, her expression firm. "There," she said. "Dust."

Mara swiveled to look and at first saw nothing. But after a moment, it appeared: a cloud of dun-colored dust, rising in the distance like the trail of a snake.

"Could be animals," she said.

"It's not." Keera and Rey moved up behind the log, rifles readied, no tension in their faces. Keera looked back at Mara and nodded. Mara nodded in return and shifted in the copse, coating herself in shadows.

They waited silently. Mara scratched an itch on her nose; Rey shook his head fiercely to dislodge a fly. *It's too long,* Mara thought. *They're taking too long. They must have seen us.*

Keera lifted a hand, never taking her eyes from the road. "Scythes," she whispered. Rey nodded and readied himself. Mara counted the seconds, lips moving silently—one, two, three, four, five, six—

Keera fired, shuddering back with the recoil, then Rey fired. The shots were deafening in the little copse, the shock of them traveling through Mara's blood and leaving her shaky. She saw Keera's trigger hand go to the bolt on her rifle and tense, then relax. The men were dead.

"Easy," Keera said, pulling back the bolt to release the spent cartridge. A curl of smoke and the smell of gunpowder wafted out and disappeared into the warm air. Keera's hand shook a little, like it always did after she killed. Rey clapped her on the shoulder and she smiled at him.

Mara scrambled forward to the downed log, hooking her elbows over the top and peering out into the road. "They were harvesters?"

"Scythes on their backs," Rey said.

Mara hesitated. "We've got to do something with the bodies."

"Leave them for the birds," Rey said, and chuffed something like a laugh.

"We'll pull them into the woods." Keera got to her feet. "No harvester deserves a burial—the animals will take care of them."

They stepped out of the copse and onto the road, sunlight flooding Mara's eyes and making her blink.

The bodies lay half on, half off the trail, heaped in careless piles. Two men in rough-spun and denim. One wore a black hat that had slipped back when he fell and cradled the back of his skull where it lay on the ground. A gray horse stood away from them with its head down.

Both men were headshot, as Mara and Keera had been trained to do. One had a round dark hole in the middle of his forehead, like a bloody third eye. The other shot had nearly missed—the second man's face was blown off from cheek to ear, a red ruin with the white of bone and broken teeth standing out.

"Wait," Keera said. Mara turned and saw her face was pale. "Where are their scythes?"

Neither man carried anything like a scythe. They were empty-handed, in fact; the horse was laden with supplies, but the men had nothing but their own blood in their hands.

"I saw them," Keera said, her voice ticking higher.

Mara looked to Rey.

"I saw them, too." Rey's hand closed convulsively on the stock of his rifle. "They had them on their backs; they reflected the sun. I *saw them*."

"All right," Mara said, softly. "It's fine."

She knelt down by the body of the man who'd been neatly shot and tipped its head so its neck was not so unnaturally crooked. Its eyes were open, but she didn't bother closing them. They wouldn't have stayed. She picked up its right hand and examined it, running her thumb over the palm and the mounts of the fingers, feeling for calluses. The hand was as smooth as a preacher's.

"It's no matter," Keera said. "No one comes this way if they don't mean us harm."

"You're right." Mara pressed the dead hand back to its chest, lying across the heart. "The Lady said they were harvesters, anyway."

Ray said, "We still have to move them."

"I'll get the horse," Mara offered, and left them standing quiet in the road. Her sister and her sister's husband. The two dead men.

The horse had gotten tangled in brush, its long split bridle reins wrapped around the branches. She stooped to untangle them, saying quiet nonsense to the horse to settle it. The reins were tacky with blood all along their length. She thought it might try to run as soon as it was free, but it didn't. It stood next to her and leaned into her touch. She stroked its neck and then led it away. Its gray coat was spattered with red.

She tied the horse short to a tree limb, so it wouldn't run. Sacks of grain lay across its back, she saw, and supplies enough for a pair of travelers. She riffled through the packs, wondering. They seemed to be traveling heavy for men planning to raid and kill. Then she closed everything back up and tried to put it from her mind. She went back to help with the bodies.

Rey took one body by the armpits and dragged it away himself. Mara and Keera managed the one with the ruined face, each taking an arm. They dragged it to a low spot with tall grass and spreading trees and left it lying next to the other one. The razor grass folded around them and hid them from view, and it sliced at Mara's arms and ankles as she knelt to lay the body down, then stepped away.

Rey closed the dead eyes and put flat river stones over the lids to weigh them down.

"Let's go," Keera said. She had folded her arms across her chest, elbows in tight to her sides. "We've spent too much time here already."

They left the bodies and returned to the path. The razor grass left long red scratches wherever their skin was bare, but no one complained. Keera went ahead to gather their things, Rey stepping quickly after. Mara hung back as they knelt together, slinging the rifles back over their shoulders. Rey said something quietly to Keera and she shook her head once, very sharply.

Mara untied the horse from its tree and looped the bloody reins around her fist. It twitched away at the smell and she laid a hand flat on its thin neck, whispering to it. Then they left: Mara, Keera, Rey, and the dead men's horse. They walked slower than they had on the way there, and quieter.

Before she got far, Mara turned back to look at the

river road. Some big bird had settled down where they'd left the bodies, pleased for the meal. A big dark bird with hulking shoulders. It ducked its head and came up with something stringy and dripping in its beak.

She turned back to the Goldwater road and didn't look back again.

Mara dropped the horse off in her little post-and-rail barn that for years now had housed nothing but possums. Then she took the things it had carried and went up to store them in the house. Enough provisions in there to keep a pair of travelers for a couple weeks, plus the sacks of grain. Maybe for trading.

But Keera and Rey both had seen scythes.

She piled the supplies away and thought on it. But every time she got close to it, she saw instead the dead man's eyes slipped closed, weighted down with rocks. The ruin that was his face.

By the time she finally made it back to the barn to feed the horse and rub it down, Rey was already doing it.

"Oh," she said stupidly, watching him rubbing the horse with a rag in brisk circles. He had nice hands, long-fingered and deft. She'd liked that about him, before her sight went cloudy and everything got complicated. "Thanks."

"It's nothing," he said. "It's a nice horse."

"Too thin," she said.

He shrugged. "That ain't his fault."

They lapsed quiet. Rey kept rubbing the dirt up out of the horse's coat and Mara stepped over to pet its nose. The horse had its eyes half closed.

"Your eyes still good?"

"Yeah," Mara said. "They are. For now."

Rey nodded, made some approving noise. "That's pretty long, ain't it?"

"Yeah."

Mostly the Lady's treatments came and went in a blink, Mara's vision clearing and then fading within the space of a day. Never long enough to make a difference. Once it had lasted three days. This time—

"Well, I hope it's for good," Rey said.

"Me too." She smiled a hard smile. "Of course, it's a little late now, right."

Rey kept silent.

Mara retreated back to sit on the beam between the two tie-stalls, splintery and slightly too tall for comfort. The tips of her boots just kissed the ground if she stretched her legs. "You must have known it would be you, even before our parents arranged it," she said. "Didn't you?"

Rey stilled for a moment, then returned to his work. His hands found an itchy spot on the horse's withers and the horse stretched out its neck, wiggling its upper lip in happiness. "Yeah, I did."

"And that was all right with you?"

"It was an honor," he said. "I was the best shot in the Goldwater. I was chosen to help guard it from harvesters."

Mara picked at the wood of the rail, peeling back loose, stringy pieces with her fingernails. "You never had anything else you wanted to do?"

"Nothing that mattered." He patted the horse on the shoulder and stepped back, putting the rag aside. "What's this all about?"

She didn't respond. Rey waited, fussing with the horse. "I think sometimes that it's a sad place we live in, where a little girl gets raised with a gun in her hand and her husband's picked for her because he's the best at killing."

"Someone's got to keep this town safe," Rey said, quietly.

"Yeah," Mara said, looking up at him. "But it should be me. Keera's life should be mine. She wasn't raised to this, like I was."

"Keera does a fine job," Rey said, shoulders stiff. "It ain't nobody's fault what happened."

"I know," Mara said. "I know."

Rey stepped forward and touched her shoulder gently, as if she might spook. "Come on out of here. It's been a strange day, but it's done, yeah? Tomorrow things'll look different."

He winced as he thought over what he'd said but Mara laughed. "Maybe they will," she said. "What do I know?"

She hopped down off the rail and they left the horse in the barn for the night with a little of the grain it'd carried on its back. The next day she'd have to go to one of the neighbors, arrange to pick up some hay. It might be good, having something living to care for.

They didn't talk as they left the barn and walked the bare-dirt path that led back to their houses. When they came to the fork, where Rey would go on straight and Mara would turn right, he hesitated as if he would say something, but Mara cut him off with an easy smile. "Thanks for the help with the horse," she said. "Tell Keera I'll see her tomorrow out in the field."

He nodded and they parted. The smile slipped from Mara's face as quickly as it had come.

The shadows were long when she got to the front porch of her house, the last of the sun gleaming through the scrubby trees. She stood a moment watching the sun set, squinting into the light. And then she heard a scrabble of claws over her roof, and the whirr of gears. A clockwork finch launched itself off the edge of her house and into the air.

"What the hell're you doing here?" she said, her heart hammering.

The finch didn't answer. It flew in low loops overhead, crying the same thing over and over in its shrill, rusty voice: "Well? Did you see it? Did you see it? Did you see it?"

Mara watched the bird for a while, and then went inside and closed the door.

Two weeks after the incident on the river road, Mara woke early in the morning, lay still under her quilts, and counted wood grains in the ceiling. As she counted, something in her gut relaxed, something that awoke every morning tight and scared that this morning, she wouldn't be able to count them.

Then she got up, dressed, and made herself some chicory. She looked out the narrow kitchen window that faced the turnip field and wondered if Keera was there already. She finished her chicory and rinsed the cup. Then she went to the barn and tacked up the dead man's horse.

If the gray horse thought this strange, he made no mention, taking the saddle and the bridle with the same quiet timidity he showed lipping carrots from her hand. He was a good-natured horse, respectful and docile. The last horse they'd taken from a dead harvester had been headstrong and young, a barely broke roan gelding that they'd given to Rey. That one was still prone to little displays of temper and meanness, with a wicked sideways spin. Not the sort of horse she would choose to ride on a hunt, to be certain.

Mara tied the gray to a rail outside the barn and then stepped back inside. In the empty stall where she kept the hay there were three trunks, each one small and neat and locked. She took a silver key from the pocket of her coat and fitted it to the lock on the first trunk. The lid opened easily, without a catch or hesitation. The inside smelled of oil and metal. She pulled a wrapped bundle from the trunk, about the length of her arm. She closed the trunk, locked it, and returned to the horse.

She stepped into the stirrup and swung her leg over the gray's back. She settled the wrapped bundle over the front of the saddle, balanced atop her thighs. The horse shifted his weight uneasily but didn't move. She nudged him with her heel and they set off at a swinging jog, away from her little house, away from the turnip field.

On horseback, the trip out to the river road would take half the time it had on foot. She didn't hurry, though, and let the gray set his own pace. His ears twitched back and forth like bird's wings and she wondered if he remembered this path. How at the end of it lay a slick of dried blood.

But the air was very fine, warm and still with nothing stirring but insects, *click-click-click*ing in the grass. So she kept a loose rein, her face turned up to the sun, and didn't think too much about what she planned to do.

Most of the fields stood empty. She saw only one man out, paused over his crops and leaning on his hoe. He hailed her and she stopped. He asked Mara if she and her sister would attend the wedding in town, a few weeks away. She said they would, though she hadn't talked to Keera about it.

When the path ran into the river road she turned right, the way they'd gone to ambush the harvesters. She rode up to the place and stopped the horse but there wasn't much trace left. All the blood had churned into dust and flaked away. She got down and toed at the dirt with her boot. The horse stood by her shoulder and snorted long bursts of breath—catching some scent in the air, or maybe just ghosts.

Mara returned to the vale where the bodies were hidden. Though some part of her expected them to be gone, they were still there, lying in the razor grass. Scavengers had been at them, and everything soft was eaten, leaving sunken holes in their faces and their bellies and their throats. The smell of rot was strong enough to make Mara's eyes water and her throat sting.

"What were you?" she asked the dead men. "Why did you come here?"

A black beetle crawled out the bottom of one man's jaw.

She turned and left the bodies where they lay and went back up to the river road. She walked on foot with the horse beside her. When she reached a clearing on the side of the road, with open space and big, mature trees, she stopped and pulled down the long bundle she'd taken from the chest that morning. She unwrapped it and let the cloth fall to the ground. The feeling of the wood and metal under her fingers was just as familiar as she'd known it would be, as if she'd never put it away.

She fussed with the rifle for a few minutes, making sure all the parts were clean and working. Then she breathed in and raised it to her shoulder. There was a tree with a big burl in the center, like a target, and she squinted one eye shut to aim.

She breathed out, and fired.

Much later she sat on the grass in the clearing with the rifle leaning against her shoulder and looked up at the spattering of shot deep in the burl. She couldn't put a shot just where she wanted it anymore.

"Missed you in the field this morning," Keera said behind her.

Mara leapt to her feet, the rifle in her hands. "Don't sneak up on me like that."

"Didn't think you were gonna shoot me," Keera said, eyeing the gun.

"Did you walk all the way out here?"

"Yeah. I thought I might find you here." For the first time, Mara noticed the bag lying on the ground by her feet. Keera's rifle was there, too. "I've got something I need to do," Keera said. "Figured this was as good a time as any."

"What're you saying?"

Keera didn't answer. She stepped up next to her sister and looked over at the trees, with their peppering of deep pits. "Looks pretty good. I didn't know you were gonna take it up again."

"It's been two weeks." She didn't want to say it out loud, that she might be able to see again, forever. Things like that couldn't be said, lest the sound of them in the air prove them false. "I thought I'd try."

"You don't need to," Keera said. "Rey and I, we do all right. You don't need to do anything if you don't want to."

"I want to."

"Why?" Keera asked, quietly.

"Because you shouldn't have to," Mara said, sharp as a shot.

Keera flinched, her face shuttering. "It's my job now, by rights. You can't change that just by shooting holes in a couple of trees."

Mara looked down at her sister's hands, crooked into loose fists, tense and steady. She remembered how they had shaken after Keera shot the man whose body lay rotting in the razor grass. "I was meant to do it."

"I know," Keera said. "I know! But you got out of it, fair and square, your damned *eyes,* and you can't come back now. I won't let you."

They stared across the dry ground, Keera tense and bright, a high flush of color in her cheeks, Mara just tired. Tired with the weight trapped in her gut, the weight of what she had done to her sister with her inability to do her damn job right in the first place. "You hate it," she said. "I know you do."

"That doesn't matter."

"It should."

"But it doesn't," Keera said. She stepped away from Mara and picked up her rifle. "I'm going to go down the river road."

"No," Mara said. "What would you do that for? It's not safe."

"I have to know where the harvesters come from, don't you see? And what if there are other people out there fighting them? We could help each other."

"There's not," Mara said. "Nobody comes here, and nobody who leaves ever comes back. That's how it's always been."

"That doesn't mean it's law." Keera turned and faced across the road, over the broad expanse of the river. The sun sparkled off it, clean and beautiful. "I've just got to know. About—"

She stopped. Mara finished for her: about those men lying there dead.

"I thought you just told me you were going to do your job," Mara said. "Protecting the Goldwater."

"And I am," Keera snapped. "I'm doing it. I'm figuring it out, and then I'm coming back."

Mara didn't say anything.

"If you want to put those rifle skills to the test, you can help Rey mind the place while I'm gone." Keera bent, got her pack, and slung it over her shoulder. "I'm sure he'd be glad for the help."

"Does he know where you're going?"

"He knows I always try to do right by this town." Keera's voice had lost its edge. She sounded weary.

"All right." Mara closed her eyes for a moment, let everything go black. Would she have done the same in Keera's place?

"I came to ask if I could borrow that horse," Keera said. "It'd make the trip quicker. Ours is a spooky little devil so I won't take him."

JAMES J. EADS

"Take him. You can't go on foot." She moved off to the horse, tied at the edge of the clearing. On the way, she stopped next to her sister and softly rapped their elbows together. "Come back soon."

"I'll do my best."

They packed Keera's things onto the gray in silence, and then Keera swung into the saddle and stepped the horse back toward the road.

"I'll figure it out," Keera said. "Who the harvesters are, where they're coming from."

"Be safe," Mara said. "Shoot straight."

Keera nodded and moved off down the road. Mara stood for a long time, watching her sister and the horse grow small and indistinct in the distance. Then she wrapped up her rifle and walked home, alone and on foot. Everything was quiet except the sound of her footsteps on the packed dirt and the low burble of the river. In the trees, one bird called and another one answered it.

A wind swept through the Lady's crooked house, licking through all the open windows and sending doors swinging, open-shut-open. But the door to the Lady's parlor stayed closed. That door had never been shut before when Mara came to visit. She stood frozen with her hand on the knob, then leaned in close and put her ear to the wood. But she could hear nothing inside. The Lady was very still, or she was gone.

Mara opened the door and stepped into the room.

The Lady came upon her in a rush of puckered bird skin and heavy green velveteen and an open beak, hissing and snapping. The Lady slammed Mara back into the doorframe, her hands digging hard into Mara's shoulders.

Mara choked and leaned her head back, despite herself. Her hands gripped and relaxed but there was nothing to grab, no purchase on the smooth wood. Her rifle at home and her knife still in her boot—not that she would dare use it on the Lady, who had healed her. She steadied herself and gazed into the gap of the Lady's beak, the wide black hole that led into her gullet. Mara thought, *Her fingers are so strong. She's always looked frail, but she's not. She's not.*

"Why did you let her go?" the Lady hissed, her beak so close to Mara's face, the sour blood stink of her breath gusting out.

"Because I couldn't stop her," Mara said evenly. "And because she was right."

The Lady backed away. Her fingers left hot impressions in Mara's skin.

"I never took you to be simple before, girl," she said. "What good could possibly come of this? You know as well as I do, no one ever comes back."

"No one has before. But Keera will. She's strong, and she's armed."

The Lady made some croaking noise deep in her throat. "And you think that will make a difference?"

Mara held her gaze, then looked away. "She was right about the harvesters. We should know where they come from, and why they come. We need to know."

"You don't," the Lady said. She turned and went to the window, clacking across the wood floor on what could have been heeled shoes or taloned bird feet. "I'll tell you now, girl: no good ever comes of looking for trouble where none exists. Things were fine as they were. Everyone in the Goldwater is happy. Your family kept everyone safe."

The Lady's shoulders shook under the heavy cowl of her dress. Mara watched her for a moment, not speaking, before she realized that the Lady was crying. But her black bird's eyes didn't make any tears.

Mara lifted herself off the doorframe and went a little farther into the room. In the quiet, she could hear the wind outside. "Lady," she said. "Are you crying for Keera?"

The Lady lifted her head. "Yes, I suppose I am."

"Why?"

"Because she's one of my people. Like you are, and everyone down there." She gestured out the window with a loose hand. One of the many rings she wore slid off her finger and dropped to the floor. She didn't bend to get it. "I care about all of them. You don't understand, girl, how much I love you all."

Mara stayed quiet, working her jaw.

"You don't understand," the Lady repeated.

"But Keera will be back," Mara said. "I know it."

The Lady's neck shrank back into the cowl of her dress and her shoulders shook in another dry sob. "I will watch for her," she said, her voice strange and choked.

Mara stepped up and stood beside the Lady at the window. She wondered how to comfort her. If she even could. But the Lady seemed barely to notice her. She stood shrunk in on herself, plucking at the sides of her dress with her hands crooked into claws.

After a while, Mara turned to go.

"Your eyes," the Lady said.

Mara stopped.

"Are they still well?"

"Yes," Mara said. "They have been well since the last time I saw you."

"Good. Very good. I'm glad," the Lady said.

"I can't thank you enough for your treatment."

The Lady said nothing to that, and kept on looking out the window, so Mara stepped to the door and opened it. There was a clean streak on the doorframe where her back had wiped away the dust.

"It's well that you can see," the Lady said abruptly. "Because now you'll have to do your sister's job, won't you? All alone."

Mara stood there for a moment, and then she said, "Yes."

"You'll do fine."

"Until Keera comes back."

"Of course," the Lady said.

Mara slipped out the door. The wind kicked flecks of dirt into her eyes, and she blinked against the sting. She walked away from the house slower than she'd walked coming there.

One of the clockwork finches swept down out of a sheltered place in the eaves as she stepped onto the bluff. It swooped overhead, fighting against the wind. "We're all watching for Keera," it said.

"My thanks." Mara didn't stop for it, but kept on toward the trailhead.

"Of course, it might be better if she didn't come back." The finch trilled a laugh.

Mara bit her cheek, a spike of pain and a rush of

blood in her mouth. "Shut up," she said. "You don't know what you're talking about."

"I always know what I'm talking about. My dear mother told me 'Never tell lies,' didn't she?" The finch settled on her shoulder and its wings brushed her hair. It crowded in to speak directly into her ear. "Bad things happen to creatures that lie."

"Go away," she said, whirling to dislodge it.

The finch lifted into the air. "What do you see, Mara?" it said. "What do you see?"

She rushed down the trail, nearly running. She heard the finch behind her for a long while, until she got far enough and the wind carried away its words.

Mara walked the edges of the turnip field in the half light of dusk, so the shadows splayed long down the furrows and she couldn't see so well that the weeds were growing up, choking out the plants. She didn't make it out to the field as often as she should anymore. It was hard to manage it by herself.

But everyone was safe, everyone was fine. She should have been happy. The wedding her neighbor had mentioned was the next day, off in town. A cattleman's son and a weaver's second daughter. Mara and Rey would go, wish them luck and happiness.

But Keera hadn't returned.

Mara scuffed her toe in the dirt and kicked out a stone. It skittered across the edge of the field.

It was true that Mara had trained for this job all her childhood, until her sight went bad before her sixteenth birthday. She knew how to handle herself. Everyone in the Goldwater was as safe as they'd ever been.

But she didn't feel right. The waiting set her on edge. Every morning, getting up and not knowing if she'd see Keera and the gray horse trudging home.

She couldn't be certain if she was looking forward to that day, or dreading it.

She looked up to judge the light in the sky. Less than an hour until full dark. Even so, she stepped over into the soft, turned dirt of the field and planted herself in the middle of a row. She found a tall weed, and pulled it out. She pulled weeds until well past dark, until her hands were black with dirt and sticky with sap. Until her mind filled with the monotony of the task, and she didn't think about anything else anymore.

The married couple jumped over a broomstick, held by a pair of their closest neighbors. Everyone cheered, circling in a dizzy spin. Mara clapped, too, and Rey beside her. She didn't know the girl well, or the groom. It didn't matter. They were Goldwater; they were home.

"They look so happy," Mara said, watching the rosy bloom across the young bride's face. The girl grinned and grabbed her new husband's arm, staggering with weakness from the heat of the room—or maybe just pretending so.

"They do," Rey agreed. "I wish them the best."

He sat with his hands clasped across his knees, and he didn't smile.

Mara chewed on the side of her lip, then rose to her feet, letting the crowd in the middle of the barn sweep her up. "Do you want to dance?"

"No," Rey said. "You go ahead."

"Fine." Mara let her feet carry her, away from Rey and his solemnly bowed head, away from the bench where she'd sat all evening and into the crowd of her people. Someone took her hands and twirled her, and her feet knew what to do even if she did not.

"It's good to see you here," the man dancing with her said. "We don't see enough of you and your sister, for all you do."

"You know," Mara said, following the flow of the dance. She swung under the man's arm and came up on the other side. "We do what we must. There's not much time for anything else."

"Of course," he said.

The steps of the dance swung her away and into the arms of another partner. This one smiled politely and didn't seem to care much who she was.

She danced for a long while.

When the night grew dark and everything was winding down, Mara stepped outside and found Rey sitting alone on a stump. She went to him.

He looked up. "Have a nice time?"

"I did. It's good to be friendly with the people in town. You must have seen some old friends."

"Yeah. But that was a long time ago." He got up and brushed dirt off his pants. "You wanna head back?"

"Sure." She twisted her hands in her skirt, feeling suddenly guilty for the flush in her cheeks and the pleasant tired ache in her feet.

Rey nodded at her and they started walking. A few other couples walked by them and waved, and they waved back. But soon enough they lost all the townsfolk, and they were walking by themselves on the path to their farmstead. And the night was so dark, so still.

"I didn't mean to make you come, if you didn't want to," Mara said.

Rey turned to look at her, startled from some thought. "No, it's all right. I'm just in a mood."

"Sure," Mara said. "Because you couldn't be dancing with Keera."

Something in her gut twisted sharply when she said it.

"I just miss her, is all."

"Right," Mara said. "I miss her too."

Rey frowned, then his face smoothed out. He grabbed Mara by the wrists and tangled his fingers in hers. "Come on, then, dance with me."

"What, here?" She looked down the empty road, dark and quiet.

"Sure, here," Rey said, and pulled her into a quick waltz step. Mara laughed and followed his lead, winging down the path with his arm snug around her waist.

Her smiled faded when she noticed the fixed set of his grin, and the stiffness of his shoulders under her hand. But they still danced.

"You two make a fine pair."

Rey stopped dead and Mara just a hair after him, dragging out of his grip. The hand that he'd held was warm, and she gripped it against her stomach as she peered out into the darkness. They had danced almost all the way to the crossroads between their two houses. "Who's there?"

Quiet in the dim of the crossroads, just barely visible by the glint of the moon off all that metal, sat the clockwork finch. When it saw that they had spotted it, it shuffled its wings back and forth with a tinny clink. "All apologies for disturbing your frivolities," it said.

Mara walked closer to the little bird. "What is it?"

"A harvester," it said. "Coming by the river road. Tomorrow."

She looked up at Rey, and he stared back at her without expression. She nodded. "All right," she told the finch. "We'll take care of it."

Mara and Rey walked a little farther up the river road this time before settling in to a good-looking spot, all bushes and low-hanging branches. It wouldn't do to go back to the copse they'd used before, wouldn't do to establish a pattern. Routines made people sloppy.

"So there's only the one," Rey said. "Shouldn't be bad."

"No." Mara adjusted herself in the underbrush, made sure she had enough room to move and aim and fire without being seen. "Don't you wonder why one would come alone, though?"

He shrugged. "It's still a harvester. Who knows what even one of them could do?"

"They die as easy as anything else."

Rey had nothing to say to that. They settled back in the bushes and waited, rifles over their knees. Something splashed in the river and Mara startled up to look at it—the river ran so shallow this time of year, anyone could walk in it—but it was only a fish jumping, its tailfin slipping back under the surface and the rings of its splash warping and disappearing into the current.

"Be still," Rey said softly. "I think I see something."

She squinted down the road and was still. Dust coming.

"You ready?" Rey said.

"Of course." She breathed out between her teeth and put the butt of the rifle's stock to her shoulder. They waited in silence. Not even birdsong. The sound of Mara's own pulse strangely loud in her ears, pounding high in her throat.

The harvester rounded the bend. A thickset man on a gray horse. His scythe rode naked on his back, the blade shining in the sun.

"Got it," Mara said. She aimed a little high to compensate for the distance. The trigger at half pressure. Breathe out, fire.

The stock thumped into her shoulder and the shot cracked out. The man slumped in the saddle and the horse shied violently, scooting sideways into the trees. The harvester's body slid from the saddle and landed crumpled on the edge of the road, twitching.

"Good shot," Rey said.

"Thank you." Mara looked at her hands. They didn't shake. She laid her rifle down. "Let's go pull him off the road."

The harvester had fallen on his shoulder, his face in the dirt. Blood streaked the ground and Mara's hands as she went to turn him over, but there wasn't much of it. His scythe had jammed up through its bindings in the fall and its crescent blade stuck out over his back like a wing.

"Harvester for sure," Rey said, after Mara had wrestled the body onto its back. "Still got the scythe. Mean-looking bastard, ain't he?"

Mara nodded, but the man's face swam in and out of her vision in a blur. There was his heavy brow, a hole through the middle of it; there were his ruined teeth, exposed by a slack eerie grin–

But there, too, was something else, someone else. Some other face she almost recognized.

She blinked twice and her vision cleared. The dead man came into solid focus. She brought a hand up and pressed hard over her eyelids. Not now, it couldn't be going now. Not when it seemed as if she finally had a chance.

"Come on, help me get this ugly lug off the road."

Mara grabbed the man's feet and Rey took him by the shoulders. They didn't have to carry him far, since he was practically off the road anyway. They took the body into the trees and down a little slope to a place where the tall brush would hide it. They laid him at the base of the slope without ceremony.

Mara stepped back to study him, the way he lay in the brush. Before she could think better of it, she stooped down to the body and turned it roughly, holding its shoulder off the ground with one hand while she fumbled with the straps on its back. The dead man's arm felt like clay under her hands, cooling and softly pliant. After a moment's work, she had the scythe free, and she let the man drop back to the ground.

"What the hell do you want that for?" Rey said. He stood back from her as she swung the scythe up to rest against her shoulder.

"Don't know," she said, running her fingers down its haft. "Just working something out. The last pair didn't have them when they died, right?"

It felt solid enough, and heavy. Not a well-balanced thing, with all its weight in the blade.

Rey stared at her. "That's damn creepy."

"Yeah," Mara said, and shrugged, and then turned and walked back to the road. Rey followed her after a moment.

When she was almost there, she stopped.

The harvester's horse hadn't gone far. They found it by the roadside, facing away from them. Its white-gray tail swishing.

A sick feeling rose in Mara's gut.

"That horse," Rey said. His voice was strained, rough.

Mara held up her hand, telling Rey to stay where he was. She put the scythe on the ground and crept forward, going slow and careful to avoid startling the horse. She talked nonsense to it under her breath, so it would hear her voice and know she was there. "Hey there," she whispered. "It's okay; it's all right. Everything is going to be fine."

She took up the broken tangle of its reins, threading her hand down familiar leather. The horse stood its ground, skin shuddering, eyes white-rimmed with panic.

"It's fine," she said again, but something hot welled in her eyes. "You're all right." Her throat closed up on the words. She couldn't say more. Instead, she touched the softness of the gray horse's nose and stood petting it, her head bowed, blinking fast.

"Mara," Rey said. He hadn't come any closer. "It's the same horse, isn't it."

Mara tried to respond, but her mouth was dry. She said nothing.

"Isn't it?"

She nodded, jerkily.

"Oh, damn," Rey whispered. He'd gone sandstone-pale. Stood there with his hands out like he was looking for something to steady him, but could find nothing.

Mara turned the horse away from the tree. Behind its saddle, it carried Keera's pack, hooked to the flaps.

A cold pit opened up in Mara's gut. That was it, then. No chance that she'd just traded the horse away or anything like that. Everything she'd had was in that pack, everything but her gun.

"What does it mean?" Rey said, his voice shaky. "Did that bastard—did he kill her?"

"I don't know. Could be he just stole the horse. Could be she's fine."

She twined her hand in the horse's mane. Maybe that could be, but she didn't think so.

She should never have let Keera go. It should have been her responsibility. And now look at it, her baby sister dead. Killed away from home where they couldn't even bury her. It wasn't right.

"Yeah, that could be," Rey said. He didn't sound like he believed it, either.

They stood there by the side of the road in quiet, Mara scratching the crest of the horse's neck and thinking about her sister being dead. Then Rey folded up as if someone had punched him in the gut and dropped to sit on his heels. "I don't know what to do, Mara."

She said nothing.

"It'd be easier if I'd seen her," he said. "But now I don't know for sure. I don't know if we've killed the man that killed her, or if she's even dead at all."

"I know," she said.

"What are we gonna do?"

She considered. Then she walked forward, pulling the horse along by the reins. It didn't want to move. "We'll go home," she said. "Keera would hate us if we fell apart now. The town still needs protecting."

Rey nodded, very small. Mara bent and offered her hand; he took it, and she helped him to his feet. His eyes were glassy with unshed tears.

Mara didn't feel like crying at all, anymore. She just felt that cold pit yawning inside her, as if something dead had its hand stuck through her stomach to grip at her heart.

"Come on," she said.

She picked up the harvester's scythe again, from where it lay in the weeds. Rey said nothing. They walked the long road back together and no one spoke.

Mara woke the next morning twisted up in her bed, the blankets twined through her arms, panting and damp with sweat. She couldn't remember what she'd dreamed. But it had been something bad, and something loud, and echoes of it still rang through her head even in the stark pale light of morning.

"What did I do?" she said aloud. "What have I done?"

She got up and wiped her face clean and made

herself some chicory. She drank it standing by the window, looking out at the Lady's house, barely visible on its distant hill. High up, set away. Where she could look down on everyone.

The chicory burned her throat and settled her nerves. When it was done, she left the window and went to the place in the corner where she'd propped the harvester's scythe, covered in sackcloth. It seemed smaller than it had been the day before.

With a hand that still didn't shake, she twitched the cloth away. Keera's rifle leaned against the wall where last night Mara had left the long-bladed scythe of a harvester.

"Damn it," she said, very softly.

If only she'd felt surprised, though. That would have made it better. But no part of her was shocked. There was only the creep of horror up her spine, a cold twist in her gut. And the slow burn of shame. Because hadn't some part of her known it already? Hadn't some part of her seen it, out on the river road?

She set her back to the wall beside her sister's gun and slid down until she sat in a heap on the floor. She pressed her forehead against her knees and closed her eyes. She stayed like that for a long time.

Rey didn't need to know yet, not until she'd figured it all out. He was mourning enough. She took the gray horse and rode out as soon as the sun came up. The horse jigged underneath her, spooked at phantoms. She spoke quiet words to him but he wouldn't calm.

The sun crept higher as she rode, already a white glow in a pale sky. The last dying gasp of summer. The day would be mercilessly hot.

The trip to the river road felt long, though she urged the horse to a trot. But she finally turned onto the road and went to the place where they'd left the dead harvester. She swung down from the horse and left it tied to a tree while she made her way down the slope. Her boots skidded on loose dirt. For a moment, she couldn't remember exactly the spot where they'd left the body and she circled round, riffling through bushes and weeds, but then she saw a flash of bright color on the ground. The color of one of Keera's shirts.

She brushed the leaves out of her sister's face with the flat of her hand, straightened the fall of her hair over her shoulders.

But Keera would never pass for sleeping.

"I'm so sorry," Mara whispered.

And there, alone, she let herself cry.

After a while, she dried her eyes on the back of her hand, went back to the horse, and got the coat she'd worn that morning. She took the coat back to Keera's body and snugged it up over her shoulders.

"I'm going to make things right," Mara said, voice hoarse. "And then I'll come back for you."

But of course, Keera couldn't answer.

Mara lingered a while longer, and then went back up to the road. She untied the horse and swept into the saddle. If she needed answers, she had a good idea of where to look.

Don't go," the finch warned, but Mara went on up the hill to the Lady's house. The clockwork finch fluttered around her head, its movements quick and uncertain.

"You knew, didn't you?" she said, never stopping her mad charge up the path. "And you did nothing."

"I am her creature. What do you expect me to do?" The finch swooped and dove and the clanking sounds in its belly were louder than ever. "I tried to make you see."

"I see fine!"

At the crest of the hill, Mara left the finch behind and burst through the Lady's front door. Dead things crunched under her feet, rodent bones and bug wings. The clockwork birds shrieked on the rafters, all together, a mad chorus. She rounded the corner and hit the Lady's door with her arms outstretched. It flew open and Mara half-fell into the room, stumbling and skidding over the floor. The Lady whirled from the window, her head high. Mara stopped and stood, fists clenched so her nails bit into her palms. "My sister is dead."

The Lady moved to her armchair and sat. She folded her hands in her lap. "I know. I am sorry."

"I don't give a damn. Somehow, you did this." Mara stalked the floor, gripped by a teeth-grinding feeling that wouldn't let her rest. She had to keep moving, or it would all spill out.

"It wasn't me that killed her," the Lady said softly.

And didn't that cut as sharp as a harvester's scythe.

"You changed her," Mara said.

The Lady moved her hands in her lap, stretching her thin fingers. They were different than before, slimmer and less wrinkled. The rings hung loosely on them. "Why are you so quick to blame me?"

"Because only you could do it." She swept around the back of the Lady's chair, passing by the green tapestry with the eagle gripping a man in its claws. "Because you've got to be doing something up here other than watching the road and fixing my eyes. You've got to be getting something out of it."

"Yes," the Lady said. "That's true. I protect my town, and in return, I am fed. Each of you will feed me, in time."

Mara stopped dead. "What do you mean?"

"It is as I say." The Lady stretched out her long bare neck, turning it as if to work the kinks out. "Don't you see it every time you look at me? I am a creature that feeds on death, girl. When someone dies here, their spirit feeds me. Makes me stronger. I was weak when you killed those two on the road. Now I am strong again."

"No."

The Lady had always helped her, been nothing but generous to her. Made her able to see again.

"It's so."

"So we're only food for you," Mara said, her voice tightly controlled.

The Lady wrung her head back and forth. "It's not like that. You are my people and I love you. My greatest wish is for everyone in the Goldwater to live to old age and die happy, surrounded by the ones you love."

"So the reason no one comes here, no one leaves?"

The Lady drew into herself, tucking her elbows close to her sides and pulling her head back into the shade of her big cowl neckline. "The towns where I lived before were not understanding. Accepting. I could not stay anywhere for long. So I thought it best to take this town and keep it small. To take one group of people and their families who would grow to know me as a guardian. No need for outsiders. No need to stir up trouble."

"The harvesters don't exist."

"No."

Mara exhaled a long breath and went to the window. She put her hand on the sill in case she needed the support. It wasn't even that she didn't know what to think, what to say—but that she *couldn't* think. Every thought felt like spring ice, cold and thin and so brittle.

"None of those men Keera killed were harvesters."

"No," the Lady said. "Travelers, traders. But you understand, you were still right in your job. You kept the Goldwater safe."

Mara clenched her fingers on the edge of the sill. Paint cracked and flaked. She whirled and faced the Lady. "You made Keera look like a harvester. She could have come back!"

"But she knew. And she would have told you and her man. No one would have been safe here anymore."

"*You* wouldn't be," Mara said. "How could we know the truth and still let you live up here, a stinking carrion bird, picking our corpses clean."

The Lady hissed and sprang from her chair. "Keep a civil tongue around me, girl," she said, beak clacking. "And how thin is your outrage when now you have what you've always wanted. Your old job back, your old man. Isn't that so?"

Mara froze.

"And don't forget who gave you those *eyes*." The Lady's chuckle grated on Mara, an unnatural thick sound.

"Take them back, then," Mara said, and took three long strides to meet the Lady in front of her chair, where they'd always sat when Mara came for treatment. Only this time Mara reached for the knife in her boot and came up with it gleaming in her hand like a tooth.

The clockwork finches on the rooftop screamed louder and louder.

"You don't know what you have said, girl," the Lady said, and she drew closer.

Mara looked at how the tip of the Lady's beak curved down into a cruel point. She raised the knife.

The Lady's head darted out of her cowl faster than Mara could track, and her beak gaped open. Mara fell back, wrenching her head back and slashing out with the knife at the same time. She caught the edge of the Lady's dress. But the tip of the Lady's beak caught Mara's left eye, raking through it and popping it free of its socket, tearing through the flesh of her eyelid down to her cheekbone.

Mara fell to her knees. She was screaming, she knew, but it didn't really feel like her. She was only this white-hot pain, the run of blood and fluid down her face and over her hands.

The Lady stooped over her, and Mara could do nothing. Blood dripped from the Lady's beak, and she clicked it back and forth as if she were chewing. She brought the beak down against Mara's jawbone, and then slowly slid it up to rest against her right cheekbone, below her other eye.

Mara could only gasp for air. Blood ran into her mouth.

"Let her be, Lady," said a finch. Mara's finch. The

one who had warned her. "I think you have hurt her enough."

The Lady withdrew. "She knows."

"She'll keep quiet," the finch said. "She knows now not to cross you."

Mara curled on the floor with her hands to her face, trying to press everything back in, hold it all together. Her knife was useless on the floor next to her.

The Lady spoke to Mara, though she didn't look back. "I didn't want to do it, girl. I've always been fond of you."

"You need her," the finch said. "No one else has her training. Her family is the work. You need them to carry on."

The Lady fell quiet a moment, then grasped Mara by the shoulder and pulled them both upright. "Let's get you fixed up."

Mara followed mutely. She couldn't have walked anywhere on her own—the world through her good eye was edged round in white and prone to spin if she moved too quickly. The Lady sat her down in the velveteen chair and got a pot of cream and a winding of linen bandage. Mara faded in and out of consciousness while the Lady treated the hole where her eye had been.

She saw Keera, once, and her parents who had gone before, but then she blinked and her vision cleared. The Lady was there once again, twisting her bandage into place.

When she was done, the Lady looked Mara squarely in the eye and said, "Now that you know, you must choose for yourself what to do. I hope you choose well."

She reached up and dabbed a little blood away from the corner of her beak.

Mara nodded and got up. She had to lever herself out of the chair, leaning hard on the armrests.

The Lady called after her as she shuffled to the doorway. "I don't do anyone any harm, you see? The Goldwater is happy because of me."

Mara didn't look back. She kept putting one foot in front of the other until she was down the long hallway and pushing through the door to the outside. The clockwork finch kept pace, flying close beside her.

She stood at the top of the trailhead, but didn't start down. Instead, she stared at the town spread below her, the collection of little houses and barns and green fields. Harvest time wasn't far away.

"What will you do?" the finch said.

Mara worked her mouth to clear out the taste of blood. She spat on the rocks below. The copper tang didn't clear. "I have to tell everyone," she said. "It's my job to protect the Goldwater. Not some vulture."

"You know everything will change," the finch said. "You'll lose everything. Lose that life you were building."

"I know." She thought about Rey, waiting back in the little house by the turnip field. She raised a hand to the ruin of her eye, but couldn't stand to touch it. "It wasn't mine anyway."

The finch said nothing. It chirped instead, a sad rusty sound.

Then she turned and started down the hill. Above her the sky stretched pale blue and cloudless. Below, the gray horse stood waiting for directions, with blind animal faith.

She walked down cautiously and the finch flew beside her. In time she reached the bottom and the horse was there waiting, standing where the path forked in many directions. One way led to home, to Rey. The other to town—she would go there soon. She would tell them about the Lady's lies. But there was something she had to do first. She turned the horse in the direction of the river road and urged it on faster.

First, she would bury her sister.

Dreameater

written by

Andrea Stewart

illustrated by

LUCAS DURHAM

ABOUT THE AUTHOR

Andrea Stewart was born in Canada and raised in a number of places across the United States. She spent an inordinate amount of time during her childhood reading and remembers often being told to quit reading and pay attention! Her love of fantasy and science fiction began when she was in grade school. She grew up in a family where Star Trek marathons and questions such as "When are you building me that FTL drive?" were the norm. Weekly trips to the library led her to discover authors she still enjoys reading—Peter S. Beagle, Isaac Asimov, and J.R.R. Tolkien. She now lives in California with her husband and a veritable menagerie of animals on her suburban microfarm. When she's not writing, she works as a contract analyst and paints on the side. This is her first professional sale.

ABOUT THE ILLUSTRATOR

Lucas Durham grew up in a creative environment and was introduced to his first Macintosh computer drawing program by age two. By four, his mom was reading him Heinlein before bed. At six, his bedroom was decorated with prints from sci-fi and comic book artists, including James Gurney, and papered with drawings of his own.

It was inevitable that Lucas would move toward a career in illustration. His formal training began at the American Academy of Art in Chicago, while he independently explored digital illustration software.

As he studied traditional art fundamentals, Lucas developed a passion for the Renaissance and Baroque schools of art. This led him to fill out an application to study at the Florence Academy of Art. It was in Italy that he merged his interests in classical art with modern illustration narratives.

Upon graduation, Lucas worked as a concept design intern at The Bradford Exchange, where he was introduced to the legal disciplines of working with image licensing. During this time he plunged into the exploding online illustration community. Live streams became a staple of his continuing education and led to networking opportunities.

Today, Lucas works full time as a freelance illustrator.

Dreameater

Spring in Arizona feels like summer anywhere else. My palms stick to the vinyl seat of the truck as I lift my legs to get some air goin' beneath my thighs.

Mama looks over briefly, and then clicks her manicured nails against the steering wheel. Rat-a-tat-tat-tat, over and over, like the beat of a song only she can hear. "Honey, I'll get the A/C fixed next city we stop in. Promise."

My fidgeting is rubbing off on her, so I settle back into the seat and fight the urge to whine. The clicking dies down, stops. Mama makes a lot of promises, and best I can tell, she tries to keep 'em. She cries when she don't, when she remembers she made a promise in the first place.

The truck slows, then pulls into the parking lot of a run-down motel. Even the asphalt is covered with brown dust. It lifts off the ground with the wind, and falls over everything, makin' the bright blue hood of the truck look like the sky just after sunset.

There's a man waiting for us, leaned against one of the pillars supporting the second-floor balcony.

His white tank top is stained yellow at the pits and tucked into torn jeans. He's got his thumbs hooked into his belt, one knee jutting out like he's some sort of model, but I know he ain't and never been. He's too fat, too ugly, too sweaty and greasy and hairy. I don't like the look of him, but then, I never do.

He swaggers up to the window while Mama puts the truck into park. She rolls it down when she's finished and gives him a long look.

"You Linda?" the man asks.

"That's me," Mama says.

"You told me you was pretty."

I bristle at that remark. Mama *is* pretty. She's the prettiest woman in the world. But before I can let my mouth run off at him, Mama reaches up and undoes the pins in her hair. She shakes it out in black, shining waves. Something changes about her. Every move she makes is smooth, graceful, like dandelion seeds in a breeze.

The man can't barely keep his mouth shut. He's staring at her like a man does at a steak after he hasn't eaten in three days. He stares so hard he don't even notice me 'til Mama gets out of the truck. His eyes narrow—thin, dark slits beneath his brow. "You didn't tell me you got a kid."

Mama ignores him, turns, and reaches behind my seat. She hands me my worn-out workbook. "Do a page of math, and write a couple pages on the things we've seen in Arizona. I won't be more'n a couple hours." She rolls up the driver's side window until there's just a crack left. "Don't open the door for anyone."

The man nods his head in my direction. "Who's her daddy? Someone like me?"

"No," Mama says, "not like you."

It ain't the leer the man gives me, or even the heat in the cabin of the truck that turns my stomach—it's the way Mama don't sound sure. She won't tell me who my daddy is, but now, for the first time, I wonder if she can't.

She shuts the door behind her and takes the man's hand. As soon as she does, the leer and the narrowed eyes fade away. He looks like someone who just won the lottery, all smiles and breathless disbelief. They go up the stairs together and disappear into a room marked with a brass number fifteen.

I may only be eleven, but even I know that Mama ain't too bright sometimes. Or maybe it's the forgetting. Forgetting that we're in the heat of Arizona, not in Oregon. Soon as she's gone, I open the door and dangle my feet out. Should I even do the workbook pages? Mama don't score 'em, just draws hearts and smiley faces, and tells me how I'm gonna be so much smarter than her.

Across the street in an empty field, a dad kicks a ball with his kids. Can't tell the game. They don't seem to be keeping any sort of score, just kicking it over the dried-out grass, laughing, and falling over one another. When the dad sees me watching, he beckons for me to come join 'em. I duck my head at first, pretending I didn't see, my gaze focusing on my toes, the cheap flip-flops rubbing black dye onto my skin.

When I shyly lift my head, the dad is still looking in my direction, and this time his three kids are, too, and they all wave at me. Well, why the hell not? The street's nearly empty, so it ain't hard to cross.

They're good people. I can tell by the way they smile at me, the way they shake my hand, tryin' to make me feel welcome. When I tell 'em my name—Alexis—the daughter says it's pretty.

Turns out there are no rules, no real game. We just kick the ball back and forth, the dad calling out random directions, and us laughing as we try to follow 'em. It gets to where I'm as bad as Mama, forgetting. I'm forgetting I'm s'posed to be in the truck, with the window rolled up, writing pages. I'm forgetting these people ain't my kin, that Mama and I got each other, and that's all we need. I'm just feelin' the grass against my feet, my breath quick in my throat, the sun hot on my back.

I don't see her 'til it's too late. "Alexis!" Mama's striding 'cross the field in her wedge heels. She's got her hair pinned up again, and she's stuffin' a roll of bills into her jean shorts. She takes me by the upper arm. "Didn't I tell you to wait in the truck?"

"Sorry, Mama." I could tell her it was too hot, but it'd just make her feel bad.

"We kept an eye on her," the dad says. He picks up the ball and tucks it under an arm. He sticks out a hand as he approaches. "I'm David."

She drops my arm to shake it, but she don't look like his friendliness makes her comfortable, not the way it made me. "Linda."

He tilts his head at her. "Alexis—does she have any other family?"

Mama takes my arm again, her nails resting lightly

against my skin. "No. Just me and Alexis. Our own little party o' two!" She lets out a laugh, but I don't think she actually thinks it's funny.

David leans in close, and Mama stiffens, her whole body goin' rigid as a popsicle. "Doesn't really seem like the sort of life a little girl should have. You want what's best for her, right?"

When Mama speaks again, her voice is low and cold. "Don't you be tellin' me how to raise my daughter."

I'm suddenly so afraid I can't barely catch my breath. If he says one more word, if he don't back down, she's gonna kill him. She'll do it right in front of his three kids, and they ain't never gonna be able to scrub their minds clean again.

So I reach up with my other hand and grab her shirt. "Mama, let's just go." For a second, I think she'll toss off my hand and do him in anyways. *"Please,"* I add. And just like that, the death goes outta her eyes.

Maybe David saw it too, 'cause when we turn to go, he don't say anything else. Once we get in the truck, Mama reaches behind her seat and pulls out a flask. She tips it over her mouth and takes a long pull. When she swallows, a shudder runs through her. It ain't alcohol she's drinking—truth is, I don't know what it is, only smelled it once when she was with one of her men. Smelled weird, green and spicy. Whatever it is, seems to help when she's mad.

Mama lets out a sigh after she swallows, and leans her head 'gainst the steering wheel.

Now, I ain't a fortuneteller, but I know, sure as I know the sun rises in the east, that she ain't gonna remember about fixing the A/C.

We come back to the motel once a day for the next four days. I don't see no one in the field 'cross the street. Part of me's relieved, and part's sort of sad. Each time, Mama takes the greasy man's hand and comes back with a roll of bills.

The last time we come to the motel, it's dark, past midnight. I fall asleep in the truck, a blanket pulled up to my chin. I wake at the crack of dawn, to the sound of something heavy being thrown into the bed of the truck, then shuffling as it gets covered with tarp.

Mama appears at the driver's side door. She opens it and slides inside. I pretend not to notice the smear of blood on her chin. She starts drivin', and sees it soon enough in the rearview mirror. She wipes it off with the back of her hand.

"He weren't a good man, Alexis," she says. I don't know if she means to reassure me, or herself.

"I know, Mama," I say. "I know." But I don't reach out or pat her back or nothin'.

She dumps the body in a canal, and burns the bloody sheet she had him wrapped in. I just watch, and wish I weren't watchin', wish I were back in that field, kickin' that ball with the three kids and David.

We pull onto the interstate, and she drives into New Mexico before we stop for anything more'n a meal or a bathroom break. It's afternoon. Mama don't need a lot of sleep, when she sleeps at all. She parks at a Hyatt.

"Alexis." Mama turns to me, a girlish grin on her face. "Wanna have some fun?"

She gets us a room, payin' for it with all those rolled-up bills. We order room service, have a pillow fight and watch cartoons, cuddled up on the king-sized bed. I lean against her. She has her hair undone, and I rest my head in it. Mama strokes my face, so lightly I can't feel her nails. "Honey, you know I love you, right?"

I shift and breathe in her smell. She smells like me. She smells like home. "'Course I do. Love you too."

When I sleep, I dream of nothing at all.

Who's she?" the man says. He ain't fat or ugly, like most of 'em, but when his tongue darts out to lick his lips, I decide he's ugly after all. "That your sister?"

"My daughter," Mama says. She moves a little, so she's standin' between me and the man. It's an easy mistake to make. At sixteen, people tell me I look older'n my age, and Mama's always looked younger.

"I'll pay double for the both of you," he says. He's got the look of a person who got too much money, too fast. His hair's slicked back, the top two buttons on his shirt open, the watch on his wrist gold, with a black face. And like any person who's got too much money, I think he actually expects Mama'll take him up on the offer.

"You stay away from my daughter," Mama says.

For a second, he looks dismayed, like he just seen someone kick a puppy, but then his face starts gettin' red. Before he can say anything, Mama lets her hair down. And then he's like the rest of 'em, practically drooling, fallin' all over himself just to look her in the eye. Mama takes his hand.

"I'm gonna go 'cross the street," I tell her. There's a Marshalls there, and window-shopping sure beats sittin' in the truck.

She don't turn, just leads the man towards a room on the first floor of the motel. "That's fine, honey. Just be back in an hour or so."

The whole thing gives me the creeps. She hasn't taken a man for a while now—keeps tellin' me the next one'll be the last. Sometimes I wish I were younger, back to a time when I thought this was normal, like everyone's Mama did the things mine did. I try to shrug off the memory of the man lickin' his lips as I walk into the store. Maybe I oughtta drink some of Mama's juice—seems to do the trick for her.

I look 'round the housewares, pretending Mama and I got a house to decorate with all the useless crap they got on the shelves. There's a little ceramic frog I think's meant to hold business cards, or maybe just pennies or something. I kinda wish I had the money to buy it, and put it on the dashboard of the truck. Ain't nothin' in the truck feels like it's mine sometimes.

I try on a couple of outfits, even a nice dress—like I got a prom to go to. The blue satin hugs my curves, and I give myself a pouty look in the mirror. I sass Mama sometimes, just to feel like a regular teenager, but I never push too hard, and Mama don't take it too seriously. She can be scary when she's really mad.

By the time I put the dress back on the rack, I'm bored. I head to the front of the shop. When I look through the glass doors, I freeze.

There's cars outside the motel, more'n there was before, black cars. They ain't parked in any spots, just set up in a semicircle 'round the blue truck. Guys start spillin' out of 'em, dressed in black, wearin' vests and helmets, carryin' guns.

I'm running over there before I can stop myself,

my heart poundin' in my ears, loud as the slap of my flip-flops against the pavement. Some guy without a helmet or a gun puts his hands out to stop me when I set foot in the parking lot, but I ain't as weak as I look. I barrel into him, puttin' him off balance, then spin, so he can't get a grip on me. The men with guns ain't in their positions yet, so I find a gap between 'em and dash through.

Someone yells somethin', but I don't pay attention. I'm focused on the door I saw my Mama go through.

She didn't even lock it. She must've been in a bad way, to get so careless. I open the door and see somethin' I ain't never gonna be able to un-see.

Mama's on the floor, naked, crouched over the man who licked his lips at me not an hour before. His head's opened up, nice and neat, like someone took a razorblade to a melon. She's got his brain in her bloody hands, and she's eatin' it. Even as she gags on it, she makes these soft sounds of pleasure in the back of her throat.

I can't say nothin', all the words stick on my tongue. I can't even scream. I hear footsteps coming up behind me, the rattle of guns as things click into place. The first guy who gets up next to me ends up retching onto the floor when he sees Mama, his gun limp at his side.

Someone's forgotten to say "Freeze!" or "Put your hands in the air!", 'cause even though they got their guns pointed at her, Mama don't stop eating. A hand grabs my arm from behind, and I let 'em. The world is ending, so it don't matter who puts their hands on me. They pull me back, away from Mama, away from the men with guns.

It's the guy from earlier, the one I ran into. "It's okay," he says. He looks kinda like David, with dark hair and soft gray eyes. "It's okay."

Why's he tellin' me it's gonna be okay? Then I realize I got tears running down my cheeks, and I'm shaking so hard I don't even feel like me anymore, like I'm just ridin' in this other girl's skin and I left the steering up to someone else. I barely even feel it when he puts an arm 'round me and guides me away from the crime scene. Damn, that's what it is, ain't it? Funny that I never thought of it as a crime 'til I saw the cops.

He sits me in the passenger side of one of 'em black cars, and tells me to put my head between my legs and to breathe. I try that, and the world slows down. He's talkin' over me, talkin' to someone else, all the while he's got his hand on my shoulder.

"Call the coroner out here. Tell him we've got a body."

"What about the girl?"

The man's hand shakes me a little, like he's trying to wake me up. "Hey sweetie," he says gently, "how old are you?"

I still can't talk. Closest I can get is a moan.

When I lift my head, I see Mama bein' led outta the motel room in cuffs, a sheet wrapped 'round her body. She's still covered in blood. How's she gonna cope without her juice, the one that makes her forget, the one that helps her when she's mad? Right now she's dull from feeding, her eyes glazed, her steps heavy.

And then the guy's coaxing my feet into the car, and closin' the door. In the silence of the cab, I can hear my ragged breathing, like someone tore into my lungs.

The man tries to get me to talk on the way to the station. "I'm Detective Carlson." "What's your name?" "Was that your mother?" "How long have you known her?" "Do you have any other family?" I just stare out the window and don't say a word. I wish he'd crash, and I'd die, right now.

But he don't.

Some middle-aged lady with a clipboard meets us at the station and asks all the same questions. I keep hopin' I'll wake up with Mama next to me, that none of this day happened at all. The lady tells me she's takin' me to a foster home and they're gonna look for my family. By then, I get strength enough to nod. She reaches out, squeezes my hand, and gives me a smile. I wanna wipe it right off her face. If she'd been there, seen Mama eatin' that man's brain, she'd never smile again.

I don't think I will.

My foster parents are nice enough, but I still don't get the urge to talk to 'em. It's summer, so they don't make me go to school. I'm glad for that. I stopped doin' the workbook pages when I was fifteen.

I hear 'em talking sometimes, like if I can't talk, I can't hear neither.

"Has she said anything to you?" my foster mom asks.

"No," my foster dad says. "She's traumatized; give her time."

"Poor thing. I saw the news. Her mother's been

killing men for years, and all in that awful fashion. Can you imagine?"

"I'd rather not."

I kinda wanna burst in on 'em, tell 'em what a good mother Mama's been, takin' care of me herself all these years, but I feel like I'm waiting for something that hasn't happened yet.

A week after Mama's arrested, the social worker comes to see me. She asks if I wanna see Mama in prison. I shake my head no. Still waiting.

It takes a month before I know what it is, and I don't know it 'til I hear it. Mama's juice wears off slowly, 'til she starts remembering things. Remembering everything. The social worker comes again, and tells me what I've been waitin' for.

Mama's remembered who my daddy is.

He lives nearby, and for that I'm lucky. Mama's driven me all over the continental states, one to the next, never stayin' in one spot long enough to get our bearings. So I'm surprised when it turns out he's only a couple hours from the foster home I'm stayin' at. The social worker's so pleased she found my daddy that when she drives me out there, she's hummin' show tunes the whole way.

I think I'm gonna be mad when I see him, or maybe just sad and broken. I ain't never seen his face—how can I go live with him? She pulls into a long driveway, with potholes in it. The house at the end looks nice enough though, and it's on a lot of land. I don't look around too much, 'cause my daddy's standing on the porch.

I know it as soon as I see him. He's got long black hair, like Mama, and it's pulled into a ponytail. He's got a nose like mine, and the same jaw. When I step outta the car, he walks towards me, his eyes shinin'. He tries to smile and can't, he's so choked up.

"Alexis."

There's so much meanin' in that one word. I'm not angry, not even sad or broken. Before I know it, I'm huggin' him and crying, like I'm in a stupid Hallmark movie. He's crying too. He pulls back and puts his hands on either side of my face.

"My daughter. You don't know how long I've dreamt of meeting you."

Suddenly I wanna talk again, 'cause I've got questions, so many questions.

It's not like my heart ain't still broken, but my daddy does his best. He sets me up in his spare bedroom and cooks dinner. I ain't had a home-cooked meal in practically forever. He lets me serve myself. He don't urge me to take more or less, or place things on my plate I'm not sure I want. I can feel him watchin' me out the corner of his eye, like he's afraid I'm gonna make a run for it.

"I'll take you shopping tomorrow," he tells me, once we start eating. "You'll need new clothes, shoes."

I wiggle my toes. I'm still wearin' those flip-flops, same ones I ran across the street in. Moving my feet makes me realize how cold they are. I don't know how to thank him when he ain't done anything yet, so I just focus on eatin'. He talks 'bout how his week was as we eat, his voice deep and steady. I didn't think I was tense, but as he talks my muscles relax, one at a time.

"How'd you meet my mama?" I ask him, once I've taken the edge off my appetite.

"At a laundromat. We lived in the same part of town," he tells me. His shoulders stiffen up, the way mine do when I'm gettin' ready to lie. "Your mother was the prettiest thing I ever saw. I won't say I loved her. I barely got the chance to know her. But I'm glad we had you."

And there it is, the lie, at the end. It confuses me. It's not like he seems unhappy I'm here—he seems to really like me, and I think he's glad to meet me. But he's hidin' something. "Did you know she was crazy when you met her?"

A shadow passes over his face. "Alexis—there are things I need to explain to you. Things that you won't want to hear."

"Look, you may be my daddy, but you don't really know me. Mama didn't tell me nothin', so I wanna hear what you gotta say."

He gives me a long look before he stands up. "Hold on, I'll be right back."

I don't eat anything else once he leaves. I don't have an appetite no more. When he comes back, he's holdin' something in his hands. He tips it onto the table and it drops with a rattle of beads. It's a dreamcatcher—one of those kitschy ones that looks like it's been made in someone's fifth-grade craft class. "Do you know what this is?"

I ain't stupid, so I just glare at him. He laughs. "Yeah, well, I don't know how much your mother told you about your heritage." He reaches back and undoes his hair. It's black as night, shimmering 'neath the chandelier's light. If I look hard enough, I think I see stars in it.

"I'm a dreamcatcher," he says. "I can sort of hypnotize people. I make sure they have good dreams, and no bad ones. It has other benefits. I'm stronger, and no one notices me much until I let my hair loose. Dreamcatchers run in my family. They run in your mother's too."

"Mama's family," I whisper. "How come Mama's different?"

"I don't know how much you know about genetics," my daddy says, "but sometimes things go wrong. When they do, you get disorders—illnesses. Those run in the family too. Your mother isn't a dreamcatcher. Something's messed up in her genetic code. She takes all dreams, not just bad ones, and eats them. She's not dangerous to women, just to men. The more she eats their dreams, the more she wants." He stops, swallows. "It's why she did the things she did. Once she's had a taste of a man's dreams, she wants the whole thing. She's a dreameater."

I'm still puzzlin' things out, putting things together and seein' the big picture. "Mama's juice?"

"A medicine. My brother's a doctor. He made it for her. It dampens her urge to eat. It doesn't always work, and it's not foolproof. And it's got bad side effects. It makes her forget things, lots of things. But the first few times my brother brewed it up, it worked like a charm. When it stopped working as well, she left, probably started making it herself."

"She ever eat your dreams?"

"Yes," he says, and now he's whisperin', just like me.

And then the last pieces click together, and I see why he didn't wanna explain things to me in the first place, why he lied. "If you're a dreamcatcher, and Mama's a dreameater, what's that make me?"

He takes a deep breath, like he's fortifyin' himself against his next words. "Like I said, it's genetic. Your mother wrote to me after you were born, the only letter from her I ever got, before she forgot who I was. When I found out I'd fathered a child, I went to my brother and he helped me figure out the chances. There's a twenty-five percent chance you didn't get any of this, twenty-five percent chance you're a dreamcatcher, and a fifty percent chance you're a dreameater."

Not only am I not hungry anymore, I think I'm gonna puke. Fifty percent chance I'm gonna be just like Mama.

The chair I'm sittin' in ain't as comfortable as it looks. I flip a quarter, watch it turn in the air, and catch it when it comes back down. Heads. I do it again. Tails. This is how my life's been decided. I just don't know yet which one it's gonna be. Heads or tails.

"Alexis?"

The lady at the desk's callin' my name. Daddy's waiting outside, in his car. He didn't think it a good idea for him to get any closer to Mama, not with her craving his dreams. I gotta leave everything in the waiting room, includin' the quarter I was tossing around.

LUCAS DURHAM

When I see Mama, dressed in an orange jumpsuit, I feel sorta numb. She's got her hair in a ponytail. She gives me this sheepish little smile when she sees me. Like being in jail's not as big a deal as I thought it was.

She picks up her phone on her side of the glass, and I pick up mine. For a while, neither of us says nothin', and all I hear is her breathing and mine, in-out, in synch.

"I'm sorry, honey," she says finally.

And just like that, the numbness goes outta me. "Sorry for killin' all those men, eatin' their brains, or sorry for getting caught? Sorry for draggin' me around all those years when I got a daddy? Or sorry you had me at all?"

"Alexis," she reaches out, touches the glass near my face. I don't move an inch. Mama looks frail, her fingers delicate, the lines in her face deeper'n I remember.

She opens her mouth, but I ride on over her, 'cause I'm gonna finish what I gotta say before she soothes away my anger. "Daddy told me what you was. He told me what he is, too. And he told me how much a chance I got of bein' just like you. Fifty percent, Mama. Fifty!"

Her fingers trail down the glass, her eyes distant, like she don't even hear me.

"Why'd you do it?"

Her eyes focus again. Mama and I've spent so much time together, she knows I'm askin' 'bout me, and not the men. "Lots of reasons, honey. I thought maybe someone'd come up with a cure by the time you were grown. I wanted a baby—I didn't think it fair I'd be denied having my own children for somethin' that ain't my fault. When I was pregnant, I didn't think it'd be fair to not give you a chance at life. And when you was born, Alexis, it was like the sun risin' in the sky after a long, cold night. I weren't lonely no more, and I've been lonely a long time."

"But I'm the one who's gotta live with this. How long I got?"

"I started feelin' the urges when I was twenty. Didn't know what it was 'til I was twenty-two."

Four more years before I find out what I am. A few years after that, and I might be just where Mama is right now. "It's not right, what you done." I wanna say it with strength, but I hear the wobble in my voice.

"Honey, you know I love you, right?"

The funny thing is, even though I'm still angry and feelin' like I'm gonna cry, I wanna say it back to her. I don't know if it's just years of habit, or if it's 'cause I can't stop loving her, no matter what. But I bite my tongue, and hang up the phone.

I can't sleep that night, hard as I try. My daddy offered to do his dreamcatchin' thing on me, but I ain't keen on it after all the things I just found out. Besides, I ain't never had any dreams. I asked Daddy what it meant, if it meant anything at all. He told me it was nothing, and started talkin' about putting posters on my walls.

Maybe it means I'm like Mama. Or maybe Mama's been eating 'em so many years my brain's forgotten how.

I'm tossin' and turning, so I get out of bed and start walkin' 'round the house. Turns out Daddy ain't sleeping neither. He's in his study, leaning over his desk, polishing something with a little yellow rag.

"Hey," I say.

He whirls in his chair, lifting what he's got in his

417

hand, only a little bit, but enough for me to see it. It's a gun—an ol' fashioned one, like they used in the Wild West. Soon as he sees me, he lets it fall into his lap, coverin' it a bit with the rag. I think he knows well as I do it's a silly move. I already seen it.

I clear my throat, tryin' to dispel the awkwardness that's risen up. "You said you was stronger'n most people. How much stronger?" Some of the men Mama took was huge.

"Much stronger." He turns and lays the gun on the desk.

"But you ain't got nothin' on Mama, do you?" I take another step into the room and see the shine of sweat on his upper lip. "You're afraid that prison's not gonna hold her."

"Alexis . . ." He holds up his hands, warding me off. Huh. So he don't wanna talk about it. He's scared. Me? I've been scared my whole life, so this ain't anything new.

"If she gets out and comes for you, you gonna shoot her?"

He just sits there, fixing me with his black eyes. I got no idea what he's thinkin'.

I point a finger at him. "You remember, that's my mama you're thinkin' of killing. My mama. Someday I might be just like her. You gonna shoot me then too?" I don't wait for an answer. I go out of the room, my face so hot I'm sure it's steaming. Part of me wishes I didn't say those things to my daddy. He's a good man, and he's been nice to me. I don't want Mama to kill him, and he got a right to defend himself. I just don't know what's right no more.

I go outside onto the wooden porch, and lean on

the railin'. The night air feels good 'gainst my skin. My eyes adjust to the darkness. 'Cross the yard, in the cottage on Daddy's property, I see the renter's still awake too. He's got the curtains open, the lights on, and he's hunched over a desk, head cradled in his palm as he reads a book. Curly brown hair falls over his eyes. Daddy told me he was a graduate student.

"Alexis." Daddy's voice sounds from behind me, but I don't turn around. His feet shuffle 'gainst the wood, and then he's next to me, looking out where I'm lookin'. "I don't want you to worry about your mother, or me either. I want you to think about you."

I nod in the direction of the cottage. "I wanna be like that someday—learnin'."

"How about in a couple days?"

I look up at him. "Really?"

He nods. "I'll see if I can get you a tutor, get you up to speed before school starts. I should have done it earlier, but I didn't know if you'd be up for it."

I smile for the first time since I seen Mama crouched over that man's body. "Yeah, thanks."

"Come on," my daddy says. He puts his arm 'round me. "Go get some sleep."

I lean into him. "Sorry 'bout what I said earlier."

"Sweetheart, out of everyone, you've got things the hardest. Don't you apologize to me."

Daddy comes to an agreement with the renter— Josh. Lowers his rent in exchange for him tutoring me. I do my best, but I can't stop thinking 'bout Mama and Daddy and the gun and the flip of a coin. Josh's real sweet, and he's patient even when my mind's elsewhere.

I go to see Mama again at the end of July. She looks like hell. She's got dark circles 'neath her eyes, and she walks like she's still asleep.

I pick up the phone before she even sits down. "Mama, you okay?"

"You still mad at me, honey?"

I am, but she's the only mama I got. "No."

"I'm not doin' so well," she says. She gives me a confused-lookin' frown.

"You gotta tell 'em you need your juice."

"Don't matter," Mama says. "They ain't never gonna let me have it and it's too late anyway."

Too late? She grips that phone like a lifeline. Her nails dig into the plastic, and they shave off pieces of it that curl and drop to the table. I reach out, but I can't touch her, can't tug on her shirt, like I did that time with David. There ain't nothing to help her 'cept the sound of my voice. "You need to calm down, Mama. No use gettin' angry."

"You know they got men for guards here? Sometimes one of 'em dozes off, and I get just a taste." She ain't angry, she's hungry. "Least when I was out and about I could pick who I fed on. Tried to always pick the bad ones."

"I know you did." I keep my voice soft.

"They gonna try to keep me here forever."

"Mama, you're gonna get a trial."

"What, you think I'll walk outta here?"

"Sure, maybe someday."

Must be one lie too many, 'cause her lips curl back, her whole face goin' tight. This what she looks like to those men before she kills 'em? She hurls the phone at the window. I must've jumped up, 'cause I'm standing 'bout three feet away, watching Mama make a spectacle of herself, tearin' and slammin' at everything in reach. The glass don't break, but her phone's in little black pieces, all over the table and floor.

She gets a hold of herself before the guards come and get her. I thank God, Jesus, Buddha, anyone I can think of that she does. I don't wanna watch her kill no one else.

I bite into the back of my pencil, taste the wood and paint in my mouth. I try to focus on the numbers on the page, but it ain't easy. Finally, I toss the pencil onto the table. "I don't think I can do this."

"Sure you can." Josh gets up and comes 'round to my side. "You're smart, Alexis. You just need to concentrate." He puts the pencil next to my paper.

"You really think I'm smart?" Maybe I *can* do this—be just like all those other teenagers.

"Of course I do. You learn much faster than most of the kids I tutor."

"Am I gonna be ready once school starts?"

He tilts his head to the side, purses his already-thin lips. "Maybe, maybe not. You're making a lot of progress. Just don't be afraid to make mistakes."

The breath goes outta me and I remember why I couldn't think in the first place. I *am* afraid. I'm terrified. I don't know why I'm sittin' here with Josh, acting like I'm a normal girl learning math. Seventy-five percent chance I ain't normal. Fifty percent chance I ain't anything close to normal.

"Hey, did I say something wrong?" He wrinkles his brow.

Daddy. Mama. The flip of a coin and a gun in the

drawer of the desk in the study. "If I asked you to shoot me, right in the head, would you do it?"

His brow wrinkles even more, like he's one of them pug dogs. "Alexis, why would you say something like that?"

I suck on my upper lip, run my teeth down it. "Don't know," I say finally.

I wake to the sound of tappin' at my window. Rat-a-tat-tat-tat. In two seconds I go from sleepy to wide awake. I'm trying to calm down, tellin' myself it's just a branch or a bird or a raccoon, when I hear it again.

I hear it a third time before I decide to get up. A fourth time before I actually do. When I go to the window, I'm breathin' through my mouth. Can't seem to get enough air through my nose. I draw back the curtain.

I don't see nothin'.

But then a hand pops up, the nails tapping 'gainst the window. They're not painted no more. They gleam 'neath the light of the moon.

"Mama?" I whisper. I open the window, just a crack, so she can hear me. "Mama, that you?"

She rises from where she's been crouching under my window. "Alexis, honey." Maybe she tried to clean herself up before she got here, but there's still dried flakes of blood on her face. She's got on that undershirt the prisoners wear 'neath the jumpsuit, and a pair of jeans. "You were right, they let me out this mornin'. I walked all the way out here just to see you. Took me damn near forever."

I didn't hear nothin' on the news. She must've broke out tonight, and took someone's car. Probably killed 'em too. "Mama," I breathe out, "you can't be here." I keep real still.

Mama's swaying back and forth, like she's drunk. Daddy must be sleepin', and she's close enough to eat his dreams. She'll want the whole thing, and I can't let her have it.

"But I came so far," she says.

"Can't you come back tomorrow morning? I'm still sleepin'."

Her face goes hard. "No." She closes her eyes, takes a breath and looks calmer when she opens 'em. "You should come with me, honey. Now I'm out, you don't have to stay here no more. Could be just like it was before."

Maybe I can stall her somehow, grab the phone, call 911. "Can I grab a few things, Mama?"

She sways harder, like she needs to piss. "I can't wait no longer." She licks her lips. "Did you want me to come in and help you?"

I don't want her any nearer to my daddy. "No, no. I'm comin'. I'll come right through the window. Just like old times, right? You, me, and a beat-up truck."

She lets out a low laugh.

I open the window all the way, and find the edges of the screen. My fingers tremble. I probably won't see Daddy again. I won't be goin' to school in the fall, neither. But maybe that's the way my life's gonna be anyways. Me 'n Mama—a couple of dreameaters.

A click sounds behind me. "You leave Alexis alone," Daddy says. He's got the gun in his hand, and he points it at Mama. I move to the side, outta the line of fire. I get a trickle of shame in the back of my throat, but I don't wanna go with Mama, not really. Daddy's hand shakes a little, but I look in his eye, and I know he won't budge.

Mama's face goes tight, like it did when I visited her. She flexes her fingers. "She's my daughter too. I raised her."

"You gave her life, Linda. Doesn't mean you own her."

She looks at me, her eyes cloudy. "Honey?"

"I just don't want you to hurt Daddy," I whisper. *"Please."*

But she's too far gone for that. She snarls, and shreds the screen with one swipe of her hand. She leaps into the house, like the wall below my window ain't any obstacle at all. Daddy's still got the gun pointed at her, but he shakes harder now, and he don't pull the trigger. Maybe he's thinking 'bout what I said earlier, thinking 'bout how Mama and I look kinda alike.

He kneels, real quick, and slides the gun away. Then he rises, and goes to meet Mama, his jaw set, his hands in fists. He swings at her hard, and gets a hit on her. She flies back, hits my closet, the doors cavin' in like they're made of cardboard. I may be stronger'n I look, but I ain't that strong. Nothin' I can do but watch.

Mama pushes herself outta the broken doors with a growl, and launches herself at Daddy. She swipes at him, like a cat at a toy. He jumps outta the way, but the third one catches him 'cross the ribs. He lets out a grunt—the green shirt he sleeps in ripping and goin' dark with his blood. While he's distracted, she rushes him, shoving him with her shoulder. He falls 'gainst the bed, one hand to his side.

Before she can get too close, he kicks her in the stomach. She don't go back as far this time. She's prepared. Daddy can't get up from the bed 'cause she's standin' over him. He tries to shove her. His hands connect, but she's quicker. She grabs his wrists, her nails slidin' 'neath his skin. He don't grunt this time, he groans as the blood starts running down his arms.

I can't just watch no more. The gun's slid under my desk. I start crawling towards it. Daddy groans again. He can't die. Not my daddy. I'm not gonna let Mama do it. Seems like a lifetime, but I finally close my fingers 'round the cool metal and scramble to my feet. Mama's standin' over Daddy, and his wrists are bleeding onto my blankets. She got her hands 'round the top of his head.

I lift the gun. "Mama, you get your hands off my daddy."

She turns, but don't move her hands. "Alexis, what you doin'?"

"What's it look like I'm doin'?" My words are tough, but I'm shakin' way harder than Daddy did. Now I know why he couldn't shoot her. I'd never have forgiven him if he did.

Her eyes narrow. She turns back 'round, and slides one nail 'neath the skin of his forehead. Daddy screams.

I squeeze the trigger. The gun goes off.

Mama's absolutely still. Then blood blooms on the back of her shirt. She crumples to the floor.

"Mama?" I must've dropped the gun at some point, 'cause I got both hands on her shoulder. I turn her over and grab her head. "Mama?"

She's still breathin', and some of the fog's gone outta her eyes. "Alexis," she whispers, "you remember, I done the best I can." Her eyelids start to close.

"Mama," I say. Her eyes open a bit. "You know I love you, right?"

She don't answer, but she smiles a little, and then she's gone.

Josh comes barrelin' in the door to find me with my dead mama, and Daddy in a bad way. Turns out he called 911 soon as he heard the gun go off. He helps me put pressure on Daddy's wounds 'til the ambulance gets there. Daddy's sorta out of it, but he tries to give me a smile as the paramedics load him into the ambulance. They let me sit with him on the way to the hospital.

They whisk my daddy away once we get there, and make me stay in the waiting room. I still got his blood on my clothes, and Mama's. Smells strongly of copper and antiseptic.

After what seems like forever, someone comes for me—a lady in green, a surgical mask 'round her neck. Her sneakers squeak 'gainst the linoleum.

"Your father's going to be fine," she tells me. "He lost a lot of blood, and he's going to have scars, but he'll be up and about in no time."

I sink into the chair with a sigh. She starts to leave, but then turns and looks at me, like she just seen the blood all over me.

"Are you okay?"

I don't even know how I'm s'posed to answer that question. I'm not okay, not sure I'm ever gonna be.

I'm thinking 'bout how I maybe only got four years, how I had to kill my own mama, how I'd rather put the gun to my head than be a dreameater. But then, I might not be a dreameater, I might have more control'n Mama, or Daddy's brother might come up with a real cure. "I ain't hurt," I say finally. It's close as I can get to the truth. She gives me a quick smile and leaves.

I lean my head back, lookin' at the white ceiling panels and the fluorescent lights, their pattern stuck into my head. They swirl in front of me, like snow bein' blown by the wind. Been a long night. I close my eyes, intending to open 'em a second later, but I don't. I'm in a blizzard, but I ain't cold at all. I'm grabbin' the flakes as they pass me by, and they gather on my fingertips, glowin' bright as the moon. I can't stop laughing—it's the craziest and most beautiful thing I ever seen.

For the first time in my life, I'm dreamin'.

Master Belladino's Mask

written by

Marina J. Lostetter

illustrated by

TIFFANY ENGLAND

ABOUT THE AUTHOR

The open skies and dense forests of the Pacific Northwest are ideal for growing speculative fiction authors—or, at least, Marina J. Lostetter would like to think so. Originally from Oregon, she grew up with a mother whose idea of a great family outing was half a day at the bookstore, a father who placed The Hobbit *in her hands when she was nine and a brother who insisted that she'd publish one day—even before he'd read anything she'd written.*

Now she resides in Arkansas with her husband, Alex, who is the most supportive and understanding partner in the world. After Marina graduated from Southern Oregon University with a history degree, she expressed a desire to do something crazy: write fiction for a living. Alex insisted that she jump right in, and Marina has been writing full time ever since.

This marks Marina's third finalist story in the Writers of the Future Contest, as well as her second professional publication. Her work has also appeared in Orson Scott Card's InterGalactic Medicine Show, Mirror Shards: Volume 2 *and* Penumbra.

ABOUT THE ILLUSTRATOR

Tiffany England works from Los Angeles doing freelance illustration and art restoration. She is a recent student of Jim Garrison and Laguna College of Art & Design, where she received her bachelor's in illustration. Her work has been shown at the Society of Illustrators Student Competition as well as at galleries from coast to coast. Artistically, she takes her inspiration from various styles of artists from the Golden Age of Illustration, such as Arthur Rackham, Edmund Dulac, and Gustaf Tenggren. Classically trained, Tiffany finds that art history provides a firm foundation for her technique and illustrative ideals, making it possible to combine elements of representational form with effective storytelling and design sensitivity. Recently she has been apprenticed by Aleksei Tivetsky in the fine work of icon painting and construction, using old master techniques and materials. Currently she is creating a secular illuminated manuscript, an amalgamation of her knowledge of character and story with the delicate work of writing an icon.

Master Belladino's Mask

The chiming of the store's bell smacked of luxury, like everything else in the city. Bells in the country always tinkled with a tin echo that indicated they were made of lesser things, just like the country people: their rolling drawl was the calling card of an unrefined upbringing.

Melanie was all too aware of this when she opened her mouth to address the clerk. "I'm interested in a mask," she said, as crisp and clear as possible. *And saving my mother,* she silently added.

His dull eyes traced her from mud-crusted skirt up to moth-eaten best hat, his lips maintaining a scowl the entire way. He had a long, lithe torso, with the limbs and nose to match. When he answered, he answered slowly. Melanie wasn't sure if it was because it took a long time for the words to climb out of his lengthy chest, or if he considered her dull-witted.

"You are in a mask shop. I'd expect you're interested in a mask. What kind?"

She sneaked glances left and right. On the walls hung carvings of every possible shape and design.

Bright and dark colors made sweeping patterns, twisting together to tell a variety of stories. Exotic animals displayed gaping maws. Demons grinned through grotesque, asymmetrical features. Human likeness twisted into caricatures through exaggerated expressions.

She hunched her shoulders, shrinking from their cold, empty stares. They watched, waiting expectantly for her to choose. *So many dead faces.* A shiver crawled up her spine.

"A healer's mask. His name was August Belladino. Is he here?"

The clerk grinned, as if he knew something she did not. A private joke, perhaps. "He is. Were you looking to rent, or buy? The knowledge of Master Belladino does not come—" he frowned deeply—"cheap."

What did he consider cheap? Any sort of magic carried a hefty price in the country. But city and country definitions of "expensive" weren't the same.

"I'd like to rent," she said, reaching into her purse. She pulled out all but a few vials of minutes. "Is this enough?" In the country the ratio was usually 60:1. One hour of use for every bottled minute.

She glanced down at the time, a little guilty. She could have given it to her mother. But, no, that wouldn't be proper. What were a few more minutes of agony when she could have years of health?

The store bell rang again, and Melanie glanced over her shoulder at the new patron. He was a dark-skinned young man, about her age. He looked as if he belonged in the city—all sharp edges and clean lines.

Her cheeks grew hot. Melanie felt embarrassed to have her exchange with the clerk overheard.

The clerk glowered, and his annoyance intensified. He opened his mouth to say something to the man, but seemed to think better of it. Instead, he counted up Melanie's minutes. "Enough for a day and a half."

Her heart sank. "I'd hoped for three. The healer in my town said I'd need three."

"Then come back when you have the full fare." Impatiently, he drummed his fingers against the countertop.

"Please," her voice shook. She gulped. "I don't have time to raise more." She dumped the rest of the bottles from her purse. The last minutes were meant for the innkeeper, but the mask was more important. Melanie and her mother could sleep on the streets a few nights, if they had to.

"Still not enough," he said coldly.

Smooth skin brushed past hers, and a dark hand laid a generous pile of time beside hers. "That should cover it," said the young man.

Deep, black eyes held Melanie's gaze for a moment. She opened her mouth, but didn't know what to say.

"I told you not to come in here again," the clerk said. "You scare away my customers."

"I'm not scaring anyone," he said indignantly. "I'm helping her pay. I'm giving you money. Are you refusing to rent to her?"

Without another word the clerk stomped from behind the counter and over to the far wall. Taking great care, he lifted one of the wooden masks from its hook—one of the animal effigies. "Master Belladino's mask," he said, offering it to her. "Covered for a week."

"It's so light," she said, balancing it delicately. In the country people had to carve their death masks out of cedar or pine instead of imported balsa, and no one she knew could afford paint, let alone enchantment. Clutching it to her chest, she turned to the young man. "Thank you," she said, "I'll repay you, somehow. I'll come up with the time—or I can work the minutes off straight. I might not look it, but I can plow fields all day, or clean house, or—"

"We'll come up with something." His face was gentle, but his expression stern. "Where are you staying?"

"The inn at—" In her sudden elation, she'd forgotten. Her eyes strayed to the bottles.

He read her mind. "I'll cover that, too. I work at the Creek Side Inn; I can get you a room, if you'd like."

"That would be wonderful. Thank you so much, Master—?"

"Leiwood."

"Melanie Dupont. I'll get my mother and we'll be right over. I can't, I mean..." She was so happy she couldn't get her tongue to behave properly. "It's just, I didn't think—" She shuffled her feet, wanting to be off as quickly as she could.

"Go. I'll see you this evening."

Giddy with excitement and gratitude, she skipped away. Before she could cue the bell's tinkling once more, Master Leiwood caught her by the shoulder. "Be careful," he said darkly. "Keep your guard up."

She nodded absently, her hand already on the door.

As she left, Melanie caught the beginning of a new

conversation between Leiwood and the clerk. She paused outside the door to listen.

"You didn't explain it," Leiwood said.

"It's a healer's mask; she'll be fine."

"Not like me?"

"Not like you."

The conversation ended, and she hurried on. Melanie was too happy to wonder what they'd meant.

Mother. Mother, look." Melanie turned her mother's pale face toward the mask. "Isn't it beautiful?" The focal point was a tree frog—the full frog, climbing up a vine, looking over its shoulder—and around it were leaves, branches, and a couple of small exotic birds. The frog's eyes had been cut out for the wearer.

Melanie wanted to put it on this instant, to learn Master Belladino's healing techniques as soon as possible.

But she forced herself to wait, just until they moved to the Creek Side Inn.

Using the board they'd brought, Melanie was able to leverage her mother out of bed and partially onto her feet. She buckled her into a harness, then looped the straps—like those on a traveler's pack—over her own shoulders.

Limply, her mother hugged her from behind. "Good girl. My good girl," she breathed.

Melanie slowly took her mother's full weight onto her back. "You feel lighter today," she said, worried.

"Easier for you to carry, that way," her mother said. "Soon you won't have to worry about me anymore. You'll be able to live your own life, as a young woman should."

Yes, Melanie thought, *but not for the reason you think.* "You'll feel better soon," she said.

Her mother sighed. "Yes, I'm sure I will."

Melanie gathered up the rest of their meager belongings, then hobbled out of the room.

Is this acceptable, Mistress Dupont?" Master Leiwood asked, but not of Melanie. He was addressing her mother.

No one had spoken directly to her mother in a long time. They always acted as if she couldn't hear, or as though she weren't there at all.

"Fine," Dawn-Lyn Dupont whispered, snuggling into the covers. "It's a lovely room."

The tables and wardrobe were polished mahogany. Fine sheets—so fresh that Melanie wondered if they'd ever been slept in before—covered the feather bed. These were posh lodgings.

Master Leiwood nodded and came away from the bedside. "For her?" he asked Melanie, nodding to the mask which sat on the windowsill, propped against the pane.

"Yes. She has the muscle illness. The one that makes everything quit moving. Even the heart, in the end." She dropped down onto a chaise, and looked out the window to the bustling afternoon street below. "I asked every healer I could find to have a look at her. In the end they kept telling me, 'You need August Belladino.' When I learned he was dead, I was sure he must have a mask—a real one, an enchanted one. An expert craftsman wouldn't let his knowledge disappear when he died."

"Some experts can't afford to enchant their masks," he said, "and some would rather cash in their time, live it out."

"Yes. But luckily, Master Belladino could...and didn't."

He sat down beside her, keeping a respectful distance.

"You own the inn, don't you?" she asked suddenly.

"I do," he said.

They were quiet for awhile. Eventually Dawn-Lyn's breathing evened out. Melanie could tell she was asleep.

"Would you like to go to the lounge?" Master Leiwood asked. "Let your mother rest?"

She nodded and followed him out and down the stairs.

They sat at a small table, bent over full mugs of beer that neither touched. "You sounded concerned when I left the shop," Melanie said.

He laughed in a caustic sort of way. "I had a bad experience with a mask." He nodded toward the bar. "It's on the wall there. Would you like to see it?"

She wasn't sure she would, but he got up and she trailed behind. Several masks decorated the room, but the one he indicated was different from the rest. It looked like a crow, with a long black beak and shining metal feathers—and it was hewn in half.

"My father's," he said. "We had an...*unhealthy* relationship. When he died I thought I'd be able to understand him better if I bought his mask and wore it for a little while. Turns out that wasn't a good idea."

Twisting a fold in her skirt, she waited for him to explain. He didn't look as if he wanted to—more like he *had* to. "My father was a bad man. And for the short time that I wore his mask, so was I. Thankfully, I don't remember much of what happened, and no one got hurt. Once the mask came off, I was me, and the memories of being in his mind drifted away.

"That's why I hang around the shop. I try to warn people. It's not just knowledge that gets transferred, it's personality, too. Maybe even more than that…" He put his hand over his mouth, as if he were about to be sick. "Just be careful. Stay yourself and stay strong. I don't know much about Master Belladino, but they say he was a genius. And sometimes geniuses have a funny way of looking at the world, be it good or bad."

Melanie patted his hand. "Thank you. For warning me, for everything. I better get back; mother will be hungry when she wakes."

"Sure. If you need anything, my room's at the top of the stairs."

The sun and her mother had both gone down for the night when Melanie decided that it was time. She lit a candle, then pulled out her inkpot, a pen, and a roll of parchment.

With slight trepidation roiling in her gut, she turned the mask over, laying it carving side down on the table. It was padded inside, with a silk lining—very inviting. She slowly slipped it over her face, letting it settle against her features. Then she tied the black ribbons under her hair and waited for the magic to take hold.

The quill was in her hand before she recognized what she was doing. Words, processes, formulas—an ocean's worth of information came flooding through. It felt as if it bypassed her brain and splattered straight onto the paper. She saw the words appear, and they turned in on themselves, again and again. Soon she had a collection of giant, worthless inkblots.

With her left hand she grabbed her writing wrist and wrenched it away from the page. She drew several deep breaths, steadying herself. Her heart seemed to be running a desperate race, and her fingers and toes twitched with barely subdued energy. Everything was trying to escape the mask at once. Too much information was being channeled through her. She had to figure out how to control the deluge.

One word at a time. She told herself. *Concentrate. Focus on the muscle illness. What needs to be done?*

Her writing hand tried to get away, but she reeled it in. Only letting one word seep out at a time, she continued. Her mind began filtering more and more. She caught wisps of ideas, portions of equations. A list of ingredients sprang from amongst the rest, and she patiently wrote it down.

Why had her local healer told her it would take days? All of the information was here, now. It took only moments to fall out of the mask.

But getting a tight grasp on the process was taking longer.

Yes, I remember. She recalled everything the ailment required to be canceled. For the first time she realized that medicine and potion-making were all mathematical, with the illness on one side and the cure on the other. Both sides of the equation had to balance, to cancel each other out. The ending answer always needed to be zero.

To cancel the muscle illness...

She made notes next to each ingredient. It was slow going, writing and making her calculations. The characters came out at an agonizing pace, but if she didn't hold back, the words would be illegible.

The muscle illness didn't behave the same in each person, so the makeup of the medicine was always slightly different. She had to recall all the specifics she could about her mother's sickness. Retrieving the memories was difficult—Master Belladino, with his overwhelming mental faculties, didn't want to share her consciousness.

Melanie worked through the morning, only stopping when her mother asked for food. She went to the kitchen to order her a meal and some water and bread to last out the day. The boy who wrote down her request deftly ignored the mask.

That was the only time she left the room. Leiwood came to the door once to be sure she was alright. She shooed him away without leaving her chair, assuring him they were fine.

Night had come again by the time she finished. Next she would need to visit the apothecary. But the stars were bright through the window, and all lamps in the hall had been extinguished. The inn had settled down for the evening.

But she needed to start mixing the medicine as soon as possible. Her mother had been sick long enough. Making up her mind, she decided to go to Master Leiwood's room and ask him to escort her now.

Reaching up, she pulled the ribbons loose, and the mask slid away. Not wanting to waste any time, she gathered her cloak and the annotated list, then scurried out the door.

Halfway to his room she stopped and pulled out the list. The items were familiar, but the notes were gibberish. It was as if someone else had written them, and in code. What did that mean? Had she only imagined that she knew how to cure her mother? No, she'd had the information, but now it slipped out of her like water through a sieve. In the next moment even some of the ingredients became foreign.

She needed the mask. Without it she was helpless.

When Leiwood answered the door, he looked as though he'd seen a specter. He quickly shook his surprise, but she'd caught it. Melanie hadn't considered what she looked like with a frog where her face should be. "We must go to the apothecary," she said, demanding. That wasn't like her: impatient. But this was her mother's life on the line. She didn't need to waste time on courtesies.

He stepped aside and motioned for her to come in. A small fire crackled in the hearth behind him, and the room smelled spicy. "You country people keep strange hours."

It was a joke, but she didn't find it funny. "I need these things." The list appeared, and she held it firmly before his eyes. "Quickly—we must have balance."

Nodding absently to himself, he took up his night jacket. "You're lucky the apothecary owner's a friend of mine. He might open for us."

She brushed past him into the hallway, with her

posture tight and tall. She could feel it—a stiffness she didn't usually carry.

A cheery whistle on his lips, Leiwood locked his door. Then he held out his arm for her to take. She refused, and realized something.

"You're Victor's boy."

The lively flush faded from his cheeks. "I am."

"How's he doing?"

Leiwood turned his eyes away, focusing on his brass key-ring instead. "He's dead. I told you. Been gone four years."

She started down the stairs. The information seemed simultaneously new and old. Had she heard of Victor's death before? "He was a bit odd, wasn't he? A little... off kilter?" Unbalanced.

Work, she remembered. *I was studying... something ... And Victor—* Refocusing, she shook the feeling. *No, I never knew Leiwood's father.* She let the conversation fade, and they headed out of the inn and down the street.

In the poorer quarter where she and her mother had previously stayed, the streets had hummed all night. Melanie had thought the constant ebb and flow of the city was a dance that never ended, but this district was quiet. All of the respectable people had gone home to bed.

They passed a few vendors, a heap of sleeping vagabonds, and one woman dressed similarly to Melanie—but with paint on her face—who asked Leiwood if he wanted to "trade up."

"You like 'em masked?" she shouted when he didn't answer.

They turned a corner and Melanie had the sense to look indignant.

"What, they don't have 'nightingales' where you come from?" he asked.

"None who would be so rude to a pair of gentlemen."

"What?"

"Nothing."

The apothecary was a strangely shaped building, with a hexagonal domed ceiling made entirely of blue glass. It gave the place a peculiar watery glow when Leiwood lit the oil lamps.

The apothecary owner had not liked being awakened. Despite that, he'd given Leiwood the key and told him to return it with payment in the morning. Melanie was grateful they hadn't had to wait for the man to change out of his dressing gown so that he could accompany them.

Now, in the thick of pots, tubes, and vials of components, Melanie hurriedly read off the ingredients. Directing Leiwood to one end of the shop, she took the other.

"Slow down," he said, taking her hand. "You act like there's no time. She's bad off, but I think she'll keep until morning." Leiwood grinned at her, trying to coax a smile back.

"But, balance—" She felt awkward. Things weren't in their place. The world wouldn't be right until her mother was cured. "My time's not my own until she's better."

"Real time, or bottled time?"

"Both." She saw a mineral she needed—a clump of yellow sulfur—and snatched it off the shelf.

"What will you do? When you don't have to spend the whole day watching over her?" Leiwood abruptly let Melanie's hand go, as though aware of how intimate the gesture seemed in the dim light.

She sighed and stared at the list for a moment. He was prying, and she wasn't sure she wanted to be opened. "I don't know. She's been ill since I can remember. My father was much older than her—I had to take care of them both for awhile. To be honest I never really thought there would be a day when she wouldn't need me." She looked up. "You're right. What will I do?"

"At least you'll have time to think about it. Time to discover how to spend your time."

They gathered a few more items in silence. A locked glass case held a large specialized syringe with intricate designs covering its barrel—a tool essential to the cure. Melanie worked at the lock for several minutes before giving in to frustration and smashing the case with a weight from the balance scale.

"What was that?" Leiwood called.

"Nothing. I broke a box. I'll replace it." She waved away his concern.

"Be careful, please."

"Sure, sure."

More silence. She glanced in his direction every now and again and found him watching her. It gave her strange, contradictory feelings in the pit of her stomach.

"I remember having my time bottled," he said suddenly.

"You can't," she laughed. *He must think me in a dull*

mood, telling me a joke. Time was taken only from newborns.

"I do. I had it done late, because my father was trying to cheat the Tax Man. He never declared my birth."

She stopped her searching, and closed the cabinet she'd been investigating. "What was it like?"

"Painful. But I felt lightheaded after, kind of euphoric. They took extra, as interest."

"That's not fair. It's your father who should have paid."

"You can't take time from adults—not without killing them. But it made me realize something—about life. It's why I've worked so hard.

"I didn't inherit the inn from my parents. I earned it all myself. Real time is far more valuable than bottled time. It has a better exchange rate. I decided I wanted to spend mine as productively as possible, get the biggest payout I could. That way, when I'm close to dying, I won't feel the need to cash in. Because I won't have any regrets. I think only people who waste their lives scrape for those extra minutes."

"It's kind of unfair," Melanie said, thinking about her mother, "that the time can only be tacked on at the end, not in the middle."

"And who spends those last cashed minutes well? People who die young never think to cash out. Only the old do it. They're all invalid and incontinent when they get them. Those aren't extra minutes I want—extra minutes being incapable." He came over to her with a sack filled with half the list. "And you know what? If people stopped cashing in, I don't think we'd have to harvest anymore. Babies would get to keep their time, as they should."

"Sounds ideal," she said.

He shrugged. "It's the way things were meant to be."

An hour later they returned to the inn with sacks of minerals, chemicals, and dried herbs. As they walked, Leiwood seemed to drag his feet, which she found galling. Her impatience was restored post-haste.

Was he trying to exasperate her? Did he not see how important it was to restore the equilibrium? The asymmetry fed on her nerves, tore at her muscles, weighed heavy in her chest. There was a struggle going on in every fiber of her body, demanding she cure the problem.

An image of a dead cat and a weeping, disheveled girl came to her mind, unbidden. It frightened her, and she vehemently shooed it away.

Back at the inn, Melanie didn't want to wake her mother, so they went to Leiwood's room instead. "Mortar, pestle," she demanded, snapping her fingers at him. Obediently, he drew the tools from one of the bags. While she worked, he set out the rest of the gear: a small burner, some test tubes, a beaker, and the syringe.

Into the crucible went sulfur, calcium, and dried reishi mushrooms. She topped it off with a liquid catalyst that glowed an eerie, subtle green. "It has to rest for a day," she declared after thoroughly mixing the substances. "This cure demands time."

Leiwood sat on his bed, giving her a sideways look. He'd been staring at her strangely since they'd gone out to get the ingredients. It worried her. Annoyed her. Disturbed her.

Just like his father, she thought harshly. *Brutal man...
killed my daughter's cat.*

But that couldn't be right. She wasn't a mother.

Confused, she wandered over to the fireplace, and
looked deep into the red coals. "They say I'm a great
healer."

Leiwood's answer came tentatively. "Master
Belladino was, yes."

"I could cure any ailment. Save the dead from
dying."

"Melanie?"

My unfinished work. The thoughts didn't seem her
own. *I died before I could finish my work.* "But there was
one thing I couldn't figure out how to balance. One
illness I couldn't find a cure for." *Cat. Dead cat.*

"You mean August Belladino. There was something
he couldn't cure?"

The cat. Then he... Then he... She...

"Cruelty." She picked up the iron poker and thrust
it into the hearth. "It resides deep, somewhere most
medicine can't reach. And I never could figure it out."
She whirled around. Leiwood's eyes were wide, and
sad. His expression made her angry. "Did you know
that a lot of sickness stays in the family? That it passes
from parent to child?"

"Melanie..." There was a warning in his voice.

She raised the poker, pointing it at him. There he
was; she could see Victor Leiwood hiding under that
shocked expression. Sick man. *Do you know what he
did to her?* she screeched.

Leiwood was on his feet, arms out, imploring.
"What? Who?"

"My daughter!" Melanie ran at him, swinging

447

and thrusting the iron. Claw-like fingers sought to curl around his collar and draw him in. She wanted to impale him, to open him up. "Let me see it!" she shouted. "Where is it? Where does the abuse live? Down in your belly? In your spine? Show me, Victor!"

"Melanie!" he said. "It's not you. Fight the mask. Fight it! I didn't do it." He launched pillows and oil lamps and a table in her path—anything to stop her. "I'm not my father. I'm *not*."

Wrath blurring her vision, she plunged the poker forward, barely missed Leiwood, and embedded the point in a plush chair.

This isn't right, she realized backing away. *Leiwood has done nothing but help me. He's a good man.* But an image of his father flashed before her eyes, and the hatred returned with a vengeance. She fought it, trying to keep separate from the feelings. "Leiwood," she said, distress pervading her voice.

"Melanie? Take off the mask!"

She curled her fingers around the edges and pulled with all her strength. The mask wouldn't budge. It had fused to her face, holding on like a leech. "It won't— It—"

In the next instant she was flying after him again. Deep, rumbling accusations spewed from her mouth. She didn't even sound like herself.

But now there was a duality within her. There was Master Belladino, enraged, hell-bent on tearing Leiwood apart—and Melanie, who wouldn't hurt a thing. Especially not someone who had been so good to her.

"Help me!" she cried. And in her next breath, "You *filth*."

TIFFANY ENGLAND

Melanie wrestled with herself, desperate to escape the essence that possessed her body. "The fire!" she yelled, and moved in its direction. But she tripped on her own feet and fell short.

"What are you doing?" He didn't flee, but he kept away.

"Burn it," she urged. *"Burn!"* Inch by wavering inch, she crawled across the floor toward the fireplace. Melanie urged him to hurry, and Belladino damned him the whole way. She felt sick, insane. She wasn't worried about the flames—about burning skin. She just wanted to be alone again.

Leiwood rushed forward, grasped the mask, and pulled. It didn't come loose. Melanie grabbed his wrists and growled.

"I can't get it off," he said, defeated, searching her eyes—half hidden behind the wood—for another idea.

Melanie pleaded, "Put it in the fire anyway."

Melanie's words said *do it,* but her body writhed, desperate to escape. "No," Leiwood said, "you'll— There's got to be something else." But the memory of his father's mask—then the hatchet, which Leiwood had swung toward his own face—his own brush with death… Perhaps fire was the only answer.

But then he thought of plunging her face into the coals. It made him sick, and he knew he couldn't do it.

Leiwood backed away, leaving Melanie to grapple with herself. She clawed at the neck of her blouse, tore at her hair. At one moment she looked like she was strung out on an invisible rack, her spine pulled taut, then it snapped loose again like a band of rubber.

Trying to think fast, he spun toward the heap of apothecary items. With shaking hands, he picked up each substance and read label after label. At a loss, he thumbed the syringe, then the burner. None of the items provided an answer.

He heard a scraping of wood on wood and looked up. Melanie was dragging herself toward the fire once more, face down, mask grating against the floor. She didn't look as if she could stand much more.

"Wait!" he shouted, bounding over to her. Heart pounding, he grasped one ankle, stopping her progress toward ruin. "Fight it. Give me a little time, I'll think of a better way."

"Son of grime," she raged, reaching forward and grasping the hearth's hot grate. The rancid scent of charring human skin wafted into Leiwood's face.

With a hefty yank he hauled her in reverse, simultaneously scanning the room for something to restrain her. The only things that seemed reasonable were the drape cords.

The cords were tied neatly around wrought-iron window hooks. He struggled with the knots—distress made him clumsy. He bumped the nightstand that held a lamp and his pocketbook and they tumbled to the ground.

His purse burst open, and bottles of time went bouncing across the room.

Stunned, he watched one roll to the foot of the table. His gaze went back to the apothecary items. An idea struck him.

451

Scooping up one of the time vials—a fiver—he leapt over Melanie's twisted form, then skidded to a halt next to the medicines. In the next instant the syringe was in his hand, poised above the cork that kept the time contained.

It was illegal—and nearly impossible—to release time without a Tax Collector present. The time was kept in by enchantment, and only things designed to contain enchantment could break the magic seal.

He should have flashed on the needle before—he'd only seen one other like it. Leiwood remembered the needle from when he was young. From when they'd made him pay the tax.

It was special, and rare, something you had to have a license to obtain. Probably Belladino had such a license, so Melanie hadn't thought twice about taking it from the apothecary.

What would happen when the time was let go? He'd never heard of anyone setting it free before. All he knew was that he needed some—more than what he had. Time to think before Melanie threw herself into the flames.

He jammed the needle deep into the spongy cork and pulled back on the plunger. As the barrel filled with a swirling pink and turquoise essence, the bottle cracked. Once empty, it turned to dust.

Without another thought Leiwood pointed the needle in Melanie's direction and shot time into the air.

Everything stopped. There was a stillness to the room, like on a winter's morning after a heavy snow. When he noticed even his breathing had stopped, he started to panic, but quickly focused.

He was seeing double—as if two stained-glass images were superimposed. But not quite, because the images weren't identical.

There were new things in the room—wispy, ethereal things, the same color as the essence of time. There was a new plant in one corner, a handprint on the windowpane, and smoke—as from a pipe—over the bed.

Melanie was frozen, her rigid, burnt fingers outstretched for the grate once more. He was grateful that the mask hid her expression, because surrounding her head was a *creature*. It was something between an amorphous blob and a tentacled sea monster. The bulbous body grew out of the center of the mask, and the translucent arms reached out behind her, like streamers caught in a high wind.

He wanted to lunge at it, but wasn't sure if that was the right thing to do.

What were they, these newly revealed things? They couldn't be physical objects; he'd stood right where the new plant sat.

Perhaps they were things that existed in time only, separate from space.

A faint pulsing drew his attention to the ceiling. Splayed across it were symbols, constantly shifting. They weren't words, or astrological signs. The speed at which they changed reminded him of a countdown.

There had been five minutes in the bottle—that was all the time he had to decide what to do.

He moved to put the syringe down, but caught sight of what it had become. The superimposed version of the needle was bigger—almost like a dagger. And the two metal circles of the finger grip now extended up and over his hand to his wrist in a partial gauntlet. Things that looked like spiny vines wound up his arm from there, all the way to his shoulder, where a protective plate with moving— living?—parts rested.

The syringe let him interact with time without being caught in it, like Melanie was. It was the key.

And the cure.

Leiwood ran at her. Diving forward he plunged the dagger-needle between the frog's eyes—Melanie's eyes—and pulled on the plunger. A small drop of blood entered the barrel with a faint fog of time. He'd pushed too deep, failing to consider the softness of the balsa. Lightly, he scaled back, pulling the needle out just a tad.

When he pulled on the plunger again, the creature on the mask suddenly moved. Its tentacles clamped down around Melanie and its body quivered. The bulbous portion shimmered and resolved into an ugly caricature of a human face—Belladino's face, tainted and twisted with hate. It bit and howled at Leiwood.

"I'm sorry, I—" But there was no use in Leiwood apologizing to a half-formed time-specter of a man for things that he had never done.

He struggled with the creature, sucking at it, more desperate to separate it from Melanie than before. His arm shook as he applied force to the plunger. Soon the thing began to shrink, absorbed into the mask and then drawn up the needle and into the barrel.

The last airy bit of the creature caught, Leiwood withdrew the needle and backed away, examining the syringe. The mass inside swirled like an angry, bottled storm.

One moment Melanie had been fighting the torturous rift in her mind, struggling to plunge herself into the fire. And the next she was in Leiwood's lap, his arms wrapped tightly around her, holding her close. The mask no longer covered her face.

"It's gone," she said, amazed. Leiwood smiled a sad, scared smile, and her heart dropped out of her stomach. "I'm sorry." She felt like slime. What had she done? "I couldn't—I—"

He rocked her back and forth. "Shh. It's all right."

With his thumb he wiped away a drop of blood from her forehead. How had that gotten there? She stared at the smear for a long moment. *Did I black out?*

There was a quick, sharp tap on her forehead, and then another. He was crying. "I didn't know," he said. "My mother took me away when I was ten. I didn't come back until he was gone. He hurt a lot of people, but Master Belladino's daughter...I didn't know." His arms suddenly tensed around Melanie. "And your mother. Your poor mother."

Melanie began to cry herself, and the tears burned as though they were molten. The idea that something had happened and she couldn't remember it was frightening, but the thought of her mother sent her over the edge. The solution in the crucible had to cure, but then what? The next steps had been lost with the—

But no. She thought hard, and found she knew the process. And it was not fading; it was strong and clear in her mind.

How—?

Yes, there were more formulas in her memory, more healing potions and techniques. She was almost sure she knew them all. But the anger and hatred had fluttered away. All that was left was knowledge.

"I can still save her," she whispered. "But, why do I still know how?"

"Perhaps when I pricked you..." he started, then took a shaky breath. "I took the poison out, but maybe I locked some things in, too."

She didn't understand, but the joy at realizing her mother could be saved shoved the curiosity aside. "She'll be all right. Leiwood—" He looked into her eyes. "I'm sorry I didn't resist hard enough. I should have kept him back. There was more I should have done."

"No," he smiled. "It's not your fault. It was Belladino's mask."

They sat locked in silence for a long while. Melanie let relief, and sadness, and terror, and calm, and happiness flood through her freely.

Eventually Leiwood helped her stand. "We need to get you to a healer." He gazed mournfully at her ruined hand. She hadn't even noticed it.

"I can do it myself," she said firmly. "I know how." She smiled, and curled the blackened fingers despite the pain. *"I know how."* She had a gift now—a master healer's knowledge and all the long years of life to improve upon it. She'd always been a helper, devoting her life to her ailing parents. But they hadn't sucked away her time—they'd enriched it. "And I know what to do with my life. I can share Master Belladino's genius with the world. Just the brilliance. Hopefully his loathing is gone forever."

Leiwood glanced over to the syringe on the floor, but didn't say anything.

She hugged him close. "I'll make sure people don't have to waste their lives being sick."

He nodded. "Because real time is worth more than bottled time."

Melanie's heart fluttered. "Life is always worth more when it's lived."

The Year in the Contests

Each year, our past writers, illustrators and judges make major accomplishments. In 2012, this trend continued. We had three Writers of the Future alumni nominated for World Fantasy Awards: Ken Liu (WotF 19), Tim Powers (WotF judge), and Karen Joy Fowler (WotF 1). Ken Liu won the short story category with "The Paper Menagerie," while Tim Powers won the collection category with his *The Bible Repairman and Other Stories*.

For the Hugo Awards, Ken Liu won Best Short Story with "The Paper Menagerie," and Jim C. Hines (WotF 15) won the award of Best Fan Writer. Ken Liu and Carolyn Ives Gilman (WotF 3) were also nominated for Best Novella, Brad R. Torgersen (WotF 26) was nominated for Best Novelette and Mike Resnick (WotF judge) was nominated for Best Short Story. Bob Eggleton and Stephan Martiniere (IotF judges) were both nominated for Best Professional Artist.

With the Nebula Awards, we had five nominees: Carolyn Ives Gilman and Ken Liu for Best Novella; Brad R. Torgersen for Best Novelette; and for Best

Short Story, Tom Crosshill (WotF 26) and Aliette de Bodard (WotF 23). Ken Liu won in his category with "The Paper Menagerie."

Brad R. Torgersen was nominated for the John W. Campbell Award for Best New Writer and Nnedi Okorafor (WotF 18 and Contest judge) was nominated for the Andre Norton Award for Young Adult Science Fiction and Fantasy Book.

David Farland (WotF 3 and Coordinating Judge) won seven awards this past year for his novel *Nightingale,* including the International Book Award for Best Young Adult Novel of the Year, and the Hollywood Book Festival Award for Best Book of the Year.

Omar Rayyan (IotF 8) won the Chesley Award for Best Color Work and Shaun Tan (IotF 8 and Contest judge) won the Locus Best Artist Award.

Also this past year, several past illustrator winners were featured in *Spectrum, the Year's Best Fantasy Illustrations.* These included Fiona Meng (WotF 28), Omar Rayyan, Shaun Tan and IotF judges Bob Eggleton, Stephen Hickman and Stephan Martiniere.

In 2012, 193 short stories and over a dozen novels were published by Writers of the Future winners. Heather McDougal (WotF 25) released her first published novel *Songs for a Machine Age* in November.

Tom Doyle (WotF 28) sold his novel *American Craftsmen,* the first in a series featuring ancient American magic and espionage, to Tor in a major auction. A collection of his short fiction, *The Wizard of Macatawa and Other Stories,* also sold.

Each year, the contest administration undergoes changes and growth. In 2012, Leo Dillon, one of our dear illustrator judges, passed away. Leo had been illustrating for over fifty years, with his work gracing many children's books and publications, and had served as a judge for fourteen of them, inspiring countless new artists.

K. D. Wentworth, who acted as Coordinating Judge for the writing contest and editor of the anthology, also passed away. K. D. had won the contest in 1988, and she served as a judge since 2000. She was a prolific short story writer, novelist and educator, and was beloved by all of the writers whom she taught during her twelve years with the Contest.

We've added a fantastic new writing judge: Nnedi Okorafor, an American-born author with her roots in Nigeria. She was a Writers of the Future published finalist in 2002 and went on to publish prolifically and win dozens of honors on the international stage, including the 2011 World Fantasy Award for Best Novel with her book *Who Fears Death*.

We also added a new illustrating judge: Larry Elmore, who is well known for his work as a fantasy artist for TSR. He has worked on Dragonlance and done artwork for dozens of magazines and book covers.

Additionally, we gained another Coordinating Judge, Dave Wolverton, also known in fantasy as David Farland, who acts as first reader for story submissions. He forwards the best entries on to the other writing judges, edits the anthology and teaches the writing workshop.

We will miss and remember Leo Dillon and K. D. Wentworth as we look forward to another successful year of Writers and Illustrators of the Future.

For Contest year 29, the L. Ron Hubbard Writers of the Future Contest winners are:

FIRST QUARTER

> 1. *Tina Gower*
> TWELVE SECONDS

> 2. *Marina J. Lostetter*
> MASTER BELLADINO'S MASK

> 3. *Stephen Sottong*
> PLANETARY SCOUTS

SECOND QUARTER

> 1. *Alisa Alering*
> EVERYTHING YOU HAVE SEEN

> 2. *Eric Cline*
> GONNA REACH OUT AND
> GRAB YA

> 3. *Kodiak Julian*
> HOLY DAYS

THIRD QUARTER

> 1. *Andrea Stewart*
> DREAMEATER

> 2. *Marilyn Guttridge*
> THE GHOST WIFE OF ARLINGTON

> 3. *Alex Wilson*
> VESTIGIAL GIRL

FOURTH QUARTER

> 1. *Christopher Reynaga*
> THE GRANDE COMPLICATION

2. Brian Trent
WAR HERO

3. Shannon Peavey
SCAVENGERS

Published Finalist: Chrome Oxide
COP FOR A DAY

For the year 2012, the L. Ron Hubbard Illustrators of the Future Contest winners are:

FIRST QUARTER
> *Jackie Albano*
> *Sida Chen*
> *Olivia Xu*

SECOND QUARTER
> *Jon Eno*
> *Luis Menacho*
> *Karsen Slater*

THIRD QUARTER
> *Lucas Durham*
> *Tiffany England*
> *Aldo Katayanagi*

FOURTH QUARTER
> *James J. Eads*
> *Joshua Meehan*
> *Daniel Reneau*

Our heartiest congratulations to all the winners! May we see much more of their work in the future.

WRITERS' CONTEST RULES

1. No entry fee is required, and all rights in the story remain the property of the author. All types of science fiction, fantasy and dark fantasy are welcome.

2. By submitting to the Contest, the entrant agrees to abide by all Contest rules.

3. All entries must be original works, in English. Plagiarism, which includes the use of third-party poetry, song lyrics, characters or another person's universe, without written permission, will result in disqualification. Excessive violence or sex, determined by the judges, will result in disqualification. Entries may not have been previously published in professional media.

4. To be eligible, entries must be works of prose, up to 17,000 words in length. We regret we cannot consider poetry, or works intended for children.

5. The Contest is open only to those who have not professionally published a novel or short novel, or more than one novelette, or more than three short stories, in any medium. Professional publication is deemed to be payment of at least five cents per word, and at least 5,000 copies, or 5,000 hits.

6. Entries submitted in hard copy must be typewritten or a computer printout in black ink on white paper, printed only on the front of the paper, double-spaced, with numbered pages. All other formats will be disqualified. Each entry must have a cover page with the title of the work, the author's legal name, a pen name if applicable, address, telephone number, e-mail address and an approximate

word count. Every subsequent page must carry the title and a page number, but the author's name must be deleted to facilitate fair, anonymous judging.

Entries submitted electronically must be double-spaced and must include the title and page number on each page, but not the author's name. Electronic submissions will separately include the author's legal name, pen name if applicable, address, telephone number, e-mail address and approximate word count.

7. Manuscripts will be returned after judging only if the author has provided return postage on a self-addressed envelope.

8. We accept only entries that do not require a delivery signature for us to receive them.

9. There shall be three cash prizes in each quarter: a First Prize of $1,000, a Second Prize of $750, and a Third Prize of $500, in US dollars. In addition, at the end of the year the winners will have their entries rejudged, and a Grand Prize winner shall be determined and receive an additional $5,000. All winners will also receive trophies.

10. The Contest has four quarters, beginning on October 1, January 1, April 1 and July 1. The year will end on September 30. To be eligible for judging in its quarter, an entry must be postmarked or received electronically no later than midnight on the last day of the quarter. Late entries will be included in the following quarter and the Contest Administration will so notify the entrant.

11. Each entrant may submit only one manuscript per quarter. Winners are ineligible to make further entries in the Contest.

12. All entries for each quarter are final. No revisions are accepted.

13. Entries will be judged by professional authors. The decisions of the judges are entirely their own, and are final.

14. Winners in each quarter will be individually notified of the results by phone, mail or e-mail.

15. This Contest is void where prohibited by law.

16. To send your entry electronically, go to:
www.writersofthefuture.com/submit-your-story
and follow the instructions.

To send your entry in hard copy, mail it to:
    L. Ron Hubbard's
    Writers of the Future Contest
    PO Box 1630
    Los Angeles, California 90078

17. Visit the website for any Contest rules updates at www.writersofthefuture.com.

ILLUSTRATORS' CONTEST RULES

1. The Contest is open to entrants from all nations. (However, entrants should provide themselves with some means for written communication in English.) All themes of science fiction and fantasy illustrations are welcome: every entry is judged on its own merits only. No entry fee is required and all rights to the entry remain the property of the artist.

2. By submitting to the Contest, the entrant agrees to abide by all Contest rules.

3. The Contest is open to new and amateur artists who have not been professionally published and paid for more than three black-and-white story illustrations, or more than one process-color painting, in media distributed broadly to the general public. The ultimate eligibility criterion, however, is defined by the word "amateur"—in other words, the artist has not been paid for his artwork. If you are not sure of your eligibility, please write a letter to the Contest Administration with details regarding your publication history. Include a self-addressed and stamped envelope for the reply. You may also send your questions to the Contest Administration via e-mail.

4. Each entrant may submit only one set of illustrations in each Contest quarter. The entry must be original to the entrant and previously unpublished. Plagiarism, infringement of the rights of others, or other violations of the Contest rules will result in disqualification. Winners in previous quarters are not eligible to make further entries.

5. The entry shall consist of three illustrations done by the entrant in a color or black-and-white medium created from

the artist's imagination. Use of gray scale in illustrations and mixed media, computer generated art, and the use of photography in the illustrations are accepted. Each illustration must represent a subject different from the other two.

6.   ENTRIES SHOULD NOT BE THE ORIGINAL DRAWINGS, but should be color or black-and-white reproductions of the originals of a quality satisfactory to the entrant. Entries must be submitted unfolded and flat, in an envelope no larger than 9 inches by 12 inches.

7. All hardcopy entries must be accompanied by a self-addressed return envelope of the appropriate size, with the correct US postage affixed. (Non-US entrants should enclose international postage reply coupons.) If the entrant does not want the reproductions returned, the entry should be clearly marked DISPOSABLE COPIES: DO NOT RETURN. A business-size self-addressed envelope with correct postage (or valid e-mail address) should be included so that the judging results may be returned to the entrant.

We only accept entries that do not require a delivery signature for us to receive them.

8. To facilitate anonymous judging, each of the three photocopies must be accompanied by a removable cover sheet bearing the artist's name, address, telephone number, e-mail address and an identifying title for that work. The reproduction of the work should carry the same identifying title on the front of the illustration and the artist's signature should be deleted. The Contest Administration will remove and file the cover sheets, and forward only the anonymous entry to the judges.

9. There will be three co-winners in each quarter. Each winner will receive an outright cash grant of US $500 and a trophy. Winners will also receive eligibility to compete for the annual Grand Prize of an additional cash grant of $5,000 together with the annual Grand Prize trophy.

10. For the annual Grand Prize Contest, the quarterly winners will be furnished with a specification sheet and a winning story from the Writers of the Future Contest to illustrate. In order to retain eligibility for the Grand Prize, each winner shall send to the Contest address his/her illustration of the assigned story within thirty (30) days of receipt of the story assignment.

The yearly Grand Prize winner shall be determined by the judges on the following basis only: Each Grand Prize judge's personal opinion on the extent to which it makes the judge want to read the story it illustrates.

The Grand Prize winner shall be announced at the L. Ron Hubbard Awards Event held in the following year.

11. The Contest has four quarters, beginning on October 1, January 1, April 1 and July 1. The year will end on September 30. To be eligible for judging in its quarter, an entry must be postmarked no later than midnight on the last day of the quarter. Late entries will be included in the following quarter and the Contest Administration will so notify the entrant.

12. Entries will be judged by professional artists only. Each quarterly judging and the Grand Prize judging may have different panels of judges. The decisions of the judges are entirely their own and are final.

13. Winners in each quarter will be individually notified of the results by mail or e-mail.

14. This Contest is void where prohibited by law.

15. To send your entry electronically, go to:
www.writersofthefuture.com/submit-your-illustration
and follow the instructions.

To send your entry via mail send it to:
  L. Ron Hubbard's
  Illustrators of the Future Contest
  PO Box 3190
  Los Angeles, California 90078

16. Visit the website for any Contest rules updates at www.writersofthefuture.com.